"Cox has a gift of creating characters who, no matter how outwardly different, can resonate with a reader at the deepest level of the soul. Callie and Beckett, the two women at the heart of *He Should Have Told the Bees*, are no exception. Equal parts heartbreaking and hopeful, this novel speaks to each heart's yearning for home—but one that is more than just a place on a map. A beautiful and poignant must-read."

**Jennifer L. Wright**, author of *If It Rains* and *The Girl from the Papers*

"Amanda Cox has woven an enchanting story about two women who find they have more in common than it first seems. With family secrets that are gently nudged into the open, an honest look at anxiety and recovery from childhood trauma, and two charming romances, *He Should Have Told the Bees* is the type of book that is destined to become an often-visited friend."

**Kimberly Duffy**, author of *The Weight of Air* and *A Tapestry of Light*

"With its compelling characters, riveting family drama, and illustrations of God's redemptive love, *He Should Have Told the Bees* is a honey of a tale! This is contemporary Christian fiction at its finest. Amanda Cox has crafted another winner!"

**Amanda Wen**, award-winning author of *Roots of Wood and Stone* and *The Songs That Could Have Been*

"*He Should Have Told the Bees* is a heart-deep journey of courage, compassion, and connection. With an expert hand, Amanda Cox offers a tale that resonates with masterful metaphor, captivating story, and a conclusion that wraps reader and characters alike in a cloak of belonging, hope, and healing. A powerful offering, rich with themes of trust, sacrifice, and treasure unexpected."

**Amanda Dykes**, bestselling and award-winning author of *All the Lost Places*

"Buzzing with emotion that brought me to tears, *He Should Have Told the Bees* will keep you turning its pages until the very end. Cox's hope-filled approach to generational trauma frames the complex relationship between brokenness and the faith that sustains us. With true-to-life characters and an unpredictable plot, this redemption story will challenge you in the very best ways as you root for the characters to find reconciliation and healing. Sweet as honey, beautiful as nectar, sharp as a sting—I never knew I could love bees so much. My favorite read of the year!"

**Ashley Clark,** acclaimed author of The Heirloom Secrets series

# HE
# SHOULD
# HAVE
# TOLD
# THE BEES

## Books by Amanda Cox

*The Edge of Belonging*
*The Secret Keepers of Old Depot Grocery*
*He Should Have Told the Bees*

# HE SHOULD HAVE HAVE TOLD THE BEES

*a novel*

## AMANDA COX

Revell

*a division of Baker Publishing Group*
Grand Rapids, Michigan

© 2023 by Amanda Cox

Published by Revell
a division of Baker Publishing Group
Grand Rapids, Michigan
www.revellbooks.com

Printed in the United States of America

Library of Congress Cataloging-in-Publication Data
Names: Cox, Amanda, 1984– author.
Title: He should have told the bees / Amanda Cox.
Description: Grand Rapids, MI : Revell, a division of Baker Publishing Group, [2023]
Identifiers: LCCN 2022057516 | ISBN 9780800742737 (paperback) | ISBN 9780800743116 (casebound) | ISBN 9781493441280 (ebook)
Classification: LCC PS3603.O88948 H4 2023 | DDC 813/.6—dc23/eng/20221205
LC record available at https://lccn.loc.gov/2022057516

This book is a work of fiction. Names, characters, places, and incidents are the product of the author's imagination or are used fictitiously. Any resemblance to actual events, locales, or persons, living or dead, is coincidental.

Baker Publishing Group publications use paper produced from sustainable forestry practices and post-consumer waste whenever possible.

23  24  25  26  27  28  29      7  6  5  4  3  2  1

For Caleb, Ellie, and Levi.
Your encouragement and faith in me are
like honey for my soul. May you always chase
after your dreams with the same fervency
with which you support mine.

Before them, under the garden wall,
  Forward and back,
Went drearily singing the chore-girl small,
  Draping each hive with a shred of black.

Trembling, I listened: the summer sun
  Had the chill of snow;
For I knew she was telling the bees of one
  Gone on the journey we all must go!

from "Telling the Bees,"
by John Greenleaf Whittier

# PROLOGUE

Callie's ears filled with the sound of windshield wipers slapping and Momma's incessant muttering. Prayers or curses, Callie couldn't tell. She wished Momma would turn the car around—that for once in their lives they could just stay.

The feeling that had clenched Callie's chest while they shoved their few belongings into duffel bags early that evening hadn't let up an inch in the hours they'd traveled.

Her mother had tried to hide behind smiles and promises of adventure, even in the dark of night. Didn't she know by now that Callie knew the difference between the truth and a lie? Momma's smiles were as dependable as the flimsy dress-up costumes from the bargain store that ripped halfway through trick-or-treating.

She studied the back of her mother's head, wishing she could crawl inside and see what lived there.

Sometimes she wondered if Momma was like the neighbor's cat that had gotten hit by a car. It lived, but it was never right again, given to darting wildly about the yard but not escaping. Running and running until it fell over.

Callie pushed out a heavy breath and leaned forward to pick up the canary yellow teapot resting by her feet.

Her mother glanced over her shoulder. "Go back to sleep, sweetie. When you wake up, we'll be at our new place," she said with too-bright sunshine in her voice.

Callie cradled the teapot against her middle and shut her eyes.

Instead of sleeping, she imagined Ms. Ruthie's round kitchen table, sliced by a ray of sunlight, with the bright teapot at its center, warm next to the robin's-egg blue walls.

Momma had swiped it from the apartment before Ms. Ruthie's real relatives arrived to sort through her belongings. She'd pressed that cool, ceramic vessel into Callie's hands as though a teapot could compensate for a living, breathing human being. Momma promised tea parties and a lot of other things. But the only thing Ms. Ruthie's teapot held since the day she died was air.

Ms. Ruthie. The tea party queen. Her pretend parent at Open House at school. The baker of cookies so Callie hadn't come to bake sales empty-handed. The drier of tears when Callie cried for a mother who too often disappeared without warning.

She stared out the window and sniffled. Headlights reflected off the droplets jittering across the panes, and Callie pretended they were squirming slugs racing for safety. Some made it across. Others grew heavy from the weight of water and dropped into the deep darkness beyond her car window. She silently cheered the droplets on, even those that struggled, doomed to fall.

Callie was sucked into repetitive dreams in which she fell in unending dark alongside the plummeting raindrops, never reaching the ground. Windshield wiper slaps. Ms. Ruthie. Water droplets.

A jarring motion woke her. The round teapot slipped from Callie's sleep-laxed hands and hit the floorboard with a sickening crack.

The car jerked again, and Callie's mother cursed at potholes and rainstorms and the absence of streetlights on the winding road.

Momma slowed. Rain drummed against the pane at a frantic rate.

Moments later, the car turned. The scratchy slosh of deep, wet gravel met Callie's ears as the single beam of Momma's one working headlight shone on a wooden sign.

Walsh Farm.

# ONE

Twenty-Two Years Later

*T*he field dotted with white boxes hummed a song Beckett Walsh had tuned her life to. Arms loaded with black cloths, she tramped through the field, the tall grass thwacking against her rubber boots. At the center of the apiary, she set down her burden. Though she'd never believed in these superstitions, she'd made him a promise.

One by one she unfolded the repurposed tablecloths and draped each hive. Every time, she said the same thing.

"He's gone. He's not coming back. It's just me now."

She swallowed and blinked her dry eyes. The bees' capacity to understand this loss was probably about as good as hers.

The early summer fever broke as the sun lowered behind the distant hills. Thank goodness for that. She wanted to keep her promise, but wouldn't these cloths overheat her bees? Her bees. They were supposed to be their bees. They'd always been theirs.

He'd brought home their first package of bees twenty-three years ago, when she was only five. She could still remember stretching her hand up to the mesh that made the sides of the small wooden box. The tight cluster of bees clung to the top, the power of their delicate wings stirring air against her palm.

At the memory, the ache inside her swelled, cutting away her breath. The days, hours, years they'd spent in this field. Working side by side. Checking queens. Diagnosing hive issues. Collecting liquid gold. Talking.

He'd always been a quiet man, but being out among the bees changed him. Here, his pent-up words flowed freely, like the gentle brook that formed the border between their field and the woods.

Mere days ago she'd listened to those low tones for the last time. Had she known it, she might have paused her work, leaned in, and let his talk of bees and their mysterious ways cradle her like an embrace. She clenched the black shroud in her fists and swallowed hard as she draped another hive. "He's gone. He's not coming back." The words scraped past the knot in her throat.

"Hey! What are you doing?"

Beck turned, searching for the small lilting voice that had jolted her.

A slender girl emerged from the brush at the edge of the field. She pulled a bramble from the end of a honey-colored plait.

"This is private property."

But the girl traversed Beck's invisible boundary in her shorts and mismatched knee socks. She marched up to Beck, picked a bur from the flower-patterned sock, tugged the striped sock higher, and swiped at the angry red scratch on her thigh.

"This is private property," Beck repeated more slowly this time.

The girl plucked a long piece of grass and stuck it behind her ear. "I'm sorry. I didn't know. Where I come from there is no such thing as private property. We are all one people. One land." The girl pulled a small notebook and a nub of a pencil from a neon fanny pack at her waist. She scrawled something on it and stuffed it back into her pack. "I am learning so many interesting things on your planet."

Beck sighed. This child had to be at least nine. Maybe ten. Beck didn't know much about kids, but surely the girl was too old to pretend to be a life-form from another planet. Too young to be wandering by herself all the way out here. Beck put her hands on her hips. "Here on Earth we frown upon things like trespassing." She motioned to the hives surrounding them. "You could get yourself hurt if you don't know what you're walking into."

The girl edged away from the nearest bee box. "They'll sting?"

"They're bees. Of course they'll sting." Beck pursed her lips. She'd never been one to instill fear in people about her beloved bees, but the last thing she needed was an unchaperoned child hovering about her hives.

The girl shivered and rubbed her bare arms despite the soft blanket of heat lingering in the early evening air. "But you're not even wearing one of those suits."

"My bees know me. It's strangers they don't like."

The girl stuck out her hand.

Beck eyed her skinny, briar-scratched arm.

The girl tilted her head. "Is this not the customary earthling greeting? My name is Katya Amadeus Cimmaron. I hail from the planet Zirthwyth of the Vesper Galaxy."

Beck crossed her arms over her chest. "You look like an earthling to me." She glanced to the descending sun. "You'd better head home. I'm sure some other earthling is looking for you."

Katya shrugged and dropped her waiting hand. "I only look like an earthling. I am a shapeshifter. It is my gift. To you, I look like a mere child. But to my people, I am two hundred of your Earth years old. How old are you?"

Beck did not have time for this nonsense, and yet this imp of a girl had a gravitational pull that tugged Beck into her fictional orbit. Or maybe she was simply a convenient delay from facing the painful things beckoning her back to the farmhouse.

Beck propped her hands on her hips. "I am twenty-eight in Earth years, if you must know."

"What's your name?"

"Beckett Walsh, but everyone calls me Beck."

Katya scrunched her nose in animated concentration. "Beck, why are you covering up the bees? Does it protect them? I hear there is a crisis of dying bees on your planet. And if bees die out, human life will become unsustainable. Funny how such a tiny thing can keep the earth going." The girl pulled out the notebook again and poised her pencil at the ready position. "How do these black cloths save your bees?"

Beck raised an eyebrow. This kid was some piece of work. "Why the interest? Do you have a bee crisis on your planet too?"

Katya shook her head, her expression somber. "I am not here to find out how to save my planet. I am here to see if there is still time to save yours."

Something about the solemnity of this child in her jester's attire made Beck's reservations fade. Or maybe it was the way deep down she wished someone would swoop in and save her, so much so that even the words of a wayward child served as a life preserver. "How kind of you to make the attempt. You can help me cover the hives if you'd like."

Katya chewed her lip. "But I am a stranger. You said they don't like strangers."

Beck took a deep breath and projected her voice. "Hey, bees. This is Katya. She's an alien, but I think she's all right." She smiled. "There. Now they know you. Truth is, honeybees rarely sting unless they feel threatened. When they sting, they die. They prefer to avoid that if they can help it. Just promise me you won't come around here without a grown-up."

With her index finger, Katya drew an *X* over her chest. "Cross my heart. I won't bother your bees."

"Take this end of the cloth, and we'll drape it together."

Katya pinched the hem between her fingers and edged toward the nearest hive. "You never told me. What do these cloths do?"

"Absolutely nothing."

"Then why do you do it?"

"It's an old superstition that if the beekeeper dies, you must tell the bees of his passing or the bees will die too. The cloths are supposed to help them properly mourn. The keeper made me promise I'd do it if anything ever happened to him."

"I thought you were the beekeeper."

"I'm just the apprentice. Well, I was." Beck bit down on the inside of her cheek, focusing on that ache instead of the one welling in her chest.

Katya stared at the hive in front of her, eyes wide. "What happened?"

Beck swallowed hard. "Heart attack."

"Oh." Tension left the girl's body, and she tugged the fabric until the wrinkle on the top of the hive disappeared.

Beck placed a hand on top of the box. "He's gone. He's not coming back. It's just me now."

The notebook reappeared from the fanny pack. Katya peered at her over the top of the spiral wire and scrawled as she spoke. "I don't think it's just superstition. If your whole world is getting turned upside down, then someone should tell you to your face. The bees have a right to know."

Beck picked up another cloth from the pile. "Their world isn't getting turned upside down. Nothing changes for bees. The world just keeps spinning, and they keep on doing their thing."

"Humans never count what the little things in the world notice." By the look in Katya's eyes, Beck would almost believe the child was two hundred Earth years old.

"We've got two hives left. You cover one and I'll cover the other." She motioned to the waiting UTV. "And I can give you a ride to . . . to wherever you're staying during your visit to Earth." She stooped, picking up the remaining shrouds, and turned back to find herself alone again with her hives. "Katya?"

She scanned the uncleared land, looking for sounds and sights indicating movement in the brush, but it was as though the child had vanished into thin air.

Beck finished covering the hives and called for the girl a few more times before climbing in the UTV. She rolled her shoulders to shake off the tension resting there. The girl was probably a guest at the neighboring farm. A few years back, the Baileys had started renting out the loft apartment in their barn for the summers. With a little hand-holding, they let suburbanites and city slickers try their hand at farm life. Surely her mismatched sock alien had just wandered back to where she belonged.

Beck cranked the engine and rambled back to the house, giving one final glance to the shrouded hives, the wind toying with the edges of the cloths, lifting and waving them. A silent farewell. Her father really was gone. He wasn't coming back. It was just her now.

# TWO

The next morning, Beck swept her short, wavy hair into a stubby ponytail and tugged her faded ball cap low over her eyes, sparing a glance in the mirror on her way out of her bedroom. Golden light spilled through the east-facing window, its warmth chasing away the ghost of a childhood nightmare that had come back to haunt her last night. She crept down the wooden stairs, boots in hand, then tiptoed down the hall, passing the kitchen.

Her aunt stood in front of the sink, gazing wordlessly into her mug. Aunt Kate's normally sleek bob was frizzy and tousled. Beck slipped an apple from the basket at the edge of the countertop and stepped toward the back door. A board squeaked beneath her foot. She cringed.

"Beck-Anne?" Good ole Aunt Kate, always trying to soften Beck's edges.

"Yeah?" Beck backtracked.

Her aunt blinked red-rimmed eyes. "I can make you some breakfast."

Beck lifted the apple. "This'll do. I'm not that hungry."

Aunt Kate sighed and sank into a chair at the rectangular table in the center of the kitchen. "Me neither."

"Well, I better hurry. I've got to get out to the bees to take those cloths off before it gets too hot. They'll beat their wings until they die from exhaustion trying to cool the hive. It's been hot for early May."

Aunt Kate straightened in her seat, her no-nonsense demeanor momentarily eclipsing her grief. "Don't you dare be late, Beck-Anne. It just won't do to be late today of all days. I'll lay out the dress I bought for you. I think it should fit."

"Aunt Kate . . ." Beck ground out the words, reaching deep for patience and finding the well dry. The woman never ceased trying to get her in something other than her worn jeans and tees. Every Christmas of Beck's growing up, her aunt had sent a box containing something girly and impractical from a boutique near her house in Asheville, North Carolina. You would have thought the woman would have surrendered by now.

Her aunt's attempted smile wobbled at its corners. "Don't worry. I also bought you a pair of black slacks and a simple blouse. I knew it was a long shot with the dress."

Beck softened. "Thank you."

Aunt Kate narrowed her eyes.

"I mean it," Beck said. "You knew I hadn't put an iota of thought into what I'd wear today. I should be nothing but grateful, even if you were trying to strong-arm me into a dress."

Aunt Kate dipped her chin. "Martin sends his respects. He wanted to be here, but his flight from California got canceled last minute. Some issue with the plane."

Beck nodded. It must be hard for her to have her husband stuck on a business trip the day she buried her brother. "I know he'd be here if he could." Beck gave her aunt a peck on the cheek before hurrying out the door.

Henrietta, her Rhode Island Red hen, stood on the welcome mat, head tilted, inspecting Beck with one beady eye.

Beck gently shooed her away from the door. "Sorry, girl. Aunt

Kate is strictly opposed to house chickens." She shut the door behind her and lowered her voice. "Don't worry, she'll be out of your feathers before too long."

She crossed the gravel drive and ducked into the barn, inhaling the sweet scent of horse and hay. The raw emotions that had been clawing for the surface since she'd opened her eyes that morning settled. As she walked, she ran her hand along the top of the stalls her father had built, pretending something of him still lingered in everything he had touched.

A soft nicker greeted her.

"Hey, Sparks." Her buckskin gelding stuck his head over the stall door. She took a bite of her apple and offered him the rest. Smiling at the sounds of his slobbery crunching, she headed to the tack room for his bridle.

She wasn't much of a horsewoman, but Sparks was a gentle old boy who worked at two speeds, ambling walk and, if you insisted, long-striding trot. She led him outside and used a fence rail to boost herself onto his bare back.

Swaying with his stride, she lost herself in the soft clomp of horse hooves and the swish of grass against his nimble legs. Twittering birds took flight as they entered the wooded trail leading to the farthest field where the bees were kept.

When they broke into the clearing, a herd of deer in the adjacent field lifted their heads in unison, ears sticking out from the sides of their heads like warning flags. Sparks chuffed softly but plodded along on their normal route that curved away from the herd. Satisfied that she and Sparks weren't a threat after all, the deer returned to their grazing. Even in the quiet beauty, that old nightmare poked at Beck's consciousness. Why had that dream revisited her? Because her father was gone and could no longer come to her rescue? Or because his funeral would force her to venture beyond the boundaries of Walsh Farm?

Several yards from the hives, Beck halted and slid from the horse's back. She unclipped the reins from his bitless bridle and draped them over her shoulder, leaving him to graze while she worked.

Beck slipped the black shrouds from the hives as the first bees were beginning to stir, eager for their day's work. If only she could join them, buzz to and fro with purpose. Work herself until there was no space left for thinking. Feeling.

"You have a horse? He's beautiful."

Beck turned. The mismatched sock alien emerged from the brush munching on a banana and looking freshly showered. Today's knee socks featured puffy clouds on one leg and monkeys on the other. How long had she waited there? Why didn't anyone care that this child wandered alone?

"Good morning, Katya Amadeus Cimmaron from the planet Zirthwyth of the Vesper Galaxy."

The girl graced Beck with a nod of approval and then pointed to the hive as Beck removed another cloth. "You're taking them off? You just put them on yesterday."

"A worker bee only lives about six weeks," Beck said. "One day for them is like a year of your life."

Katya Amadeus Cimmaron crossed her arms over her chest and cocked out her hip. "You mean it is like one Earth year. Years are different on my planet."

Beck mimicked her stance. "So how does one Earth year compare to yours?"

Katya looked at the ground and shook her head slowly. "I would try and explain it, but sadly it is beyond an earthling's understanding. It would only give you a headache."

Beck laughed under her breath. "Do you want to help me with uncovering the hives?"

Katya brightened. "Sure!"

"Make sure you stand behind the hive when you remove it. There might be some anxious little ladies bursting to get to work."

"How do you know they're girls?"

"All worker bees are girls."

She lifted her chin. "Cool."

Beck smiled, remembering the way she felt when she'd learned that fact about bees. Even though she was so different from Aunt Kate, from all the girls she knew, in that instant she'd gained a sense of camaraderie with these tiny pollinators who made the world go 'round.

Together, she and Katya uncovered the fifty hives that dotted the field in neat rows. Surrounding the edges of the field, the black cloths draped over the scrub brush waved in the wind.

Katya surveyed their work. "You should leave it like that. The bees have to go on with their work, but the cloth will help them remember the beekeeper."

Moisture welled up in Beck's eyes, and she turned away under the guise of considering the lay of the land. If she left this evidence of her mourning draped about this field, the sun would eventually fade those stark black mourning cloths to a soft gray. She could only hope that was how grief worked. "I like your idea."

"Really?" Katya straightened. "You do?"

"Sure."

"Do you miss the beekeeper too?"

"He was my dad." Her words came out thin and airy as they squeezed past the lump in her throat.

"Oh. That must be hard. Earthlings are close to their parents, aren't they?"

Beck narrowed her eyes. "You're not close to your parents, Katya?"

She shrugged and ambled in a lopsided circle with her arms clasped behind her back—an extraterrestrial philosopher. "It's different on my planet, remember? One people. One land. Whoever is available to take care of the younglings does. Parents are interchangeable. Like earthling light bulbs."

Beck nodded. Sometimes earthling parents acted as though they were as interchangeable as light bulbs too. But never Beck's father. He had been the one person she could count on. "And who is taking care of you right now?"

Katya shot her a withering look. "I am two hundred Earth years old. I do not require a caregiver."

Beck tried to read past the facade presented by the pink-cheeked girl with sweat beading on her nose. "Maybe not. But surely someone is looking for you."

"Yeah, I better go." Katya scurried into the undergrowth, despite Beck's protests. The distant clang of the triangular dinner bell sounded, and Sparks lifted his head.

It was time to dress for Dad's funeral.

# THREE

The building inspector glared over the top of his clipboard. "I'm sorry, but you're going to have to get the electrical and plumbing up to code before you open." The man gave a curt farewell nod before exiting. The door swung closed behind him, leaving Callie Peterson with a half-uttered protest hanging from her lips. The grand opening banner flapped in the breeze, mocking her.

She turned to her contractor, who scratched at the back of his neck, avoiding her gaze.

"This office space was fully operational when I bought the place two months ago," she said. "How can they keep me from opening?"

Mike let out a breath and hitched the waist of his worn jeans. "I did warn you before we started taking those walls down. On an old building like this, you start making improvements and the city is going to go over it with a fine-tooth comb to make sure everything gets updated to the current code. And it's your bad luck they passed a new one the week before you closed on the place. You might be able to appeal it, but . . ."

All she'd wanted was to take down a few walls and do a facelift on the bathroom. A simple transformation to turn the neglected brick building near Frazier Avenue from sectioned-off offices to an airy showroom for all her artisan candles and skin-care products.

She hadn't even started on the project to revamp the back half into a workshop in an effort to be cautious with her funds.

"How long will the updates take?" She couldn't face her real question. What was the price tag? However much Mike quoted her, the inspector's list of changes would drain the remainder of her business loan. Money she'd allocated to furnish the place and restock supplies.

He crossed his arms over his chest. "My plumbing and electrical guys are tied up on another project for at least two weeks. Then, once we start, I'd say at least another two weeks on all the things the inspector mentioned. And that's if everything is straightforward once we get in there. On buildings like this—"

"It's never straightforward," she finished his sentence with a groan. "I know. I know. But, Mike, I had my heart set on opening in two weeks."

"I'm not going to say I told you so, but—"

"You just did," she said through clenched teeth.

Mike stuffed his hands in his pockets. "So, what do you want to do, boss? You can try to argue the decision, but that could take months."

Callie massaged her temples and sighed. "Get me an estimate with whatever needs to be done to get this place open, and we'll go from there."

She left Mike standing in Sheetrock dust and hiked to her car. Better head home and get to work making as many online sales as she could.

Callie drove away from the shop, taking the few turns necessary to drive past the riverfront on her way home. Chattanooga was called the Scenic City for a reason. The view it offered never failed to lift her spirits.

But no matter how gorgeous the iconic blue arches of the Walnut Street Bridge looked against the pink sunset, they did nothing to soothe the tightness in her chest today.

She'd timed her grand opening perfectly. Memorial Day weekend coincided with a nearby arts festival and a women's conference at the convention center with over five hundred attendees. With her prime location near Coolidge Park, catnip for locals and tourists alike, it was sure to have been a banner day. But now . . .

She stopped her car in front of the large cottage that had been split into apartments. At thirty-one, she didn't exactly fit in with the revolving college-age residents, but they certainly gave the location some flavor.

Callie climbed the steps and lifted her hand in greeting as she passed a guy on the front porch wearing a beanie, despite the summer heat, and strumming his guitar. She shook her head and smiled, fairly certain this porch sitter didn't even live there. She grabbed her mail from the box for apartment 3 and headed inside.

In the combination living space and kitchen, she scooted aside bundles of wicks and beeswax bars to make room for her laptop on the scuffed breakfast table. What she needed was a little pick-me-up and a plan. She'd run the numbers. Numbers were one thing that never lied.

But first, coffee.

She dumped the spent grounds from her portafilter and refilled it with fresh espresso, inhaling the comforting scent. Once the hiss of her machine faded, Callie opened her laptop and settled herself in front of her screen.

The first thing she needed was a realistic assessment of what she could hope to bring in over the next several months. She studied the sales spreadsheets comparing this spring's sales to last. She was growing, nice and steady. Quite honestly, she was exactly where she wanted to be in her third year of running Solace Naturals. Purchasing the small building had been a huge step of faith, but one she'd felt so ready for. If only she had researched the building codes further. She'd been too impulsive. She was never impulsive. With good reason, apparently.

She pulled her long brown hair into a high bun and then leaned back against the chair, stretching out a tight spot in her shoulder blade.

Her email notification dinged. Mike's estimate. That was prompt. She clicked print without reading it and massaged her forehead while the printer hummed. Normally she was so good with details, thinking through every possible way something could go wrong and planning a solution. It was a survival skill that had often been the topic of the sessions with her therapist, Joanne. "Be spontaneous. Try something new. Have faith that it could go right." Maybe she'd gone a little too far trying to implement her therapist's advice.

Six months spent outside of Mom's constant state of crisis had lulled Callie into the belief that the world could be a predictable place where things went according to plan.

Callie closed her laptop and laid her head down on the computer. *God, help me know what to do next. Help me to make the next move. I don't want to be motivated by my fear of all the things that could go wrong or to plow ahead on my own strength. Teach me how to rely on you. To trust You.*

She blew out a breath and straightened. Faith in something outside of herself had never come naturally. Not with a raising like hers.

She glanced to the crunchy, brown peace lily on her cluttered counter and cringed. If someone opened her up, the little mustard seed of faith that had sprouted in her heart when she was sixteen probably looked a little bit like that poor plant.

She picked up Mike's estimate from the printer and scanned over the line items. If only these were things that she could work on over time and not things she had to have completed and in place before the doors opened. Then it would be fine. But having to make mortgage payments on this empty space that wasn't making any income on top of that?

She flipped through her mail stack. Bills already paid through autopay, junk mail. She smirked at the envelope from River City Trust Company. They sure had gotten good at making junk mail look official. But these folks had missed their target audience. The closest thing she had to something worth putting in a trust was her scuffed oak breakfast table and her espresso machine. She could bequeath those to any of her adjacent caffeine-addicted college kids just by sticking them outside on the wide front porch.

A knock sounded on her door, and she pushed the mail to the side. It was probably one of her neighbors asking if they could borrow some milk because theirs had gone sour or someone who needed to vent their roommate issues.

Her friendly gesture of dropping off little gift baskets and welcoming them to stop by any time may have been overkill. She was starting to feel more like a dorm mother than a fellow resident.

She fixed a friendly smile on her face as she pulled the door open. "Hey, baby."

Callie dropped the neighborly smile.

A faded bruise colored one of her mother's hollowed cheekbones. She had to be at least twenty pounds lighter than the last time they'd spoken. It had been a long time since Callie had seen her looking this bad.

"It's me. Your momma." She attempted a teasing, sugary tone, but emotion caused her voice to warble. "I found you." Her chin trembled, and she held out her arms, reaching.

Callie's heart pounded like a bass drum, and her chest grew tight. The words shouted between them the last time she'd seen her mother resounded in her cranium. Sleepless nights had followed, imagining her mother spiraling into darker and darker places. By the look of her thin, unwashed frame, it seemed her imagination had not been far off.

Her mother dropped her outstretched arms. "Say something, Callie."

"I . . ." Callie had said all she'd needed to say that night six months ago. Standing outside the bar where her mother had called for a ride after she'd been ousted for harassing the bartender who refused to overserve her.

*I pushed her too hard.* "I tried to call you after that night. It said your phone was disconnected. I've been worried." She shook herself out of it. *Her decline isn't my fault.*

Her mother swiped a clump of hair from her face. "You know, I've found that not being in constant contact with the world is kind of freeing. Life is more peaceful without that thing dinging all the time."

Translation: Mom had probably spent her money on booze instead of her phone bill.

She glanced over her shoulder to her cramped one-bedroom apartment. Her shoulders tensed, creeping toward her ears. She could offer a shower and a night on the couch. But let her move in again?

No. Callie had gone with a smaller place for a reason. Maybe she hadn't realized it at the time, but this was why, wasn't it? To make it easier to hold the line she'd drawn in the sand. There was a problem with sand though—a strong puff of wind was all it took to erase that guide mark.

Callie sighed and forced the words past the mountain of guilt crushing her chest. "Nothing's changed from what I told you that night. You need help. More help than I can give you. I wish—"

Her mother stepped forward, her toe crossing the threshold of Callie's doorway. She grasped her hands. "I'm ready, baby. That's why I came." Her eyes were wide and pleading. "I want to get help, but I can't think straight. I don't know where to go or what to do. I need you to help me. Just this one last time, I promise."

The tremor in her mother's voice cut into Callie's heart and flowed through her veins. As much as she hated to admit it, the little girl inside Callie Peterson still desperately wanted to believe her mother had the power to keep her promises.

# FOUR

*a* few days later, Beck rounded the house, dewy grass clippings adhering to her bare toes. There was something about feeling the cool earth beneath her feet that always settled her soul. She knelt beside a bed of lupine in fiery pinks, oranges, and cool purples. She pulled a few weeds sprouting up in the river rock border. Already a few little early-rising worker bees hovered about and nestled in the blossoms, drinking in all they could carry.

The percussive slap of the screen door punctured Beck's world.

"I just don't know, Martin. I know I've been here a whole week, but I'm not sure I should leave her yet." Aunt Kate's voice, coming from the sweeping front porch, reached Beck's ears crisp and clear, as though she stood right beside her. "I'm supposed to be back to work Monday, but maybe they could spare me a little longer."

*No. Go back home.* All Beck wanted was to mourn her father in peace without her aunt hovering, psychoanalyzing Beck's every move.

"I don't know how she'll manage," Aunt Kate continued. "It's what I've been telling you. Beck never even leaves the place. George made a world where she never had to. How is she supposed to manage alone when something as simple as running to the grocery store sets her off?"

Aunt Kate went silent, no doubt listening to her husband on the other end of the line. Beck's chest ached. Wanting to deny her words. Knowing she couldn't.

"She did go to the funeral. I'll give her that. But I arranged all the details while she wandered aimlessly, acting like weeding the garden and messing with those bees was her number one priority. At the funeral, she was a bundle of nerves the whole time. She didn't calm back down until we were back on the farm."

Beck sat on the largest of the river rocks bordering the beds, her strength drained. She'd tried to play it off like she was handling everything just fine. Apparently Aunt Kate saw right through her. Pinpricks fired off behind her eyes. Her aunt may have been embarrassed by her issues, but Dad would've understood. He always had.

Aunt Kate's clipped footsteps sounded on the front porch. Back and forth. Back and forth. "No, I know. She's twenty-eight. I've got to let her stand on her own two feet. Sink or swim and all that. But is the timing right? She hasn't touched the mail. There will be bills, papers to be signed to transfer the property. She can't afford to let things like this slide."

Beck stood and went for the barn, driven by a force outside of herself. Check the fence lines. That's what she needed to do. A branch could have fallen in the winds last night. The last thing she needed was her animals escaping onto the neighbors' property. That was something she couldn't let slide.

With the necessary tools for the job at hand in her backpack, she swung atop Sparks and nudged her reluctant steed into a slow trot. She focused on the low-lying fog floating over the fields, trying to deny the pain and shame Aunt Kate's words stirred to life.

Beck rode along the edge of the property making sure the fence was in working order. Where there were weeds and brambles obscuring the fence, she cut them away. Any low-hanging branches that looked like a threat, she cut back. The physical exertion unwound knots inside her. Just because she'd never had to take care of things like farm finances didn't mean she couldn't. And just because leaving the farm proved . . . difficult . . . didn't mean it was impossible.

Her last stop before returning back to the house for lunch was the beeyard. Already, the color of the black fabric draped along the border had softened slightly. She wished she could say the same about the pain in her chest.

Beck dismounted Sparks and left him to graze. She picked the nearest hive and sat beside the entrance, watching the bees come and go. It had been one of her favorite games for as long as she could remember. By observing returning worker bees, studying the color of the pollen packed onto their rear legs, she'd learned how to identify what flower they'd foraged from by pollen color. Today's abundance of dark yellow bundles indicated sweet white clover as the delicacy of the day.

What would it be like to be a honeybee? Never an ounce of question in their purpose. No wondering what to do next.

"Whatcha doing?" Katya wandered over. Maybe she should still be surprised by this little wood nymph who always seemed to know the exact moment Beck arrived in the field, but something about her presence had started to feel comfortable. Still, she needed to figure out where this kid belonged. Make sure she was as okay as she seemed.

Beck waved her over and pointed out the bees' "pollen pants."

Katya wrinkled her nose as she took a spot on the grass beside Beck. "Isn't that the stuff that makes people sneeze?"

"Some people are allergic, yes, but for bees, it is a food source. It's rich in the fats and proteins they need."

Katya scribbled furiously in her notebook as though Beck spilled the secrets of the universe for her ears only. She paused and peered over her notes. "Did you know that elephants are terrified of tiny little honeybees?"

Beck raised her eyebrows. "I didn't know that."

Katya sat extra tall, obviously pleased that she knew something about bees the keeper did not. "Yup. In Africa, they were having trouble keeping the elephants from destroying crops. They'd plow right through fences. So, they started making fences out of beehives. And bam, no more elephant problems. It's cool 'cause it helps the farmers with their crops, it protects the elephants from being harmed, and it helps bees."

She pictured the girl tugging at the arm of some parental figure, nagging them to help her research bee facts to impress Beck. "That is pretty cool." Beck leaned back on her elbows, watching young bees fly spirals around the hive, orienting themselves to their home base.

Her stomach rumbled, and she stood and stretched. "My earthling body is in need of food. You can come if you want. We can call whatever earthling you're staying with and let them know where you are so they aren't worried. You may have noticed we earthlings have a great propensity for worry."

Katya stood and shook her head. "I told you that I do not require a caregiver."

Beck shrugged, striving to match Katya's nonchalance despite her growing concern. "Of course, little shapeshifter. But an earthling body does require hydration and nutrition. Do you want to come back to my place and get some lemonade and a PB&J, or do you want to keep lurking around in the woods?"

Katya bit her lip, glancing behind her to the brush she'd emerged from earlier. She shrugged. "I could eat."

The child followed her to the perimeter of the beeyard. Beck paused and placed her thumb and forefinger in her mouth, emitting a shrill whistle.

Sparks lifted his head and trotted toward them. Katya edged behind her, staring.

Beck clipped on the lead line. Sparks leaned his head low and snuffed in Katya's face.

A suffocated squeal squeezed out of the girl's tight-closed lips.

"He's just saying hello. That's how horses greet each other. They breathe each other's air."

Katya reached for his nose with a shaky hand. "It feels like velvet." Sparks tossed his head, and she jerked her hand back.

"Don't worry. He's not a biter."

Katya's eyes widened. "Horses bite?"

"Some horses bite and some bees sting. But most don't if you don't give them a reason to." Beck straightened her ball cap and mopped the sweat from her forehead, then she tugged Sparks toward the wooded trail and Katya fell into step beside her.

They let out a simultaneous sigh of relief when they entered the shaded path.

Back at the barn, she put Sparks in his stall and filled his water bucket, then she turned to Katya. "I'm going to run inside the house to make some sandwiches. If you want, take a peek into the last stall—our barn cat had a litter of kittens. But keep your distance. Sassy is as wild as a mink. She will bite and scratch, and she'd sting, too, if the good Lord had seen fit to equip her with a stinger."

"I'll just look." The girl tiptoed over and peeked through the slats to where Sassy nursed her newborns.

Beck turned to go. To her back, the girl said, "You know, you should spay and neuter your pets. I thought all earthlings knew this."

Beck smirked over her shoulder. "She arrived in that condition, thank you very much. I guess she thought my house looked like a place she could be safe for a while."

Katya nodded. "I could see that."

Rational or not, Walsh Farm had become the one place in the world Beck felt safe.

She climbed the steps to the wraparound porch, then she slipped off her boots by the door and went inside, letting the screen door slap closed behind her. "Aunt Kate?"

"I'm in the living room. Was that a little girl with you?"

Thank goodness for the buffer that sock alien provided. She padded through the foyer and leaned against the entryway. Aunt Kate sat on the couch folding towels. "Yep. She showed up at the apiary a few days ago, and she was back again this morning. She seems clean and well fed, but she shouldn't be on her own like that. Any thoughts on what I should do?"

Aunt Kate scrunched her nose, thinking. "I can call the Baileys and see if they know anything. You'd mentioned they had started taking on guests. You know, that wouldn't be a bad idea for you. You could turn the upstairs into a B&B. This house will feel pretty empty with just you here. It might be good for you."

Beck nodded, keeping her expression still as pond water. "Sure. I'll get on that right after I get back from the cross-country road trip I've planned."

Kate froze midfold and narrowed her eyes. "Your what?"

The corners of Beck's mouth twitched.

"Oh, you. Get out of here, you snarky thing." Kate winged a balled pair of socks at her, hitting Beck in the thigh. "I thought you were serious there for a second."

Beck laughed and tossed the socks back into the pile but cringed inside at the hopeful spark that had bloomed in her aunt's eyes before fading when she realized Beck was only joking. "Well, I better get in here and make some lunch for our visitor and try to keep her entertained until we can figure out whose she is." She snickered. "Shouldn't be too hard to keep her busy. She's researching life on our planet to see if it's still possible to save it."

"Sounds like you when you were little," Aunt Kate said.

"And here I've always prided myself on being down to earth." She went into the kitchen and made two sandwiches, licking the excess peanut spread off the butter knife before tossing it in the sink. On the porch, she called for the girl.

Katya skipped out of the barn in a very un-alienlike fashion. She reached for the sandwich on top. But she froze when a white hatchback pulled down the drive. Beck squinted, trying to discern the driver.

As the car pulled to a stop, Katya jumped off the porch and sprinted for the barn.

"Katya!" Beck called after her.

"Fern!"

Beck turned to the source of the male voice. He unfolded from the driver's seat gazing toward the barn, horn-rimmed glasses askew, button-up half-untucked. The expression on his face appeared hopeless and harried.

"Fern?" she asked.

He ran his hand through his mussed hair, the same color as the alien girl's. He smiled weakly, one eyebrow raised. "Katya?"

Beck gave him a lopsided grin. "That's what she's been going by. She yours?"

His mouth opened and closed, and he nodded once. "I'm Isaac Wesley. Fern and I are staying on Bailey Farm for the summer." He motioned to the barn. "May I?"

She studied him. Though Katya/Fern had fled at the sight of him, he looked less like a threat and more like a drowning man desperate for a life preserver. "Of course."

He strode after the girl in ankle-length khakis that looked like they'd been left to cool in the dryer.

Beck followed at enough of a distance to give them space, but close enough to detect if anything was amiss with this new stranger.

The man entered the empty stall the girl occupied. She sat in the fresh hay, hugging her knees, looking away from him. Her expression placid.

He knelt to her level. "Fern, I know I said you could explore while I was working, but I meant for you to stay on the Baileys' property and to tell me where you were going. I missed a meeting yesterday trying to figure out where you'd wandered off to, and if we don't hurry back, I'm going to be late for another. They weren't too keen on me working remotely this summer, and if I miss any more meetings, I'm worried that—"

Fern stood, fists clenched at her sides. "Sorry. I didn't mean to mess up your life. I never even wanted to come here. But nobody gave me the choice."

She strode past both him and Beck. The man stood. He grimaced when the car door slammed. He shifted his loafer-clad feet, coating his shoes and bare ankles with a film of sawdust. "I hope she wasn't too much trouble."

The space between Beck's shoulder blades tightened. "You really shouldn't let her wander like that. She could get hurt. Or lost."

His eyes closed and he swallowed. "I know. I . . ." His eyes flashed open, and he glanced at the smartwatch vibrating on his wrist. He froze. "I'm sorry, I really have to go."

He hurried out of the barn and drove away in a cloud of dust.

Fern gazed out the back passenger window as if thoroughly bored with all her studies of Planet Earth, ready to return to her home planet.

# FIVE

Callie strolled through Renaissance Park, Hydro Flask in hand. She smiled at a petite woman who quickstepped to keep up with her Great Dane's longish stride. Going the opposite direction, a tall man walked a mincing Pekinese.

Someday she would be one of them. She'd have the steady type of life a dog required.

She toyed with the loop that kept the lid attached to her water bottle. There had been a dog once. She'd never forget her giddy excitement when her mom took her to the shelter the week before Christmas and they brought home that scruffy terrier mix. They'd had to be sneaky about it. The extended-stay hotel they were living out of didn't permit pets. But it had been love at first sight between her and Scout.

When her mother slid back into a bad place—coming home later and later, and hot dinners around the table were replaced with Callie fixing herself a bowl of carefully rationed cereal—things seemed easier with Scout to commiserate with.

A few months later, her mother's shaky foundation gave way. In the dead of night, her mother had jostled a half-awake Callie from her bed and ushered her into the back seat before peeling out of the parking lot. As they rode away, Callie's hand had automatically reached for Scout's wiry fur to settle the angst constricting her chest, but for the first time in months, he wasn't by her side.

She'd screeched and wailed until her throat ached, begging her mother to go back, to turn around. Nonchalant, her mother replied that she'd found a nice family to take Scout. But Callie knew better. He had been left behind. She'd never asked for another pet after that. It was better if she was the only one who had to endure her mother's endless cycles of abandonment.

Callie sank onto a picnic table bench and pushed the memories back into the mental boxes she stored them in. What was the sense in letting her mind go back there? She was here to enjoy watching other people and their adorable pets.

The warmth and sunshine seemed the right setting for facing the less-than-promising outlook represented on the paperwork in her bag. She pulled the file folder from her satchel and lined up the itemized price list of the renovations the building inspector required alongside the list of her personal expenses. She might be living off cereal and ramen for the foreseeable future, but it wasn't totally impossible to make it work.

The irony was not lost on her—the repairs needed were the things within the walls that no one else could see. She let her head fall back with a sigh and stared into the cloudless sky. *God, if You're trying to send me a message, I read You loud and clear. No offense, but I think I could have done without this tangible reminder.*

Her phone rang. An unfamiliar number showed on the caller ID. Her thumb hovered over the dismiss button. It was probably just another spam call about the nonexistent extended warranty on her car. Although it could be Mom begging her for a ride from the rehab center she'd entered a few days ago. It wouldn't be her shortest stint.

Callie swiped to accept the call and put the phone to her ear. "Hello?"

"Hello, this is Charity Benton from Sunrise Recovery Center. I'm calling for Callie Peterson on behalf of Lindy Peterson." The woman had a sweet North Georgia drawl, not the tinny sound of a spam recording she'd anticipated.

She drew in a breath, steeling herself for what would come next, refusing to consider the amount of trouble her mother could have caused in a such short time span. "This is she."

"Well, I was calling because there's been a bit of a hiccup with your mother's paperwork."

Callie stomach clenched in the woman's pregnant pause.

"As we were finalizing everything with her intake, it came to our attention that your mother's current health insurance plan is going to lapse at the end of this week. It seems she was terminated from her place of employment several weeks ago, which is especially unfortunate, because her plan would have left her paying next to nothing out of pocket for the six weeks of inpatient care recommended. Here at Sunrise, we're committed to do our best to work with the families we serve to get them the care they need at an affordable rate. Now, there are a few different options we can look at . . ."

The woman's voice took on a distant quality, leaving Callie feeling as though she stood at the end of a long tunnel explaining a complex algebraic equation beyond Callie's comprehension.

The words bounced against the walls of Callie's mind as memories replayed. Other rehab centers. Reckless, undying hope that her mother was going to get the help she needed, always dashed to bits. But this was different. This was the first time Mom had been the one to say she needed help. Not Callie. Not the courts.

The tiny bloom of hope that had sprouted in Callie's heart withered.

"We do offer payment plans as well as loan services. Also, we can make adjustments to the treatment plan—"

"I'm sorry. Hold on just a moment." Callie shook her head to clear it, bringing herself back to the here and now. "My mother is the one who checked herself in. I simply provided the ride to your location. Why are you speaking to me instead of her about this?"

"Oh, pardon me. I didn't realize you hadn't been informed." Charity cleared her throat. "Your mother listed you as her health-care proxy. That way we can keep you in the loop. It also gives her health-care providers the allowance to speak candidly with you. Loved ones find this access gives them peace of mind, especially during those initial weeks in which we don't allow the residents any outside contact. Your mother was certainly free to leave that line blank, but she chose you."

Callie's head spun at the woman's continued stream of words about the benefits of her involvement in her mother's care. "That's uh . . ." She trailed off. Maybe it was wrong, resenting this entanglement her mother had forced upon her, but distance was the only thing Callie had found helpful in holding any semblance of healthy boundaries with her mother. "But this call is about the finances. That's a decision my mother needs to make."

"Ms. Peterson, she also listed you as the responsible party for costs incurred during the course of treatment in the event something is not covered by insurance. We tried speaking to your mother for clarification. She reported feeling too unwell to make decisions at this time and asked that we call you to handle the arrangements. Is this a role you are willing to accept?"

Callie's pulse pounded. All the dog walkers and their charges seemed to move in slow motion around her. A part of a different world. One without cares.

"Ms. Peterson, are you there?"

"Oh. Uh. Yes. Yes, I am willing to help her move forward." Lindy Peterson was never, ever going to be able to use Callie as an excuse for her problems. Callie would see to that. Even if this bankrupted her.

Charity rattled off numbers at a dizzying rate. Everything from the cost of simply finishing out the two-week detox program to the full six weeks of inpatient care. Payment plans that might be available depending on her income. Callie grabbed a pen from her bag and started scrawling numbers as fast as she could on the nearest sheet of paper.

She hung up the phone and laid her head in her hands as her throat grew tight. She bit down on her lip to keep the welling tears in check.

Crying wouldn't fix anything. The only thing Callie had ever found useful in making anything better was prayer and hard work. Although, if she was honest, she tended to depend a little more on the latter.

She looked down at the number she'd written down. Of course, of all the papers she could have scribbled on, she'd grabbed Mike's estimate.

Callie shook her head. Even though she'd tried to disentangle herself from her mother's affairs, Lindy Peterson had found a way to cross Callie's boundaries without even being present. Like with a million other instances, Callie would be forced to choose between finally grasping her just-out-of-reach dreams and bailing her mother out of another mess. Maybe now was a good time to restart her therapy sessions. She'd thought she'd made so much progress, but maybe it had just been the fact that her mom hadn't been around.

She studied the other parkgoers.

All around her, parents played with their kids on blankets or under trees. Well-dressed people walked their dogs with wide smiles on their faces. A lady at the other picnic table, with her coffee in hand, gazed across the river with a contemplative smile on her face. The lives Callie imagined for these happy strangers flashed before her eyes. Childhoods involving two healthy, caring parents. Free from the weight of loved ones' self-destruction. Callie drained the last of the water from her bottle. Her therapist's words came back to haunt her.

"Fantasizing about having a 'normal' life is very common among adult children of alcoholics. It's often a tough battle to let go of the perceived normal that it seems everyone else was afforded."

She couldn't quite remember how old she'd been when she realized her mother was not like other mothers. But she could remember the guilt she'd felt wishing she could trade with someone else.

# SIX

*C*lipboard in hand, Beck trekked across the yard. Aunt Kate had left yesterday morning, brows drawn so tight in worry, they'd leave permanent lines across her forehead. Beck practically had to drag her aunt from the house, dousing her in promises that she would manage just fine on her own.

Starting today she'd prove her words true.

Gray clouds hung low in the sky. It was a good day to get some organization and prep work in. She headed to the honey house, the large metal building where she and her father stored their supplies and processed honey, beeswax, and pollen. She pushed open the sliding door and inhaled the smell—sweet, rich, and woodsy, just like the inside of a hive.

Sunlight streamed in, glinting off the jars on the shelf just waiting to be filled with liquid gold. She wove her way through the stacks of extra honey supers ready to be added to the hives in the coming weeks. She'd inspected most of the six-inch-high wooden boxes weeks ago, making sure each one was in good condition.

With everything in bloom, the bees were feasting on the abundant nectar flow. The hives would need another round of empty supers added soon. It was forecasted to be hot and sunny tomorrow. Low wind. A prime day for inspections.

She took a super down from the last stack and looked for signs of peeling paint or instability in the wooden joints. She removed all ten frames inside, making sure none of them needed repairs. She worked through the remaining stacks in that same way and set aside anything that required mending.

On her way to the back of the room where the rest of the supplies were kept, she paused in front of the beekeeping suits hanging on their pegs. Her smaller one next to a taller one. Beck walked over and rubbed the canvas of her father's suit between her fingers. Was she really capable of managing without him?

She sorted through miscellaneous items, organizing things that had been left in the wrong places in moments of haste and noting what she needed to add to the Apiary Supply order. Dad had always taken the forty-five minute drive to the supplier, but surely they had shipping options. She'd check online tonight.

She went to the plastic tub in the corner and ran her hands over the last of the wood her father had cut for building new brood boxes. Those deeper boxes were where the real magic of the hive happened. The queen, the mother of them all, constantly bringing forth new daughters. Those daughters emerging into the orderly life in which each one was given a distinct role in the survival of the hive.

She picked up a couple pieces of wood and fit the tongue and groove together before returning it to the pile. There were a few hives with burgeoning populations that she needed to split before they got a mind to swarm.

She straightened and looked over the checklist she'd started. All she had to do was get organized, take one step at a time, and everything would work out fine.

The phone on the wall jangled, and she grabbed it from the cradle. "Walsh Farm, this is Beckett Walsh."

"Hey there, Beckett. This is Louis over at the fire department. We've had a call about a swarm of bees hanging out in a cherry tree near State Route 322 and wondered if you'd like to handle that for us. Your farm was the top one to call in case of bees. I thought you might want them."

Free bees hanging out in a tree in search of somewhere to call home? Her dad had loved to get these calls. "Well, I . . ."

She visualized pulling her bee suit from the hook. Grabbing the swarm kit. Placing it in the back of Dad's truck. Pulling the keys off the hook. Inserting the keys in the ignition. Her chest grew tight. Pulling to the end of the drive. Making that right turn. Her breath came in pants. Images of her wrecked truck on the side of the road where she'd lost control mid–panic attack consumed her. The fingers of her free hand, of their own volition, started their tap dance. Each one against her thumb in progression. Index finger, middle finger, ring finger, pinky. Index, middle, ring, pinky.

"Beckett, you still there? You want to come get 'em?"

Fingers still tapping, she said, "No. I . . . I'm not able to get out that way." She blew a long breath. "I'm a little tied up at the moment, but if you ring the Sweetwater Beekeepers Association, I know there'll be somebody who'd love to have them." She swallowed hard.

She hung up the phone, leaned against the wall, and slid down to sit.

She focused on the repetitive motion of her fingertips, bringing all the frantic buzzing inside her head in line with that steady march. Index, middle, ring, pinky.

One thing at a time. She'd start with handling everything that could be ordered and shipped. The things that required venturing beyond the driveway—she'd face those when it came to it. Bee swarms could go to another keeper. Carrying on her father's legacy didn't mean doing things just like him. She had to find her own way.

Aunt Kate's concerned face popped into her mind. She'd better see to that mail stack though. See what bills were outstanding and all that. She headed out of the honey house and slid the barn-style door closed behind her.

Although, the grass around the house was looking a little shaggy. Might as well get on that before the rain that was forecasted for the afternoon. Paperwork was for bad weather and when the sun went down. She grabbed the mower keys off the peg in the barn.

As she rode the mower in careful circles around the house, noise canceling headphones on her ears blasting classical cello, her thoughts wandered to her little alien friend. Had Fern ceased her roaming, or was she even now prowling about in the woods like Huck Finn, waiting for Beck to reappear?

Movement in her peripherals snagged her attention. A tall woman who looked to be close to her father's age waved frantically from the driveway in a hot pink sun visor and floral print pedal pushers. Beck slipped the headphones from her ears, letting them rest around her neck.

"Yoohoo! Hello!" The woman's shrill voice cut through the roar of the mower.

With a sigh, Beck cut the engine and hopped off. She squinted. Was that Annette?

Beck sighed. At the funeral, Annette had cornered Beck, ruining her attempt to find a quiet place to decompress. Annette had tearfully recounted the many meals she and George had shared after church on Sundays and how much he'd meant to her. Though Annette had come to the farm only a handful of times over the years, the woman never failed to rub Beck the wrong way.

Her cloud of perfume reached Beck six feet in advance. Beck swiped the moisture from her forehead and winced. She was currently drenched in Eau de Grass and Sweat and was likely equally as pungent. The woman held a pile of mail in her arms, her lower lip trembling.

"Can I help you?" Beck asked.

"It's me, Annette. Your father's friend."

Beck inwardly recoiled at the emphasis placed on her last word. "I remember."

"I was stopping by to bring you a casserole. I made too much for myself. Then I saw your mailbox overflowin', but when I stopped the car, my bee flew right out my window. Have you seen her anywhere?" The woman's eyes welled, and her last sentence came out in a pathetic squeak.

"Uh . . ." Was this some sort of joke, or was this woman struggling with her mental faculties? "I have over a million on the property. I'm not sure I could pick yours out of a lineup."

She tilted her head, brow furrowed. "Well, she's about yea big." She held her hands about a foot apart.

"In that case, I'd know if I'd seen her." Beck chuckled. "Never in my life have I seen a bee that size."

Now the woman was looking at Beck as if she questioned her sanity. "She's tan, has a curled tail and a black smoosh-nosed face. Answers to Beatrice or Bea."

Beck snorted. "Oh! You mean a dog."

The lady squinted and adjusted her sun visor, dropping an envelope off the top of the sliding mail stack. "Of course, dear. What did you think I meant?" She stooped to pick up the envelope and dropped three more.

Beck went to her aid, scooping the mail from her arms. "I haven't seen your dog, but I don't mind helping you look around. Or you can leave me your number and I can call if she turns up."

Annette took Beck's free hand and squeezed it. "I don't want to interrupt your work, but I'd feel ever so much better if I could look around."

Beck slipped her slick and gritty hand away from the lady's tidy French manicured vice. Boy, could she go for a quick dip in the creek about now. "Of course."

"Oh, thank you, Beckett."

Beck forced a smile. "I just have a few more rounds on the mower and I'll help you look." She popped inside and set the mail on the hall table where another pile was waiting to be opened. She'd better see to all that tonight. Otherwise the lights and water were going to be cut off and Aunt Kate proved right.

Annette's sharp cries of "Bea! Beatrice!" sounded outside. Beck shook her head and placed her headphones back over her ears. Just when she thought she'd have a nice quiet day to herself.

After she finished the yard and the grass around the barn, she parked the mower in the shed and rinsed the sweat and grit from her arms and face with the chilly water from the hose.

Annette sat on the porch steps, tears dripping down her heavily rouged cheeks.

"Are . . . are you okay?" Beck scuffed the toe of her boot against the pea gravel walkway, scattering pebbles.

The woman looked up, blinking her pale blue eyes. "I'm sorry. I know she's just a dog, but after losing George and now maybe her too—" Annette stifled a sob. "It's just too much."

Beck patted her on the shoulder, which felt just about as comfortable as walking around with her shoes on the wrong feet. She knew her dad and Annette had been friends, but the way she had cried at the funeral, maybe there had been a little more between them than Beck allowed herself to see. She climbed the porch steps and grabbed the box of tissues Aunt Kate had left on the entryway table, then set them beside the crying woman. She went back inside for a glass of water for each of them, searching for the right way to respond.

Outside again, she passed the glass to Annette who was mopping her tears with her already tattered tissue. "Thank you, dear. I know it must seem so foolish, going all to pieces over a dog. My son bought her for me right after my husband passed, and she's been my constant companion for the past six years."

Beck sat beside her. "Animals have quite the knack for worming themselves deep into your heart."

"Your daddy just loved that little dog." Annette twisted the damp tissue in her hands. "Bea would jump in his lap and wriggle like an earthworm on hot pavement, and George would just laugh."

Beck choked on her sip of water. She couldn't imagine her stoic father being wild about a smoosh-nosed lapdog. Or throwing his head back in laughter about anything, for that matter.

That. That was why Annette got under her skin—the way she talked about him like she knew him in a way Beck didn't. "I'll continue to keep my eye out for her, and I'll let you know if she turns up. I know all the best hiding spots around here."

"Do you really think you'll find her?" Annette's forlorn expression made her look like a distraught child who'd misplaced their best-loved toy.

"I'll put the word out to the neighboring farm. She'll turn up." Beck took Annette's empty glass inside, then walked her to her car.

"Oh my, I forgot the whole reason I came in the first place," Annette said, lifting a casserole dish from the back seat of the car. "I wanted to bring you a meal. I always make too much for myself, and thought I'd be neighborly and share. It's chicken poppy seed. It was your daddy's favorite."

Beck's jaw tightened, and she forced a smile she did not feel. "That was kind of you."

Annette squeezed her arm. "We've got to look after each other now. We who loved him best."

She gave a small nod in reply. If Dad and Annette were as close as she implied, why hadn't he talked about her more?

"Call me if Bea turns up." She took a shuddering breath. "Even if you just find her remains, please call. At least I won't wonder."

"I will."

As Annette backed out of the drive, Beck let out the breath she'd been holding. She went inside and deposited the casserole into the fridge. Henrietta strutted through the open doorway. The hen hopped on top of the mail pile and shook, fluffing her feathers into a poof. She pecked at one of the envelope corners.

Beck shooed the hen through the door. "I'll deal with the bills tonight. Promise." She went back out to finish up her daily list, doing everything in her power not to think of her father or Annette.

# SEVEN

The low rumble of thunder underscored the jazz band warming up on the Sizzle Stage. Callie scanned the meager crowd, hopes dashed for a banner day at the weekly Chattanooga market. At least all the vendors and their products were safe under the massive pavilion.

"Need a knife?"

"Huh?" Swiping away the hair stuck to her cheek, Callie turned toward the male voice.

"To cut this humidity." Her booth neighbor Luke grinned as he straightened a black-and-white photograph of the Walnut Street Bridge on his display. "The weather needs to just go ahead and throw her fit and get all her frustration out and clear on up."

"Her? Why is the weather a her?" She cut a playful glare his direction, dropping lavender bath bombs into a glass bowl.

Luke shrugged and adjusted the bandanna that corralled his shaggy hair. "'Cause it wouldn't aggravate you if I said it was a him."

She shook her head and finished her display, then started organizing the boxes beneath her tablecloth. Over the past two summers, Callie had grown attached to her booth neighbor and his good-natured teasing. Her gaze traveled the circuit a handful of shoppers had begun to stroll, finding the farmers, the beekeepers, the crafters, the photographers, the artisans, and the musicians. These were her people. A Sunday afternoon crowd that walked to their own beat. Some of them regulars. Some who spent their summers traveling from market to market.

The rain filled the air with a staccato beat and the scent of damp pavement. A few more diehard marketgoers jogged beneath the cover of the large pavilion, closing their dripping umbrellas and heading to the produce booths.

Callie heaved a sigh and braced her hands on the table.

"Why so glum, chum? The rain will pass."

She lifted her head. Luke stood in front of her booth, hands in the pockets of his camo cargo pants.

"I needed today to be a good day."

"Ah, the life of the starving artist. You never know what you're gonna get." He motioned to one of his photographs displayed on canvas. "Take this shot, for instance. I spent a whole day hiking to this waterfall way back in the mountains only to find that a flash flood had washed out the trail and the path was blocked by fallen trees. The whole day was a complete bust. But as I hiked back, I noticed the sun streaming out of the clouds over the mountains. Perfect lighting on a perfect fall day. The hand of God, they call it, when the rays come down like that. Some people even say that it's evidence that a miracle is taking place in that spot."

Callie peered out at the pouring rain, nary a crack in the clouds. "I'd take some light breaking through right now, miracle or not." She motioned to the photograph. "So, do you really believe those sun rays mean something miraculous happened?"

He tilted his head. "You don't believe in miracles, Callie?"

"I . . ." The thing was, she did believe miracles happened. Just not when she'd asked for them.

He lifted his hands, palms up. "Forget miracles for a minute." He pointed to the photograph. "Do you know the scientific reason those sunbeams appear?"

She straightened her beeswax candle display. "No, but I have a feeling you're going to tell me."

"They're called crepuscular rays. And they happen because of light hitting dust. It's just ordinary, boring particulate floating all around us like it always does, and then bam, the light hits it and suddenly it's something that makes people stop and take pictures. If that's not a miracle, then I guess I don't know what a miracle is."

Callie couldn't explain it, but something about his words eased the weight on her shoulders. He always seemed to have that effect on her.

"Watch my booth for me and I'll go grab us some tacos from the food truck," he said. "I have a feeling this rain is going to clear and it's going to be an amazing day." Luke walked away with a familiar jaunt in his step.

Callie never had trouble seeing the dust particles infiltrating her life. Luke always saw the sunshine.

The rain slowed its pounding and transitioned into a fine mist.

She glared again at the gray-bellied sky. This booth wasn't even going to remedy the deficit in this week's bills, much less the avalanche coming her way.

Luke returned ten minutes later, set Styrofoam containers on his table, and grabbed his camera. He pointed back the way he came. "Miracles everywhere, I tell ya." His face was luminous.

She couldn't help but follow him as he retraced his steps from the pavilion. As she left its cover, delicate mist clung to her skin. A sunbeam had cut through the gloom, creating a rainbow that framed Lookout Mountain in a full arch. Luke snapped a few photographs. He grinned back at her. The tiny droplets clinging to his hair glinted in the glow. "It's amazing what light can do with everyday, ordinary things like dust and water."

Callie smiled at her friend. Her friend who had two parents, happily married for thirty-five years, who'd been accountants at the same firm for almost that long. It wasn't his fault he didn't understand her cynicism. She was grateful he didn't.

Back at their booths, he passed her one of the Styrofoam containers. "Fess up. What's going on?"

Between bites, Callie mentioned the change in the building code and how that had affected her recent real estate purchase. "Next weekend was supposed to be my grand opening."

"Well, setbacks are never fun, but you'll get there."

"Sure. If I can keep sales on the upswing. I'm paying the mortgage on a building that isn't making money and spending way more on the reno than I had anticipated. That might have a little something to do with why I'm so edgy about the weather."

He motioned to the thinning clouds. "Well, at least that's looking up."

The voice inside her nudged hard. *Why did you stop there? Why didn't you tell him about what's really bothering you? He's your friend.*

She opened her mouth to spill the words, and her stomach roiled. Maybe one day she'd conquer her lifelong compulsion to protect Lindy Peterson. Someday she'd take the risk of letting someone see the truth. But today was not that day.

Already the crowd had started to pick up. "You're right. It will work out in the end. One way or another."

⬡⬡⬡⬡

Yesterday had turned out far better than Callie had expected. So much so that she was almost completely out of stock of several of her soaps and bath bombs. A plethora of online orders had come in overnight. That meant today was going to be a busy day. Which was exactly what she needed. Distractions. There would be time enough to hash out all her emotions at therapy later this week.

Callie put on her safety goggles and opened her kitchen window before carefully pouring lye into water. When she finished, she set the container aside to cool, then turned on her small fan to push the fumes toward the open window. Then she mixed the oils she used for her calendula soap.

A knock sounded on the front door, and she slipped off her protective gloves to answer. Luke stood outside her door with a brown paper bag in hand. He grinned and said, "Somebody is up and at 'em early."

"Ha. Yeah." She glanced at the mess behind her and brushed her ponytail from her shoulder, offering him a tight smile. Luke had occasionally picked her up to carpool to events with their church small group, but she'd never let him bear witness to this mess.

He leaned around her. "Wow. So this is where all the magic happens? You really make everything out of this little apartment? Impressive."

Her embarrassment dissolved and a laugh slipped out. She shouldn't have feared he'd judge her. If anyone could appreciate the creativity that came out of this chaos, it was him. "Yeah. It's probably a good thing I live with college students as my neighbors, otherwise there might be some complaints about the smells with the lye and all the essential oils I use."

He raised the paper bag in his hand. "You seemed a little off yesterday. I just wanted to check in on you. I know how much you love cinnamon rolls."

Off? That was one way to describe it. "That was kind of you. I guess I'm just a little stressed. But it will all be fine." Eventually. "Do you want to step out to the stoop? My apartment is a little pungent with the lye reaction going on in there. I can bring some coffee. I make a mean latte."

"Sure."

She made one for each of them, complete with clumsy foam art. He followed her out to the wide front porch of the historic home. They sat side by side on the front step. He passed her one of the wrapped cinnamon rolls and pointed to his temple with a smile. "Nice specs, by the way. It's a good look."

She swiped off the safety goggles she'd forgotten were on her face and shook her head, smiling. "Yeah. I bet."

He took a long drink of his coffee and looked over the quaint neighborhood filled with small cottages. "So, it's just the stuff with the shop bothering you?"

"Yep." The word slipped out, driven by habit instead of conscious choice. She'd learned long ago how to give answers that would hold people at just the right distance so they wouldn't worry or ask questions. What age had she'd been when she'd perfected that defense mechanism?

*Tell him*, the little voice inside her head urged. She took a bite of her cinnamon roll instead, comforted by the sweet, yeasty warmth.

"Okay, Callie. I'll take your word for it. Something just seemed different yesterday." He motioned to her door. "I don't want to keep you from your work."

*Tell him. This isn't like when you were a kid. Your life won't implode if people find out the truth about her.* The still, small voice gently nudged again, but Callie's words stayed safe behind a padlocked door in her heart. "You came at the perfect time," she said. "Right now I'm just waiting for everything to cool."

The phone in her front pocket rang. Another unfamiliar number. *Great. What has Mom gotten me involved in this time?* She set her coffee on the stoop. "I better take this. Give me just a minute." She stood and walked across the lawn to the sidewalk.

"Hello?"

"This is Hope Callahan with the River City Trust Company. I am calling for Callie Peterson."

Callie blinked, remembering the junk mail she'd gotten from the same company several days ago. "This is she, but I am not in need of your services at this time. Thank y—"

"Ms. Peterson, I just wanted to make sure that you got the notice in the mail about the upcoming trustee meeting regarding the trust of Mr. George Walsh. It's on Thursday, June eighth at 4:00 p.m. here at our offices."

"Um." *George Walsh? Trust?* "I think you may have the wrong Callie Peterson."

"Your mother is a Ms. Lindy Peterson?" Hope spoke slowly.

Callie swallowed hard. "Yes . . ."

"Great. I've got the right person! Will you be able to attend?"

"I'm sorry. I'm a little confused. Who is George Walsh? What trust?"

"Did you not read the letter we sent?"

"Uh, I think I better call you back."

"All right, then! I'll look forward to your call. I want to make sure that both parties are able to attend to go over the particulars of the trust. We'll talk soon. Have a nice day."

Callie stood staring at the phone in her hand as if looking at it hard enough would help her make better sense of the words that had just come through the speaker.

"Callie? You okay?" Luke watched her from his seat on the step.

She walked to him, feeling like she was moving in fast-forward and slow motion all at the same time. "Uh, yeah, I'm fine. Something just came up that I need to deal with. So, thanks for the breakfast, but I'm going to need to run." She collected their empty coffee mugs and left Luke on the stoop.

She hurried inside and frantically sifted through the bills until she found the unopened envelope from the trust company. But reading the words on the page didn't make anything clearer.

Who in the world was George Walsh and why would he leave her anything worth putting in a trust?

# EIGHT

Beck cast a critical eye at the dark clouds skating past her property. She finished repairing the section of the pen the goats had damaged straining for the grass on the other side and stashed her tools. Best to get in and get showered. She wouldn't be able to get anything else done before the storm blew in.

She headed inside, past the house phone ringing on the wall. Probably Annette wondering about her pup that Beck had yet to locate since her escape last week. Or another call about a swarm of bees she felt powerless to collect.

She climbed the stairs and entered the bathroom. Beck stripped out of her sweaty clothes and stepped into a cool shower. Afterwards she'd tackle the last remaining letter of the stack she'd been slowly whittling down. The missive from the trust company haunted her. If she opened that envelope, read what needed to be done to transfer the property to her name . . . somehow it made it real that her father was gone. That it was just her here on this farm.

How could she be living in a reality in which there were no more chances to ask for his wisdom? No more hugs to squeeze her tight—hugs that held a strength stronger than anxiety's grip.

Hot tears fell unchecked under the cold shower stream. The first real cry she'd allowed herself in days. Who would be her anchor if those roaring emotions took over, sweeping her into one of the panic attacks that had come to rule her life?

Emptied of her tears, she wrapped herself in a towel and headed to her room. Beck dressed in terry cloth shorts and a thin tank and sat on the edge of the bed. She needed to bite the bullet and open the letter.

Thunder rumbled, low and long. The sky opened and rain pounded on the tin roof. She closed her eyes and soaked in the sound for a few moments, letting it drive every thought from her mind.

Beck stood and looked out the window to the barn and adjacent pasture. At the sight of something white and brown zipping past her view, Beck groaned. She'd forgotten to put Oslo in the barn.

She raced down the stairs and out the front door, letting the screen door slam behind her. She slipped into her muck boots and splashed across the puddle-ridden ground. The rain instantly soaked through her pajamas.

That crazed donkey. Something about storms made him bonkers and brought out this wildness in him. The fool thing thought himself a caged mustang desperate for freedom instead of a coddled miniature donkey.

She dashed in the barn and grabbed a lead rope. She needed to get him in before he hurt himself trying to jump the fence like he did that one time a few years back.

Inside the pasture fence, he raced circles around her, braying.

"Oslo, come here, buddy." She reached for his halter as he dashed by, grumbling under her breath when she missed.

Oslo first belonged to the Baileys. After learning the mother rejected him and the Baileys were unable to devote the time needed for his care, Beck had begged her father to let her keep him. He'd warned Beck of how much work bottle-feeding was and how animals raised without their mother often had lifelong behavioral issues. Beck, full of the kind of confidence only a teenager possesses, told him that she could handle it. She figured she'd turned out just fine despite having a mother who had rejected her. So would Oslo.

She might have been a little quick to judge on both their accounts.

She backed the donkey into a corner. Crooning softly, she edged closer and reached for the halter's cheekpiece. "There, boy, that wasn't so bad." She clipped the lead rope. As if set off by the click of the clasp, Oslo attempted to bolt. Beck tried to hold her ground, but the terrain had softened in the sudden downpour. She fell to her knees trying to keep hold of the rain-slick rope, locked in a ridiculous tug-of-war with a rebellious miniature equine. She was afraid that if she tried to stand, she'd slip and lose him.

Thunder pealed, and Oslo ceased his tugging for a split second. Beck used that momentary diversion to stand and regain control of his head. "Come on, you dingbat. Let's get out of this mess." She squelched across the pasture, Oslo prancing at her side like the struggle had never occurred. Muddy water ran down her shins and into her boots. So much for that shower. She walked Oslo into the stall next to Sparks.

"Could you teach that goof some manners and sense while he's in here with you?"

Sparks lifted his head over the wall separating the two stalls and snuffed, looking down his nose at the diminutive steed.

"I know, bud. It's a lost cause but do try." She exited the barn and closed the door behind her. Lightning forked across the darkening sky.

A pair of headlights sliced through the fog and rain. The white hatchback slid to a stop, and Isaac's lanky figure rose from the car. He jogged through the rain to the front porch.

She cupped her hands around her mouth. "I'm over here." When he didn't seem to hear her, she called louder, waving.

Isaac turned and dashed across the yard, dodging puddles. Panting, he said, "Is Fern here? Please say she's here." His wide eyes peered at her over the top of his droplet-covered glasses. His gaze flicked down and immediately flicked back up. He turned away.

She crossed her arms over her thin, soaked tank top, cheeks blazing. Steam probably rose from the top of her head. She ground her teeth. *Thanks a lot, Oslo.* At least the mud provided a little extra coverage. "I haven't seen her. She's missing?"

Eyes still averted, he nodded. "I'd hoped she'd come back here." He scrubbed a hand over his forehead.

She hurried to the tack room and grabbed two rain slickers from the hook. She slipped one over her drenched pajamas, zipping it to her chin, and gave the spare to Isaac. She grabbed the keys to the UTV. "I'll help you look."

She drove the vehicle at its top speed, bouncing them over the terrain in the slanting rain. Mud splattered her bare legs. Her passenger gripped the roll bar, his jaw set.

He glanced sideways, blinking hard. "Thank you."

She nodded and swiped water from her face. "Of course." Beck grimaced as another splatter of mud hit her cheek. "Let's check over by the apiary. That's where she's been the past three times."

"Three times?"

This guy really was a clueless mess.

"I brought her out here to make it easier on everyone," he told her. "But I'm making a disaster of it. I'm not cut out for this."

She narrowed her eyes. Was he one of those dads? A divorcé who thought taking on a caregiver role was a favor to the mother? She clamped her lips tight and focused on the trail ahead. She wasn't doing this for him. She was doing it for Fern.

She pulled to a stop at the apiary. The wet black cloths clung to the brush, transforming the foliage into a hoard of monstrous creatures closing in. "I think we should check along the brush."

Thunder rumbled and the wind kicked up.

Isaac nodded. "And if she's not here?"

"Then . . . then we just have to keep looking." Beck jogged across the field, squinting through the rain. "Fern? Fern, it's Beck. Where are you?"

She paused between each call, listening. But all she could detect was the rustle of rain on the foliage and Isaac's deeper tones calling out.

She sighed, cupping her hand around her mouth. "Katya? Katya Amadeus Cimmaron?"

A whimper came from within the brush. Not human. Animal.

Beck trudged forward, briars tearing at her bare legs between her thigh-length slicker and her muck boots. "Fern? Katya?"

"Beck?" A small, tremulous voice reached her ears.

Beck rushed forward, ducking under drenched branches and slapping away bramble.

Fern knelt on the ground, pale and wide-eyed. Rain diluted the blood dripping from her hands, turning it pink. Beck rushed forward, taking her hands. "Where are you hurt? What happened?"

Fern shook her head, face pinched. "It's not me. It's her."

It was then that Beck registered the small tan form by Fern's side. The dog whimpered and then yelped when it moved. Its hind leg was wrapped tight in rusted barbed wire, a remnant of a fence from long ago.

"I found her, and I tried to help. But then the storm started." Fern sobbed. "I couldn't leave her."

Beck patted the girl's drenched back. "Of course not. I have some wire cutters in the UTV. Sit tight."

Thunder rolled and Fern's lower lip trembled.

Beck tore out of the undergrowth and jogged for the vehicle. "Isaac! Isaac! I found her." She could only hope he heard her over the storm. She grabbed a pair of wire cutters from the toolbox.

As she hurried back to Fern, Isaac caught up to her with his long stride. His forehead was creased and his eyes wide. "You said you found her. Where's Fern?" He saw the wire cutters and the blood on her hands and blanched. "What happened? Is she hurt?"

Beck shook her head. "She's fine. Just follow me."

At the sight of his daughter, Isaac rushed forward. He removed his slicker and draped it over Fern, pulling her close to his chest.

Beck knelt in the mud and stroked the pug's side. She cut the barbed wire away from the post, and then trimmed the wire close to where it tangled around the dog's leg. Though Beck moved as delicately as possible, both Fern and the pup whimpered as she worked.

Beck made low soothing sounds, but she doubted they heard her over the rain. When the dog was finally free, she scooped it to her chest. Without a word, Isaac and Fern followed in her wake.

At the UTV, Beck motioned for Fern to climb in. She placed the pup in the girl's lap, then she and Isaac sandwiched Fern in.

As Beck raced back to the farmhouse, she glanced at Isaac who'd been silent since finding Fern. His normal rumpled appearance had been doused in the rain, plastering the longer wavy hair on the top of his head to the short-shorn sides. His fogged-up glasses had slipped down his nose. The expression behind them was so pained, she'd have thought he'd been the one tangled in barbed wire.

He gripped the roll bar to keep from sliding on the leather bench. His once-wrinkled button-up clung to his skin. He glanced at her, and she refocused on the path ahead. She navigated around a dip in the terrain that was collecting rainwater.

Fern cradled the bleeding dog, murmuring softly to it. The little runaway girl had found Annette's runaway Bea.

She slid to a stop in front of the barn, hopped out, and motioned them to follow her inside. "Lay her in the straw, Fern. It's nice and soft."

The girl set the shivering pup down, stroking the place between her ears with her long pale fingers.

"Okay, go in the tack room—there's a stack of towels in there. You can dry her off a bit while I wrap up this leg."

Fern scurried away in her mud-splattered knee socks. Isaac hovered near the stall door.

By the time Fern returned, Beck was finishing wrapping the leg. She rocked back on her heels. "That should do until Annette can get this little girl to the vet."

Fern looked up sharply. "You know who she belongs to? She has an owner?" Her round chin quivered. "When I found her, I thought . . . I thought . . ." Moisture welled in her eyes.

Isaac knelt beside her and placed a hand on Fern's slim shoulder. She shrugged it off.

"A lady came by looking for her a few days ago," Beck said. "She was very upset."

Fern sniffled.

"I bet you saved this dog's life."

Fern shook her head. "You saved her, not me. I couldn't free her. I tried, but it was too hard."

"And I wouldn't have ever found her without you." Beck stood. "I'm going to call Annette and let her know we found her dog."

Isaac and Fern rose from their seats next to the dog. Like Beck, they were muddy and shivering. She thumbed over her shoulder. "You can come inside and dry off if you want."

Isaac placed an arm on Fern's shoulder. "We've imposed enough already. Come along, Fern. Let's get you home."

Fern glanced at the pug and gave a doleful sigh, then trudged to the car, the hem of the rain slicker nearly dragging the ground.

Isaac turned to Beck. "I'll return the jacket tomorrow, if that's all right."

Beck shrugged. "Sure. No rush."

He scrubbed his hand over the back of his neck. "Well, um . . . thanks again." He turned to go.

"Isaac, wait." Beck grimaced. She would regret this next move, no doubt about it. But she couldn't ignore that tug on her heart any longer.

He turned, one eyebrow raised.

"If . . . if you want to drop Fern off for a few hours while you work, you can. I can teach her about animals and the bees. She's a smart kid. I think she gets bored easily. I can keep her busy and maybe stop her from wandering off unannounced."

Isaac blinked. "Really? You'd do that?"

Beck straightened her stance and propped her hands on her hips. "Just a few hours a day. Not all day."

He released a breath and a corner of his mouth lifted. He stepped to her and grabbed her hand and pumped it twice before letting go. "That would be amazing. You have no idea how grateful I am."

"It's no big deal." Beck's cheeks flamed. She would definitely regret this arrangement at some point, but she couldn't bring herself to think about that yet.

"No, it is. Thank you. Thank you so much. Fern will be thrilled. Seriously. Thank you."

It nettled her that he was such an inept father to such a bright young girl, but she couldn't deny the sense of accomplishment she felt watching some of the tension melt from Isaac's shoulders. She could tell he loved Fern, even if he seemed a little lost.

She jogged toward the house to call Annette. Her Bea was in need of a few stitches.

# NINE

Callie peeled the silicone mold away from four loaves of rosemary-lavender soap and set it aside to cut into bars later. She grabbed a pizza from the freezer and popped it in the oven to bake while she transformed the space back into her kitchen.

Someday there would be a workshop with large basin sinks, multiple stovetops, wide work surfaces, and a plethora of cabinetry. At least that was supposed to be phase two of the renovations before the city's demand that she update the plumbing and electrical.

It would be nice to have a kitchen that only functioned as a kitchen again. As she tidied her overcrowded counter space, her eyes kept drifting back to the letter she'd pinned to the center of her corkboard a couple of days ago.

George Walsh.

She'd been digging through her memories, but his name still didn't ring any bells. She didn't know of any relatives with that name. Not that she had any relatives to speak of, besides her mother.

She'd asked questions about her family when she was old enough to realize the other kids at school had grandparents, aunts and uncles, cousins. "We have each other and that's enough," was her mother's invariable reply. The only information she'd ever gleaned was that

Callie's grandfather had been a mean drunk, and her grandmother had died in an accident when her mother was just a girl.

With regard to Callie's father, her mother said he didn't exist, an explanation Callie accepted for the majority of her childhood until she'd gained enough understanding of human biology to recognize the impossibility of that statement. Somebody had to be her father. Somebody, somewhere.

She glanced back to the letter pinned to the wall.

Had it been George Walsh's name hiding behind her mother's closed lips all these years?

She grabbed the large pot she'd used for her last batch of soap and took it to the small single-basin sink. She struggled to get the large vessel cleaned inside that tight space, wrestling just as hard with the memories banging around inside her head.

She'd gone through a phase in which questions about her parentage gnawed at her like a teething puppy with a rawhide bone. She'd become more creative with her inquiries, hoping to trick her mother into dropping a clue. But the more Callie probed, the more agitated her mother had become. When Callie noticed her drinking starting earlier and earlier in the day, she'd finally let it go for good.

Who else but her father would have named her in a trust? And there was a cotrustee. Could she have a sibling? Or would this be someone's wife, learning for the first time about their husband's secret past life? Callie shuddered. Would she have to prove her biological connection?

She buried her face in her hands. So many thoughts. Possibilities. She needed answers.

The timer beeped, interrupting her spiraling thoughts. She pulled her thin-crust pizza from the oven and left it on the stovetop to cool.

Callie eyed the cell phone resting on top of a stool. Maybe the rehab center made exceptions to their rules.

She dialed.

"Sunrise Recovery Center, this is Stephen."

"Uh. Hi. This is Callie Peterson. I was calling to speak to my mother, Lindy Peterson." The click-clack of keys sounded in the background.

"I'm sorry, ma'am. Her record shows she is unable to have outside contact at this time, but as you are her health-care proxy, I can make a note for her case manager to call and update you when they have a chance."

Callie bit back her protest. "Sure, that would be great." Maybe if she spoke with someone directly involved in her mother's care and explained the situation, they'd let her ask just one question. She couldn't fathom attending this trustee meeting completely blind.

Her phone dinged. A text from Luke.

---

You were quiet all weekend and you barely said two words at small group last night. Are you going to tell me what that phone call was about or am I going to need to ambush you with more cinnamon-laced carbs?

---

She stared at the screen a moment before firing off her text.

---

Everything's okay. We'll talk on Sunday.

---

Callie finished her pizza and spent the next hour affixing her hyacinth logo to her lotion and liquid soap bottles. She slid her thumb over the floral silhouette, noting the chip in the blush nail polish she'd carefully painted only the night before.

This business represented every dream little girl Callie had concocted while sitting alone in innumerable hovels, not knowing when her mother would return.

Solace Naturals was supposed to represent her freedom—never having to rely on another person for her stability and peace. And then she'd gone and chosen her mother's favorite flower for her logo.

Despite the bravado and feelings of emancipation from her past, something in her could not let go. No matter how hard she tried to hate her mother over the years, all she'd really ever wanted to do was love her.

The phone rang. The number from Sunrise. "This is Callie Peterson."

"Hi, Ms. Peterson. This is your mother's case manager, Teri Smith. I am returning your call with an update about Lindy."

Callie let out a slow breath to steady herself.

"Because of her many years of substance abuse, detox has proved to be quite intense," Teri said, "but our medical staff has been able to help her through the worst of it. As she's started to come out on the other side of this, we do have some concerns that underlying mental illness has perpetuated her struggles with alcohol and other substances. While symptoms of detox can mimic certain mental health diagnoses, there have been some red flags during her stay that lead us to believe there might be some significant, unaddressed trauma in her past."

Callie flashed back to all the nights she'd woken to her mother sobbing in her sleep, curled into a ball on her bed. She'd always assumed that her mother was simply feeling guilty for her inability to get her life together. "What are you telling me?"

There was a heavy pause on the line. "Well, Ms. Peterson, we could continue to take her through our full program here, and while I am sure that would give her some useful tools and coping skills for her substance use disorder, we believe that your mother would benefit from something more specialized to her needs. Intensive mental healthcare would serve her better in the long run. We have a sister campus that provides an excellent therapeutic community. They'll help with diagnosis and finding the correct medications to give her a much better quality of life. Essentially, we think that alcohol has been her means of self-medicating her underlying mental health issues."

A strange sort of peace settled over Callie as she listened to this woman's words.

"Both individual and group counseling are incorporated into the program," Teri continued. "Over time, clients are slowly adjusted from the strictly controlled environment into independent living. We've seen so many Sunrise clients who were repeat rehab attenders finally be able to find healing at this program. A healing that lasts."

The hope that had shriveled like an old balloon reinflated a fraction. Her mother's issues were more nuanced than simply lacking willpower. She dropped her chin, swallowing the pain in the back of her throat as all her mother's unkept promises replayed in her head. Her childhood yearning dashed over and over again.

Because addiction always won.

As Teri continued on about the wonderful prognosis she saw for her mother, Callie couldn't help but visualize zeros being added to the ends of already large numbers on the total bill for her mother's care. Callie slumped in her chair and squeezed her eyes shut. This could be the chance her mother needed to finally be whole and here Callie was worried as everything she'd worked toward for herself slipped further and further from reach.

Callie ended the call with Teri, grabbed her purse, and headed out the door for her therapy session. There would be no shortage of things to discuss today.

∞∞∞

Once Callie was settled across from Joanne in her office, she filled her in on the latest with her mother's rehab situation.

Joanne nodded and made a few notes on her notepad. "I know that touched on some sensitive themes we've previously discussed, like the promises your mother made to get well. Tell me more about what it was like for you to hear there may be some previously unidentified issues perpetuating her addictions."

Callie fidgeted with her hands and then folded them in her lap, squeezing them tight to ground herself. "When her caseworker was telling me this, I flashed back to my seventh birthday. My mother had promised to take me out for dinner, but of course, she didn't show. Ms. Ruthie made a big fuss, digging around in her cabinet for cake mix and ingredients, saying things like, 'Well, let's just see what I can find lying around this ole pantry.'"

Callie's heart softened, visualizing the woman's kindness. "In the hall closet, she 'found' a roll of streamers that just so happened to be my favorite shade of purple. We sang silly songs while we baked, and she giggled while I tried to blow out trick candles." Callie lifted her chin. "I never told Ms. Ruthie that I spied the grocery receipt from earlier that week sticking out of her purse. I wasn't a great reader, but I recognized the words *cake* and *mix*. She'd known my mother couldn't keep her promises, even if I hadn't accepted that yet."

Joanne sat quietly across from her, her face open and compassionate.

"Just like that, my seventh birthday was over. Right as I was climbing into bed, Mom came stumbling in. She hugged me so tight it hurt, and the smell coming off her was so bad, I was sure I'd vomit birthday cake all over Ms. Ruthie's floor.

"She apologized, of course. She wasn't good at much, but she had a lot of practice saying sorry. She begged to know what I wished for, and I told her I wanted her to get better. I wanted her not to go away anymore.

"Things actually did get better for a while. We went on hikes and wild pretend adventures. After I was supposed to be asleep, I'd hear Ms. Ruthie scolding her about how she'd let me stay up too late and eat too much junk."

Callie shook her head. "But just like always, the darkness trickled back in little by little. She'd start coming home later and later again. Until some nights she didn't come home at all." Callie took a shaky breath. "What the caseworker said today didn't erase the pain of my mother's actions, but it reminded me of some of the lies you and I have talked about together, and it made me see how that lie still lives on inside me—the belief that my mother loved alcohol more than me."

Joanne nodded. "You're right, Callie. Addiction and the solution to addiction seem so simple on the surface. What is the truth that replaces that lie?"

Callie picked at the cuticle on her thumb and then lifted her eyes to meet Joanne's. "My mother has a substance use disorder. It was not a result of me not being enough for her. It wasn't a result of anything I did or didn't do."

# TEN

Beck reviewed her to-do list, set it down on the counter with a thunk, and scrubbed her eyes. As if she didn't have enough problems trying to run a farm on her own, now she'd taken on babysitting on top of it. What had she been thinking?

Beck couldn't deny that there was something magnetic about that girl. An image of Isaac's panicked eyes from that stormy night flashed in her mind, and a strange warmth infiltrated her chest.

At the familiar sound of rumbling gravel, Beck glanced at the stove clock. Seven thirty on the dot, just like Isaac had promised. They had gone out of town for some family function the past two days, and Isaac had said Fern was so eager for her first day on the farm that she'd been driving him up the walls, begging to leave early.

She gulped the last of her cooled coffee before placing her mug in the cluttered sink and heading for the door. She jogged down the porch steps, hand lifted in greeting to Isaac and Fern who stood by his car, engaged in what looked to be a serious conversation.

"Good morning, y'all."

Fern spun toward her. "Beck! What are we going to do today? Collect honey? Learn to ride your horse? Go swimming in the creek? Is Bea going to be okay?"

Beck blinked, frozen by Fern's bombardment. "Maybe we'll get to do one of those things on your to-do list. Except the honey. It's not the right time of year quite yet. But soon.

"And Bea is fine," she added. "Ms. Annette called and said she'd needed a few stitches and some fluids, but the pup's on the mend, thanks to you." Beck crossed her arms over her chest and cocked her hip to the side to mirror Fern's posture. She smirked. "Did that cover all your inquiries?"

Fern nodded and then adjusted her knee socks—one hearts, the other butterflies. "Let's do it."

The girl headed for the barn without a backward glance at Isaac.

He stuffed his hands in his pockets. "Thanks again for agreeing to watch her for a little while. I know she'll love it. She gets bored with me, and I feel bad about that. But I gotta pay the bills, you know." He ducked his chin and rolled some gravel beneath his loafer.

Beck shrugged. "Sure." She supposed not all parents could be like her father, who'd dropped his job at the bank to run this farm. He'd always told her that he'd done it because he was tired of having an office job, but she had a feeling it had really all been about giving Beck a world that felt safe after her mother left them.

Isaac adjusted his glasses on the bridge of his nose. "I'll be back in a few hours. Call me if you have any issues with her. She's a pretty sweet kid, but I know she can be a real handful sometimes. Especially lately. Her mom and—"

A whinny sounded from the barn.

"Beck!"

Fern appeared at her side and tugged on her arm. "Beck, are you coming, or what? This horse is going crazy. He's eyeballing me and keeps banging his bucket against the stall."

Isaac gave her a lopsided smile. "I better let you get to it. Thanks again."

Beck nodded. "It will be fun." It certainly wouldn't be boring.

Isaac ducked his tall frame into the compact car and drove away.

In the barn, Sparks was certainly putting on a display. Oslo, who occupied the paddock connected to the barn whenever it wasn't storming, contributed boisterous braying.

As Beck gathered the feed buckets, Fern bounced alongside her. "These animals are crazy."

"Just typical breakfast time at the farm. They normally eat earlier, but I waited on you."

"I'll come earlier next time."

"I don't know if your dad will be up for that."

Fern scrunched her face like she'd been offered bitter greens. "That's not my dad. That's my uncle. My parents are dead."

Had Beck actually recoiled at the child's detached words, or had it just been her heart reeling inside of her? "I'm so sorry, Fern. I didn't know."

A million questions fought to burst from her, but she kept her lips clamped tight. She'd better let Fern take the lead in that domain. She filled a bucket with grain for Sparks and one for Oslo, making a mental note to order more food from the feed store later that afternoon. She watched Fern in her periphery.

Fern noticed her attention. "Uncle Isaac thought it would be good to get away for the summer, so he brought me here. I'd rather be home. I just want everything to go back to normal." Fern picked up Sparks's feed bucket. "Who's this one for?"

"Uh." Beck's mind refused to process the question, still stuck on the emotion-free way Fern spoke about the death of her parents.

Her own loss was still so fresh and raw, simply hearing of Fern's tragedy made the back of her eyes burn and her throat tighten. Fern was just a girl and yet she didn't struggle to speak the words.

Every morning when Beck woke, her heart bled like a fresh wound as reality settled in.

Fern lifted the bucket again and swung it back and forth for emphasis. "Beck? Whose food bucket?"

She blinked hard and pushed air out of her chest. "That's Sparks's feed. Go ahead and dump it in the bigger bucket in his stall, and then come back and we'll bring him a flake of hay."

Fern's eyebrows shot up. "Won't he want more than a single flake?"

Beck smiled despite the throbbing in her chest. "A flake is not what you think. I'll show you." A loud bray filled the air. She picked up the second bucket. "I'm going to feed Oslo before he has a conniption fit."

As she carried the bucket out the side door of the barn, her thoughts collected like a flock of birds on branches. Should she press in? Ask Fern more questions about her parents? Pretend the conversation never happened? Maybe she shouldn't have run Aunt Kate off. She'd make a far better mother hen to an orphaned girl than Beck.

Oslo continued his noisy complaints as she walked to his food trough. Blessed silence descended as he buried his muzzle in the grain. Beck scratched the space between Oslo's ears. He came up crunching, affectionately bumping her arm.

Fern appeared at her side. "Aw, he's so cute. I never knew donkeys were so little."

Beck ruffled his short mane. "He's a mini. But don't let his size fool you. He's a feisty thing."

"I fed Sparks his grain."

"Good deal. All right, let's get them their morning hay. And then we'll feed the chickens and collect the eggs."

"Milk the cow?"

Beck laughed. "We don't have a cow."

Fern's shoulders drooped. "Aw, man. I wanted to learn how to milk a cow."

"We have goats. They've already been milked this morning, but I have a couple that are about to wean their babies, and we can milk them this afternoon if you want to."

Fern wrinkled her nose. "You can milk goats? Weird."

"Yep. It makes great cheese."

Fern toyed with the end of one of her long plaits. "So . . . there's baby goats? Can I play with them?"

"Sure." After she gave Sparks and Oslo some hay, Beck walked her to the goat pen. "Stay here and play for a minute if you'd like. I need to call the Feed and Seed and make an order. We're getting a little low."

Fern skipped to the pen and carefully latched the gate behind her, crooning to the baby goats that were already starting to gather.

Beck went to the office Dad had built into the corner of the honey house. She opened a window and sank into his chair, then stared at the cluttered desk. His were the last hands to touch these things. She shifted a page hanging off the edge as it waved in the breeze. Every little move she made felt like erasing marks on a chalkboard. It felt wrong.

She squared her shoulders and opened the drawer, her eyes scanning over the neatly labeled files. She pulled out his receipt from the latest feed order from a month ago to use as her guide. She grabbed the phone off the desk and dialed the number.

"This is Davy at Sweetwater Feed and Seed. What can I do ya for?" His voice was twangy and young.

"Hi, Davy. This is Beckett over at Walsh Farm. I need to put in an order." She listed her needed supplies.

"Alrighty. I've got ya. What time you wanna pick all this up? This afternoon? Tomorrow?"

Beck's chest grew tight. "Actually, I was going to see about having it delivered."

The line grew quiet, and there was the muffled sound of conversation like someone had placed their hand over the receiver. "Uh. Ma'am, we actually don't deliver."

Beck gulped. "Yeah. Yeah, of course. I . . . I'll be over later this afternoon."

She hung up the phone and laid her head on the desk. She could do this. She had to do this. If her bees could fly miles to forage nectar, she could make it the ten miles down the road to the Feed and Seed. Unless . . .

She redialed the number.

"This is Davy at Sweetwater Feed and Seed."

"Hey, Davy. Beckett Walsh here again. Say, you don't happen to own a pickup truck, do you?"

"Sure do." She could hear the pride in his voice. Classic country boy.

She forced her request out in a rush of words. "Well, I know the store doesn't deliver, but I realized I can't make it out there today, and I was wondering if you'd be willing to drop my order off after your shift ends. I'll pay you, of course. How does twenty bucks sound?"

"Dude, yeah. You're the Walsh place, right? It's right on my way home."

Beck relaxed. "Great. I'll see you whenever you get off of work. No rush."

She collapsed against the back of the chair. Everything would turn out just fine. It might take a little ingenuity here and there, but she could find a way to make this work. She hurried back to Fern, who was giggling at the baby goats frolicking at her feet.

"Hey, you. We'd better get on to our next task. We've got eggs to collect."

Fern exited the goat pen, careful to latch the gate behind her. She turned to Beck and then squinted, looking beyond her. "Who's that?"

Beck turned, following Fern's pointing finger. A short, portly man in a seersucker blazer and creased khakis stood beside a Mercedes sedan. He placed a straw boater hat on his head and picked up a clipboard from his passenger seat. Aside from the car, he looked like he stepped straight out of the 1930s.

"I have no idea. Wait here." Beck jogged down the hill to the time-traveling trespasser. Small footsteps crunched behind her. Beck shook her head. *Nosy kid.*

The stranger stood outside the farmhouse. He made a few notes and then started to walk around the side of the house.

"Hello? Excuse me?" Beck called out. "Can I help you?"

The man lifted a hand in greeting but continued scribbling on his paper. Beck quickened her pace. "Sir, this is private property."

Undeterred, he showed no response to her change in tone.

As she approached, the man ceased writing and stepped to her, extending his hand. "Hi there. I'm Henry Blake with Blake Appraisers." The man's voice carried a heavy southern drawl.

"I didn't order an appraisal." She tried to get a glimpse of his notes. The property was hers, wasn't it? Who else was there?

He dropped his hand and consulted the paperwork. "This here appraisal was requested by the River City Trust Company in preparation for the trustees' meeting next week."

*The what?* Beck followed Henry as he walked the perimeter of her house.

"My name is Beckett Walsh, and this is my property. What trustee meeting?"

"I don't know the specifics, ma'am. I'm just fulfilling this appraisal request from River City Trust Company."

Beck's stomach dropped. The envelope still waiting on her kitchen table flashed in her mind. The one she'd thought was safe to avoid a little longer. "There must be some mistake." Surely Dad hadn't intended to have the place sold upon his passing. But why else would an appraisal be required?

"It's the normal practice to order an appraisal when property is passed from the trust holder to a trustee. As far as what all is in the trust and who it's going to, I have no information on that."

Beck let out a breath. Everything was fine. There was no reason to get worked up. Dad probably left something for Aunt Kate and maybe even Uncle Chris, the mystery man she'd only heard stories about from Aunt Kate.

If Dad was so bent on her telling the bees when he died to protect them, surely he would have told her if he'd decided he wanted to sell her home.

"How many acres is the property?" The appraiser held his pen at the ready.

"Sixty."

He nodded as he jotted down her answer. "Is income generated from the land?"

"I . . . I . . . not much. Enough to keep this place running and pay the bills."

"And is any of the property in the floodway?"

"I don't really know. I—"

He waved his hand as if shooing away a pesky insect. "I'm sorry. I can consult the property records while I'm typing up the report. I just need to make a few more notes and then I'll get out of your hair."

All Beck could manage was a nod. She backed away with Fern lingering at her side, silent as a hoverfly.

"Who was that guy? Do you know him? He looked too fancy for here."

Beck blinked hard. "Hey, kiddo. Go check on Sassy. She has a food and water bowl in the tack room. Make sure they're both full."

"Are you okay? You don't look so good."

She swallowed. "Uh. I just need to check on something real quick and then we'll go feed the chickens." Beck strode to the porch. Her shadow had thankfully detached herself from Beck's side and headed into the barn. Beck jogged up the porch steps and hurried inside. The echo of her boots on the hardwood reverberated through the empty house.

She unearthed the envelope from the pile, then slid her finger beneath the corner to break the seal.

Pacing the kitchen, she scanned the short letter from the trust company. It simply informed her that upon her father's death, his trust became irrevocable—she swallowed hard—and as one of the named trustees, her presence was requested in Chattanooga, Tennessee, next Thursday at 4:00 p.m.

She dialed Aunt Kate's number, but it just rang and rang in her ear with no answer. She watched out the window as Henry Blake's Mercedes disappeared down her drive in a cloud of dust. Apparently he had obtained the information he needed. To be so lucky.

Beck walked back to the barn, propelled onward by some part of her brain not consumed with questions.

Fern hurried to her side. "I fed the cat. She only hissed twice. I think we're making friends. Can we go feed the chickens now?"

Beck blinked and nodded. *Chattanooga on Thursday. One of the trustees. One of them? How many could there be?*

*Chattanooga on Thursday.*

"Beck?" Fern stood with her head tipped sideways and her hands on her hips. "Did you hear me?"

She pressed her lips tight. "Chickens. Yeah. Let me show you where the feed is." By muscle memory she filled the bucket and grabbed a basket for the eggs. Beck passed the basket to Fern and scrubbed a hand over her face. She walked to the pen on autopilot.

Fern stopped short and crossed her arms over her chest. "I thought this was going to be fun, but you're just like Uncle Isaac. Busy. Acting like I don't exist." She punctuated each sentence with a little stomp.

Beck stared at the glowering child beside her. "I'm sorry. I just got some really upsetting news and I'm trying to figure some things out. Here, can you finish feeding these guys?" She offered the bucket with an apologetic smile.

Fern's stance softened and she took the offered bucket. "I'm sorry you're having a bad day. Probably doesn't help being stuck with me."

Beck's heart melted at Fern's solemn expression. "You've been great. My mood has nothing to do with you. Cross my heart."

Fern tossed some chicken feed over the wire fence, watching them scurry and peck. "Is there anything I can do to help?"

"No, there's nothing to be done." Beck passed her the basket. "But while the hens are busy eating, we can slip in and gather some eggs."

∞∞

Later that afternoon, while Beck watched Fern splash in the creek, she dialed Aunt Kate's number again with unsteady hands. Surely Aunt Kate knew more than the letter revealed. This was the sort of thing her dad would tell his sister, wasn't it? Something that for whatever reason he'd not seen fit to tell Beck.

On the third ring, Aunt Kate's voice came through the line. "Beck-Anne? What's wrong?" Worry filled her voice before Beck had the chance to say a word.

That woman had zero faith in her. Beck pushed out a breath. Or maybe that lilt of panic in her aunt's voice was because the last time Beck called, it had been to tell her she'd found her brother slumped over his tractor in the lower forty.

"Did Dad tell you he'd put the farm in a trust?" Beck's shaky hand gripped the phone tighter, the fingers on her free hand started their rhythmic tapping pattern on her thumb. "Have you gotten a letter about a trustee meeting? This guy in a boat hat looking like he should be a part of a barbershop quartet showed up to do an appraisal on behalf of River City Trust Company." She clutched the phone so tight her knuckles ached. "And I'm supposed to be in Chattanooga one week from today to go over the trust."

"An appraiser was there? Haven't you gotten anything from your dad's estate?"

"There's a letter from a trust company about the meeting, but it didn't give any details about the contents of the trust or who the other trustees are."

"Oh, Beck. Do you need me to come down? I could drive you."

"No." Maybe? She tapped the pad of her index finger harder and faster against her thumb, then ceased her tapping altogether and propped her forehead in her hand. "Did Dad tell you anything about any of this?"

"I knew your dad was putting everything in a trust. We talked about it when he had it drawn up. Told me that he hoped I wasn't offended, but everything was going to you. Unless . . ."

"Unless what, Aunt Kate?"

"Unless he changed it. Added your mother."

Beck's mouth went dry, and her throat constricted. "Why would he do that?"

"No, you're right. He wouldn't have done that, no matter how tight the hold she'd had on his heart."

Hold on his heart? There was no hold that Beck was aware of. Her mother had walked out on them when Beck was five, and though Beck had waited years for her to return, she'd eventually given up. Her mother almost never came up in their conversations. They'd said all they needed to say about the woman who wouldn't stay, and together they'd made a happy life.

This time it was Aunt Kate who blew out a breath. "Chris could be involved, but when I last spoke to him, he didn't say anything about it."

"Uncle Chris? You still talk to him?"

"On occasion. He's my brother. It was his twin he had a problem with, not me. Still, I'd hoped he would've come to the funeral."

Beck stood and walked to the water's edge. She dipped her toes in the cool water, watching Fern's attempts at skipping rocks. Had Dad included an uncle she had never met in his trust as some sort of last goodwill offering? "Why would Dad include him and not you?"

"That's it, I'm coming. We'll sort this out together," Aunt Kate said. "Just because he named someone else on the trust doesn't mean you need to worry. He could have decided to give something to someone as a token of love. Like that truck he knows you're never going to drive."

Beck shrank at her aunt's words. She was twenty-eight. Twenty-eight but sheltered and protected and coddled to the point that she had no idea how to be an actual adult. Only the apprentice of one, looking on while Dad had handled all the important things. Why? Because of the way anxiety ruled her life? Because he didn't think she was up to the task at hand? Had he wanted to give her everything, but when he saw that her struggles hadn't gotten better over the years, he'd decided that she wasn't up to being the sole owner?

Aunt Kate buzzed on in her ear about getting packed, and the first steps they should take.

Beck straightened. "No."

The line grew quiet again. "What?"

"I said, no. I can handle it. I'll look through Dad's files, everything, and I'll figure out what this is about. I'll call Uncle Chris and ask him if he knows anything. I'll figure out what's going on."

"Beck, I can come back. Martin will understand. I still have some personal days saved up at work."

"I can do this. Just . . . do you have Uncle Chris's number? That's one thing I'm pretty sure I won't find in Dad's house."

# ELEVEN

The stepladder wobbled beneath Callie as she stretched to unhook the last bungee holding up her grand opening banner. She slipped the hook free, and the vinyl crumpled into a pitiful pile of bright colors. Callie lifted her gaze from the ground and looked over the landscape. Walkers, joggers, and early morning shoppers strolled the street.

One day she'd have a permanent place to call her own with her name and logo across the front. Just not now. She needed to accept that as much as she wanted it, the timing wasn't right.

She could always rehang the sign when she had a clearer picture of the future.

Leah, who owned a condo down the street, slowed her jog and lifted a hand in greeting, but her brow creased when she noticed the fallen banner.

Callie gave a quick wave and pulled her phone from her pocket as she descended the pair of steps. She said hello into the phone though nobody called, and retreated into the empty store, dragging the sign behind her, making a trail through the construction dust that coated the polished concrete floors.

Leah had been so excited about Callie's store opening up just down the street from her. She talked about how so many people had the dream to open their own shop, but so few had what it took to actually go through with it.

Callie was in no mood to confess that she had joined the ranks of dreamers who came up short. Nearing the back of the store, she lifted the banner from the dusty ground and laid it over a folding table. She rolled her shoulders and heaved a breath and then grabbed a push broom. *Stop it. Not now is not synonymous with not ever.* Starting at the back and working forward, she swept, stirring up a cloud of Sheetrock dust as she went.

She hadn't come this far in life by huddling in a corner whining about all the things that should have been. Like always, she'd do the best she could with what she had.

A knock sounded on the front glass. Luke stood with a hand cupped around his eyes to cut the glare. An unbidden smile stretched across her face. She waved him in.

He maneuvered through the front door, hampered by the large rectangular object draped in fabric that was tucked under one arm. "I was in the neighborhood, and I thought I'd stop in. I hope it's not a bad time."

"Nah. I'm just catching up on some things." She quickly swiped the grime off of her face with the collar of her T-shirt, feeling the grit that clung to her damp skin.

He surveyed the room, laying the object he carried on the folding table next to her sign.

She heaved a breath and gestured to the draped vinyl. "I've put off taking that thing down for way too long. I guess it felt like a public admission of defeat."

"I bet you'll be hanging that sign again in no time," he said.

"We'll see." Of course, she left out the fine print of what made the whole thing so impossible. She swatted at the dust particles dancing in front of her face, illuminated by the sunlight spilling through the windows.

Luke smiled. "Maybe my timing is just right. Brought you something." He lifted away the sheet covering the mysterious object he'd set down, revealing the photograph she'd admired at the market of the mountain crowned by sunbeams.

"For me?" She stepped closer.

He nodded. "Yep. For your new space. I figured if it didn't go with the decor in the store, you could hang it in your office. Or at home." Color rose in his face. "I mean, if you like it."

She lifted the canvas print. "You know I like it. It's beautiful."

He leaned his hip against the table. "I hope the photograph is a good reminder during these dusty moments."

She propped the broom against the wall and stuffed her hands in the pockets of her cut-off shorts. "Of what a mess this place was?"

He chuckled. "No. That beauty comes from the light. Dust doesn't change itself. The light does that."

She smiled. "I get what you're trying to say." Sort of. But she wasn't entirely sure how it applied to her current situation.

He shoved his hands in his pockets too, then stepped closer. "I know something's going on with you that you're not saying. If you don't want me to know, that's your prerogative. But I want you to know that somebody sees and cares, Callie. You don't have to deal with whatever it is alone."

Callie's gaze shot to the floor and she edged backward. "Thank you. That means a lot." Her heart pounded in her chest. She hated the way an offer of help always had the opposite effect that it should. She forced herself to lift her chin and meet his eyes.

He studied her with a crease between his brows. There was kindness in his gaze. A tenderness she wished she could learn to trust. How did a person learn to do that? Trust an imperfect human being who would probably let them down at some juncture or another.

He rubbed the back of his neck and shifted his feet. "Well, anyway. Please at least tell me you're going to be at the market this weekend."

"I'll be there." She'd ended up bailing on him yesterday. Instead, she came home after church and pulled the covers over her head.

"Good. When you called out, they put this woman beside me who weaves shawls from dog hair. She sang show tunes nonstop." He shivered. "And I'm allergic." He headed for the door.

"To show tunes or dogs?"

"Both," he said, mischief glinting in his gray eyes when he looked over his shoulder.

She grinned despite herself. If she ended up trying for a part-time job to supplement her income, she should put that skill on her résumé: able to smile while dying inside.

He paused with his hand on the door. "Seriously, I know you probably have a ton of friends you can turn to, but if you ever need one more, you know where to find me."

She nodded and forced another smile. "Same place every Sunday." Why couldn't she respond with something more substantive than that lame deflection? Allow him into her life instead of just leaving him to guess what was going on. What horrible thing did she imagine would happen?

He pulled the front door open.

"Luke, I really, really like you." Callie stifled a groan. Okay. That was something honest and definitely vulnerable. And she was pretty sure he felt the same way. But, of all things, why had that come out of her mouth?

She cringed. Because awkwardly blurting that she had a crush on him was somehow safer than admitting her mother was an alcoholic and her life issues were derailing her dreams for about the four thousandth time, and she was doing everything in her power not to lose hope. To pretend she wasn't doomed to repeat this same pattern for all eternity.

What a train wreck.

He turned, head tilted. His mouth stretched in a slow grin. "I really, really like you too, Callie." He waved his hand, indicating the room. "You're really overwhelmed right now, so maybe when things settle down a little bit, we'll explore that mutual liking thing we've got going on. Until then, seriously, I'm here for whatever you need."

As he exited the building, Callie snatched the broom from where it rested against the wall. The floor and that broom became a conduit for the gamut of emotions coursing through her.

He'd asked for honesty about her pain and instead she'd expressed interest in a relationship she was definitely not ready for. Unless she was prepared to tell him the truth about her mother, rehab, the whole shebang, all she had to offer him was the same facade everyone else got.

After she finished her task, she neatly folded the banner beside Luke's canvas. Maybe she didn't have the necessary funds to get this place up and running, but at least it looked more hopeful now that things were tidied up. That was her specialty, wasn't it? Giving things the outward appearance of being fine and finding some measure of safety in that.

Callie locked up the shop, the early June heat blasting her full in the face.

She headed in the direction of her apartment but then paused. Maybe she couldn't get Solace Naturals up and running just yet, but some of those shops might be willing to carry her products if they had the shelf space. She'd been so focused on online sales and getting the storefront going that she hadn't considered it before. It definitely wasn't her dream, but it would be another potential source of income while the building project was on hold.

Callie hurried to her apartment, showered, and typed up a product list. On another sheet of paper, she wrote down the names of five gift shops in the downtown area that might be a good fit for her products.

Armed with the pertinent information, product samples, and all the willpower she could muster, she headed out her front door.

# TWELVE

Despite the many things screaming for her attention over the past few days, Beck had done her best to give Fern her focus, especially after Fern's accusation of Beck being as absent-minded as her uncle. Although, after hearing about Fern's parents, she found she had far more sympathy for him. Being unexpectedly thrown into full-time care of a child? She had no idea how she would cope with something of that magnitude. In fact, she was certain she'd messed up big-time today.

When Isaac arrived, Beck mopped the sweat from her brow and stood from where they had been building new boxes for the hives Beck planned to split next week.

"Hey, Fern. Do you want to go pet the baby goats again before you go?" she said. "I'm going to go talk to your uncle for a minute."

Fern looked at her with wide eyes. "Did I do something wrong? Please tell me I'll be allowed to come back. I didn't mean to be a pest."

Beck patted her shoulder, hoping the compassion she felt somehow transferred to the girl in that action. "You were awesome. I'm gonna tell your uncle how much help you've been." Hopefully he'd still allow Fern to come back once Beck fessed up.

Fern grinned, jumped up, and trotted off to the goat pen.

Isaac walked her direction, and Beck met him halfway across the lawn, lifting a hand in greeting on her way.

He pushed his glasses up on his nose and shoved his hands in his pockets when she stopped in front of him. "Is she still behaving for you?"

"She was great."

The creases around his eyes relaxed. "I really appreciate all the time you've spent with her. She's had a tough time lately."

Beck released a breath. "There is something I wanted to give you a heads-up about. I might've royally messed up today."

Isaac blinked. "Um. Okay."

"I'm really sorry. I'm not used to kids. I should have had a better answer for her question." The words rushed out of Beck. "But while we were building the hive boxes, we were talking about the different jobs of all the bees in the hive, and um . . . then she asked me about the male bees."

Isaac tilted his head. "Okay. So . . ."

Heat filled Beck's face. It was simple biology, but should Fern possess this knowledge at her age? "Well, I tried to skip over them, and I told her that they just fly around. But you know Fern. She didn't buy that that was all they did. So I just told her."

Isaac massaged his temples. "Told her what?"

Beck bit the corner of her lip. Might as well spill it. "I was just being straightforward. I didn't know how else to say it. I told her that the drones only job was to find and mate with newly hatched queens. And she looked really, really confused and asked me what mating was." Beck cringed, shutting her eyes tight. "I told her to ask you about it when she got home."

First she heard a snort, then it erupted into a full-out laugh. Beck opened her eyes to see Isaac, hand pressed over his mouth, shoulders shaking. She failed to see the humor, but at least he wasn't mad.

"Beck, she was playing you."

"Huh?"

"The kid watches National Geographic every day. She knows what mating is."

*That little imp.* "Is she old enough to watch that stuff?"

"She said it was okay." Isaac shrugged. "She was having such a hard time adjusting, I didn't want to be the bad guy. I figured there's worse stuff on television."

Beck tried to swallow down all the embarrassment she worked up dreading this conversation. "Yeah. Well, like I said, I'm sorry if I handled that wrong."

Isaac gave her a lopsided smile. "You're doing fine. At least she doesn't run away from you."

"Has it been any better since she's been spending a little time here?"

He said, "Well, she definitely gets her energy out. She's too tired to wander off, so that's a plus. This summer hasn't been easy on her though. One minute it's like she's so happy to be here, and the next she resents it."

Beck stepped closer, surprising herself when she reached for his upper arm. "A little advice from someone who is going through the same thing she is. Be patient. It's going to take time to figure out a new normal for the two of you, but I think she'll adjust if you give it time."

Isaac tilted his head, looking at her like she'd started talking in a language he had only a rudimentary grasp of. "Uh, yeah. I'm sure we'll figure it out over this next month or so."

Did he not hear the part about patience? "Well, okay then. You can bring her by again tomorrow if you'd like."

She and Isaac walked to the goat pen to collect Fern who was only willing to leave after Beck promised three times that she could play with the kids again tomorrow.

Beck watched the pair of them drive away. As the car drew out of sight, her attention locked on her dad's old pickup truck, collecting pollen under the carport. The vehicle that would carry her to Chattanooga three days from now. The pricks of fear that had been lingering below the surface grew until they wrapped themselves around her rib cage, squeezing away her breath. What was she supposed to do about this trust meeting?

She tried her uncle's number again, propping the phone against her ear with her shoulder as she poured herself a bowl of cereal for supper. It rang and rang, ending with an automated voice mail. Surely Dad wouldn't have put his brother on the trust. Definitely not Mom either.

Beck walked into the living room, staring at a vacant corner where they always put up their Christmas tree. She dredged up the memory.

She could still remember the scents of cinnamon and yeasty dough floating on the air. Bing Crosby was belting out "White Christmas" on the scratchy record player her dad brought out just for special occasions.

Her mother danced into the room with over-bright eyes, telling Beck she had a surprise for her. She'd made Beck close her eyes while she plopped a cardboard box at her feet. It was tied shut with a red velvet ribbon.

As Beck tugged the loose end of the bow, the box wiggled, and a plaintive meow came from within. She ripped the ribbon off and pulled out a long-haired orange tabby. Her mother had clapped her hands with delight, tugged her father over, and together they'd laughed at the cat's antics as it pounced in the leftover Christmas paper.

It had been the happiest they'd been in a long time, or so she'd thought. When Beck woke the next morning to find Christmas spent and her mother gone, the sadness that had lingered in her father's eyes despite the joyous day made a lot more sense. He'd seen signs that a naive little girl had missed.

A few weeks after her mother left, the cat slipped out the back door and ran away too. Sometimes she imagined the cat had left to find Mom. And they were happy together. As a child she never quite worked out how to feel about that—to be glad that Mom was happy or sad that she was happy without her and Dad.

Maybe most kids would have spent their life wondering why they were so defective that their mother could not stay. But not Beck. When you have . . . had . . . a father like George Walsh, there was no space to wonder such things.

She sat the cereal bowl down with a clatter and went to the door of her father's room. She had to face this. Face what was beyond his door and see if he'd left any clue about what he'd put in his trust and to whom he'd given it.

She took a steadying breath and stepped inside.

Aunt Kate must have made the bed before she left. Beck crossed to it and tugged at the blanket until there were little wrinkles across the top and then placed the pillows slightly off-kilter.

There. That looked more like the room George Walsh had occupied.

She inhaled the faint piney scent in the room. Pine and something else that was unique to her dad, not unlike the smoky sweet scent that lingered in the places bees had occupied. How long until the scents went stale and it would be like her father had never been there? She'd been shocked, losing him without warning in a single afternoon. No one had warned her about the way she would continue to lose him by infinitesimal degrees every day.

She knelt in front of the cabinet that served as his nightstand, her hand frozen on the handle. It seemed shameful, violating his privacy, especially with the room still feeling like it was his.

But he wasn't here to give her the answers she needed. Beck pulled the cabinet door open.

There were worn notebooks. The first one she pulled out was filled with thoughts about the habits of bees. Another held sketches of flowers, labeled with their names and their meanings. As she flipped through the pages, one purple bloom caught her eye. Her heart clenched when she read the words beneath it. No wonder he'd wanted to mow her mother's flowers down. Beck would have let him if she'd known.

Setting aside the sketchbook, she picked up a stack of postcards bound together with twine. She loosened the bundle and flipped through the stack, beautiful scenes from around the country displayed on each one. The only writing on them were addresses, no names, no text. She stacked them back together and rebound them, then pulled out a large leather-bound photo album she'd never seen.

Inside were pictures of Beck as a baby in the arms of her mother. Pictures of Beck sitting on her father's lap as a toddler as he gave her rides on the tractor. Family snapshots in their Easter best. To any outside observer it would look as though this album chronicled the life of the quintessential American family.

But Beck knew better. This secret photo stash of her father's was one man's fantasy. A picture of what he wanted to be real, but it was nothing more than empty images of what should have been.

She shoved the album back inside the cabinet.

All these years he'd acted as Beck's happy, nurturing father. Had that been an illusion too?

She walked to his closet, touching each of the shirts hanging there. Clothes she'd been carefully washing and placing on the rack since she was a child. The back of her eyes burned as she traced her hands over the shoulders of his favorite denim shirt. Why? Why had he never told her the burden he carried?

Had the ache in his heart from the wounds her mother inflicted been so great, so constant, that he'd been desensitized to the symptoms of the disease setting up camp in his heart?

She pressed her hand to her chest, counterpressure to the physical ache she now carried growing by the second until it made it too hard to catch her breath.

She stuffed her fist against her mouth and hurried from the room, her feet carrying her down the hall, out the door, and into the honey house. She grabbed her father's bee suit from the peg, climbed inside it, and zipped the mesh hood around her. She sat curled on the ground, rocking herself, forcing inhales to pass through her tight chest as she breathed in the scent of him and the scent of honeybees trapped in the fabric. Protective gear was meant to keep stings from piercing the skin, but it did nothing to protect her from the barbed stingers living in her chest.

# THIRTEEN

Callie fidgeted in the chair across from her therapist.

"We talked last time about opening up with Luke and telling him about what's been going on with your mother. How has that been going?" Joanne peered at her over her black frames, the picture of composure.

"I tried," Callie mumbled. "But I couldn't make myself. It's like the words are just clogged up inside."

"Because?"

Callie pushed out a breath. "Because for my entire life Mom drilled it into my head that if I told the truth about her, our lives would fall apart. I'd lose her. Get put in foster care. When I was sixteen, I finally got up the courage to tell someone. My youth pastor, Jenni. She called Mom to talk to her. The very next day, I came home from school to our packed-up apartment. I never saw Jenni again, and I lost the most stable person in my life since Ms. Ruthie."

Joanne nodded. "So, tell me how that plays into your fears about Luke now. You fear that you'll lose him?"

Callie worried her bottom lip between her teeth. "Not exactly. It's just this weird feeling that grabs ahold of me and I can't talk." She massaged away the tic starting under her eye. "Instead of telling him what I needed to tell him, I blurted out that I had a crush on him."

"Oh." Joanne tilted her head. "Do you?"

"Yeah," she admitted.

"And why do you think those words came out in that moment?"

Callie huffed, an ironic smile tugging at her mouth. "I don't know, Joanne, but I have a feeling you do. Just spill it."

Joanne chuckled. "You've already told me without knowing it. Tell me what your goal was all those times you tried to protect and care for your mom."

Callie wrapped her arms around her middle. "To stay together. To help her be okay."

"All right. To what end? What need were you trying to get your relationship with your mom to meet?"

Callie shook her head. "It was about helping her. Not me."

"Remember, having needs isn't selfish. What did you need from her?"

Callie pressed her fingers to her brow bones. "I needed my mom to be there for me. To be stable. And I tried to help her be that person."

Joanne nodded. "You needed love and care?"

"Yeah." The word came out a whisper.

Joanne raised her shoulders and let them fall. "So maybe your response to Luke makes a lot of sense. Your brain, which experienced trauma in the form of abandonment and neglect, is still trying to close a loop your mother's neglect has left open. It's still searching for a way to have that unmet need fulfilled. Your need for love and affection is all tangled up in memories of your mother's inability to provide them. That blurted comment that felt like an accident wasn't an accident. A part of you was trying to close the open loop by making a bid for the love and affection you still crave."

Callie swallowed hard. And here she thought she'd been making progress.

Joanne smiled softly. "Don't give me that look. You are making progress. Healing is like an onion. It might feel like you're going in circles, but you're actually discovering new layers."

Callie scrunched her nose. "Stop knowing what I'm thinking. It's creepy."

Joanne winked. "Just doing my job."

# FOURTEEN

*A*fter a good sleep and a morning spent with Fern's incessant energy at her side, Beck's future seemed more manageable than it had the night before. Drawing courage from the feisty whirlwind had helped her hold off on calling Aunt Kate and asking her to reconsider swooping in to take charge.

Once they reached the apiary, Fern hopped out of the utility vehicle and trailed in Beck's wake. The girl's normal stream of chatter suddenly ran dry. As excited as she'd been about getting her first peek inside the hives, now that the moment approached, she hung back a bit.

"Come here. Let me double-check you." Beck motioned Fern over. She knelt in front of the girl and looked over all the zippers and Velcro closures, especially those at the bottom of her pant legs and hat, to confirm there were no spaces where a bee could find its way in. A bee sting wouldn't be the worst thing in the world, but she wanted Fern's first experience to be as magical as Beck's first peek inside the queen's palace had been.

Beck straightened, dusted off her hands, and pulled on her purple nitrile gloves. "Ready?"

Fern nodded, her veiled hat bobbing with her.

"Now you really do look like a space traveler," Beck said tapping the brim of Fern's hat, trying to pull a smile out of the girl. It almost worked.

Beck puffed a little smoke at the entrance of the hive, while explaining how she tried to use the bare minimum. Using smoke was effective in distracting the guard bees from their post, but she hated the fact that it made her bees think their lives were in danger, that they needed to gorge themselves on their precious food stores because that smoke meant fire and fire meant they might have to leave it all behind.

Beck almost never used smoke and just kept it at the ready in case things got a little out of hand. She much preferred to just move quietly and carefully and be as unobtrusive as possible in this sacred world of theirs, always remembering that she was nothing more than an interloper in their intricate domain.

But today, for Fern's sake, she used a little more smoke than usual. Beck well remembered how intimidating the sheer number of bees could be, especially if they started to get a little fussed by human presence.

After she had both the outer and inner covers off, she called Fern closer. She pointed out the pollen and the white-capped honey stores packed in the hexagon cells at the top of the brood frame. She taught her about the brood pattern, the capped and uncapped cells that held the next generation of bees.

At first, Fern stood rigid, but as Beck worked through the frames, Fern leaned closer. Her normal stream of questions returned like an opened floodgate. She leaned in close as Beck held up a frame.

"You mean those tiny, tiny little rice-looking things are baby bees?"

Beck nodded. "Yep, those are eggs. I look to make sure there is one in each of the cells. You can even tell how many days old they are by looking to see if they are standing straight up or leaning. And you can tell how old the larvae are if the cell is still open or if they've been capped with wax."

"Why does that matter?"

"Right now I'm looking for the queen bee, and if you look carefully, you can get an idea of how long it's been since she's laid these and if she might be on this frame."

Fern stared wide-eyed at the bee-covered frame, the constant movement of striped bodies hypnotizing. "You're looking for one bee out of all of these?"

Beck nodded. "Yep. It's not easy, but it helps if you know what you're looking for."

"And why do you need to see her?"

"It's not absolutely necessary. All the signs, the various stages of the brood—from eggs to larvae to capped brood inside this hive—point to this hive having a thriving and healthy queen. But I like to see her if I can."

"Why is she so important?"

"Because she is the mother of them all. Without her, the whole hive will eventually die out if they aren't able to raise a new queen. If I find a hive without a queen and no signs that they've been able to raise a new one, I can often help them out. Bring them a new queen."

Fern edged closer, bringing her face as close to the frame Beck held as her veiled hat would allow. "Do you see her?"

Beck relaxed her eyes, letting all the individual moving insects become a single organism as she looked for the queen whose larger body and way of moving made her different from any other bee in the hive.

Fern pointed. "Is that her? That one is different from all the others."

"No, that's a drone. The males have a rounded body. Hers is long and narrow, and sometimes attendant bees will be surrounding her in a little circle." Beck pointed. "There." And then she was gone again, moving fast and covered by the high population of the hive.

Fern pouted. "I can't see her."

Beck placed the frame back in the hive body. "It takes practice. I bet you'll spot a queen by the end of the day." She replaced the inner and outer covers and stood. "One down, fifteen more to go for today's rounds." They'd better hurry the rest of the inspections. She'd taken her time with the first one so that Fern could have a good experience.

Beck unzipped her veil and let her hat and attached veil hang down her back. She motioned for Fern to do the same. "Come on. Let's get some water. We have a lot of work to do, and it's not going to get cooler."

Once Fern's head was uncovered, she pushed the damp hair back on her head. "Who knew beekeeping was such sweaty work?"

"Ready to go back home to your uncle yet?" Beck asked, testing her.

Fern shook her head, braids swinging. "Not a chance."

Beck worked through the remaining hives on her list, keeping notes in her notebook on everything she observed. Putting stars beside the ones that she had concerns about so that she could go back to them. She worked quickly, only pausing when Fern had a question.

For the most part, Fern was content to watch the work in silence and sketch in her notebook. And Beck understood. Even after all these years, all this time, opening up a hive was like entering a little planet all to itself. Katya Amadeus Cimmaron of the Vesper Galaxy fit right in here.

Hours later, sweaty and exhausted, they opened up the last hive. When Beck got to the center frame and pulled it out, Fern gasped. "What is that?"

Beck turned the frame around so that the side of the frame Fern inspected faced her. The large peanut-shell-like formation stood out from the perfect order of the typical hexagonal pattern.

"That's a supersedure cell."

Fern tried to scratch her nose through her veil. "What's supersedure?"

"It means that the hive decided they needed to raise a new queen."

"Why? What happened to the old one?"

"She may very well still be here. We'll be able to tell as we keep looking. She may be an older queen, or maybe the hive feels like she isn't as efficient as she should be. Or sometimes the bees just sense that something isn't right with her, something we can't detect yet, and they want to replace her."

"And when this little bee hatches, then what?"

Beck gave her a tight smile. "Then they fight to the death. The one who lives, the strong one, will be the queen."

"That's harsh."

"Things in the hive often are."

"Can't you stop it?"

"I could," Beck said. "I could dispose of this cell and the bee inside. But if they really feel the need to replace their queen, they'll make another queen cell. I've found it's usually best to let them sort things out themselves and keep an eye on their progress."

They finished up the final hive and hurried to the creek to cool off. There was nothing like stepping into that cold mountain-fed stream after working hours in the heat. Beck and Fern slipped out of their suits. Beck rolled up her pants legs and waded in, splashing water on her face and arms.

Fern jumped right in.

"Your uncle is going to skin you alive. You didn't bring a change of clothes."

Fern grinned, diving under the deeper vein in the middle and coming up with a whoop. "Whoa, that's cold! Come all the way in, Beck. It feels great."

Beck remembered calling out the very same words to her father who always stayed in the shallows. Had he ever wished he would have done things differently? Dove deeper instead of using bees and farm chores as his way to connect?

"Beck, please? It's fun." Fern's chattering teeth contradicted her recommendation.

Beck groaned and waded forward, doing a shallow dive into the deep middle. The icy water coursed over her, chasing every thought from her brain. She came up with a whoop just like Fern. It seemed the only possible response to that cold shock.

Both she and Fern dissolved into giggles. Laughter had chased away the subtle tension that so often lingered on Fern's face, tension that no child should know about. Fern's untainted joy was worth the chill.

⌀⌀⌀⌀

The next morning, Beck packed her bag for Chattanooga even though it was ridiculous to pack a bag for a forty-five-minute drive to a one-hour meeting. It somehow settled her nerves to know that if something came up, she'd have anything she might need.

She carried the bag out to the truck, along with a roadside emergency kit she'd hodgepodged from the tools in the barn and two copies of directions to the trust company she printed out in case her GPS failed or her phone died.

She stowed the bags in the back and laid the directions across the dash. Maybe she should do a trial run to get ready for tomorrow. Crank the truck, drive it to the end of the road, and turn around and come back.

She retrieved her dad's keys from her pocket. They jangled against each other in her shaky hand. On the second try, she managed to slip the key into the ignition. She sat back against the leather seat and let out a slow breath. "Beckett Anne Walsh, you're not five years old anymore. You have a choice about what happens to you, and so did your mother. Nothing out there's going to swallow you up and keep you from coming back home."

Yes. She knew all these things. She ran her hands over the steering wheel, hands slick with cold sweat. She knew them. That's what made her so angry at herself. When the irrational and the rational inside of her went to battle, irrational won—a defect she could not bring herself to forgive.

It had started with childhood nightmares. But even after she'd outgrown the dreams of fanged beasts devouring a lost, wandering mother, faceless fear had managed to grow and take on a life of its own, completely immune to logic.

In the face of irrational fears she was powerless to banish, her father created a world where she hardly ever had to acknowledge their existence.

She blew out a breath and turned the key. Nothing. She tried again. Still nothing. After the third attempt, she leaned back against the truck seat and pressed her palms against her eyes.

At the sound of an approaching car, she took a shaky breath and exited the vehicle.

Isaac and Fern.

She hadn't expected them today.

Fern exited the car and skipped over, a bouquet in her hands, her uncle following at a more sedate pace.

"We went to the flower farm today. Me and Uncle Ike. It was fun." She thrust the bouquet of zinnias close to Beck's face. "These are for you."

Isaac smiled. "Sorry if we're disturbing you. She insisted we bring them over right away."

Beck took the bouquet in hand, hoping her emotions hadn't left traces on her face. "That's so nice of you, Fern. Take them inside and put them in one of my big jars from the bottom cabinet, if you'd like."

She passed the flowers back to Fern who trotted merrily into the house, blooms jostling in her tightly clamped hands.

Beck motioned to the silent truck. "Do you mind giving me a jump? I think my battery is dead."

Isaac pulled his hatchback over and popped the hood. Beck hooked everything up and jumped the car off. The truck successfully started, and Beck let out a breath of relief. She left it hooked up for a little while and then disconnected to let the truck run on its own for a bit.

Fern rejoined them. "I left your flowers on your kitchen table."

Beck gave her a quick hug. "Thank you. And thanks to your uncle who helped me get the old truck started. I've got a trip planned for tomorrow."

The engine died. Beck groaned.

Isaac pushed the hair that had fallen onto his forehead back into place. "Should we try again?"

Beck shook her head. "I think I've got bigger problems." At best it was a bad battery, but she had a feeling it was the alternator. What were the chances she could find a mechanic to do a home visit who also happened to have an alternator lying around for her dad's older-model truck and could have it ready by tomorrow? Zero-to-none sounded about right.

She leaned against the truck to hold herself up.

"What can I do?" Isaac asked.

She shook her head. "Nothing. I'm just going to have to tell them I can't make the meeting tomorrow." At her side, she started tapping the fingers of her left hand against her thumb in their familiar, calming pattern.

"I could take you," Isaac said. "Mrs. Bailey and Fern already have plans tomorrow. Fern's been begging to learn how to bake bread and Mrs. Bailey is giving her a lesson."

"No, I couldn't ask you—"

"Absolutely you can ask me. I think I owe you more than a bouquet of flowers for all the help you are to Fern. And me." His face reddened slightly as he pushed his glasses higher on his nose.

"What about your work?"

"I'll bring my laptop and get some things done while I wait. I'm sure there'll be a coffee shop nearby."

As much as she needed help, the last thing she wanted was a witness to her issues. "It's really not necess—"

"It's settled," he said, cutting her off. "I'll pick you up tomorrow. Just tell me what time."

"Oh, okay . . . Okay." She blew out a breath and stretched her left hand open wide, releasing the cramp she'd worked up. "The meeting isn't until four, so if we leave by two thirty that will give us enough time."

*Lord, have mercy on my pathetic soul and don't let me lose it in front of him tomorrow.*

# FIFTEEN

Callie parked in River City Trust Company's lot. She walked into the nondescript high-rise, finding the suite number on the building directory sign in the lobby.

She clenched and unclenched her fists while she waited for the elevator. If only she could see through the walls into the meeting room. Was it a room full of George Walsh's family? Would everyone know why she was there, leaving her the only clueless one? Would they try to make her prove her connection, outraged that this interloper was robbing them of something that was rightfully theirs?

The elevator dinged, and she rode up alone. At the front desk, she gave them her name, and they walked her down a long hall to a conference room. She declined their offer of a glass of water and sat at a long table alone while the minutes crawled. Callie pulled a notebook from her satchel and fidgeted with her pen.

At exactly four, the receptionist showed another woman into the room who was shorter in stature than Callie and, if she had to guess, a few years younger. Or maybe it was the way she was dressed that gave that impression, with her worn jeans and a baggy T-shirt tucked into the waist and her hair pulled back into a short ponytail.

The woman sat at the opposite end of the long table. The receptionist reentered with a glass of water and sat it in front of the woman. Her thank-you came out barely above a whisper.

The receptionist looked at Callie. "Are you sure I can't get you anything?"

"No, ma'am. I'm fine, thank you."

The other woman seemed to stare through the wall. She sat tapping each finger against her thumb, over and over again in the same pattern. Index finger, middle finger, ring finger, pinky. Index, middle, ring, pinky. She looked at her watch. She looked at the door. She looked at Callie.

Callie had opened her mouth to introduce herself when the woman said, "Are we about to get started?" Her voice sounded pinched, like it was a struggle to get the words out.

"Should be any minute, I'm guessing."

This girl, whoever she was, must have somewhere pressing to be.

The door opened, and a man in a navy suit walked into the room with a file in his hand. "Good afternoon. Sorry to keep you waiting. I had a client meeting that ran a little long." He flipped through the pages in his file and then smiled at each of them. "Let's jump right into this. My name is Craig Avery. We're here today to go over the contents of the irrevocable trust of George Walsh. To be clear, now that he has passed, nothing in this trust can be changed or altered, and once the trust property has been transferred to the named beneficiaries—"

A clatter and splash came from the opposite end of the table. "I'm so sorry." The woman stared helplessly at the spilled water stretching across the table.

"I'll grab some paper towels." Callie hurried from the room before the man could call anyone else to clean it up. She needed to get out of there, to escape if only for a moment.

When she returned with wads of paper towels in each hand, the woman still sat staring at the spill like she was trying to figure out how it got there. Callie wasn't sure what was going on with her, but the woman definitely wasn't okay.

Callie wiped up the water and returned to her seat. Mr. Avery gave her a kind smile. "As I was explaining, once the assets have been distributed, there will no longer be a need for the trust, and it will be dissolved. Today you will receive copies of the trust, as well as copies of the paperwork you'll need to sign for the transfer of assets. Mr. Walsh entrusted our company to administrate his trust and requested that this take place in person rather than simply sending a letter of distribution. It was his original intention to hold this meeting with him in attendance."

As the man continued on, sharing legal detail in language she didn't quite grasp, Callie dared a glance at the other woman from the corner of her eye. She had her hands clasped at chest level, her knuckles white. Callie looked back to Mr. Avery.

He gestured to the woman. "To Beckett Anne Walsh, your father wished to have all the farm equipment and livestock transferred to you, entrusted into your care." He gestured first to Callie and then to Beckett. "Callie Peterson and Beckett Anne Walsh, you have been named as cotenants of George Walsh's apiary, Walsh Farm. This means that you each have equal holding in the property. You may either continue in co-owning the property as equal owners, or you may jointly choose to sell—"

A gasp came from Beckett. She panted for air, her hand pressed to her chest.

"Ma'am. Are you okay?" Mr. Avery rose from his seat and approached her.

"My-my . . . my heart. I can't . . . b-b-bree . . . It hurts . . ."

Callie stood helplessly by her side while Mr. Avery poked his head out the conference door. "Martha, call an ambulance."

"N-n-no . . . it's n-not . . ." The girl doubled over, and another low guttural sound slipped out of her.

Mr. Avery put his hand on Beckett's shoulder and looked at Callie. "Don't worry. The hospital is less than five minutes from here. We'll get your sister some help."

She started to explain that Beckett Anne Walsh was not her sister, but maybe this man knew something about her family tree Callie did not.

A lanky man swept into the room, eyes wide behind his glasses. "Beck?" He knelt in front of her.

Beck sat up, both hands pressed to her chest like she was about to give herself CPR. Her eyes bulged, and she gasped for air. "Home . . . Take me home."

"Okay. Okay," he said under his breath. "But I'm taking you to get checked out first."

Sister or not, Callie and this stranger now owned a farm together thanks to one George Walsh. And his daughter sure wasn't taking it well.

# SIXTEEN

Beck sat on the end of the exam table, waiting for the nurse to come with her discharge papers. She swung her foot like a recalcitrant child. She crossed her arms over her chest that still ached and sat tall when what she really wanted to do was collapse in a ball and sleep. She glared at Isaac who sat in the vacant chair beside the door. "I told you I didn't need to go to the hospital."

He looked up from the newspaper he'd been reading, his glasses having slipped down his nose. "Yeah, well, I might have taken your word for it if you'd been able to talk in complete sentences and take a solid breath. And if you hadn't mentioned your father's heart problems."

She stopped swinging her leg and drew her knees up under her chin. "All I needed was to get back home." There was nothing more embarrassing than losing control like that in public.

He stood and stepped closer to her. "Was it something that happened in the meeting?"

The man's words in the conference room pushed into the edges of her thoughts, and she shoved them away. She bit her lip. "I was already having a hard time before it started."

He folded the newspaper and stuck it under his chair. "You were pretty edgy on the way here. Which is why I stayed in the lobby instead of leaving for the coffee shop."

The door to the exam room opened and a young nurse entered. "All right, Ms. Walsh, we're still waiting on that discharge paperwork. Dr. Johnston asked me to bring the prescription for a mild sedative he'd mentioned to you." She held out a small paper square.

"Thanks," Beck said as she took it.

As soon as the nurse left the room, Beck wadded the slip and tossed it into the trash can by the door. "Nothing but net." She smiled weakly.

Isaac crossed to it and plucked the wad from the trash. He carried it over to her, pinched between his finger and thumb. "Pretty sure you should at least shred this or something." When she didn't take it, he set it on the exam table. "And, I don't know, maybe you ought to give the prescription a try. It could help."

Beck lifted her gaze from her lap and stared at the abstract art on the wall. "I should've warned you this could happen, but I wanted to pretend I could handle this. I should be able to handle this."

"You lost your dad," Isaac said, his voice soft. "Give yourself some—"

Beck buried her face in her hands. "It's not that. At least, not just that. I've had issues for a long time. Panic attacks since I was a little kid. But only when I was away from home." She shrugged, heat rising in her face. "So I stay home. If I do that, the panic attacks don't affect me. I shouldn't need medicine just to leave my house. It's pathetic."

Isaac grimaced. He took off his glasses and wiped away a smudge with the hem of his shirt as he sat back down. "What happened in the meeting?"

She inhaled and exhaled slowly, trying to expand her tight chest. "I'm not even sure if I heard everything right, because this weird auditory thing happens when I have a panic attack where this buzzing in my ears takes over. There was this other woman in the room that I thought was just somebody who worked there, but then the guy said that . . . that she and I . . ." Beck's pulse rose. "I think he said that she and I— That my dad left the farm to us. That we are cotenants. I don't know what that even means."

Isaac shifted in his seat. "Uh, well, it means that you and her equally own property together. You can either decide to continue in that arrangement, or the two of you can decide to sell."

Beck bit down on the side of her cheek until she tasted blood, trying to force her post–panic attack fogged mind to process his words. "So she could decide to sell her part, and some other person would own half the farm?"

"Well . . ." The look on his face was pained. "The way cotenant arrangements work in Tennessee is that the property would either need to be held by the two of you in its entirety or sold in its entirety and the profits split. Now, you could be the buyer and choose to buy the farm in its entirety. But you'd need to be able to offer fair market value, unless the other person wasn't interested in getting their full value out of the place."

Her peripheral vision blurred, and the room seemed suddenly off-kilter. Any penny she had to her name was already invested in the farm.

A strong, steadying hand braced her. "Beck?" His voice seemed to carry from somewhere far away.

She blinked hard and clenched her hands tight, until her short nails bit her palms, grounding her. "I can't lose my farm, Isaac. I can't." She struggled for a solid breath. "I need to get home. Please, take me back home."

He went to the door. "I'll go check on their progress with the discharge paperwork." He paused, his mouth opening like he wanted to say something else, but then he turned and left the room.

Tears gathered at the corners of her eyes, and she laid down on the exam table, the protective paper cover crackling against her cheek. Her body felt so heavy, like somebody had turned up Earth's gravity. Though she wished otherwise, this feeling was familiar, the

aftermath of the battle between mind and body in which both parties lost.

Beck racked her memory. Not one recollection of her father men-
tioning Callie Peterson.

She rolled to her back, staring at the ceiling. The tiles had been
painted to look like the sky. She wished those ceiling tiles would
open wide and she could shout loud enough for her father to hear.
To ask him why he'd taken what had been theirs and given half of
it to a stranger, never breathing a word about why.

Beck's chest grew tighter and tighter. He'd thought she couldn't
handle the place on her own. Considering how a simple meeting
landed her in the ER, she couldn't argue. But why not Aunt Kate?
Why not the mysterious and noncommunicative Uncle Chris? Either
of them would have made more sense than this outsider.

Half an hour later, they were free to go. Beck sank into the passenger seat, and Isaac came around with a fluffy, purple unicorn
blanket. He leaned her seat back and tucked the fleece up to her
chin.

She was too tired to protest. "Nice blanket."

"It's Fern's."

She closed her eyes. "Uh-huh. Sure."

"Take a nap and we'll be home soon." The tenderness of his words
was more comforting than the blanket.

The tension coursing through her lessened the closer they got to
home, and before long exhaustion won and she drifted off to sleep.

She woke when the car slowed as it traveled down the exit ramp.
She shifted to sitting, watching the rolling land zip past the windows.

"Did you have a good nap?"

"Yeah. Surprisingly."

"You have a cute snore."

If he was trying to tease her, his efforts were in vain. After all he'd witnessed this afternoon, snoring in front of him ranked pretty low on the embarrassment scale.

Isaac turned off the road and passed the sign her father had crafted by hand.

Walsh Farm.

Home sweet home.

But now her safe haven didn't feel so safe. Half held by a girl who lived and breathed that land, its very soil embedded in the whorls of her fingerprints, and half held by a woman in a pantsuit and heels, who looked like she'd never set foot off pavement.

Isaac carried her bag and a folder that must have come from the trust company inside the house, with Beck following like a lost pup. He put the folder on the table, then took a glass from the dish drainer and filled it with tap water with the ease and comfort of someone who lived there.

He put the glass on the counter beside her. "Do yourself a favor and leave that folder sitting right where it's at. Drink some water, take a long hot shower, and then go to bed. I'm going to go get Fern. She can walk me through whatever needs to be done here for the night."

Beck took a long drink. "No. I can handle it."

He gave her shoulder a gentle squeeze. "Of course you can." The steadiness of his voice and the way he looked into her eyes made her believe he was talking about more than farm chores. "And I promise you'll be able to handle it even better after a good night's sleep." He placed the crumpled prescription on the table beside her. "Maybe think more about trying out the prescription before you shred it." He shrugged. "I've taken something similar for anxiety. It helps."

She lifted her chin and met his eyes. "You have anxiety?"

He nodded. "It used to be really bad. It still flares up from time to time, but I've found things that make it more manageable. Maybe you can too."

He picked up the cup of water from where she'd left it and handed it to her. "Now scoot. Go upstairs and let Fern and me do a kindness for our favorite neighbor."

# SEVENTEEN

Still reeling from the interrupted trust meeting that afternoon, Callie stopped by her favorite coffee shop before parking on the street in front of her store. Coffee shop prices weren't exactly in her budget anymore, but desperate times called for desperate measures.

Armed with caffeine and a stack of paperwork, she unlocked her shop.

She laid out the file from the trust company that included the appraisal. Next to the file, she laid out the bill from the contractor for the needed electrical and plumbing upgrades and the latest quote from Sunrise Recovery. Finally, she pulled out a piece of grid paper where she'd jotted down small expenses. Callie took a bracing sip of her honey lavender latte.

At the bottom of the grid paper, she totaled all her expenses.

She took another sip and flipped open the file from the trust office, searching for the appraisal. The panic-stricken face of Beckett Walsh floated into her thoughts, and Callie shoved it away.

She would consider how all of this might impact Beckett in a moment. First, she just needed to know how the trust of George Walsh factored into her magic number—the number that meant that everything she had been working toward and had been thwarted over and over could become possible again.

On the summary page, she found the estimated property value, and her eyes went wide. Next to that sum, her bills were nothing.

Heat coursed through her body, and then it ran cold. She had to talk to her mother. Find out who this man was.

Beckett's crumpled face pressed harder on her conscience. How could Callie claim rights to half of the property? Property that belonged to a daughter, not to whoever Callie might be to him. Property that the woman might even live on.

Unless Callie was his daughter too.

That would change everything. Didn't a father who had left her to live with her unstable mother owe her something?

Was this man one of the many reasons Mom picked up and ran? Had it not always been her addictions dictating their lives? A someone instead of a something? Someone Mom was trying to protect her from?

Callie shook her head to clear it. There was no use letting her imagination run away with her.

She ran her finger over her name, typed out in black ink, declaring her half owner of an apiary. Until getting the business loan for the storefront, the biggest ticket items she'd ever had to her name were her gently used Honda Civic and the credit card she paid off every month.

Callie pushed out a breath. She should simply deny her right to the inheritance and then it would go to Beckett. Taking from that fragile woman felt like taking from a child.

But what if accepting this gift from this stranger meant Callie could have the life she'd been struggling toward for as long as she could remember? A stable life with a dog, a thriving business, and a healthy mother who could finally act like a mom.

All she had to do was go back to the trust company and sign her name to that deed and then find a buyer for a piece of property she'd never even laid eyes on.

She pressed her fingers against her aching brow bones. As much as the idea of a mysterious benefactor magically appearing and carrying off all her concerns tempted her, it couldn't be that simple. There were strings attached somewhere. She just hadn't found them yet.

Callie sat back in her chair and rubbed her hands over her face. The list of people she could call for advice was pretty short. When your parent is an addict, you learn how important it is to keep the decent human beings in your life at arm's-length. Compelled to help the hurting, those people could inflict the most damage on her and her mother's delicate situation.

Her last conversation with Joanne played in her mind.

Would it be weird to call Luke about this? The only reason she'd ended up with his phone number in her contacts was because they texted each other pictures of food truck menus when they took turns standing in line for each other.

But he had shown up at the shop with that gift for her the other day. That was more than just market booth–neighbor friendship, right? Then they'd kind of admitted that they were attracted to each other. Did that make it more or less okay to call him with her dilemma?

She picked up her phone and turned it over and over in her hand, Joanne's advice nudging at her. It's okay to take chances and see what happens. She rolled her shoulders and dialed Luke's number.

He answered on the second ring. "Callie?"

"Um. Yeah. Sorry, is this a bad time?"

"Not at all. Just doing a little editing and looking for any reason I can to take another break from staring at the screen. What's up?"

"Okay. Something really crazy happened and I was wondering if I could get a little advice."

"Of course, yeah. I'll help if I can."

"I just got back from a meeting at a trust company where I learned that I inherited half ownership in an apiary, which is apparently a farm that raises honeybees. I googled it." She rattled on, explaining how she had no idea who the person was or why he would have done such a thing. And in this outpouring, she forced the words past her lips—the real reason this sum of money coming to her at this moment in time mattered so much to her.

"You're paying for your mom's rehab?"

Callie cringed. "I . . . yeah. She lost her job and her insurance lapsed. And I think this is the first time she not only admitted that she had a problem but said she wanted to do something about it. I'm pretty sure rehab was where she'd disappear to when I was little and she'd leave me with our elderly neighbor for months at a time, but whenever she came back home, nothing had really changed. If anything, it was worse." Callie took a breath to slow her rapid speech. "As much as my cynical side says I'd be better off lighting my cash on fire than footing her bill, I just can't stop believing that things could get better. That I—" Her throat constricted and her face contorted against her will. She gasped for air, unable to finish her words.

"Callie?"

Words couldn't make their way past the tightness in her throat.

"Where are you?"

"Shop." She gasped out the word.

"I'm coming over."

"Don't." But she hadn't been able to squeeze the word out before the disconnecting beep.

She folded in half in her seat, trying to get a solid inhale. A war raged inside of her, but this time she couldn't identify which was the friend and which was foe—control or release.

Survival had always depended upon control. When the person

who is supposed to take care of you falls apart at the slightest puff of wind, you learn to be the strong one. The one who is never shaken. Her chest grew tighter and tighter.

Luke was coming. Luke who could not see her like this. She didn't even let herself see her like this. *Pull it together, Callie.*

For as long as she could remember, Callie lived her life carefully perched on a precipice. Every time her mother's life collapsed, the person who was supposed to take care of her chipped away a little more of the rock beneath Callie's feet until there was almost nothing left to stand on. If she leaned one way or the other, she would plummet. For the first time in her life, it felt like balancing on the precipice would be what killed her. Not the fall.

She let the first tear drop, the weight she'd been holding all her life plunging with it. A wet splash dampened the film of dust between her feet.

Emotions poured out of her in a jumbled rush she could not name. Release. Release when she'd spent her life holding so, so tight. She wanted to scream. Smash things. Crawl under the rickety folding table and cry. The force of it all was terrifying, but she could breathe again. At least she could breathe again.

She wasn't sure how long she sat there sobbing in a way she hadn't since she was a little girl sitting at Ms. Ruthie's table the Christmas she was eight. There'd been a plate of cookies in front of her she felt too heartbroken to touch. Momma had run off again, skipping Christmas, and Ms. Ruthie was dying of cancer.

A knock sounded at the front glass. Callie stood and scrubbed her sleeve across her eyes. She took several shaky breaths. The knock became louder.

Walking to that door felt more dangerous than all the emotions she'd just let free—let herself feel. She stepped over a haphazard stack of boards and Sheetrock scraps left behind. The building inspector might consider the place unsafe for the public, but that didn't compare to the dangers of the space she was about to let Luke Matthews traverse.

With a shaking hand, she turned the bolt. Luke swung the door open and slipped inside. He froze in front of her, taking in her disheveled state, and in the next moment she was wrapped in his arms.

When was the last time someone had held her like this? Had they ever?

Her mother's embraces were always a desperate clinging that left Callie feeling like she was the one doing the comforting even if it had been Callie who'd fallen and scraped her knee. Luke's arms seemed to offer something entirely different.

Into her hair he whispered, "I'm right here."

New tears found a trail down her face, a foreign emotion springing up in her that felt a whole lot like relief.

# EIGHTEEN

Beck rolled over in her bed, swathed in a ray of light. She stretched, feeling like a barn cat. The warmth of the sun was a balm for the aching places in her heart, but then she scrambled upright. She'd missed the sunrise, which meant she'd overslept. She blinked wide awake, sniffing the air. Bacon. Someone was in her house.

For the briefest moment her heart stutter-stepped at an illogical imagining of Callie Peterson in her kitchen, having already moved in.

Fern's giggle broke through Beck's dread.

She rose and wiped the sleep from her eyes, then slipped into her favorite T-shirt and denim overalls. She tucked her cropped hair behind her ears, stuffed a ball cap on her head, and descended the stairs.

Fern stood doubled over and giggling as Isaac pulled a smoking pan from the oven. The pile of dishes she'd left sitting in the sink had been washed and placed on the draining rack, but there was flour everywhere. The smell of bacon had gone from savory to charred.

"Uh, good morning."

Fern and Isaac turned in unison. At that exact moment a pancake fell from above and hit Isaac on the shoulder before it slipped off and landed with a resounding splat on the linoleum. Fern collapsed, literally rolling on the floor laughing. Balancing the sheet pan, Isaac gingerly plucked the pancake from the floor and tossed it onto the overcooked bacon that still smoked on the tray. "We wanted to make you breakfast."

Between gasps of laughter, Fern said, "I bet him ten bucks he couldn't flip the pancake higher than his head, and he . . . he . . . he stuck it to the ceiling!"

Fern's laughter infected both Beck and Isaac.

He attempted to rein in his mirth. "At least we did a decent job feeding all the animals their breakfast."

Beck bit the corners of her lips in an unsuccessful attempt at keeping a straight face, imagining pancakes hanging from the barn rafters. "You know they don't eat pancakes, right?"

He put the pan down on a trivet and crossed his arms over his chest. "I know that." He grinned. "Actually, I know nothing. I just did whatever Fern said. She's the boss."

A now-composed Fern beamed. "Trust me. I did way better in the barn than Uncle Ike did in the kitchen." She flounced to the counter where she picked up two glasses of orange juice. She placed them on the table and then went back for the third. Today's knee socks were a mixture of bananas and apples.

Isaac rolled his eyes in a very dramatic, Fern-like manner. "Uh, rude. You love my breakfast. Besides, I just got distracted by your fancy pancake-flip dares." To Beck he said, "Sorry about the bacon. But aside from the ceiling pancake, I'm pretty sure the rest of them turned out okay. Grab a seat and we'll bring you a plate and some coffee."

Fern slid a pancake stack in front of her. "He really does make the best pancakes." She hid her mouth behind her hand and whispered, "Although I'm pretty sure that's the only thing he knows how to make."

Beck grinned. It was nice to see Fern lighten up with her uncle.

Isaac set a cup of coffee in front of her. "I promise we'll clean up the mess. We tidied up and then we went and wrecked it worse."

Beck's cheeks heated at the thought of all the dishes she'd let pile up. Since Dad was gone and she was alone, she'd found it hard to care about the details she'd once dutifully tended to.

Isaac and Fern joined her at the table.

"Can I say the blessing, Uncle Ike?"

"Sure thing, kiddo."

"Jesus, thank You for today and for Beck letting us learn about her farm. Let this food nourish our bodies. Amen."

The memory of her father's baritone voice blessing the meals the two of them shared played in Beck's mind. He had closed every prayer with the same phrase. *"We trust You, Lord, with our today and with our tomorrow."*

That momentary floating feeling lent to her by Fern's laughter shrank away. For a moment she'd forgotten the pain of losing him. The confusion about the trust. Callie Peterson.

How could the man she'd trusted with her todays and tomorrows have left things so unsettled and uncertain?

*"If anything ever happens to me, tell the bees,"* he'd often said. *"They need to know or they'll die too."*

That dumb superstition.

When was he planning to tell her what he'd done? He must have known this would kill her.

It was then she noticed Fern watching her, looking from the untouched pancakes to Beck's face and back, waiting for Beck's verdict.

Beck drizzled maple syrup she'd harvested last winter over her stack, then cut off a bite and paused with the pancakes balanced on her fork. "You two really outdid yourselves this morning. You didn't have to come back and do all of this."

"We wanted to help, Beck," Fern said through a mouthful of pancakes. "Uncle Ike said you'd had a hard day and needed your rest."

Her gaze drifted to the file one of them had relocated from the kitchen table to the counter. She'd have to face that today, read through the legal jargon and figure out what it meant for her future.

Her father, who had so carefully protected her all his life, had chosen the moment of his death to leave her vulnerable. The facts refused to compute.

"I can help you with the paperwork if you'd like."

Isaac's words snapped her out of her trance, and she put the pancakes into her mouth. They were light and fluffy on her tongue, but she couldn't seem to taste them.

"I'm not great with farm animals or multitasking breakfast, but financial planning is what I do for a living. I've walked a lot of people through trust documentation, so if you feel lost in it, I'd be happy to help."

Beck offered a tight smile. "I'm pretty sure I have kept you from your work enough."

He glanced at his watch and winced. "Actually, I do have a meeting in fifteen minutes. Is there any way I could borrow your Wi-Fi for a quick meeting?"

Beck laughed under her breath. "I don't have Wi-Fi, but if you want to go into the office in the honey house, there is an Ethernet plug-in."

"Perfect." He stood and grabbed his laptop bag from the counter. He gestured around the kitchen. "And do not touch this mess. As soon as I finish up this meeting, I'm going to be back, and Fern and I will clean this up."

Fern groaned.

The back door squeaked, signaling his exit.

Fern nudged her. "Go on. Eat your pancakes. They're really good."

Beck attempted a smile and took a few bites to pacify Fern. The last thing she wanted was her lack of appetite to hurt the girl's feelings.

Fern fidgeted in the seat next to her. "I know Uncle Ike said we had to clean up, but do you think I could go play with the baby goats while I wait for him?"

Beck nodded, and Fern was out the door before Beck could accompany the gesture with words.

Rising from her seat, she picked up the file folder from the kitchen counter. Everything from the day before was such a blur. She returned to the table and started to flip through the documents, her eyes finding the property appraisal. Her heart pounded in her ears. There was no way Callie Peterson wouldn't want to sell. Her dad might as well have dropped a sack full of cash in the stranger's lap. Who wouldn't take it and run?

Beck would be forced to leave. And Oslo and Sparks, the chickens and goats—Beck would have to sell them off. And what about her bees? How could Dad have left their bees unprotected?

She laid her head on her arms. She knew exactly who would be in the market to buy a barely profitable farm. There were new industrial plants going in all around Sweetwater. New work opportunities meant new subdivisions. Land developers had stopped by on more than one occasion in recent years, looking for a steal.

She sighed and lifted her head. The only conceivable way to save this place, and her sanity, was to convince Callie Peterson that keeping the farm could be a long-term investment opportunity—enough of one that she'd be willing to pass up the lump sum indicated on the appraisal.

But Dad had been the one who kept financial things afloat. Afloat had been all that the two of them cared about. They'd lived day to day, seeking peace from an encroaching world and nothing more. At least she had.

If she was so dependent on this place, she should have planned for how to survive in the event of disaster. But she hadn't. Because she'd trusted in her father to do that for her.

She flipped to the front page of the packet and reread the trust. Surely some hidden fine print would make this make sense.

# NINETEEN

Callie lined up the ingredients for a batch of body butter on her countertop, the only semblance of order in the chaotic kitchen. She grabbed a bar of beeswax and grated it into her double boiler. She'd never put much thought into the tiny creators of the wax she so often used in her products and found it ironic that she was now half owner of a farm whose chief focus was bees.

Unless, of course, she chose to relinquish her share to Beckett.

Callie grated faster, trying to work off the tension rising in her shoulders. Nothing about this felt right, but she couldn't deny the fact that the inheritance, deserved or not, could solve her financial concerns.

She and Luke had talked at length sitting in the vacant shop two nights ago. He'd encouraged her to reach out to Beckett, and maybe he was right. But Beckett, antsy and cold, had not seemed all that easy to talk to at the trust company. The last thing Callie wanted to do was cause her another panic attack with a phone call.

But the two of them had to figure something out.

Once the beeswax, olive oil, and cocoa butter were melting down in the double boiler, she dialed the phone number the trust company had provided.

"Hello, this is Beckett Walsh." The voice coming through her speaker was clear and steady. So different from the woman she'd met on Thursday.

Callie drew in a long breath. "This is Callie Peterson. I just wanted to check in with you. See how you're doing. See if we could maybe figure out a time to talk? I have some questions. I'm sure you do too . . ." She trailed off.

Callie stirred the oils together, busying herself in the ensuing silence.

Beckett cleared her throat. "How did you know my father?"

"I didn't." Empty, hollow words.

"Then you don't know why—"

"I'm sorry. I don't." Callie almost blurted out her questions about her paternity but refrained. She shouldn't stab in the dark for the truth not knowing who she might wound in the process. Would her question imply George had been unfaithful to Beckett's mother? "I thought maybe we could get together and talk through things. Nothing fancy. Maybe meet at a coffee shop or a park? Between the two of us, we could figure something out about what's best moving forward. Maybe connect some dots?"

"No." That strangled quality reentered Beckett's tone.

"Okay, um . . ." She wrestled her racing thoughts into submission. How were they supposed to work this out, then?

"I . . . I meant I can't meet you for coffee. But you could come here."

Callie blinked. That was not the turn she thought the conversation was taking. "Sure. Yeah. That would be amazing, actually."

∞∞∞

Beck hung up the phone and sank into a kitchen chair. In two weeks, Callie was coming here. It would have been better if they could meet on neutral ground. This could be Beck's one chance to convince Callie that the farm was worth keeping. Was there any way she could get a solid plan together in that amount of time?

She groaned as she stood from the chair. Convincing Callie would be a lot easier if the farm actually made much of a profit. She walked out onto the wide front porch, taking in the peeling paint on the barn and the threadbare gravel driveway that was slowly becoming more of a dirt road with rocks poking through.

As a little girl, Beck had seen Walsh Farm as an enchanted land where all the best things in life existed. She blew out a breath. Even though the farm had come to represent a lot more to her than that, like hard work and productivity and purpose, there was a part of her that had never grown out of the feeling that nothing could touch her here in this kingdom.

To Callie Peterson, how could this place look like anything more than a bedraggled money pit?

Isaac arrived with Fern. He had called the night before and asked if it would be all right for them to come over after lunchtime. It wasn't Fern's normal day to come, and she sincerely hoped this wasn't some ploy to check up on her.

Fern bounded from the car like a cottontail bunny with cabin fever. "Hey, Beck!"

Beck waved. "Some new chicks hatched earlier today, if you want to go see them."

"Yay!" Fern skipped off to the chicken coop.

Isaac emerged from the car in a more human fashion. Beck did a double take. Instead of his typical button-down, khakis, and loafers, he wore a T-shirt, a pair of faded jeans, and work boots that had seen better days.

He shrugged. "The farm bug bit me as bad as it did Fern. She begged me to come work at the farm with her."

"The Baileys have chickens and ducks and goats you guys could help with."

There was a softness in his eyes. "She likes you."

Beck's cheeks warmed.

"You make her feel like she's important. Needed. Not a pesky kid getting in the way." He smiled. "That means a lot to her."

Beck tugged at her short ponytail. She was so needy it was apparent, even to a child.

Davy's beat-up truck rumbled and rattled its way down the drive. He braked hard, sending up a cloud of dust.

Beck gestured to Davy who exited the cab and lowered the tailgate. "Good thing I don't need eggs. They'd never make it in one piece." She turned to Isaac. "Let me pay him and get these in and then we can find a fun project for Fern."

As she walked to the truck, Isaac fell into step beside her. "I'll give you a hand."

She paid Davy for delivering her groceries, plus she tacked on a little extra to what they'd agreed upon as a thank-you. It wasn't much, but hopefully every little bit would help with his college fund.

As she and Isaac carried the groceries inside, she said, "He delivers supplies from the Feed and Seed for me, and it turns out he was looking for odd jobs, so he's been shopping and delivering for me. It saves me a lot of time."

As if she needed to make up a reason to explain her need for grocery delivery to the same guy who had witnessed her full-scale panic attack.

"The grocery store here doesn't do delivery? Most of the ones back home do."

Beck grinned. "No, the Save-A-Ton isn't exactly up with the times."

She had just enough groceries to fill both her and Isaac's arms in one trip. Alone, she didn't need much.

They set the bags on the counter, and Beck started loading the refrigerator. Isaac motioned to the paperwork spread across the table. "How are things going?"

Beck blew out a breath. "The way I figure it, the only way I don't lose the farm is if I can convince Callie that it would be better for her to keep this place as an ongoing source of income."

Isaac looked up from the paperwork. "And um . . . you can make a case for that?"

As Beck put her blueberry yogurt in the fridge, all the half-formed plans of how she could increase the productivity of the farm died on her lips. "No." She faced him. "If I'm honest, it's the opposite." She bit down on the inside of her cheek in a bid to rein in the emotions tightening her throat. "But I can't lose my home."

He pressed his lips in a line, and a fraction of her sorrow reflected back to her in his eyes. Even though him witnessing her panic attack had completely humiliated her, there was some comfort having someone understand the truth behind her concerns. Unlike Aunt Kate, Isaac didn't seem bent on trying to fix her or rationalize that being forced to function off the farm could be for her ultimate good.

"I can help if you want." He picked up a page and studied it. "Like I said, it's kind of what I do. Help people take the resources they already have and harness them for their full potential."

"Oh. I couldn't—"

"I want to."

"You're already so busy," she said. "And I know I can't afford to pay whatever fees your company charges."

"I wasn't trying to take you on as a client, Beck. I was asking to help you as a friend."

"The last thing I want is to be forced to sell. But I can't ask you—"

He stepped closer to her. "It's me that's doing the asking. Because you matter to Fern." He swallowed hard. "And I know we barely know each other, but—"

"You're going to lose the farm?" Fern stood in the doorway, wide-eyed—one of her knee socks slouching down to her ankle. With a fluffy chick cupped in her hands, she strode to her uncle. "You have to help her." She turned to Beck. "He's helping you. You aren't losing this place. It's too special."

She spoke with the bold determination of a reigning monarch standing before a warring nation.

It seemed the fate of Walsh Farm was now in the determined hands of a sassy sock alien.

# TWENTY

*C*allie gazed out the passenger window of Luke's Jeep, the wild-flowers along the side of the highway blurring into streaks of orange and white against a backdrop of green. She still couldn't believe that Beckett Walsh had suggested they meet at the estate. Maybe even more than that, she couldn't believe she'd accepted when Luke asked if she'd like him to tag along for moral support.

He probably didn't think anything of it, this hour drive to Sweet-water. Maybe that's what normal people did together. Normal people who knew how to ask for help instead of carefully constructing the image that everything was fine.

After Ms. Ruthie passed away and her mother became Callie's full-time "caregiver," Callie figured out that if she was clean, prompt, had unrumpled hair, and made her face bright and interested, others wouldn't notice how truly exhausted she was. They'd see the fresh-baked cookies just like all the other kids brought to the bake sale, but they wouldn't notice the Band-Aids on her burned fingertips.

Her mom always said that the two of them were different. Outsiders wouldn't understand what a special girl Callie was to be able to take care of herself at such a young age.

Callie had comforted her conscience, telling herself that she never outright lied. It wasn't her fault that people saw what they wanted to see—a smart, polite, well-cared-for little girl.

Because Momma said . . .

Callie scoffed, breaking away from those long-ago days. "Better the devil you know than the devil you don't."

"Huh?" Luke's gaze darted to her.

Callie swallowed. Had she really said that out loud? "I was just thinking about my childhood." She inched down in the seat, the weight of Luke's expectant silence filling the air. *I can do this. I can tell him one gut-honest thing.*

He nudged her hunched shoulder gently. "This is the part where you tell me what's on your mind."

She squeezed her eyes shut. *Lord, give me strength.* "I was thinking about how my mother convinced me that the best thing I could do was to make sure no one knew how much we struggled." She swallowed and dared a glance at Luke. "I wonder sometimes if it would have been better for both of us if I'd told people how bad it was. Maybe she would have gotten help sooner."

Luke picked at a loose thread on the steering wheel's stitching. "You did your best. That's far too heavy a load for a kid to carry."

Was it? It was so much a part of her life, she'd become accustomed to the weight. Callie sighed. "I would get so close sometimes, to telling a teacher how bad things were. I even fantasized about getting taken away and my mom getting better, fighting to get me back. But then the question became, What if she didn't? What if I wasn't enough?"

Luke remained laser-focused on the highway in front of him. "You couldn't have saved her. You couldn't have been enough for her. You know that, right?"

"It's a hard lesson to learn, you know. When you just want your parent to put you first. To love you more than the things they are addicted to. Something every other kid on the planet seems to have and you don't."

"Does it sound trite if I say that you have that in Jesus, even if you don't have that in a parent."

Callie sat straighter, stretching out the tension building in the middle of her back. She pondered his words, knowing he meant well. "In my mind, I recognize the truth of that statement. But it doesn't take away the craving for a mom who still lives in my heart. Sometimes I get really angry at myself. Like I shouldn't need that. Especially from her." She huffed out a breath. "But right or wrong, that's how I feel."

Luke nodded, his features drawn in concentration. "That makes sense."

Those words comforted her more than she knew how to express, hearing that the struggle between her head and her heart seemed remotely reasonable to another human being. Her anxiety quieted as she watched the scenery beyond the glass. "You know the story of Lazarus?"

He nodded.

"Jesus mourned at the guy's tomb with Mary and Martha, even knowing he was about to raise Lazarus from the dead. Sometimes when the pain cuts the deepest, I picture Jesus weeping for me too, even though he knows he can fill the holes my mother left behind."

Luke smiled softly and nodded again, letting her words linger in the air between them.

⬡⬡⬡

Fifteen minutes later, Luke took the Sweetwater exit, and Callie soaked in the beauty of the rolling land, the farmhouses, and the town square, which looked like something right out of a small-town movie set. They drove a few more miles and then Luke made the final turn. A hand-painted sign marked the entrance.

"Stop the car." Her voice echoed in her ears. She stared at the sign. An image that had been long buried in her memories prodded at her consciousness.

She'd been here before.

She squeezed her eyes tight, trying to call the memory out of the depths. Sitting in the back seat of Mom's car. Staring out the windshield, peering through the pounding rain. Mom just stared at the sign, her hands gripping the steering wheel.

She never had figured out why the sign held her mother captive for half an hour. Was George Walsh the father her mother said didn't exist? What had kept her suspended at the end of that driveway instead of taking the graveled path before her?

Luke continued on down the drive and parked beside the house. "You ready?"

"As I'll ever be." She looked out the passenger window. Beckett and a little girl waited at the sidewalk, seemingly engaged in serious conversation.

When they exited the Jeep, Beckett approached them. "Hello, Mr. and Mrs. Peterson?"

Callie toed the gravel with her leather sandal and fidgeted with her purse. "No. I . . . uh . . . he's just a friend. This is Luke Matthews."

Beckett's face grew red. "Sorry. I shouldn't have assumed. I just thought with you coming to discuss the property that this must be your husband."

Callie swallowed hard. "I should have asked. Is . . . is this all right? I didn't mean to—"

"No, no, it's fine."

"Is this your daughter?" Callie motioned to the little girl, who'd stepped closer to her side as if offering a defense.

Beckett gave a breathy laugh. "No. This is Fern. She's been helping me out, learning about farm life this summer. I'm not married. No children. It's just me."

Fern propped her hands on her hips. "I'm just a guest. I have about as much right to this place as you do."

Beckett cringed.

Callie let out a loud laugh and then clapped her hand over her mouth. "I'm sorry. I-I'm just so nervous. And I'm just as confused as Fern is on why I'm here right now. I don't know what to say or where to start."

Luke stepped back. "Callie, I should head out and let you two have some time, if you're okay with that. You can call or text anytime you're ready to go."

It was probably for the best. She hadn't meant for Beckett to feel ganged up on. "Okay."

Fern flicked her braid over her shoulder. "You should stay, Luke. I can give you the tour. We can check out the barn, the beehives, the creek. It's a real cool place." She gave him a winsome smile and then her face became serious. "Just make sure to watch out for a few hives on the end. They're infested with killer b—"

Beckett's eyes went wide, and she clamped a hand over the girl's mouth. She shook her head. "There's no killer bees here." To the girl she said, "I'm sure Luke would much rather go into town and stroll around for a few hours."

Luke bent slightly at the waist as if trying to be more on eye level with Fern, his expression open and kind. "No, that sounds great. I'd love the VIP tour."

"I never said you were a VIP." Fern was solemn as a monk.

He simply laughed in response like she was the funniest person he'd ever met. Fern grabbed him by the hand and led him off toward the chicken coop.

Beckett looked at Callie and then back to Fern and Luke. "Just a warning, I can't be held responsible for whatever Fern does next."

Callie smiled. "Luke is really good with kids. He does photography classes for kids her age at our church. Volunteers with the children's ministry. He'll survive." Callie cleared her throat. "So, have you had any more ideas about how all this came about?" Her smile faltered and then dropped away.

Beckett shook her head. "Nope."

# TWENTY-ONE

Callie followed Beckett inside the house, accepting her offer of lemonade. Once inside the kitchen, she took in the worn linoleum and the old-fashioned wallpaper that peeled in places. Maybe Beckett was looking forward to selling. It had to be quite the burden managing everything alone.

She heard an odd rustling sound behind her and turned. A shriek squeezed out of her, and she took two steps back. "Um. There's a chicken in your hallway."

"That's just Henrietta."

"You have a . . . a house chicken?"

Beckett shrugged. "Not on purpose. She's sneaky." She crossed to the sink to wash her hands. Callie did a double take when she noticed the hyacinth logo on the front of the hand soap. A bottle her own hands had touched. Next to it a lotion bottle. She turned, scanning the room. On the center of the table rested one of her large candles. Beckett hadn't mentioned being a previous customer.

"That's my soap." Her voice sounded distant in her own ears. "I-I meant that I make it. Solace Naturals is my company."

Beckett turned slowly, studying her. "There's more. In the bathroom. And the bedrooms. My dad bought all of this, not me." She went to the fridge and pulled out the pitcher of lemonade and poured two glasses, her brow furrowed. "I couldn't tell you why. As you've probably noticed, I'm not exactly the frilly soap type."

Callie crossed her arms over her chest as if it would guard her from any more jabs Beckett might aim her direction about her "frilly" business.

"No offense," she said, probably noticing Callie's defensive posture. "It's really nice. It's just that I've been raised by a man who bought Irish Spring and Dial from the Dollar General and called it good. When this stuff started showing up, I mostly wondered if it was some weird way of trying to make up for me not having a mom. It's the kind of stuff my aunt Kate loves."

That tidbit of information drew Callie farther into the kitchen. She knew what it was to lack a mother, at least a normal one. But her mother had never tried to make up for an absent father. How could she when she couldn't even manage to fill one role in Callie's life?

Callie smoothed her finger over her polished pink thumbnail, trying to figure out the next move in the conversation. Not wanting to say anything insensitive but craving information. "Did your dad ever have a booth at the Chattanooga Farmers' Market? I do a lot of business there."

Beckett nodded, eyes narrowed. "He did go to the market in Chattanooga on occasion."

"You never went with him?"

She shook her head. "Not my scene." She paced the floor. "That's how you knew my dad? He was a customer at your booth. And that's why you get half my farm?"

Beckett's use of "my" resounded inside Callie's head. There was such a difference between the woman she'd met at the trust company and the one standing before her now. It was like she was meeting two different people. This one self-possessed, skeptical, and firm.

Callie dried her sweaty palms on her jeans. "I'm sorry. I don't understand why this happened. Not at all. It's the only connection

I can see as of this moment." She crossed the room and picked up a framed picture sitting on the end of the counter. "Is this him?"

"Don't—" Beckett cringed and dropped the arm reaching for the photo in Callie's hands. "Yeah. That's my dad."

*Tread carefully, Callie.*

The man in the photograph stood beside an old tractor, smiling. Those kind yet solemn eyes so familiar.

He'd come to the booth a few different times over last year's market season. With his overalls on and a straw hat on his head, he looked every inch country born and bred. One time in particular rang out like a bell in her memory. He'd picked up one of her jars of body butter, ran his work-roughed thumb over the label.

"It's a hyacinth, right?" he'd asked.

She nodded.

He'd studied her face, his eyes full of questions, and said, "They are a honeybee favorite."

Callie gently placed the frame back on the countertop. "I remember him. He was always very kind." She smiled at Beckett. "You have his eyes."

Beckett's face creased in concentration. "So, the two of you talked. Anything specific that stands out?"

"Just general pleasantries, mostly. He'd ask about my business. How I got started." There had been that one time when things got a little more personal. It had been her birthday, and Luke had brought her balloons and had royally embarrassed her, singing "Happy Birthday" over the loudspeakers from the Sizzle Stage.

The stranger had asked her how old she was and where she was from. The intensity with which he'd asked struck her as odd. But she'd smiled and told him she was from a little bit of everywhere.

She chewed her lip. "One of the last times we spoke, we got into conversation about my logo, and he told me that in the language of flowers, purple hyacinth means 'please forgive me.' It surprised me, him knowing that. He didn't really come across as the type of guy that was up on the Victorian language of flowers." His words had caused Callie to remember all the times her mother had brought the purple blossoms home to her, probably nicked from some person's flower bed as she stumbled home. Had it been intentional, her apologies?

Beckett's gaze went flinty.

Callie backpedaled. "I didn't mean anything by that. I just meant it's not like the kind of thing people go around saying all the time. Was your dad a lover of flowers?"

She took a shaky breath, the lines of her face still taut. "Other than the fact that flowers fed his bees, he had no use for them."

Having no response to the bitterness flavoring Beckett's tone, Callie drained the tart lemonade and set her glass on the table.

◯◯◯◯

Beck picked up Callie's empty glass, her thoughts whirling. He'd told Callie, a stranger, about the meaning of that flower but not her. Not when her own mother left behind a sea of them with no explanation.

As she ran the glass under hot water, she gazed out the window over the sink to the flower beds, that last Christmas with her mother replaying in her mind. Her mother's fevered energy. The intensity of her love those days leading up to Christmas had felt like looking square into the sun.

Beck pinched her lips tight, remembering her mother's hands gripping hers as they'd spun madly about the living room. They'd been dirt-stained, and the places around her nails were cracked and raw from the morning she'd spent digging in the cold ground.

When Beck asked her why she was working in the garden when it was too cold for anything to grow, she'd said, "A present for you for later. You'll see." And then she hugged Beck so tight she couldn't breathe.

That spring, an ocean of purple hyacinths had sprouted up from the ground. Their riot of color mocked the sorrow that lingered in the eaves of her and her father's home.

It had been one of the few times she'd seen her father angry. At least like that. He'd slammed about in the shed and brought out the mower. He cranked it and approached the flowers. Beck had stepped in front of him, refusing to move. They stayed in a silent standoff that seemed to last forever for little Beck.

He'd finally turned the motor off and knelt in front of her.

"Please, don't mow them, Daddy."

He should have told her then about the secret language—that those purple blooms were meant to be her mother's perennial apology, coming back every year as a fresh reminder. She would have let him mow them down. Would've helped him rip the rooted bulbs from the ground.

Instead, she'd pointed at the flowers and said, "They like them."

She'd dragged him closer, showing him the honeybees burying themselves in the blossoms. "If you mow Momma's flowers down, you'll hurt the bees. And they didn't do anything wrong."

A few weeks later he'd brought home the cluster of bees in that mesh box, and they'd started their first hive.

Beck dried the glass she'd washed four times over while staring out that window and then placed it back in the cupboard. Those hyacinths had bloomed for years, but because neither she nor her father cared for them the proper way, most of them had eventually ceased to bloom. Every now and then one would pop up out of the blue.

She turned back to Callie. "I should give you the tour so you can see what this place is all about." She picked up the business plan she and Isaac had roughed together and pretended she was as confident as Isaac sounded when he'd coached her the night before. "I know it probably doesn't look like much at the moment, but this place could really work well as a long-term investment for you. This farm is my lifeblood, and I'm perfectly content to keep running things as I have been. We can work out a way to split the profits."

◇◇◇◇

Callie gripped the UTV's roll bar as they bounced over the field, heading back toward the house after touring all sixty acres. Her head was practically swimming from Beckett's endless descriptions of the farm's current assets and the five-year growth plan to expand the apiary as well as the goat dairy. She'd even mentioned setting up glamping tents on the unused land as a possible third stream of income, though she'd sounded far less passionate about that option.

Callie certainly hadn't expected the girl she'd met at the trust company to be a business maven, but Beckett threw around terms Callie often heard on the entrepreneurial podcasts she followed.

It did make her wonder though. If Beckett was so business driven, why hadn't the farm made those moves until now? Had it been her father blocking the progress? Or was this simply Beckett's desperation talking?

"So that's Walsh Farm," Beckett said. "As you can see, there is a lot of untapped potential out there. Just imagine. You could continue working your business, have access to all the beeswax, goat's milk, and dried flowers and herbs for your products at no cost to you, plus you'd get a check from this place every quarter. Or maybe we could work out some sort of lease agreement, where I'd pay you for the use of your half of everything."

Keeping the place had never occurred to her. She'd planned to either relinquish her right to the trust or sell. "I don't know . . . I . . ."

Fear crept into Beckett's expression, and that anxious girl from the trust meeting took over her assertive spiel. "I can't lose this place. It's all I have."

How could Callie consider robbing this woman of her sense of stability just so she could gain hers? If only she understood George

Walsh and his motives. If only someone would show up and say, "George Walsh was your father." Then it would be so much easier to understand how she'd landed in this position. "I'll think about all you've said and give you an update on where I'm at by Friday. Will that work for you?" She'd relinquish her rights to Beckett, no matter how much that influx of cash would relieve her stress.

Beckett pushed a wild strand of hair out of her face and tucked it under her ball cap. "I'd better check in on Fern. I know you said Luke was good with kids, but Fern is . . . well she's, uh . . . not your average kid." Beckett made a wide turn, and Callie tightened her handhold and didn't loosen it until they eased to a stop again.

Beckett pointed to a wooded trail. "Fern likes the creek a lot. I'm going to check here first."

Callie hopped to the ground. "I'll come with you."

The crunch of their footsteps was the only break in the silence. Beckett glanced her way, fingers tapping against her thumb. "So, the soaps and things, that's what you do full-time?"

Callie nodded. "Yeah, I love it. Making things that not only smell good but have restorative qualities too." She wasn't quite sure why she felt this sudden urge to make this stranger see how much her business meant to her. That this wasn't just some passing fancy, even if it meant being more vulnerable than she'd like to be with someone she'd just met. "My upbringing was a little rough," she started. "I lived in some sketchy places. None of them smelled very good."

Beckett smiled. "Probably better than my barnyard smells though, right?"

"While there are some pungent smells, it smells like life here. I don't know how to explain it, but it's different."

"When I was a teenager," Callie continued, "I met this lady, Jenni, who kinda took me under her wing. She had this dish of tiny soaps in her guest bathroom that smelled like lavender." Her heart throbbed in her chest remembering her younger self occasionally swiping one.

At night when she was home in bed, she would press the soap to her nose and pretend she was still at Jenni's house.

The trail narrowed, and Callie filed in behind Beckett. She studied her relaxed stride, wishing she could figure out what she was thinking.

Callie took another breath and made herself finish the abridged version of how she lost contact with Jenni. "Anyway, life happened and I had to move away. Anytime I smelled lavender after that, I'd think of Jenni and her kindness. The way scents connect to memory is such a powerful thing. So, when I make my products, I hope those aromas that fill my customers' homes will connect them to pleasant memories."

The trail ended at the banks of a burbling creek. Luke and Fern stood on the bank skipping stones. Luke strode over to meet them.

Beckett's brow furrowed. "I hope she's been nice."

Luke chuckled under his breath. "She did try to convince me that your rooster really enjoyed water hose baths in hot weather. And then she tried to get me to try my hand at goat milking and pointed me to the billy goat instead of the nanny, but other than that, she's been a real peach."

Beckett cringed. "You didn't try either of those things?" Her shoulders crept higher. "Did you?"

"Nah. My grandpa had a farm. I visited often enough to know better than to follow Fern's advice."

"I'm really sorry."

"She's definitely kept me entertained. How are things going?"

Callie clasped her hands in front of her chest. "Beckett's certainly given me plenty to think about."

Fern trotted over. She propped her hands on her hips. "So? What's going on? What's going to happen to the farm, Beck?"

Beckett put a hand on Fern's shoulder. "We'll talk later, okay?"

"Do you prefer to be called Beck?" Callie asked.

Fern turned to Callie. She twirled her braid around her finger with downturned eyes. "Well . . . only her friends call her Beck. So . . ."

Beck cleared her throat. "Beck is fine, thanks." She shot Fern a withering glare. Through gritted teeth, she said, "Remember what we talked about earlier. Please."

Fern huffed, then nodded. "C'mon, Luke. I want to show you the barn cat, Sassy. She's really sweet."

They filed behind Luke and Fern as they walked back to the utility vehicle. Luke and Fern folded down the jump seat bench in the back, and Beck drove them all back to the barn.

Beck stopped beside the structure. Fern dragged Luke inside, and Beck smiled at Callie, the corners of her mouth trembling. "I know my father's trust gives you just as much right to live here as it does me, so if you want, there are a lot of buildable sites. So that's an option as well. You know, if you're looking to build a home."

"Okay, I . . ."

A silver car pulled down the drive, and Beck groaned. "Of course she'd come today of all days." She sighed. "I'm sorry. She was friends with my father. Let me go say hi real quick and then we can get back to this."

At a loss for what else to do with herself, Callie trailed in Beck's wake.

A middle-aged woman in a purple tracksuit emerged from the car with a casserole dish in hand. She smiled apologetically at Beck. "I made too much again. Thought I'd share. It's tater tot casserole."

"Thanks, Annette. I'd offer for you to come inside for a bit, but now isn't a good time." She gestured to Callie. "This is Callie. According to Dad's trust, she and I co-own the place now."

Callie stepped out from behind Beck and lifted her hand in greeting.

Annette's eyes widened. "Oh, my."

A pained look crossed Beck's face. "He never said anything about the trust to you, did he?"

"No."

It might have been Callie's imagination, but Beck seemed relieved by that answer.

"No, he never mentioned it," Annette said. "Land sakes, Callie, you really favor Lindy."

"My mother?"

Callie turned sharply to Beck. Had she misheard or had the two of them spoken in unison?

Beck's eyes were wide and haunted.

Callie shut hers tight and drew in a slow breath, trying to wrangle her racing thoughts. She turned to Beck. "Lindy Peterson is your mother?"

The lines of Beck's face pulled like she'd been force-fed something bitter. "Lindy Walsh is the name on my birth certificate. She cut out of here when I was five, and I never saw the woman again. I hardly remember her."

Callie looked to Annette. "My mother was married to George Walsh?"

Annette nodded, her eyes forlorn. "I knew Lindy from high school. Her name was Peterson then."

Callie squeezed her eyes shut and shook her head. "I'm thirty-one. Beck?"

"Twenty-eight."

"That makes you three years younger than me. If she left when you were five, I would have been eight." Callie massaged her forehead. "Why don't I remember him? Or you? I would remember if I'd ever been here, right?" The solitary memory of the farm sign from the back seat of her mother's car flashed in her head.

They'd gone on to Little Rock, Arkansas, after her mother had driven away. They'd lived out of her car for three months until her mother met a "friend" who let them move in. That's what she'd chosen for them instead of the farm waiting at the end of that driveway. She shifted her gaze to Annette. "Did he know about me? Am I . . . his?"

Annette adjusted the casserole dish in her arms. "Dears, why don't we go inside? I'll put a pot of tea on if you have any, Beck. And I'll tell you all I know about George and Lindy. Granted, it's not much, but maybe it will help."

Callie walked slowly to the house, looking to the left and the right, searching for any memory of the place. Of being here. Of this life.

Her steps halted, fragmented memories and timelines clicking into place. Her mother would have left George the same year Ms. Ruthie died. She turned a slow circle, taking in the surrounding beauty. All those times Mom disappeared, had this been where she'd gone? Another life with another family in this beautiful place while Callie had been left in a cramped, run-down apartment.

Had George Walsh rejected Callie, unwilling to raise another man's child? Then what? Had he grown a conscience in his later life and wanted to make it up to his ex-wife's fatherless child?

What she wouldn't give to shake an explanation out of her mother right now.

"Callie?"

Annette and Beck stood on the porch, looking back to where Callie stood, frozen on the path. "I'm coming."

Inside the house, Callie and Beck sat at the kitchen table. Beck looked as ransacked as Callie felt. Callie blinked. *That's my sister. I have a sister.* The connection felt so empty. So hollow. Not real.

Annette fumbled around the kitchen, asking Beck so many questions about where things were, Callie couldn't figure out why Beck didn't just stand up and make the tea herself. Once the kettle was on and the jadeite teacups laid out, Annette turned to them.

"So, George and Lindy . . . I knew George's family my whole life. I came up in school with both George and Chris. The only twins in our itty-bitty school. Not that they really looked like twins. George was always smaller, had trouble with his eyes. He was always more drawn to academics. Chris was bigger, faster, stronger. Always picked first for sports teams. Little Katie didn't come along until a long time later. Boy, did she trail those boys around, trying to mix in with them."

Annette smiled softly. "I always did hold a candle for George, even back then. Not that he noticed."

Beck cleared her throat. "Lindy. What were you going to tell us about Lindy?"

Annette laughed, the sound high and out of sync with the somber kitchen. "Right. Lindy. Well, she moved to town our junior year of high school. She mostly kept to herself. She didn't get on well with the other kids at school. It was because of that no-account father of hers. But George didn't care one iota. He befriended her. Everyone knew he was crazy about her. Except Lindy, that is. Toward the end of senior year, she started taking up with his brother. Though if you ask me, Chris did that to George on purpose. Started flirting with her. Asked her to prom before George worked up the nerve. But still, she spent most of her time with George. Plenty of gossip spread all kinds of rumors that she was two-timing those boys, but I never believed that rag." Annette rose from her place at the table and poured each of them a cup of tea. Then she settled back in her seat with a sigh.

"Let's see. Where was I? Oh, yes. The summer after graduation, something happened. I really don't know what. You never know what to believe when the rumor mill is running full tilt. George and Chris had a real big blowup. Chris left town. Lindy left town not too long after. People said it was because she was pregnant." Annette shook her head. "But I never believed it." She shrugged. "I moved away for college, so I really can't give a full account. But I understand she moved back a few years later, and George and Lindy got married. Through it all, I don't think George ever stopped loving her."

Annette sighed. "Still did, right up until the day he died, if you ask me." She sipped her tea. "He was still in love with his first love, no matter how bad she'd hurt him." She set the teacup down with a clatter. "A real shame, if you ask me. George was a good man. I wish he'd have let someone love him like he deserved." She dabbed at her eyes with her wadded napkin.

Callie glanced from Annette to Beck to see Beck's reaction to Annette's lovelorn tone. Beck stared into her peppermint tea.

Callie focused her gaze into her own mug. In Annette's story, she knew how Beck fit into everything and the role her mother played in Beck and George's life. But where was she? Could she be the baby who put George and Chris at odds? Or had that baby been merely a rumor and Callie the result of another poor choice her mother had made shortly after leaving town?

Taking a bracing sip, the heat of the brew and the cool of the menthol lingered in her throat. "What does your uncle Chris say about all this?"

Beck shook her head. "Whatever happened between him and my dad was bad enough that they wanted nothing to do with each other. I tried calling Uncle Chris before the trustee meeting, thinking that me might have some information, but he wouldn't take my call." She cradled her teacup in her hands but didn't drink. "My aunt might be able to tell us something. I know she and Uncle Chris still talk. And she lived through the rift."

Annette cleared her throat. "Your aunt was just a little girl when all this went down, so I'm not sure how much she'll remember. But his marriage to Lindy, I bet she could give you the inside scoop on that."

Callie huffed under her breath. "I just wish I could get ahold of Mom and get some answers. I've tried, but—"

Beck sucked in a breath that took all the air from the room. "You've talked to her? Recently? She's . . . part of your life?"

There was so much pain in Beck's voice, a pain Callie wanted to alleviate by telling her that a relationship with their mother was not something worth coveting.

"She's . . . uh . . . she's in rehab currently. Mom's always struggled. Never been what you'd consider stable." Callie's heart pounded, protectiveness rising up in her like a mother hen. But the words had come easier this time than they had with Luke. "She's in a program now, and her treatment providers are very optimistic that she's going to be able to make some lasting life changes."

Beck opened her mouth and closed it.

"I've been trying to pay her way through the program." More words pressed against her lips. She considered telling Beck how selling the farm could get their mother the kind of treatment she needed—that she could get healthy and be a part of both of their lives. But the rigid set of Beck's shoulders chased those unspoken things back down Callie's throat.

Annette stood from the table. "You know, I should run. You two have so much to discuss."

She said her goodbyes and patted Beck on the shoulder on her way out. It was such a micro movement, Callie almost didn't catch it—Beck's lean away from Annette's touch.

The two of them sat so silent that the ticking of the hall clock echoed off the walls. Where was Luke? Shouldn't she leave too? How did one close out a conversation like this? *Well, it's been fun touring the farm, your most prized possession that I'd love to sell in order to help the mother who abandoned you and chronically neglected me . . .* Yikes.

Callie swallowed. "So, you don't remember her? Or what she was like?"

Beck seemed dazed. "Not really. I have these random blips of memories that seemed happy. I thought she loved us. That confused me a lot as a child. What pulled her so hard from here, a place that she'd seemed happy?" Beck attempted a smile that collapsed. "I guess I get it now. It was you."

She stood and walked down the hall without explanation. Callie jittered her knee. Should she just let herself out? Leave Beck to nurse her wounds in peace?

Just as she was about to stand and seek out Luke, Beck's footfalls in the creaking hall signaled her return.

She came into the kitchen with a leather-bound photo album in her arms. "I found this in my father's things. I was a little surprised he had this. We never really talked about her or our lives before she left. Maybe you'd like to see it?" She placed the album on the table.

Callie turned the pages. Images of a stranger who looked just like her mother stared back. Same dark brown hair, blue-green eyes framed with thick lashes. Her olive-toned skin glowed with a tan that said she'd spent a lot of time outside. This version of her mother looked so . . . peaceful. Lucid. Page after page she turned, her mind trying to work out the difference between the woman in those photos and the one she knew. The clearest difference between the life displayed within these pages and the one Callie had experienced—the album chronicled a life from which Callie had been erased.

# TWENTY-TWO

Callie and Luke's Jeep disappeared down the drive. However Beck had attempted to prepare for today's meeting with the cotenant of her father's estate, finding out that they shared a mother was beyond comprehension. Beck swallowed hard. She'd never imagined she could feel such raw anger at a practical stranger.

Fern skipped over. "They're gone and not coming back, right?"

Beck narrowed her eyes at the girl. "You should not have convinced Luke to pet Sassy. That was just mean." The poor guy had been good-natured about it, but it had taken six bandages to patch him up. "While I appreciate your loyalty, it's going to take more than a grumpy cat to deter Callie Peterson from selling this place." The woman hadn't said a word, but Beck hadn't missed the desperation in her eyes when she'd said she was covering her mother's expenses.

Beck ground her teeth. Callie was not the enemy here. Although, because of the power her father had placed in Callie's hands, it sure was hard not to view her that way.

"Let's go do the evening rounds, Fern." The two of them walked to the barn in lockstep.

Callie. The chosen one.

Beck blew out a breath. She tried to channel all her emotions into the physical labor of shoveling manure out of Sparks's stall.

Growing up, Dad had made sure Beck never had any reason to want for anything, and therefore she'd tried not to dwell on not having a mother. Little Beck had concluded that her mom had left because she hadn't wanted to be a mother. Turned out, she just hadn't wanted to be a mother to Beck.

"Beck, I've fed Sparks and Oslo. I'm heading to the goat pen."

"Perfect, Fern. Thank you."

Beck snapped out of her trance and finished up Sparks's and Oslo's stalls, then she poured some cat food for Sassy, all the while trying to understand how this had happened to her. Beck turned off the lights in the barn and closed the sliding door as Isaac drove up.

He walked to her with his hands in his pockets. "So, how did it go? Did she have any response to the business plans? Did she seem interested?"

"Well, we were about to get to that when Annette showed up, and we figured out that Callie is my sister, or at least, half sister. We still don't know if she is any relation to my father. Oh, and my mother is apparently in rehab, and Callie is paying for it. She owns a natural body care shop, so she's about as flush with cash as I am."

Isaac grimaced. "Oh. Wow. That's . . . a lot."

Beck sighed. "That's one way of saying it." She wrapped her arms around her middle, hugging herself. "I don't know what to do. What to think. Feel." She squeezed her arms tighter. "I can't afford to buy the place. How can this arrangement be fair if I am not allowed to fight it if she decides we sell?"

Isaac stepped closer. "I'm sorry, Beck. I wish you weren't having to go through this." He lifted his hands. "Need a hug?"

Pushing past the awkwardness she felt about this new, sort-of friendship, she stepped into his arms and laid her head on his shoulder, allowing herself a comforting place to rest, at least for a moment.

"I'm done!" Fern called out. The sound of her jogging footsteps drew closer.

Beck extricated herself from Isaac's embrace. Fern stopped beside them, gaze darting from Isaac to Beck and back, a sly grin stretching her face.

"Let's head out, Fern. Beck's had a big day, and the last thing she needs is us in her hair."

Fern shrugged. "If you ask me, she didn't mind—"

"Ookay, you. Let's go," Isaac said as he put his hands on Fern's shoulders and guided her—quickly—to the car. Beck stifled a laugh.

She almost called out to him. To tell them to stay. He and Fern had been a godsend the day after the panic attack and in the following days, invading the heaviness of her situation with joy and light.

But she couldn't avoid a call to Aunt Kate any longer, so she smiled and waved goodbye to her little ray of sunshine and her caretaker and went inside to face whatever response her aunt might have to this latest revelation.

Inside the house, she threw together a salad from the latest offerings from the veggie garden and topped it with a boiled egg and goat cheese crumbles. There was nothing more satisfying than sitting down to a meal comprised solely of things she'd grown on this land. This place had the power to sustain. To nourish. But just like a crop could get eaten up by locusts and her chickens could be carried away by a hawk, this place could go too.

She finished her dinner and dialed her aunt's number.

It took more than a few stops and starts to get the whole story out.

Her aunt blew out a long breath. "I loathe that woman for what she did to George. And you." Beck could hear her own pulse throbbing in her eardrums in the pause. "Even if that Callie girl is Lindy's, I still can't figure why your dad would have included her on the trust."

"He never mentioned that he had another child earlier in life or that my mother had another daughter?"

"No."

Beck let the back of her head collide with the top rail of her kitchen chair. She stared at the oak leaf ceiling tiles.

"Doesn't it seem odd? This girl showing up after your father's death, claiming to be Lindy's older daughter. This sob story about a mother who needs her rehab paid for."

Beck shook her head, forgetting for a moment that Aunt Kate couldn't see the gesture. "No. You just have to meet her. She's not scam—"

"Beck-Anne, to be frank, how can you possibly know that? Raised by the unassuming George Walsh, on Walsh Farm, you're not exactly a woman of the world."

Heat crept up Beck's spine and radiated from the tips of her ears. She spoke the next sentence, her words measured and deliberate. "Her name is on Dad's trust. No matter who she is or why she wants the money, she's not faking that."

"Unless she met your father and convinced him of a connection to Lindy. He would have done anything to reconnect with her or to help her. You don't understand what it was like with him and your mother."

*"You don't understand . . ."* Beck ground her teeth. Maybe she was just a backwoods country bumpkin, perfectly content to remain tucked away at this farm, but that didn't mean she didn't understand things. Like loyalty and hard work and devotion to something bigger than herself. She wasn't an idiot.

"Sure, Aunt Kate. Callie met him, convinced him she was Lindy's daughter, and then he just so happened to die suddenly of a heart attack. Are you going to suggest she poisoned him too?" The manic tone of her voice registered in her ears, and she clamped her mouth closed.

"Calm down. I'm just trying to help you think objectively. You have to admit that it's all quite strange."

Beck tapped her fingers against her thumb in rapid succession.

Index, middle, ring, pinky. Index, middle, ring, pinky. She released a trapped breath.

Could Aunt Kate be right about Callie? Perhaps not pretending a relationship to Lindy, but was Callie a shark who smelled blood in the water that day at the trust office and knew that Beck was so desperate to keep the place that she'd agree to almost any arrangement?

"Sweetie, that's your home, and I don't want to see you taken advantage of. I don't know what in the world your father was thinking, putting some stranger on the trust. You know, I told you that I've got some PTO saved up, and I can work from your place if I need to. I'm coming down there until all this is settled."

Beck wanted to protest, to proclaim she could handle this on her own, but it was becoming abundantly clear that she could not.

# TWENTY-THREE

When they got back to Chattanooga, Luke suggested they grab some food and head to the park. Callie surprised herself by agreeing. For once she did not feel like being alone with her thoughts.

"Have I completely lost it?" Callie spoke around a bite of crust. The flavor burst of the pizza served as a balm for her nerves.

Across from her on the blanket, Luke flipped open the cardboard box and pulled out a slice. "You've been carrying your mother's needs on your shoulders your whole life." He took a bite. "I can see why selling the farm looks like a viable option. I could understand feeling relieved that you don't have to foot your mother's bill alone."

Callie gazed past Luke to the Tennessee River, sunlight glinting off the rippling current. She pushed out a breath and refocused on Luke's slate-colored eyes. "But that's crazy, right? Making Beck give up everything she loves for a mom who abandoned her."

"I doubt Beck feels like she owes her mother much," Luke said. "Her dad and that farm have been everything to her. You've lived with the shadow of a mother, all the while craving the real deal. It sounds like Beck gave up on that decades ago."

Callie should've given up on the idea a long time ago too, but somehow it was harder with that person always there, offering glimpses of the way it could be, leaving her fighting to make the better moments last.

She watched a nearby mother and her toddler play catch with an oversized beach ball, both of them giggling when it would get caught in the wind, sending it riotously off course. "I was leaning toward relinquishing my portion of the estate to Beck and refusing George's gift entirely. But then that neighbor showed up and we realized we were sisters. Even that didn't change my mind. It was when I saw that album . . ." Her voice cracked over the words. She pressed her palms against her closed eyes, trying to keep tears from forming. She blinked hard and stared out over the water. "Those pictures of a cute little family living on the farm. My mother, clear-eyed and happy. A man with his arm around her that looked kind and decent and good, unlike all the bottom-feeding creeps I've seen her with. It was a perfect little life that she conveniently wrote me out of, caught in freeze frames. I wanted it to be me in those pictures." She thumbed away the teardrop on her cheek.

"Ouch." Her pain was reflected back to her in Luke's eyes. "I can't imagine how much that hurt. But you know that anyone can smile for the instant it takes for a camera snap. But a whole life? The long haul? That's where the proof is. The only thing you truly know about your mom's second life was that she left it."

Maybe it was time to write her own life story and not worry so much if her mother was in it. But it wasn't like she hadn't already tried that. She'd stepped miles out of her comfort zone to get a business loan, collected tangible evidence that she'd escaped the clutches of her mother's hardscrabble life in which she'd begged and borrowed more than she could ever repay. And then her mother came back.

Her heart stutter-stepped. Could she make herself sell that building if it came down to choosing between her dreams and her mother's recovery? Should she?

Or should she abandon Lindy Peterson to the consequences of her own life choices?

She slid open the box and pulled out another slice. Eating her feelings probably wasn't the best course of action, but at least it was the best pizza in the city. Before taking a bite, she said, "Tell me what the right thing to do is, Luke. Surely you can see this with clearer eyes than I can."

He smiled. "As flattered as I am that you trust my judgment—or at least are desperate enough to seek it—I'm not sure I'm the one you should be talking to right now."

Who else was there?

"Have you prayed about it? I only ask because in small group you shared that was something you were working on."

Oh. She pushed out a breath, refusing to feel guilty when what she needed in that moment was grace. She lifted a corner of her mouth. "I can't believe you're just going to call me out like that, Luke Matthews."

He gave her a sheepish shrug and picked at the bandage on his finger. "That's what friends are for."

"As a kid there was no one 'bigger than me' to handle things. I was it." She worried her bottom lip between her teeth. "So reaching out to God and trusting Him to work things out often doesn't come naturally. But I'm learning." She shrugged. "When it comes to my mother, it's so easy to slip back into feeling like everything falls on me. That I'm fighting alone." Not to mention, the last big decision she'd prayed about was buying the storefront, and look how well that turned out.

He smiled softly. "How did you start trusting God in the midst of everything you've been through?"

She swallowed hard. "It's not as cinematic as one might think. At the beginning of my junior year, my mother found my stash of cash from my after-school job and spent half of it on booze. Our rent was about to be due." Callie sighed. "She told me she'd pay me back, but that didn't change the fact that I'd be going hungry at school to make sure our rent got paid. On my third day of skipping lunch, my one hot meal of the day, this girl at school handed me a flyer for a pizza party that night at the church next door. I showed up."

"It was that easy for you? You just showed up, got some pizza, and started trusting Jesus?" he asked.

Callie shook her head. "Not hardly. The youth pastor befriended me." Callie smiled though her heart ached. "Jenni was so patient with my guarded heart, continually loving me. I started to doubt that I was as alone as I felt." Callie pressed her lips together. It hadn't occurred to her until that moment, while sharing her story with Luke, that her trust in God had started with trusting a person. The very thing she'd thought herself incapable of. "With Jenni, I got a glimpse of what a 'normal' family could look like, and I started to distrust my mother's claim that it was best to hide the truth so we could stay together. It's funny how when your basic needs start getting met, the world begins to look like a different place."

"So, what happened?"

She blew out a breath. "I finally worked up the nerve to tell Jenni what my home life was like. I don't know what I thought would happen. Maybe I hoped she'd just take me in. That I could be her daughter too. Instead, she reached out to my mom. I know all she wanted was to help us. She didn't understand the effect it would have.

"I came home from school the next day and mom had all our possessions packed into her beater of a car. She said that she'd gotten a new job in the next state. I knew she was lying, but I still got in the car. I never saw Jenni again, but my relationship with Jesus that bloomed that year, that was something I could always take with me." That and one of the discs of lavender soap she swiped from Jenni's guest bathroom. "No matter what my mom did or didn't do, that was one thing no one could take from me.

"I'm still a work in progress though." She plucked a few blades of grass and rolled them between her fingers. "Sometimes I pray and tell God I'm letting go and even convince myself that I've released control, but I'm really holding on with two hands."

Luke's eyes shone. He sniffled, turned toward the river, and scrubbed his hand surreptitiously over his face before turning back to her. "That was awesome."

"I'm sorry. What?"

He ducked his chin and scrunched his face. "I mean . . . not awesome about all you've gone through. But you just opened up, and this time it didn't feel like you were editing everything you said before you said it." He shrugged, his face reddening. "I'm proud of you."

"Uh . . . th-thanks." This was awkward. But nice. Sort of.

"You should share your story in small group sometime," he said.

She laughed under her breath. "You do realize that it took me a year to just tell you that my mom has problems. You want me to turn myself inside out like a sweater and show them the mess on the other side of the pretty pattern everyone else gets to see?"

He nodded. "Yeah. That's exactly what I'm saying. Maybe that's your next big step. I think the more you tell your story, bringing your past into the light, the less hold your mother will have on you. Your whole life, she kept her problems hidden and made you carry them for her. She made it your life mission to protect her. You've started to find your footing, but with everything going on, I could see how easy it would be to get swallowed up in it all.

"So, if you really want my advice, pray. And tell the story of God bringing you through hard circumstances. That's where you'll find the strength and perspective you need to navigate all this."

The knots that had been twisting and tightening in Callie's chest ever since her mother showed up on her doorstep loosened. "Thanks."

"I don't know that I said anything remotely helpful. Just like you, I'm trying to learn and grow."

"No, really, what you said helped. Would you mind praying with me right now, or is that super weird?"

He gestured to the other parkgoers. "Maybe weird to them, but not me."

In the orange glow of the setting sun, with bowed heads and words that whispered like the lapping of water on the banks of the Tennessee River, they shared a holy moment, a beseeching for wisdom.

They sealed their prayer with an amen, and Luke squeezed her hands tight. "You're amazing. You know that, right? To come out of what you've been through the way you have."

She shook her head. She was just a girl clinging to hope for dear life.

He grinned. "You've dug deep and walked through painful things to get where you are today. You'll never convince me otherwise."

She was just opening her mouth to protest, to tell him just how far she was from where she wanted to be, when her phone rang in her purse. She pulled it out, and Beck's name lit the caller ID. She grimaced. "Here goes nothing."

⬡⬡⬡

She'd paced the riverbank while Beck talked, concerned by the strain she heard in Beck's voice. But peace still lingered in Callie's heart, despite the topic of the call. Callie disconnected and walked back over to Luke. "Her aunt is coming into town next week and has asked to meet me. Beck said that she might have more information than Annette did about George's marriage to my mother and how that whole time frame connects. Although I think I know."

She pushed out a heavy breath. "My guess is that Mom was married to George during the time we lived with this older lady in our apartment complex who let us move in when Mom couldn't make rent. After we'd lived there awhile, Mom started going away for longer and longer amounts of time. She said she was going for work so we could get our own place. I'm starting to think work meant her secret life with her other family."

Luke leaned back on his elbows, looking across the water. "Do you remember her being pregnant?"

Callie shook her head. "I would have been three." She ran her hands over the park's close-cropped grass. "Five years Mom played this game. A life with me and a life on the farm with Beck. Later on, I do remember Ms. Ruthie and Mom having arguments. Mom would say she had a plan. That we'd be out of Ms. Ruthie's hair soon. But then Ms. Ruthie passed away. My guess is that's when Mom left George. I just don't understand why it had to be an either-or situation. I don't understand why she couldn't take me there too."

# TWENTY-FOUR

*a*ll right. Let's suit up." Beck held out one of her childhood bee suits to Fern.

"We're working the hives today?" Fern skipped over and wriggled her way into the white coveralls. She pulled the attached veiled hat over her head.

"It's time to check on the hive splits we made a couple weeks back." They'd taken the carefully constructed brood boxes and split a few of the burgeoning hives to keep them from swarming.

"Tell me again why you split them in half."

Beck motioned to the UTV. "I'll tell you on the way." She raised an eyebrow. "Where's that notebook of yours with all those notes you made last time?"

"I forgot it." Fern huffed and rolled her eyes skyward. "I tried to talk Uncle Ike into going back for it, but he wouldn't."

Before the summer was up, Fern would be a master beekeeper with her incessant quest for knowledge. "In a thriving hive, it sometimes gets too crowded. The available space in the brood box for the queen to lay her eggs gets overwhelmed. In the wild, the bees raise a new queen, and usually the old queen leaves with about half the hive population and goes in search of a new home. That's called a swarm. You'll see a homeless swarm sometimes hanging in a cluster in a tree or on the side of a building, all kinds of strange places. A huge gathering of bees like that tends to freak people out, but they're super gentle, these bees. They don't have resources to defend."

"But the ones in the hives have resources to defend and that's why we need the suits? 'Cause they'll sting to defend it?"

Beck nodded. "Yep. Anyway, as a beekeeper the goal is to split the hive before the ladies orchestrate it themselves and fly off to who knows where. We like to hang on to all our bees."

"So what are we looking for today?"

"We're checking to see if they've set up house. We want to see that the queen is laying and they are starting to store pollen and nectar. Resources. When there are stored resources, you know they'll most likely stay."

Beck blinked. That was it. She needed to get Callie to become personally invested. To see the resources here. Too bad Callie wasn't a bee. Their desires were simple enough—pollen and honey for survival and a healthy brood of the next generation of bees. What was it that Callie really wanted? Needed?

They stopped in front of the first hive split. Beck groaned. She didn't have to open up the hive to make a diagnosis. Zero activity at the entrance to the hive in the middle of an early summer day meant the bees had absconded. The bees in this unsuccessful split had either attempted to return to the original hive or gone off in search of somewhere new to call home.

She'd done everything exactly right. Followed every one of her father's steps. Why had it gone wrong?

∞∞∞

Hot and weary, Beck and Fern parked in front of the house. Beck needed to make a few more notes and tidy up before she could relax, so Fern headed to the creek promising not to go farther than ankle-deep until Beck joined her.

Beck headed to the honey house to return their supplies to their rightful places. A cool dip in the creek to wash off the afternoon's disappointment sounded just right. Of the five splits they had made, two had absconded and one showed all the signs of being queenless.

Without a queen they all would have died out in a few weeks, but she had caught it in time. She'd just need to borrow an unhatched queen from a hive that was raising a spare. This time of year, that should be easy enough to find among the throngs of hives.

Beck stood in the darkened shed, the bee suits hanging over one arm and the toolbox her father had always carried into the fields in her other.

She placed the toolbox on the ground and hung up her bee suit. She took her father's suit down from the hook, folded it, and draped it over her arm, then she hung Fern's in its place.

Beck smoothed the worn white canvas across her arm. She'd thought she'd known him. She'd known that he loved grilled cheese and tomato soup from a can on rainy days and that he hated bananas but somehow loved banana pudding. That he woke every morning at 5:30 and read his Bible. That his favorite color was the first green of spring. But she had not known the man who met a girl at a market and brought her products into their home without breathing a word to Beck that she had a sister out there. She did not know the man who walked into a trust office in Chattanooga and gave a stranger half their farm.

She shoved his suit in a storage bin, then snatched a spare smoker and flung it against the wall. The tinny sound it made as it bounced from the wall to the concrete rang in her ears. Ash she'd neglected to empty was slung through the air, leaving a crescent of black on the polished floor.

*Is the man I'm missing the man you were, Dad? Why didn't I know you?*

"Beck? Fern?" Isaac called out. She glanced at her watch. He wasn't due to pick up Fern for another hour. She smoothed her straggly waves back from her face and dabbed at her eyes with the back of her hand before squaring her shoulders.

She left the honey house and found Isaac outside. Beck thumbed toward the creek. "Fern went wading."

He looked past her in the direction of the creek. "How's she doing?"

"She's been great. Really great, actually." Other than her shenanigans with Callie and Luke the other day, but she thought it kinder to leave that out. The kid meant well. "She told me that the two of you have been doing more together and that you're more fun than she originally thought."

He smiled. "I never really thought of myself as being parent material, but Fern is definitely teaching me a thing or two."

Beck patted his shoulder. "Well, for being thrown into it like this, I think you're doing a good job." She left her hand resting on his shoulder. "But how are you handling everything? You know, coping with your own loss?"

His brow furrowed, and she slipped her hand away. Isaac's head tilted. "My loss?"

"Fern's your niece, right?" How had she misunderstood this situation? "So, I assumed either her mother or her father was your sibling."

Isaac nodded, brow still furrowed. "Yeah . . . my sister."

"You weren't close with them?" Even if they were estranged like Dad and his brother, surely the loss was still felt.

"We're fairly close, sure. You mean, losing my brother-in-law? We'll always be friends no matter what happens with their marriage."

"Uh." She glanced to the goat pen where Fern played, then back to Isaac. Was this conversation completely bizarre, or had all the recent events in her own life scrambled her brain? "Fern said her parents died. That's why she's with you."

Isaac stepped back, eyes wide. "I'm sorry. What?"

Beck shrugged. There was no need to repeat it.

"When did she tell you that?"

"The first day she came to work with me."

"Her parents aren't dead. They are going through a rough patch in their marriage." He massaged his forehead. "They'd been fighting a lot and Fern started acting out. Somehow I ended up committing to keeping Fern with me for the summer while they try to sort things so Fern's not caught in the middle of it." He shook his head slowly. "I can't believe she told you they were dead."

Beck laughed under her breath, a forced, gruff sound. "Maybe she did it because it's easier to say that someone is dead instead of believing that they don't want you." Beck had pretended Lindy had died plenty of times. When she was about Fern's age, she'd even held an imaginary funeral in the back field.

Isaac shook his head. "Her parents want her. This was supposed to make it easier for Fern, not them."

"Try telling a kid that. Her parents fight and then she gets sent away? How is she not going to think she's the problem?"

The memory of Callie when she'd flipped through her father's secret album pricked Beck's heart. The broken, vulnerable look in her eyes that had said, Where was I on this day and time?

She swallowed hard. It had been a cruel thing to do, showing her that album. She hadn't meant for it to be cruel. It was all she had to answer Callie's questions about Lindy's life on Walsh Farm.

Isaac pushed the hair back from his face. "I'm sorry Fern lied to you. I'm honestly a little creeped out that she let you believe her parents were dead all this time."

She shrugged. "Weirdly, I kinda get it." One of the first things Katya Amadeus Cimmaron of the Vesper Galaxy told her was that if someone's world was being turned upside down, they had a right to be informed. Fern had been honest and raw in the only way she knew how. "I know she shouldn't have lied," Beck continued, "but when you talk to her, do me a favor and be gentle. She's obviously hurting, and I'm guessing she feels like she's been cast out and that her feelings about any of this haven't been counted. That's a lot for a kid to take on." It was a lot for anyone, no matter their age. "I'm not going to say anything else about it to her unless it comes up."

As Fern and Isaac drove away that afternoon, she reflected on her first encounter with the girl who had called herself an alien—an alien with the gift of shapeshifting. How many shapes had Fern shifted into in response to her parents' struggling marriage? Was Beck finally getting the real deal, or was this just another of the little alien's attempts to find love and acceptance on the planet she'd visited for the summer?

She sighed. Shapeshifting had not been Beck's gift. When her mother left, Beck's form had become rigid and fixed, like hardened concrete. There was only one place she could fit—on the firm footing of Walsh Farm. Anything else would cause her to crack.

Beck walked up the steps of the wide front porch and sat on the swing. She drew one knee under her chin and let the other leg dangle. The recurring nightmare she'd had for years played in her mind.

When she'd wake, crying, bathed in cold sweat, one thing had been her constant—her father had been there, cradling her in his arms as she came fully awake. In those moments she'd known the nightmare monster that had devoured her mother could never touch her. Not with him there.

He was her king, and the farm his kingdom. Nothing bad had the power to reign there.

# TWENTY-FIVE

*C*allie parked in front of the white farmhouse. An SUV sat in the drive. *Must belong to Beck's aunt*, Callie thought.

Come to think of it, she'd never seen Beck's car. She exited her own well-loved sedan and turned a slow circle. The only evidence of a motor vehicle, besides the utility vehicle, was an older model pickup parked next to a tractor under the carport. The pollen and dust was so thick on the truck, it looked like it hadn't been moved in a month of Sundays.

"Callie?"

She turned. Beck stood on the porch, hand across her brow, shielding her eyes from the sun. She was barefoot and in overalls that were patched at the knees. Callie glanced down at her own apparel, a pair of dark wash jeans, a crisp white button-down, and ballet flats. She'd apparently overdressed for the occasion, but she'd hoped to make a good impression on Callie's aunt, who no doubt saw her as the intruder that she was.

"Hey, Beck."

"Aunt Kate is inside, if you want to come on in."

Callie crossed the yard and climbed the porch steps. "She has a nice car."

Beck shrugged as she opened the front door. "I guess."

The heady scent of peaches and sugar enveloped Callie as she stepped inside. "Do you keep your car in another garage around here?"

Beck narrowed her eyes. "I don't have a secret garage where I'm hiding things from you. Besides, all the equipment on the farm went to me anyway, so—"

Callie held up her hand. "I wasn't insinuating anything. I just realized that the only vehicle I'd seen was the old truck, so I figured you must keep your car somewhere else. Just making conversation."

"It's just the truck."

"Oh, it just looked like it hadn't been moved in a while."

A melodic voice came from the kitchen, "That's because Beck-Anne never goes anywhere."

Beck's nostrils flared. "The alternator is bad, I think. I've got to get it fixed."

Only one vehicle, which was broken down, alone on this rural piece of land, at least twenty minutes from any major shopping center. Callie shuddered. How had Beck not gone completely stir-crazy? "How do you get places? Get the supplies you need?"

"I have my ways. Come meet my lovely aunt." Beck forced a smile that could only be interpreted as sarcastic and motioned for Callie to go ahead of her into the kitchen.

Kate walked to Callie and gazed into her eyes in a way that made her insides squirm. "You do favor Lindy."

She hoped the woman meant her outward appearance and not some internal defect she'd somehow discerned.

Kate clapped Callie on the shoulder. "Don't worry. I won't hold that against you."

Callie looked from Beck to Kate and back again, searching for a social cue to determine if the woman was serious or teasing.

"You girls have a seat." Kate smiled. "I've got a peach cobbler almost ready to come out of the oven. I'll pour us some sweet tea and tell you what I know about Lindy and George's marriage."

Kate puttered about and waved them both away when they offered to help serve. She grabbed a pot holder from the counter and
pulled the cobbler from the oven. The sweet, homey scent set Callie's
mouth to watering. It wasn't until there was a cold glass of tea and a
saucer of steaming cobbler in front of each of them that Kate began.

"Brace yourselves," she said. "I know Lindy is mother to you both,
but I have no interest in mincing words to spare feelings. She completely wrecked our family. Split it right down the middle." Kate
tilted her head in a gesture of concession. "Although, I'll be the first
to admit that I don't think she meant to."

She sipped her iced brew. "As a girl, I blamed her completely.
Later, after the way everything played out, I see that it was more that
she was just a haphazard stream of water that flowed into an existing
fissure that split those boys wide apart, little by little.

"I spent my childhood following Chris and George about like a
shadow, always watching for a way into their world. They had that
famed twin bond, but not in the way most people imagine. They
lived a secret game of tug-of-war, forever tethered to each other with
an invisible cord. The weak twin and the strong twin always vying
over shared ground." Kate shook her head slowly, her expression
tightening. "My mother would tell the story to anyone who would
listen. I can't count the times she told of how George was born blue
and frail and Chris lusty and hale. It was like she had to make some
excuse to people for why they looked nothin' alike.

"Throughout my childhood, I witnessed the perpetual teeter-
totter. My mother, the helpless fulcrum, striving to set to rights
something that had been off-balance from their very first cell splits.
That competition for ground continued even when they'd broken
free of the womb. Good ole Dad seemed oblivious to the whole
thing."

Kate lifted a bite of cobbler to her mouth and chewed, seeming to
travel back in time. "And then along came Lindy. I'd catch George out

the window staring all moony-eyed as she passed by before school in the morning." She shrugged and dabbed at the corners of her mouth with her napkin. "I was only eight and Chris and George eighteen when everything fell apart, so to say that my understanding of what transpired that year is limited would be an understatement. But the way it looked to me was that George and Lindy spent most of the year as friends. It was Chris who ended up taking her to the prom. I still think he asked her just because he could. To goad shy George who always had a hard time standing up for what he wanted. Maybe because he was used to Momma giving him anything she thought he might want before he'd thought to ask. That didn't translate well to life outside of our home.

Beck sat forward. "I don't think you're being very fair. Dad knew how to take care of himself."

Kate held up a hand. "He did, Beck. I'm not criticizing. We all have things from our raising that we have to overcome."

Beck slumped against the back of the chair, apparently dissatisfied with her aunt's reply.

"I have no idea how Lindy felt about either of them," Kate continued, "but the tension sure was thick after that prom date. It was late that summer that the big fight happened. At the time, I didn't know what it was about, except that Chris was leaving for college on scholarship and George was really mad about him going."

Callie glanced at Beck who stabbed at the cobbler's buttery crust but didn't eat.

"They never spoke again after that night." Kate sighed. "And they refused to tell me what happened. They always saw me as their kid sister, no matter how old I got." She drummed her fingers on the tabletop. "Over the years I caught wind of rumors of Lindy being pregnant. My best guess it that George must have thought it was Chris's. That he thought Chris owed it to her to stay and be a father instead of run off to school."

Kate motioned to the untouched dessert plate in front of Callie. "You don't like cobbler?"

Callie scooped a small bite onto her fork. "I do, I just— Your story . . . I'd forgotten everything else." She took a bite, her eyes involuntarily closing. Those peaches had not come from a can. "It's really good."

Kate beamed. "It was my mother's recipe." She tapped the fork against her chin. "Where was I? Back then, I didn't know if the baby rumor was true or if it was simply a jealous spat between two brothers that had been a long time comin'. But Lindy was gone. So was Chris. And George wouldn't say a word about either of them." She eyed Callie. "I'm guessin' it was more than a rumor."

Callie broke her gaze away from Kate's intense inspection and nudged a crumb of crust into a lake of peach juice with the edge of her spoon.

"Lindy showed up again about a year after she'd disappeared, and she and George started seeing one another sporadically. She'd come and go like a stray cat, but they married a year later." She smiled at Beck. "And then came you. George would come over to Momma and Daddy's for Sunday supper with Beck-Anne on his hip, tending to her like a pro. I got the impression he was used to being Beck-Anne's primary caregiver, though he never said as much."

Callie took a drink of her tea, leaving her hands cupped around the cold, slick glass. "So, do you think I could have been that rumored baby? Could I be George's and not Chris's?"

"To be honest, I struggle to see any trace of my brothers in you. Not like Beck." Kate tipped her head from side to side. "And if you were that baby in question, George didn't know you lived. He would've looked after you. That was his way. No matter whose you were, he would have wanted you cared for and loved, because he loved her."

The hollowness in her tone with that last word could not be ignored. Callie took another bite of cobbler.

Kate began again, "I was fourteen when Lindy left for good. I was sure George would die of a broken heart." She looked down at the table, the lines of her face collapsing. "Though I guess he did in the end. I thought for a while that Annette was going to wear him down, that he'd let himself be loved by someone with the capacity to love him back. But . . ." Her words trailed away, and she sniffled before taking another sip of tea. "My brother was a good man. And I'm sorry if it hurts the two of you, but he deserved better than whatever version of love Lindy gave him."

She raised her eyebrows and lifted her chin in Callie's direction. "I don't pretend to understand how he could rationalize giving even a square inch of this land to anyone but Beck-Anne. If sweat equity meant anything to the bank, she'd have enough invested in the place to buy it outright, two times over. But George's love for Lindy wasn't exactly rational. Whoever your father might have been, you were Lindy's girl, and I'd venture to say that was enough for George."

It was strange hearing that all this time Callie hadn't been the lone soul wishing, hoping, and praying for Lindy. "I hope it would make him happy to know that she's finally getting help," Callie said. "That I'm able to help her."

Beck stood, trembling, color rising in her face. "You want to sell my father's land to help her, don't you? After everything she's done?"

Callie took a shaky breath. "That's not what I said. I'm paying her bill all on my own. But I'm not going to lie. I'm in over my head here."

# TWENTY-SIX

*A*unt Kate rose and placed a hand on Beck's shoulder. Beck gripped the back of the chair. *Breathe in. Breathe out.* "So, you think he'd be happy seeing his estranged wife get help," she said. "Well, what about seeing his daughter homeless and kicked off the land he and I devoted our lives to? How do you think he'd feel about that?"

"I'm not asking you to pay for her rehab," Callie replied. "I'd be using my portion for that. You'd be free to buy a new farm. Maybe even a smaller one that would be easier to manage on your own."

A sound slipped out of Beck's tight throat. She'd never struck anyone before. What would it feel like? To clench her fist, step around the table, pull her arm back—

The hand on Beck's shoulder squeezed tight. Aunt Kate spoke softly next to her ear. "Why don't you freshen up in the washroom and we'll continue this discussion in a moment."

Beck shrugged out of her aunt's touch and walked to the half bath in the hall, feeling like a recalcitrant toddler. She splashed water in her face—icy against her fevered skin. She gripped the edges of the pedestal sink and gazed into the bowl, water dripping down.

*Why didn't you tell me about Callie, Dad? Whoever she is, couldn't you see that this plan to include her would destroy me?*

Beck left the bathroom. Her ears detected the tones of Aunt Kate's and Callie's hushed conversation.

Beck walked softly, dodging the boards that creaked, feeling a little bit like Fern as she crept forward.

"Well, on top of all that, Beck is agoraphobic."

Beck ground her teeth. Aunt Kate had some nerve.

Callie's words were muffled by the walls.

"You really didn't know?"

Beck tightened her fists at her sides, edging closer. Just because she preferred to stay home didn't make her agoraphobic. Being home was just simpler. If she had a panic attack, she could handle it on her own and get on with life. Her mind flashed to Isaac dragging her to the ER even though she insisted she was fine. People always overreacted and that only made things worse.

Beck edged closer to decipher Callie's response. "It does make a lot of sense after what happened at the trust company. I thought she was just upset about me."

"What happened?" Worry resounded in her aunt's voice.

"She ended up having to leave. I think her boyfriend took her to the ER."

Aunt Kate let out a little burst of a laugh she quickly stifled. "Boyfriend? Beck-Anne?"

"Maybe not. He swept into the room like a knight in shining armor, so I just assumed."

"She didn't tell me about the panic attack." Aunt Kate's voice had softened. "There might be a lot of things she's not telling me."

"I'm glad you explained about Beck. She's not just angry her dad included me on the trust. This is the only place she feels secure, and I have a say in what happens to it."

Beck leaned against the wall and wrapped her arms around her middle, sliding down the wall until she sat curled against it. Never had she felt so stripped naked by a handful of words. Words spoken by this stranger, this undesired sister who saw how weak Beck pretended not to be. Maybe Fern could give her shapeshifting lessons.

"Beck's problems started when she was little, not long after Lindy left them."

Beck clamped her hands over her ears. How dare she? She had half a mind to burst into that room and stopper her aunt's mouth.

Aunt Kate's clear tones found the tiny cracks between Beck's fingers, letting the words slip past and clang about in her battered mind.

"Over the years, I tried telling George that the girl needed to see a specialist. But he never took much stock in therapy." She scoffed. "Or talking things out. After Lindy left, he tried to work away the pain. A coping tactic I'm pretty sure Beck-Anne has adopted wholeheartedly."

There was a pause and Beck let her hands fall from her ears. There was a soft tink of a glass returning to its place on the table.

Aunt Kate cleared her throat. "And work through the pain George did, until it caught up with him in the form of a heart attack on turn six of mowing the lower forty acres." Her voice cracked over the words. She gave a loud sniffle. "I want better for Beck. I know George did too."

"She's been gone awhile," Callie said, concern coloring her tone. A chair scraped against the floor. "I'd better go check on her."

Beck scrambled to stand. She shouldered past her aunt in the hallway without meeting her eye. "Gotta see to the chores."

As she exited the house, Callie said, "Do you think she overhe—"

Beck let the screen door slam shut behind her. She slid her feet into her muck boots and strode toward the barn.

Once inside, she pulled the large barn door shut, closing herself in, and went into the tack room. She coiled a rope she'd left in a pile, sorted Sparks's brushes that were already in their proper places, stacked buckets, paced. Anything to stay in motion.

Tears attempted to blur her vision, but she blinked them away.

Twenty minutes later, after she'd rearranged a room that had been functioning just fine before, she heard the scrape of the sliding barn door. "I'm busy, Aunt Kate. I'll come back in when I'm through."

"Actually, I was coming to see if I could help." The kindness of Callie's voice speared her.

Crouched by the bin of goat wormer she'd been sorting by expiration date, Beck studied Callie who leaned in the doorway, fresh as a daisy in her dressy shoes and white button-up shirt.

Beck stood. "You want to help?"

"Sure."

A very Fern-esque thought dropped into her head. "All right, then." She pointed to the tool rack. "Grab that rake and shovel and follow me."

Beck retrieved the wheelbarrow from where it was propped against the wall. As she wheeled it onward, she glanced behind her. Callie trooped gamely along, a rake in one hand, a long-handled shovel in the other.

"This way," Beck sang out as she wheeled her way to the goat pen.

Definitely the wrong move if she was going to warm Callie to the idea of keeping this place, but after her aunt had laid all her weaknesses out on the table like a Sunday buffet, it felt awfully fitting to find a task that would leave dear Callie feeling as wrong-footed as Aunt Kate had left Beck.

She parked the wheelbarrow and unlatched the gate. "You take the shovel. I'll take the rake."

"And we're going to . . ."

Beck smiled. "Clean out the goat pen. It's a little overdue."

Callie's brows shot high, but then she schooled her expression and nodded. "Okay."

"Just watch your step. The ground is still a little soft in a few of the low spots from the recent rain. Not to mention all the goat excrement."

Callie let out a nervous chuckle and followed her inside. "Let's do this."

"There's not much to it." In one fluid motion, Beck scooped up soiled straw and deposited it in the wheelbarrow on the other side of the fence.

The largest of the nanny goats ambled over. Beck shook her head. Fern had spoiled them rotten. Now they thought everyone carried treats in their pockets.

The goat nudged Callie's rear end. She emitted a squeak and spun to face her assailant.

Beck laughed under her breath. "She's just hunting treats. Ignore her and she'll mosey on."

Callie turned back to her. Her face was red, and her shoulders had crept up to her ears. "If you say so." She adjusted her grip on the handle a few times before beginning again. "I've never been around animals much. I had a dog once, but that didn't last very long. Not . . . not with Mom being the way she was. . . . Is." Callie swallowed hard. "Anyway, I'm sure the poor dog was better off without us wherever he ended up."

Beck swallowed hard. *I sure can relate to that dog.* No matter how her mother's abandonment had impacted her, hadn't her life been better off without her? She'd never had to worry about where she'd lay her head at night. Until now, that is.

At a loss for a response, she got to work and could only hope Callie would follow suit. She'd left the house to avoid conversation, not to have one.

Thankfully, silence did follow. The level of concentration Callie put into scooping poop was almost comical.

Beck had to give her credit. She never once complained. Not even when her pastel shoe sank in muck.

# TWENTY-SEVEN

Out of the corner of her eye, Callie watched Beck's progress. Her movements were methodical and practiced. She had no doubt Beck could work for hours like this without getting winded. It was like the sweat, dirt, and sunshine of this place flowed through her like a power source.

When Callie had seen those photos of her mother with George and little Beck, when she saw the beautiful, stable life Beck had enjoyed, all she could think about was the life Beck escaped by not having a mother to care for. What opportunities might Callie have had as George Walsh's daughter instead of Lindy Peterson's?

She'd been haunted by those images, angry Beck had been shielded from the tornadic path her mother cut through people's lives. But Kate's words had revealed the truth.

Callie scooped and balanced soiled straw on her shovel, wincing as half of it splatted back onto the ground when she teetered toward the wheelbarrow in her ruined ballet flats. "I guess you probably heard me and your aunt talking about your ... uh ... struggles." Continuing to work, Callie glanced Beck's way.

Beck froze for a moment and Callie braced for what was to come. Would she storm off again? Confront her?

"Yeah," she said quietly, keeping at her task.

And that seemed to be the end of the conversation.

"I'm not crazy or anything," Beck added, several scoops of manure later. "I know, or at least part of my brain knows, that nothing terrible is going to happen if I leave this place. That some monster isn't going to swallow me up if I stray too far away."

"Monster?" Callie paused and studied Beck.

She grimaced and shook her head. "When I was little, after Mo—Lindy left, I started having nightmares. Always the same one. In the dream, she was leaving, but I'd snuck into the back of her car to find out where she always went. And every time, just as we reached the edge of town and were about to take the on-ramp, this massive beast would appear and pick up our car. He'd pull Lindy out, and I'd watch as he'd swallow her whole."

Beck swiped at her forehead with the back of her hand but kept working. "I was just a kid, and that beast was real to me. Everywhere I went, I kept my eyes peeled for that monster. I think it was easier to think something had swallowed her up than to think she chose to leave me."

Callie kept shoveling. Little Beckett Walsh hadn't been wrong. A monster had swallowed her mother whole. Callie just knew it by another name.

Beck paused. "In my dream, the monster could grow to fill any space, no matter how big or small, so I believed it could be anywhere, waiting for me. I searched for it in the stalls of the bathroom at my elementary school. Under the clothes racks at stores. Beneath the tables in children's church. Anywhere I thought it could hide.

"It just kept getting worse," she continued, "so Dad pulled me out of school to homeschool me. He left his job at the bank and became a full-time homesteader. After a while, I grew out of my fear of monsters and instead feared myself—how panic swallowed me up, turning me into someone I didn't recognize. Aunt Kate tries to give me these pep talks about how the Lord will protect me, that I don't have to constantly live in fear that something bad will happen. She doesn't understand though. I'm not afraid that something horrible will happen to me 'out there.'"

Callie paused her shoveling. "You're not?"

Beck said, "Having a panic attack is terrifying—being that out of control. Because I don't fear having a panic attack here, I don't usually have them." Beck held up her hand like a stop signal, frustration brewing in her expression. "I know what you're thinking—that if I'd just stop being afraid of having panic attacks in public, then I would stop having panic attacks in public. Sounds so simple, doesn't it? That—that right there is what is so maddening about it all. It is both true and unattainable all at the same time."

Callie propped her hands on her shovel's hilt. "Do you ever feel trapped here? Did you ever wish for anything different? Like going off to college or something?"

Beck shook her head and smiled, a wistfulness lingering in her gaze. "No. I really do love my life here. The land, the bees. Everything." She dumped another load into the wheelbarrow. "This place is like my Neverland. A place where I am strong, capable. Invincible. Every battle can be won. And that version of me feels so real. But when I have to leave, I become that scared, weak, defenseless kid again, and I hate it."

Beck left the goat pen and went to the open-sided shed where bales of straw were stacked. She swung one down in a fluid motion and walked over with it. The muscles in her arms were taut and tawny.

Callie leaned her shovel against the fence, the space between her shoulder blades aching. "I don't know how anyone could think you're weak."

Beck huffed as she dropped the bale and sliced the twine holding the straw together with her pocketknife. She glanced up, her expression full of doubt.

Callie had thought Beck a little spoiled and pampered when compared to her own life experiences. But after learning that Walsh Farm, her home, had been placed in the hands of a stranger, Beck had not wilted. She'd dug in and tried to offer Callie workable options despite how hard it must have been for her to concede that Callie had any rights at all.

She joined Beck in her task of grabbing hunks of straw and shaking them as they walked, letting the fresh bedding rain down. "When you have a panic attack, can anyone ease the burden? Take it away?"

Beck spoke softly. "I just have to weather it."

Callie went for another hunk of straw and sprinkled it across the ground. "And you live through it and keep surviving?"

Beck shook her head. "It doesn't feel like I'm surviving. Every time, I feel like I am literally going to die. Like my heart is going to leave my chest."

"But you do get through it. In my humble opinion, that's not weak."

"I should be braver."

Callie chewed her bottom lip. "I'm trying to learn that it's okay to be a little bit of a mess. To grow, I've got to be honest about where I'm really at instead of obsessing about where I think I should be by now. Otherwise, I just get paralyzed by how unattainable 'where I should be' seems. At least, that's what I tell myself when I get a little embarrassed that I'm still continuing to work on issues I've had for as long as I can remember."

Beck paused and studied Callie. "How ... um ... how did you learn how not to obsess? How not to beat yourself up when you fall apart?" She jerked her gaze to the ground, brows pinched.

Callie prayed her words would soothe Beck's searching heart. "I started by identifying the lies I unwittingly embraced and then I started confronting those faulty thoughts with the truth. Over and over and over again, every time that lie popped into my head. Until one day the truth set up residence in my heart and left no room for the lie. I started seeing a therapist and she taught me the continual process of sorting truth and lies and how to reframe those unhelpful thoughts. Plus, God continues to help me see the truth about who I am and whose I am." She shrugged. "Like I said, I'm a work in progress. And some days I am more successful than others. I just refuse to quit."

Beck stared out over the fields, more still than Callie had ever seen her.

"For whatever it's worth to you, I think the belief that you're weak is a lie, Beck."

Beck dusted off her hands and smiled. "For the record, you are a lot tougher than I gave you credit for too."

Callie ducked her chin, hiding the triumph bursting in her chest. She had passed this unspoken test. The approval of this sister of hers was something she'd craved without even knowing it. "When you've had a raising like mine, you learn to handle just about anything. Cleaning up after goats is by far not the most distasteful thing I've done."

Beck fidgeted with a tufted piece of straw that had stuck to her overalls. "I'd like to hear about it sometime, if you ever want to share." Beck met Callie's eyes, a smile teasing at the corners of her mouth. "What it was like growing up with Lindy as a mother, I mean. Not the specific tasks you deem more unsavory than shoveling goat poo."

# TWENTY-EIGHT

$S$ ide by side, Beck and Callie made their way back to the house. Beck was surprised her aunt hadn't sent out a search party for as long as they'd been gone.

On the porch, Beck slid out of her muck boots and Callie followed suit with her ruined dress shoes. She should probably offer to buy her another pair.

"Beck-Anne? Callie? I found something the two of you might want to see."

They followed the sound of Aunt Kate's voice and found her sitting on the floor in front of the coffee table. It was covered in partially unfolded sheets of paper. She looked up when they entered the room. Her eyes widened at the sight of them. Beck glanced to the left. Callie stood beside her, her once-starched white shirt wilted and dingy. The smudge of dirt, or worse, on her cheek. Barefoot, just like Beck.

Aunt Kate looked at Beck, narrowed her eyes, and pursed her lips like this was all Beck's fault. Which it was. But to assume was just plain rude.

"I found letters George sent to Lindy," she said. "There must be fifty of them. All marked 'return to sender.' You girls freshen up, then we can look through them. Beck-Anne can loan you some clothes, Callie."

Beck pushed away her annoyance at her aunt for volunteering her shower and clothes like she wouldn't have had the decency to do that herself. She focused on the pile of envelopes already open on the carpet. "You opened them? They weren't meant for you."

Aunt Kate frowned. "I thought you two wanted answers."

Beck shoved down the simmering anger and looked to gauge Callie's response to this privacy violation. Callie's eyes roved over the pile of papers. "I wonder if he mentions me in any of them?"

Beck groused. The two of them were so willing to tramp through Dad's private thoughts. She picked up an unopened envelope and traced her finger along its edges. She placed it back on the table, her eyes on Callie. "Let me grab you some clothes. The shower is upstairs."

Callie shook her head. "That's okay. I have some spare clothes in my car. I'll just run and get them."

Beck hadn't invited her to stay the night. Although, technically speaking, the house was as much Callie's as it was Beck's. The thought made her insides pucker. "You brought an overnight bag?"

"I always keep a bag of clothes in my car. Old habits die hard, I guess. Mom and I always had a just-in-case bag."

In case of what, Beck wanted to ask, but with the little she knew of Lindy, she could guess the answer.

Callie returned with a tattered and faded duffle bag that looked like it had seen its fair share of quick escapes. Beck led her upstairs to the bathroom. She motioned to the open doorway. "Towels are under the sink. Shampoo and conditioner are in the shower. Make yourself at home."

She bit down on her lip. Had she meant that? Was she really willing to let Callie feel at home here? Would that be what it took to convince Callie to keep the place? To have her feel like she belonged here too?

While Callie showered, Beck went back downstairs to confront her aunt who still sat, perusing the letters like they were sales pages from the Sunday paper. "You didn't even think to ask me first?"

Aunt Kate looked up, eyes as innocent as a six-year-old caught with their hand in the cookie jar. "I didn't think you'd mind. And don't forget. He wasn't just your father. He was my brother. I think that gives me some rights, Beck-Anne."

"This is my home. My house. And that makes the contents of this house mine too. You can't just keep coming back here, acting like I'm a child in need of a guardian."

Her aunt bristled. "Don't you mean half yours? Are you going to give Callie browsing rights?"

Beck choked, her aunt's words tasting of bile. "Are you mad at Dad? For what he did with the trust? Because he didn't give you—"

The harshness in Aunt Kate's expression dissolved. "No. I'm sorry, Beck." The lamplight reflected in the moisture welling in her eyes. "It's not that. But I can't deny that I'd like to look him in the eyes and ask what in the world he was thinking doing this without talking to you or me or anybody." She smiled through the tears that now spilled down her cheeks. "I might have been his little sister, but I still wish I could just shake him." She swiped the back of her wrist across her eyes. "I wasn't trying to horn in on you. The house was just so empty and quiet, and I wandered into his room, missing him, wanting to find something that could bring him back to me for just a minute. A shirt he wore or a picture. Something.

"I was looking in his closet. One of the shirts had slipped off the hanger, and when I went to hang it back up, I saw something sticking out of an old boot. These letters were stacked together, bound with a rubber band. I should have waited and showed them to you. No matter the trust arrangement, he was your dad and I'm sorry for what I said about them being half Callie's. Your father's memories, his things, those belong to you."

"It's okay," Beck said, even though it wasn't. She knew what it was to miss him. To want to wrap herself in something that had been his and breathe in anything of him that lingered. "Aunt Kate, I know you still have a hard time seeing me as anything other than a little girl in need of a rescue, but I'm trying to find my own two feet here—to grow—and it's real hard when I feel so small in your presence."

Her aunt pushed out a breath. "I didn't even ask you if you wanted me to come meet Callie or to talk about what I knew. I just did it." She winced. "I'm so sorry. Do you want me to go? I'll pack my things right now and leave you and Callie in peace."

Beck shook her head. "Stay. But if you and I could at least pretend like I am a capable adult, I think I might get there eventually."

Aunt Kate stood and pulled her into an embrace. "You're right. I'm going to do better. And for the record, no matter how this whole thing turns out, I sincerely believe that you are going to find a way to blossom wherever you're planted"—she smoothed Beck's hair—"without my meddling."

Beck pulled back from her embrace and offered a wry smile. "Even if I am a finicky seedling with very specific soil requirements?"

Aunt Kate kissed her on the forehead. "Even if."

The sound of a throat clearing made them turn in unison. A freshly showered Callie with her hair twisted up in a towel stood on the staircase.

Aunt Kate stepped back from Beck. "You better take your turn, Beck-Anne— Sorry, Beck. I love you, but you smell like those ruminants you are mysteriously fond of."

Beck resisted sticking out her tongue. After their conversation, it hardly set the right tone.

"I promise we won't touch another letter without you. We'll head to the kitchen, and I'll whip us up something to eat."

"I won't take long." Beck trotted up the stairs, grounded by the cool wood beneath her feet. Aunt Kate had called her Beck for probably the first time ever. That had to be a sign they'd stumbled into some sort of progress in their relationship. She could hope, anyway.

⬡⬡⬡

After Beck disappeared up the stairs, Callie held up her cell phone. "I'm happy to help you with dinner, but do you mind if I make a quick call first?"

Kate waved her on. "Based on the way you came back from helping Beck, I'd venture to say you've already done more than your fair share. Go enjoy that porch swing. Oh, and just one more thing." Kate went into the kitchen and came back a few moments later with a mason jar full of ice water. "Make sure you hydrate after all that hard work."

As she accepted the brimming glass, warmth bloomed in Callie's middle. It was just a glass of water, but the way Kate had anticipated her need before it had even been voiced affected her in ways she'd not foreseen.

Callie walked outside and was swathed in the cool night breeze that carried the sound of crickets and the throaty chirrup of frog song. Night had snuck in while she showered.

Drawn by the starry sky, she descended the porch steps and stepped onto the lawn, the grass dewy beneath her feet. She tipped her head back, enamored with the countless pinpricks of light breaking through night's dark canopy. The stars weren't nearly this visible from home.

A precious memory replayed. A night beside a bonfire, Jenni's arm around her shoulder as Callie made the decision to trust a heavenly Father with her fragile heart. She'd probably be working her whole life long to trust imperfect humanity with the same, but ever since that night, no matter how dire her situation, if she simply looked up to that light breaking through the night, she was reminded that she was never as alone as she felt.

Wind whipped her damp hair, and clouds began to gather, obscuring the clear night sky. She walked back to the porch, pulling her phone from her back pocket.

She'd missed Luke's call. Twice. He was probably starting to wonder if Beckett Walsh had decided to do Callie in and bury her inheritance problem on the back forty.

He answered on the second ring. "Hey, Callie."

"Sorry I missed your call. I stayed longer than I intended and got caught up dealing with goat excrement."

"Uh. Come again?"

Callie laughed. "You heard me right."

"Oh. That's . . . unexpected."

"It's been really good, actually."

"Um. Are you really okay? Say 'I need some decaf' to signal me if you need help."

"Beck opened up, quite a lot actually. She's agoraphobic, Luke."

The line was silent for several long seconds. "Oh."

"Yeah. You see the full picture of where this puts me," she said as she climbed the steps to the porch. "To use this inheritance to pay for my mom's rehab, I'm going to have to kick my agoraphobic half sister out of the only home she's ever known, all for a woman who abandoned her."

Callie sat on the porch swing and used her bare toes to nudge it into motion. The silence between them was filled by the chorus of night creatures. She breathed in the cooling air. "There's so much beauty here. So much peace. All the rush and striving out there in the real world just seems to cease. Am I crazy or did you feel it, too, when you were here?"

Luke chuckled softly. The sound warmed her, even from this distance. "I get it. Although my visit may have been a bit more peaceful if I hadn't had to remain constantly vigilant for Fern's subversion."

Callie stifled a snicker. "How are your cat scratches, by the way? No permanent scars, I hope."

"Just fine, thank you. I've got to hand it to the kid. She didn't give up until she got me."

How she adored the way he'd dealt with that mischievous little girl, refusing to take her tricks personally, even after he became the victim of one of them. It gave her hope that he might be the person to have the patience needed to weather her journey of discovering what healthy relationships were supposed to look like.

"So . . ." He drew out the word. "Are you thinking about keeping the place?"

She groaned, leaned her head against the swing, and stared at the whitewashed wood above. "It's the right thing to do. But so is helping Mom. And I don't know if I can do both."

Luke was quiet another moment. "You were planning to help your mom before you ever learned about the farm. What were you going to do before?"

She blew out a breath. "Go deeper into debt. Sideline growing my company and get a second job." Her chest tightened. "Sell the building even after I fought so hard to get my business loan. Something along those lines." She looked across the yard to the horizon. Stars peeped through the shifting clouds. "As much as I want it to stick this time, what if it doesn't? What if I give up my storefront and get myself buried in debt that I'll never see my way out of and she never changes? What if I sell the one thing Beck cares about, her very livelihood, and Mom just throws it all away and returns to her old ways?"

Luke cleared his throat. "And the third option where you let your mom deal with the situation she created, and you do what you want to do?"

Callie stood from the swing and walked to the edge of the porch, the tips of her toes gripping the edge. "I've thought about it. A lot. But then I get this picture in my head of standing before God someday. And I never want Him to look at me and say, 'You had the chance to help her find wholeness, to find Me, and you chased temporary things instead.' It's hard to know the difference between tough love and giving up on someone." She scrubbed a hand over her face. "My whole life has been a desperate mission to build something steady and stable, and every time, right when I think I am about to arrive in the promised land, Mom shows up and finds a way to drag me back into the wilderness. It's so hard to look at this place and not see it as my way out."

"Callie?"

She turned. Beck stood in the doorway in cutoffs and a T-shirt that had damp spots on the shoulders. Her face was stricken. Callie bit down on her lip. How much had she overheard?

Beck crossed her arms over her chest. "I just wanted to let you know Aunt Kate is almost finished with dinner. I hope you like grilled cheese and tomato soup." Her forced smile made Callie ache. "It's a rainy-day favorite around here."

Callie squinted at the dark sky. "It's not raining."

Beck lifted a shoulder and let it fall, her eyes carrying a thousand sorrows. "Not yet. But it will." She disappeared inside the house.

"You still there?" Luke's soothing voice filled her ear.

"Yeah. I'm here." The gentle breeze kicked up, ruffling her hair, carrying with it the scent of rain.

# TWENTY-NINE

Raindrops pinged against the tin roof, drawing the walls close around Beck and her company. She'd always loved nights like these when she was growing up. She and her father dunking the crusts of their grilled cheese in tomato soup. The sound of the rain filling the silence, shutting out the rest of the world. It had much the same feeling as climbing inside one of the massive pillow forts they used to build in the middle of their living room.

Beck bit into the buttery bread, toasted to perfection. If her dad had been the chef, one side would have been lightly browned and the other nearly charred. Always.

Across the table Callie peeled the crust from her sandwich and dipped it in the soup. Just like Beck, Callie saved the gooey middle for last.

The words Beck overheard on the porch reverberated inside Beck's head, driven deeper by the pounding rain.

"And every time, right when I think I am about to arrive in the promised land, Mom shows up and finds a way to drag me into the wilderness. It's so hard to look at this place and not see it as my way out."

Beck nudged her half-full bowl and saucer away from her. Sure sounded like Callie's mind was made up. Aunt Kate eyed her across the table, delicately sipping soup from her spoon.

Callie put her spoon down and stared into her lap. Warring emotions seemed to play across her face. This was it. This was the moment Callie was going to tell them that she'd decided to sell the farm. Beck braced herself, pretending she was made of steel instead of flesh and bone.

But Callie said, "Mom never was much of a cook. Cereal or anything I could microwave became my usual fare after Ms. Ruthie passed on. But on rainy nights, Mom would actually come home at a decent hour with a can of soup, a loaf of bread, and some butter and cheese."

Beck pinched off a piece of her sandwich and squeezed it between her fingers until the cheese oozed out. Callie was going to sell this place and there was precious little she could do about it. Why reminisce instead of just spilling it?

Callie tilted her head. "I wonder if that was something she got from your dad, from her time here at the farm."

Would this be all Beck would have left after the farm sold—memories and grilled cheese sandwiches and soup on rainy days? And what would happen with the bees? If she sold the farm equipment and put that with her portion of the inheritance, maybe she could afford a small acreage to keep a portion of the bees. And Sparks. She had to find a way to keep Sparks.

Some of the neighboring farms might allow her to move a few of the hives to their vacant land. Farmers sometimes let beekeepers have hives on their place and even paid for the privilege. She chewed her bottom lip. But that would involve driving to all these individual farms. Could she ever get to the point where traveling was a part of her normal life?

"Beck? Did you hear me?" Callie looked at her from across the table, a crease between her brows.

"Huh?"

"Do you think that's something that Mom did with you and George? Rainy-day grilled cheese and soup?"

What in the world did it matter? Beck shrugged, but then she noticed the way Callie leaned forward, a hunger in her eyes that could not be sated by tomato, bread, and cheese.

Aunt Kate stood from her finished meal and went to the sink.

Callie framed the bowl and saucer with her hands. "Of all the beautiful things here, why do you think this was the only thing she could share with me from this place?"

Beck blew out a breath and leaned her head back, looking up at the metallic oak leaf ceiling tiles. What was her deal with the soup? "I'm pretty sure half of America eats soup when it rains." Going along with Callie would have been wiser. She should nurse that desire for some kind of connection to this place.

A wistful smile curved Callie's lips. "Maybe so. But those rainy nights were the only nights she came home and cooked for me. That same meal every time. When the cabinets were empty, I prayed for rain."

"Oh," Beck said, at a complete loss of how to respond. She might have been abandoned, but never once in her life had she worried about where her next meal would come from.

Aunt Kate turned and looked at Callie, her expression full of pity.

Beck pushed back from the table and stood. She raked the food she could no longer stomach into the trash. "Are you two about ready to go through the letters? It's getting late and Callie's got that long drive back."

Aunt Kate gave Beck a look that could pin a fly to a wall.

*What?*

Her aunt lifted her chin and pursed her lips. An expression that said, "Go on. Say the thing that you're supposed to say in this situation, but I'm going to keep my mouth shut because you already got mad at me for walking over you."

Ugh. Beck blew out a breath. "It is pretty late, Callie. There's a trundle bed in my room if you'd rather stay the night. Or the couch if you'd prefer to have your own space." Aunt Kate already had the guest room. And there was no way she was going to offer Dad's.

Callie's shook her head. "I'd better not. A lot of orders have come in over the past few days, plus a couple of stores downtown agreed to sell my products on consignment, so I need to get an early start in the morning. The drive from here is only forty-five minutes or so. I'll be fine."

The cramp between Beck's shoulder blades relaxed.

They filed into the living room. Aunt Kate gestured to the letters she'd already read, looking appropriately sheepish when she said, "I didn't read anything in his letters so far that revealed that George knew about Callie. Mostly him pining after Lindy, asking her to come back home or to write back. And updates about you, Beck."

Beck gave a tight smile in response to her aunt's words. Lindy forfeited her right to hear about Beck's life the night she left. Was Dad naive enough to believe talking about the daughter she'd abandoned would've been enough to lure her back home?

Aunt Kate propped her hands on her hips, nodding. "Let's sort through them and see if we can learn anything new about Callie, or why Lindy left, or I don't know . . . anything that might give you girls some peace about this situation." Aunt Kate softened her executive's pose and glanced at Beck. "That is, if that's what you think we should do."

Beck laughed under her breath. Her aunt was trying. She had to give her that. "That works." She still hated that they were reading through her father's private thoughts, but if they could find anything that would make Callie want to keep the place, it was worth it. She could only hope they didn't stumble on anything that would sway her in the opposite direction.

Beck rolled her shoulders to settle her nerves. She plucked an unopened envelope from the stack. This one mailed to Phoenix,

Arizona. Her gaze darted to Callie, who was flipping through envelopes, looking at the addresses.

"You lived in Phoenix?" For some reason, maybe because Callie lived so close now, she'd imagined that Lindy and Callie had always been nearby.

"Oh, yeah, a few different places around there for a couple of years." She tapped her chin with her finger. "My favorite was this camping park we stayed at for a few months. Mom rented an RV from a nice old couple, but you could only stay on the property for fourteen consecutive days. So they'd come in and move it to another spot for us every two weeks, and we'd alternate between two neighboring RV parks.

"The air conditioner barely worked, which was unfortunate, especially in that climate. But there was a playground, and I could walk to school. The vacationers were usually nice. They'd invite me over for grilling out, so I snagged some pretty sweet meals. It beat cereal every night, that's for sure." Callie went back to flipping through envelopes, occasionally muttering things under her breath, like, "I remember that place" or "I had forgotten we lived there."

Beck settled into her chair, mystified by Callie's nomadic life. What had Lindy been running from?

She slid her finger beneath the seal and exhumed her father's words.

Dear Lindy,
    Your hyacinth bloomed.
    I wish I could tell you that Beck's adjusting. I'm thinking about pulling her out of school. They've had me come get her three times last week. I thought it might get better over time, but it's getting worse instead. The school tries with her, but they just aren't equipped to deal with her episodes. It used to only happen at night while she slept. Sometimes I wonder if she's living the nightmare

now. But she won't tell me what's happening when she comes undone. Perhaps she doesn't have the words. I know I don't.

Come back home. At least visit Beck. I think it would do her a world of good to see your face. To see that you're okay. Beck and I didn't want your apology. We wanted you. Surely you know that.

Come back and give her a real goodbye.

George

Beck let the letter fall to her lap. They'd both needed that closure more than either of them ever admitted.

Across the room Aunt Kate put down the letter she was reading. "This one was right when you started having nightmares. I'd forgotten. At first, you went on without missing a beat, but after about two months with no sign of her, you took to sitting on the sidewalk every afternoon, picking through the pea gravel. You said you were looking for quartz and little fossils, but your dad knew better. You were waiting for her car to come down the drive. Three months gone was when the nightmares started."

"It took me that long to wonder where she was? Don't normal kids cry when their moms drop them off at daycare for a few hours?"

"Oh, honey. You were so small, I guess you don't remember."

Beck pushed out a breath. "I barely remember her at all." Other than that last Christmas, which seemed permanently branded on her cerebral cortex.

"Your momma blew in and out of here like the fluff from a cottonwood," Aunt Kate said. "Always with some excuse about a friend in trouble. George would try to convince her that you all could go together, but she'd sneak out. A go-bag always in her trunk, I suspect. I was sure she was seeing somebody on the side." She looked to Callie who had been listening intently. "Now I'm guessing she was going back to you."

Callie's brow furrowed. "And you think George wouldn't have welcomed me? Or that she knew my coming along had torn the family apart, so she kept me away? Pretended that part of her story never happened?"

Aunt Kate shook her head. "I don't know." She wrung her hands. "Girls, I wish I had more information."

Beck tucked the letter in her lap back in its envelope. "I tried calling Uncle Chris when I first learned about the trust, but he never answered."

Aunt Kate stood. "I'm calling him. We're going to get to the bottom of this. Somehow. This is not my first go-round with this, pesky little sister that I am. I pushed real hard when George proposed to Lindy, sure that if he married her, my brothers would never heal the rift. But the harder I pushed, the harder they pushed back. It got to the point that I believed that if I kept at it, my relationship with them would crumble like theirs had, so I left it alone." She lifted her shoulders and let them fall. "I'd hoped they'd bury their grievance, but I ended up with a buried brother instead. I couldn't believe Chris didn't even come to the funeral."

She grabbed her phone and walked out onto the front porch, but she returned not five minutes later.

"He hung up on me."

# THIRTY

Callie lined up her custom packing boxes across her breakfast table, each one decorated with whimsical floral print and lined with lavender tissue paper. She checked and double-checked her order form as she filled each one. The first box she topped with a card offering congratulations on a new job. The next one she filled with an assortment of lotions and bath salts, then included a card asking a girl to be a bridesmaid. The rest were the usual personal orders, but the gift boxes always felt extra special, like she was getting to play a part in making someone's day.

She hadn't dedicated her life to being a doctor who rescued people from death or one of those counselors getting people like Mom through their addictions. Maybe some saw her passion as pure frivolity, but after spending her formative years trying to keep her and her mother's heads above water, it was nice to be "the little something extra" in people's lives instead of the person they depended on to survive.

Callie finished with the boxes and stacked them by the door to be shipped. In the kitchen she pulled out her leftover pasta from last night's dinner with Luke. While her bowl spun in the microwave, it wasn't her meal with her friend that captured her thoughts, but that soup and sandwich on a rainy night last week.

Watching her pasta heat, she finally grasped hold of the emotion that had swirled inside her when she'd shared the meal with Kate and Beck. On the surface it had just been canned soup, cheap bread, and processed American cheese shared with people who were practically strangers. But it had meant something to Callie.

Connection.

No. More than that.

Home.

The feeling of coming to rest in a place that was good and wholesome and safe—a feeling she'd spent a lifetime chasing.

For reasons her mother never confided, a home was something she'd never been able to provide. The closest her mother had come was the tradition of grilled cheese and tomato soup on rainy nights.

A quiet anger lived in that empty space happy childhood memories were supposed to fill. It was something she'd prayed over and laid at Jesus's feet about a thousand times, only to find that it still clung to her like tree sap.

She gripped the chair back in front of her to steady the shaking that had started in her hands, watching the color leech out of them the tighter she squeezed. *Why, Mom? Even if you couldn't stop running from your demons, why couldn't you have dropped me off on Beck and George's doorstep instead of dragging me into the hell you built for yourself?*

Why had her mother held Callie closer than Beck? Why hadn't she protected her too?

She took a few breaths, attempting to gather the emotions that lay tangled at her feet, like a yarn ball in the claws of a feral kitten.

It was a practiced motion, shoving the mess of it back into the tidy corner of her heart where she kept all the things her mother had handed her that she didn't know how to hold. But this time, she found herself unable to get the spilled emotions to fit back inside.

She picked up the phone and dialed Sunrise Recovery. She gave her mother's information to the receptionist and waited while she was transferred to her mother's caseworker.

"Hello. Stephen here. You've called to check in on Ms. Peterson?"

"Uh. Yes." Actually, she'd called to lambaste her. To verbally shake the answers to all the whys burning inside her mind, but that seemed more detail than necessary.

"She is doing quite well," Stephen said. "We're pleased with the progress she's made so far. She successfully came through detox and has been participating in group and individual counseling sessions. She's compliant and invested in her treatment. We'd like to transfer her to our sister campus sometime next week. We feel she's ready to do some deeper work on the mental health front. We truly think she is on the path for some lasting change if she continues to remain as motivated as she is to get healthy."

"Oh. That's great." The news that her mother was doing well in her rehab collided with the anger thrumming inside Callie, like two converging waves that canceled each other out. No matter how much damage her mother had done, Callie couldn't escape the bond they shared. "Can I speak to her?"

The line was silent for several moments. "Hello? Stephen?"

The sound of a clearing throat came through the speaker. "Ms. Peterson's treatment notes indicate that she is now permitted phone communication, but your mother has declined that privilege at this time."

His words were like a stone dropped into her gut. "It's urgent that I speak with her. There have been some things coming up about her past—things connected to my childhood. I've been left with some weighty decisions to make with very limited information. My mother has that information. It's vital I speak to her." Callie gripped the chair in front of her again. Mom had refused to talk to her? The person who laid her dreams aside in order to make her recovery possible?

"I understand your need to ask your mother questions. I do,"

Stephen said. "But we are at a very precarious place in your mother's treatment right now. If you intervene before she's ready and your questions trigger a trauma response, it could set her back indefinitely. Please, trust our team of professionals to walk her through this. In due time, we have confidence that she'll be willing and able to open up to you."

"I understand," she said when what she wanted to do was reach through the phone and strangle the guy. To tell him that Lindy Peterson wasn't the only traumatized person here. That she'd left a string of trauma in her wake, and the people she'd affected deserved answers.

Callie ended the call and checked her watch. This week's therapy session sure came at the right time. Callie exited the house. On the short walk to Joanne's office, anger roasted her insides and the July heat parboiled her outsides. She understood what the guy was saying. Conceptually, anyway. But she needed to hear her mother's explanation before she could make her final decision. If her mother's husband owned that beautiful, serene place, why had Callie never been closer to it than the entrance to the driveway? Why did he want to give it to her now?

Her walk brought her past the storefront. It used to be a welcome part of the trip, a symbol of hope for better days. She sighed at its slightly forlorn ambiance. Tattered brown contractor's paper covered the windows, and bits of windswept litter cluttered the shallow alcove.

Despite the setbacks, she could still envision all it could be. A beautiful sign adorning the door. Airy and bright window displays beckoning customers inside, inviting them to a world of rest and relaxation, providing quality products that would soothe mind, body, and soul. Her at the helm. Walking the floor, greeting customers, describing the benefits of the various herbs and oils she used. Hosting "Make Your Own" Fridays where she'd teach small classes on soap- or candle-making.

A well-dressed man walked from around the side of her building. He perused the structure and typed something into his phone. She was about to call out to him, to see if she could help him, but he moved farther down the street, looking at the next building, making notes, and then moving to the next and doing the same thing.

Her phone rang in her pocket. "Hello?"

"Callie, this is Kate. I've been trying and trying to reach Chris since he hung up on me that night, and I've decided that I'm just going to show up on his doorstep this weekend in hopes that he won't turn me away. I wanted to see if you'd like to come with me. I asked Beck, but you can guess how she responded."

Gaze still following the man inspecting the buildings, she nodded. "Yeah. Sure. I'll come. I tried getting in touch with Mom, but that was a no-go. For the foreseeable future, it sounds like Chris is my only hope of getting some answers. I feel I can't make the right decision unless I better understand why George wanted me to have this place and what he'd wanted me to have done with it."

# THIRTY-ONE

*W*hat's wrong, Beck?" Fern peered at the frame of the honey super Beck held.

"I would have expected to see more capped honey by now." Beck returned the frame to its proper place within the hive. "They haven't even drawn out wax on the ones on the end. This hive was thriving two weeks ago." She sighed. "The nectar flow is in full force. They've usually produced more by this time of year."

"Nectar flow?"

"All the flowers are in bloom. There is a high food supply out there. They should be thriving." Beck pulled out one of the outer frames of the super, then pointed to fresh bright-white wax hexagons on the center of the frame. "See how they've made only a little bit of the honeycomb and they haven't finished this frame or started filling it? I was expecting to add another honey super today because they would be out of storage space the way things were going."

"What's wrong?"

"Nothing I can see. The queen is busy and laying. The population seems good in the hive as far as I can tell." If Dad were here, he would know what was amiss. He always had a way of figuring out issues before they became issues. She closed up the hive and went to the next one in the row slated for today's inspections.

It looked much the same as the last. Three others were dealing with hive beetle infestations. Though they were a pest common to weaker hives, the ones she'd found them thriving in had been the strongest in that field. She closed it up, moving slowly and fluidly, doing what she could to make sure none of the bees darting in and out of the opened hive were smashed.

Beck unzipped her veil and let the hat fall against her back. She helped Fern do the same. They both breathed a sigh of relief when a breeze kicked up, ruffling their sweat-dampened hair.

After a few moments' rest, she and Fern hiked back to the UTV, their arms loaded with supplies.

Fern set the supply box on the flatbed and then pushed her hair out of her face. "Oh, I forgot to tell you that Uncle Ike said he was bringing dinner over when he comes. There's this new restaurant in town, and he thought you might like it."

Beck smiled. "That's thoughtful of him."

Fern and Isaac were good company. Fern had a way of making her forget all the things that could go wrong. And Isaac had a way of making her believe that things could go right. Tonight was definitely a good night for distraction after Aunt Kate called earlier, inviting her on a trip to see Uncle Chris—a trip she could not force herself to take no matter how curiosity pulled at her.

Fern clattered about beside her, gathering their hive tool and smoker, causing Beck's thoughts to whirl back to the issues in the apiary.

Trials came with the territory—mites, beetles, wax moths, bad weather—all things she was accustomed to battling. But nothing seemed to be thriving the way it should this season. The things going wrong just didn't fit with what she'd experienced in the past.

Maybe there was something to her father's superstitions after all. The bees knew she was an imposter, an apprentice trying to play the role of a master beekeeper. Her plan had been to prove to Callie that the farm could produce more than in the past. Not less.

"He likes you too, you know."

"Huh?" Her heart stutter-stepped in her chest, thrust from her deep concentration by Fern's gleeful declaration. She'd lost track of the last things she'd said aloud. Had she ever hinted that she liked Isaac? Surely not. At least not in the way Fern's wiggly eyebrows implied.

Beck walked around to the back and stowed the smoker and toolbox in the cargo area of the vehicle, trying to figure out how to respond.

Fern skipped after her. "I heard him talking on the phone to Dad about you. He said you were smart and hardworking."

"Hang on." Beck propped her hands on her hips. "He was talking to your dad? The same guy you told me died?"

Beck didn't think it possible for Fern's little cheeks to grow any redder than they had working the hives in the mid-summer heat, but they sure did. The little girl stared at the ground and mumbled, "I'm sorry I lied. Lying is wrong. I know it's wrong."

"Why did you? It was a cruel thing to say." Beck had decided to leave the topic alone and let her uncle handle it, but since the door had been opened, it felt right to step on through it. "Your uncle told me the truth a couple weeks ago."

Fern's bony shoulders slumped. "I was so mad at Mom and Dad. And . . . and scared. I didn't like my real life, so I made up one." She looked up and smiled tentatively. "Being an alien from another planet sure was a lot more fun than what was real. It was just pretend." She sobered again. "But I knew your dad had died, and I shouldn't have made up that lie." Her eyes watered. "'Cause no matter how mad I was at them, I'd be sad if they died, Beck. I'd be sad like you."

Beck stepped forward and pulled her into a hug. "I forgive you. But no more lies, okay?"

Her eyes went wide. "I'm not lying about Uncle Ike liking you. Promise."

Beck laughed under her breath. "That was a nice compliment for him to give. But it was just him being kind." She pulled off her gloves and tossed them in the back and then helped Fern wiggle her sweaty fingers free.

The little shapeshifter's somber expression melted away like wax under a blistering sun, and she grinned triumphantly. "You didn't see the gooey look in his eyes or hear the way he said it." Fern narrowed her eyes like a sly little fox. "And he said you were pretty."

Whew. She needed to put the brakes on this before she became Fern's next scheme. She unzipped the front of her protective suit and slid the top half off her shoulders. The tank top she wore underneath was plastered to her skin. She slipped her feet from her boots and stepped out of the suit. Tank tops and shorts were far more comfortable on a hot summer day.

"I think your uncle is smart and hardworking too, but—"

"And handsome?" Fern batted her eyes.

"Sure. But two people can admire each other, think that each other are great, but that doesn't mean they should start being boyfriend and girlfriend."

"You want to be boyfriend and girlfriend?"

Beck ground her teeth. The little stinker and her willful misunderstanding. No telling how she'd recount this conversation to Isaac later. "That is not what I said, and remember you just told me you were going to work on the lying thing. No matchmaking allowed, Fern. Besides, you guys don't even live here."

Fern pouted. "Nashville isn't that far away."

It might as well be the moon. "It's complicated. You can write that down in your research notebook."

Yep. Complicated was the right word for it.

She'd had a few bouts of loneliness over the years. Moments in time in which she wondered what it might feel like to be in love. But then she'd think of her mother and father . . .

"I hate that word." Fern kicked at a stick on the ground.

Beck brought herself back to the present. "What word?"

"*Complicated.* Grown-ups say that all the time to get out of talking about things they don't want to talk about."

Beck choked back a laugh to keep from earning another Fern glare. "All right, kiddo, our work is done. Creek time?"

Fern punched the air. "Yes. Best part of the day."

Beck grabbed the UTV's roll bar to climb in. A pain shot through her hand. She sucked air through her teeth and held her hand in front of her face.

"What happened? Are you okay?" Fern leaned across the seat to look.

Beck stared for half a second at the stinger embedded in her skin, the venom sack still pulsing.

"Oh. You got stung."

Beck gently scraped the stinger free from her skin with her nail, careful not to squeeze the venom into her hand in the process. Finger throbbing, she followed the sound of frantic buzzing at her feet. The bee's ruined body lay on the ground.

"I'm sorry," she whispered. It was one bee from among her millions. Most would mock Beck's sentimentality over a bee with a six-week life span. They weren't pets, but she couldn't help it. Her careless hand placement resulted in a sting for her, but the loss of life for another.

"Does it hurt?"

"I'm fine. This is why I told you to be careful about where you put your hands when you are in the apiary," she said. "I wasn't focused and didn't take my own advice."

"The bee will die now?" Fern asked.

"Yeah."

"That's sad."

Beck nodded and cranked the vehicle and drove away.

If she could stack up all the hurt in the world and sort the kind inflicted with malicious intent from the hurt inflicted by carelessness, how would the two compare? Was there really any difference when the result was the same?

# THIRTY-TWO

The quick double-beep of the car horn outside pulled Callie's attention from the spreadsheet she was reviewing.

Kate.

She glanced at her watch. She was fifteen minutes early. So much for getting a little work done before they set out on this ill-conceived adventure.

She opened the door and immediately backstepped, startled by Luke standing on her stoop with two coffees and a paper sack from a local bakery. "Sorry. I was just about to ring your doorbell." He gave her a lopsided smile. "I brought you and Kate some road trip fuel. I figured that was her out there in the car, but since we haven't met, I didn't want to freak her out."

Callie warmed at his thoughtful gesture. She took the cup he held out and inhaled the comforting scent of espresso laced with vanilla, brown sugar, and cinnamon. "Mmm. One of my favorites."

He shrugged. "I try to pay attention. A couple cinnamon bites are in the bag to go with it. They'll be a little easier to eat on the road than a full-size roll. So, how are you feeling about the ambush?"

She took a bracing sip. "As good as I can. At this point I just need some answers. No matter how awkward or painful they might be."

"And if there are none? Have you had any resolve about what to do?"

She blew out a long breath. "I've been taking your advice. I really have. But no answers to those prayers yet. I keep trying to trick Joanne into telling me what she thinks I should do." She gave him a wry smile. "But unfortunately she's good at what she does, and she's a firm believer that the goal of our sessions is helping me process rather than her telling me what to do."

He squeezed her shoulder. "Hang in there."

She couldn't help but wish that he'd pull her close and that gentle but firm squeeze could envelop all of her. But they remained side by side—in limbo—waiting for something to tip them into full relationship status or firmly into the friend zone. She'd like to read his mind and see which way he was leaning.

She gestured to the waiting car. "Want to meet Kate?"

After brief introductions, Kate and Callie were on the road to Valdosta, Georgia.

Kate was quiet while she navigated the streets until she merged onto the highway. "Luke seems like a nice guy. How long have you two been together?"

Callie shook her head. "Oh, we're not . . . we're friends." She drowned her stumbling words with a gulp of her cooled coffee and a cinnamon bite.

Kate laughed. "He brought you coffee and carbs and came to see you off. And to meet me. To measure me up, I think."

"Friends do that. They do . . ."

Kate smirked.

"Don't they?" In truth Callie had no idea. Friends were something she'd never been able to afford—not the kind who knew enough about her life to even have questions to ask.

Kate chuckled. "Maybe if that friend was a girl. Guys are usually only that thoughtful if they are at least a little bit in love."

Callie swallowed hard. "Love?"

"At the very least, seriously interested."

"We've known each other for about a year. We go to the same

church. Have booths next to each other at most markets. We've even kind of confessed that we're attracted to each other. But that's as far as it's gone." She sneaked a peek at Kate's profile. "I don't know how to do this whole relationship thing. I've tried dating in the past, but just when things start to feel steady, I bail. Every time. I end it before I'm the one who gets dumped. And . . . and I don't want to do that with Luke. He's too important to me."

Her heart pounded in her chest at this admission. For a girl who'd been raised to believe that showing someone the truth of your life could cause you to lose everything, she sure had jumped off the deep end recently. With Luke. Beck. Kate. She sucked in a breath through gritted teeth. Joanne would be proud.

Kate nodded slowly. "So you love him too."

Callie choked on the coffee she'd just tipped back.

"Don't croak on me. Is it so hard to admit?"

"I don't want to lose him."

"Sure. And I think his presence and patience shows that he feels the same way about you. You've got a good one there."

"I just want to get to the place where I'm good enough for him." Her voice cracked, the emotion welling in her chest like a shock of cold water on bare skin.

"Callie, honey, I've only known you for a short while, but the fact that you didn't sign that paper and put that farm on the market before my brother was cold in the ground speaks volumes to me. You didn't know him or Beck from Adam, and yet you've treaded softly and sought the truth. I'd say Luke is just as blessed as you are."

Callie released a heavy sigh. "I'm not like my mom." She gazed out the passenger window, watching the city disappear in the car's sideview mirror. "I've built a business, and I have a place to live. I don't drink. I don't use drugs. I pay my bills on time." Even if it had half killed her and she had to work through the night lately to make up for Mom's expenses and her time spent at the farm, all her responsibilities were handled. "But I still feel like I'm going to mess this up with Luke."

Kate patted her knee. "I know you're not like her. But no wonder you don't know how to have a relationship with Luke. The only thing you ever watched your mother do was leave."

⌒⌒⌒⌒

A little after noon, they took the Valdosta exit off of Hwy 75.

Kate played classical music that lulled Callie's thrumming nerves. Their drive was punctuated by small talk and questions about Chris.

Callie had tried hedging Kate into a corner, nudging to see which of the brothers she thought at fault for the rift in the family, but the adoring little sister had no answer other than to blame Lindy.

She wanted to stick up for her mom, to tell Kate that her mother may have made a mess of things, but George and Chris had a choice on how to react to it all. But knowing the kind of deep and lasting hurt her mother had the power to inflict without intending to, she wasn't sure she deserved that defense.

Kate parked in front of a white craftsman-style house, one of many in the well-maintained subdivision. The two-stall garage was open, and a car took up each space. Kate turned off the engine. "Oh good. Looks like he's home. You ready?"

Ready? Ready to drop in unannounced on the man who might be her father. Or at the very least have some information on why her life had been turned upside down lately. She swallowed back the nerves jumping in her throat. "Yeah. Sure."

When they reached the end of the short sidewalk, which seemed a mile long, Kate rang the doorbell. A very pretty blond woman who looked to be in her midfifties answered. "Kate!" She pulled her into a hug. "It's so lovely to see you. Chris didn't say anything about you coming down. I'm sorry we didn't make it to the funeral." The woman dropped her voice and muttered something that sounded like an excuse. She pulled back from the embrace, eyes widening as she noticed Callie. "Oh, hello."

Kate turned and tugged Callie closer. "This is Callie. She's a . . ."

This was about to get awkward.

"Friend." Kate motioned to the woman. "This is Heather, Chris's wife."

Callie let out the breath she'd been holding and extended her hand.

An odd expression crossed the woman's face as she no doubt tried to work out why Kate and a friend would make such a long drive and show up unannounced. Heather clasped Callie's outstretched hand and gave it a gentle squeeze. "I'll go fetch Chris. He's out back mowing. You can wait for him in the den."

She led them into a room furnished in oversized leather couches with a huge stone fireplace centering the largest wall. "Make yourselves comfortable. Can I get you anything to drink? Sweet tea? Water?"

"I'll have a glass of tea," Kate said.

"Nothing for me, thank you." Best see if Chris was going to oust her from his home brandishing one of the ornate iron fire pokers displayed next to the fireplace before she accepted any offers of hospitality.

Time ticked by on the antique clock on the mantel, and Callie began to wonder if he'd made a run for it after hearing that the sister whose phone calls he'd been avoiding had come knocking.

Twenty minutes later, he appeared in the entryway to the den. Heather lingered at his shoulder with a glass of tea for Kate.

Judging by the high color in her face, Callie was willing to bet she and her husband had had words.

"Sweetheart, give us a few minutes, please." His tone was kind, but the raspy quality of his voice surprised her. The familial relationship to George was evident, but Chris was taller and broader. The lines of his face more angular.

Though Annette had described George as a bookish teenager,

Callie hadn't been able to see that version of the farmer until now. If she mentally rewound the years on both those men and turned them back into boys, she could see how George might look slight and bookish next to his twin.

Heather pursed her lips and left the room after handing the tea to Kate. Chris's eyes had been locked on his sister since he'd walked in. He finally glanced Callie's way and then immediately jerked his gaze back to Kate like the sight of Callie had burned his retinas.

He'd seen what George Walsh had seen when he'd met Callie at that market. But whatever emotion the sight of her inspired in Chris, it was the opposite of naming her in his inheritance.

Still looking at Kate, he said, "This her?"

"This is Callie, Lindy's daughter."

"Why did you bring her here?" If those cold, soft-spoken words were able to cut through flesh, she'd have bled all over his beige carpet.

"I tried calling, Chris." Anguish crumpled Kate's proud features. "For goodness' sake, we lost George. I needed you." Her voice broke over those last words.

Callie blinked hard, caught off guard by the rush of emotion she felt on Kate's behalf.

He jabbed a finger Callie's direction. "She's not here because you need me. You brought her here for another reason." He cursed under his breath. "This is about the trust, isn't it? I didn't hear from him for years and then all of a sudden George started leaving me all these messages about finding the truth about that summer. About a baby. Something about wanting to make things right. I'm not playing his game. Leave me out of it."

Kate set her tea on the table with a clank and stood, stepping between Chris and the exit. "What game? Sit down and explain."

"And waste my breath? It's clear you believe his cockamamie story. He's poisoned you against me. I swear on my life that I am not that girl's father."

"Did you talk to George before he died? Did he tell you anything?"

"No. I wasn't letting him drag me back thirty years to his unfounded accusations." Chris paced the floor. "It didn't matter how many times I told him I was never with Lindy like that, that idiot wouldn't believe me. I don't know what guy she was running around with behind both our backs, but she wouldn't fess up. Lindy told George she was pregnant and then wouldn't say another word. Acted like a deer in headlights. Then she up and left town without telling a soul where she was going, and George never forgave me for it."

Kate stepped closer to Callie. "Slow down, Chris. He named Callie in his trust. Do you know why?"

"Oh, I know why. He found out Lindy hid the baby from him, the baby he'd convinced himself was mine. So he decided that his final act on earth would be to rub my face in the mess he thinks I left. Since I wouldn't claim the child, he's done it. That fool was so bent on trying to make me look like a jerk to the rest of the world that he ended up being the jerk. Cheating his own daughter out of an inheritance just to make a point. Unless . . ." He shook his head and rubbed at the place between his thick brows.

He sank into the oversized chair. "I always kinda wondered if it really was George who got Lindy in trouble but couldn't make himself admit it. He was the one always mooning after her. Walking her home every day. Tutoring her. I shouldn't have asked her to prom knowing the way he felt about her, but George didn't act like he was ever going to get up the nerve to do it and he'd ticked me off about something. I can't even remember what it was now. I asked her just because I could. But there was never anything between us. We weren't intimate. Didn't even kiss."

He fixed his gaze on Callie. Though his voice was cold, the sorrow in his eyes made her wonder about the man who sat across the room from her. "I'm sorry if you came here looking for a daddy, kid. 'Cause it ain't me."

# THIRTY-THREE

*I*saac stood at the kitchen counter, unpacking foil containers from a bag. A repeat supper after Beck had raved about the flavors from their takeout from a new Mediterranean eatery in town a few nights before. She'd never cross an ocean, but maybe she could become a little more adventurous in the kitchen. Experience more of the world from the comfort of her home.

Today had been her turn to introduce him to a new realm by giving him his first venture into the beeyard. She smiled, recalling his simultaneous awe and contained terror. Mingling with the joy of sharing this experience with Isaac had been the sting of seeing another man wear her father's gear.

Fern skipped into the house, letting the door slam behind her, jerking Beck from her musing. "Ms. Annette is here, and she brought chocolate cake!" She bounded right back out again.

Isaac turned to her and smiled. "Does Annette come often?"

Beck pushed a strand of hair away from her face. "Since Dad died, she's come over a few times a week." She pinched her chin between her index finger and thumb. "More than when Dad was alive. Which has been kinda weird."

"Were the two of them close?"

Beck retrieved three forks from the drawer. "Over the past few years, they'd gotten in the habit of eating Sunday lunch together. They were friends. Dad was always bringing home some dessert she'd made." Beck looked out the window. Had it been her standing in the way of the two of them being closer? The few times Dad invited Annette over, Beck hadn't exactly been warm company. Dad probably hadn't offered repeat invitations if he suspected Beck felt intruded upon. How many times had he stepped in to save her at the expense of himself?

Isaac grabbed a stack of plates from the cabinet, four instead of the three they needed. "She must really miss him. Maybe being here helps her feel close to him."

Annette walked into the kitchen with a towering cake on a crystal stand balanced precariously in her hands. Fern followed behind with sparkling eyes, probably giddy at the hope of ingesting all that sugar.

"Let me help you with that." Beck took the cake and set it on the sideboard.

"I saw Fern and Isaac at the grocery store yesterday evening, and she told me about y'all's plans. I thought you might need some sweets to go with supper."

Beck reached deep for words she'd had little practice saying. "Stay and eat with us. We have plenty." She got out another fork and glass.

Annette glanced from Beck to Isaac and back. "Oh, I couldn't possibly impose." A loneliness flashed in her expression for a moment, and then she vanished it with a wide smile and a flick of her hand. "I didn't come over here to intrude. Honestly, I just wanted to surprise Fern." She motioned behind her. "Besides, Bea is in the car."

Beck placed the fork and glass with the others. "Bring her in. I know Fern has been dying to play with her more. Just let me make sure Henrietta hasn't snuck in. I'm pretty sure a house dog and a house chicken won't mix."

◇◇◇◇

Annette stayed and brought in her domino set. They played at the kitchen table late into the night. So late that Fern and Bea gave up on them and fell asleep curled on the couch in the living room.

Eventually, Beck left Isaac and Annette debating the finer points of chicken foot dominos and went into the living room. She pulled a patchwork quilt from the back of her father's recliner, then carefully tucked it around Fern and Bea. The pug snorted and grunted as she wiggled tighter under Fern's chin. Fern with her wise-soul eyes shut tight looked so, so young sleeping with a smudge of chocolate frosting on her nose. Beck brushed a stray hair from the child's cheek.

Noise. Laughter. Games. All fueled by chocolate cake. How different this night had been from any in her memory.

She pictured her father flipping through the latest *Tennessee Farmer* in his leather recliner. She'd be sitting on the floor beside the coffee table clipping coupons or folding a load of laundry on the couch. Two people quietly closing out their day.

Her life had completely changed in the weeks since her father's passing. So much of it uncomfortable. And yet there had been this burgeoning feeling of life in it. Like the bustle inside of a thriving hive.

Her throat tightened at the comparison. What she and her father had been doing was not so much living as it was waiting. She hadn't recognized it until now.

Why had it taken his death to bring this shift in Beck's life? He hadn't been the recluse. She had.

Beck walked to the picture window that overlooked the field they let grow tall with wildflowers. The silhouettes of flowers danced in the dark, tossed by the breeze.

She reached into her pool of memories, stretching through time, searching for an answer to a question she'd yet to fully form. Her father the executive at the hometown bank quit his job and became a full-time homesteader. He built a world for Beck where she never had to fear. Sheltering her from all the things he thought her too fragile to handle.

And maybe she was fragile, like the gossamer wing of a honeybee. But hadn't he seen? Hadn't he known? Those gossamer wings could carry a bee for miles and miles, transporting a load that far exceeded its body weight.

He'd protected her instead of allowing life to test her strength. He had been the walls keeping the world's onslaught at bay. Without him here, life had trickled in, seeking her out. Fern. Isaac. Annette. Kate. Callie.

"Beck?" Annette's chipper voice called from the kitchen. "A consensus has been reached. I was right. He was wrong. As if I don't know my domino rules."

Isaac made some unintelligible comeback that set Annette to giggling.

Beck grinned.

"Are you going to join us?" Isaac called.

Beck turned away from the shadowed world beyond the glass. "Yeah. I'll join y'all for the next round."

She wasn't exactly hankering to pack her bags and set out on a grand adventure, but there was still time to choose a life with fewer walls. If she let more people into her world, might it help her learn how to step into theirs?

She reentered the homey kitchen. What an odd trio they made— the agoraphobic beekeeper, the financial advisor parenting a troubled child for the summer, and the casserole connoisseur mourning the loss of a man who hadn't had the heart space to love her back.

They laughed more that night over raucous rounds of chicken foot dominos than Beck suspected any of them had laughed in weeks.

When they disbanded, it was closer to dawn than dusk.

Isaac carried a comatose Fern to the car, her long, skinny legs swaying with this stride. The girl snuggled her head against his chest. The sweetness of Isaac carrying this little girl who was just a little too old to be carried caused a softness to bloom in Beck's heart. That softness must have found its way to her face, because Annette leaned close and whispered, "Dear one, don't be afraid to love him if you want."

Beck's face heated. She didn't know Isaac enough to love him, but she had seen enough to admire the person he was. She took the now-empty cake stand from Annette's hands and walked her to her car.

Annette paused with her hand on top of the door. "I wasn't around in the years George was married to Lindy, and I don't know how it must have been for you as a child, losing a mother in that way. Seeing the pain loving her caused him. But love is not always like that. It's not supposed to be like that. I might not have been able to convince your father to take another chance on love, but I hope I can convince you."

Beck gave her a tight smile and nod, forgoing the explanation of the impossibility of a relationship with Isaac. Instead, she said, "Dad loved you. Maybe not the way you would have liked him to. And I'm sorry if I wasn't always as welcoming as I could have been when he was alive. Letting someone else into that world didn't just scare him. It scared me too. I didn't want to see someone leave him again."

Annette's smile was sweet, though the sorrow in her eyes cut deep. "I loved him as much as he'd let me, and he loved me back with what he had to give. That can sometimes be enough. It was for me."

Beck stood in the dark, left with nothing but her thoughts to keep her company as the two cars pulled away.

No matter what Annette said, the pain in her eyes did not lie. And Beck couldn't help but wonder if it really was worth it—to love more than you could get back in return.

# THIRTY-FOUR

Callie popped in her headphones and dialed Beck's number. She'd promised to call and update her on the trip to visit Chris. She resumed stirring her latest batch of ingredients, enveloped in the invigorating scent of her lime-and-coconut salt scrub.

The phone rang in her ear.

The past month and a half had certainly taken her on a journey she never could have imagined. How weird was it that she had an hours-long heart-to-heart about Beck's father with the uncle Beck had never met?

"Hello? Callie?"

"Hey, Beck. This a good time?"

"Yep. I'm just watching Fern pick wild blackberries as we speak."

"How much longer are she and Isaac staying in Sweetwater?"

The line went quiet, and Callie could hear Fern chattering in the background. "I think until she goes back to school in the fall." There was a hollowness in Beck's tone, and no wonder. Besides her father, who else had Beck had in her life?

Callie knew just how hard an isolated life could be. Whether trying to remain invisible in the crowd like Callie had been or alone on sixty acres with only bees for company, alone was alone.

"So, Uncle Chris actually let you inside?"

Callie raised her brows. "More like Kate stuck her foot in the door and refused to move it."

"And? Did he shed light on anything? Aunt Kate called me on her drive back to Asheville, but she wouldn't say a word about what had happened. Said you'd call me when you were ready to talk about it." Beck's tone carried resignation rather than the anticipation Callie expected.

"Bottom line, he says that your dad thought Chris was my father, so he thought Chris should have taken responsibility for me. Chris thinks he named me in the trust to rub it in his face. To prove once and for all that he was the better man. He seemed to think George learned something new before he died, but Chris ignored his calls, so he doesn't know."

Callie listened for some sign of life on the other end of the line. "Beck? Are you still there?"

Her voice came through the line, scratchy and quiet. "He wouldn't do that. Dad wouldn't put me through this just to make a point. He wouldn't."

Callie reached for a response. To tell her that Chris had a far different impression of the man Beck idolized seemed too cruel a statement. "Chris says he's not my father. He said he wonders if George was my father all this time and just didn't want to own his own choices. That he wanted to project it onto someone else."

"That can't be true. That doesn't sound like him at all."

Callie let out a breath. "But we didn't know him back then."

"You didn't know him at all. Ever."

She jerked her head back at the sudden chill in Beck's tone. "You're right. I didn't. And I am trying to figure out why."

"If you were my father's child, Lindy wouldn't have kept you away. And he would have wanted to do right by you."

"But if she didn't tell him I existed—"

"That makes no sense. Do you hear yourself?" Beck's voice rose and grew high-pitched.

Did Beck hear herself? Callie had never heard her so unhinged, not even in the midst of that first panic attack. "I'm not trying to hurt you. I just want to understand why George named me in that trust so that I know what to do."

"You're looking for justification so you can sleep a little bit better at night after you sell my home out from under me. You don't care if you have to drag my memory of my father through the mud to do it. You just need a story to believe."

There was a part of Callie that wanted to roar back at the pampered beekeeper who had been sheltered away from all that was cruel in the world. Sheltered from a broken mother who wreaked havoc on every life she touched. She knew what it was to wish with all her heart that a parent was better than what they were.

But that wild part of Callie knew how to be tamed. To quiet and to retreat. She pushed her roaring emotions back into their tidy boxes so that she never showed her pain. Barely even felt it, for that matter. There was nothing more they could say at this point. All they had to go on was hurt and speculation.

She massaged her temple. "I'm sorry. I need to go. I have an appointment to get to. I'll let you know as soon as we are free to speak with our mother."

"Did you decide?" Beck's voice came softer now.

Callie blew out a breath. "I'm stopping by the trust company to sign everything later today."

"You're accepting my dad's inheritance?"

"Beck, there's still time to learn more and plan together. But for whatever reason, George wanted me a part of this, and I'm not ready to walk away until I learn what that reason was. Have you signed?"

"Of course. There was never any doubt if I had a right to my farm."

The cocktail of hurt and anger in Beck's voice left an acrid taste in

Callie's mouth. Maybe it was wrong to pretend she had any right to make decisions about Walsh Farm, but it was irresponsible to throw something away before she understood why it had been handed to her.

⬡⬡⬡

Inside her therapist's spacious office, Callie settled in her favorite chair, the plush one in the corner that hugged her when she sank into it.

Joanne sat across from her, placing her notepad and pen on the side table. She clasped her hands and leaned forward. "We talked last time about your decision with the trust money, and I know you were feeling conflicted with your limited information." Joanne left the thought hanging, waiting.

Callie blew out a breath and then relayed the trip with Kate and what little she'd learned from Chris. She told her about her mother's continued refusal or inability to speak to her, then shared how angry Beck was because Callie had decided not to relinquish her portion of the trust.

Joanne held up a hand, stopping her stream of words. "Let's pause right there for just a moment. You've given me a lot of facts about what's happened since we last met. Take me deeper, Callie. Tell me how you've been coping in light of everything going on. How is this affecting you?"

"I . . . um . . ." Callie bit down on her lip. The room throbbed with silence. "I think I made a mistake keeping the portion of the trust George gave me."

"Okay. Thoughts are good. Now tell me what you feel."

Callie squeezed her eyes tight and swallowed hard. "I feel like a terrible person. I feel like Beck didn't deserve what her father did." Callie's hands began to tremble, and she shoved them under her thighs. "Even though I still don't know if George was my father, and even

232

though selling the farm could make everything so much easier for me, Beck doesn't deserve to worry about losing the farm just because I'd like to use my portion to pay for Mom's rehab. I can survive without a shop. I've been doing fine with the online side of things. It's selfish for me to take something she needs to get something I want. I can work harder, get another job if I need to. It will be a stretch, but I have it in my power to give her what she needs, so that's what I should do."

"Callie?" Joanne's gentle voice broke through her rapid stream of words. "Are we still talking about Beck here?"

Callie's eyebrows shot high. Joanne had followed her down many a rabbit trail without ever losing the train of thought. "Yes."

Joanne nodded slowly, her thumb pressed to her lips. She shifted back in her seat. "It's just that you've used those exact words before." Compassion filled her gaze. "About your mother."

Callie sucked in her breath, wanting to deny it. To tell Joanne that she was wrong. "Beck is nothing like Mom. Nothing. She's got issues, but she's strong and capable and works hard."

Joanne folded her hands in her lap. "I hear you. I hear the emotion in your voice that my statement raised. Hang in there with me and let's explore this more. Then you can let me know if I'm completely off base.

"We've talked a lot about truth and lies in our conversations," she continued. "Let's start there. The truth is, your mother is responsible for her own actions and her decision to get help. Beck is a grown woman responsible for herself and her livelihood, with or without her father's farm."

Callie shook her head, emotions tightening her throat. "Mom's actions made Beck dependent on that place. She's why Beck is agoraphobic."

Joanne nodded. "Sure. And we've spent a lot of time together discussing some of the scars you carry as a result of your mother's actions. You have taken financial, mental, and emotional responsibility for the wounds you carry. The question is, why are you running to save Beck and your mother? Who has come to save you?"

A hot emotion without a name spilled over her. "I don't need saving. I have everything I need. I can make this work. I have what it takes to be okay."

"If that is true for you, why is it not true for them?"

"I . . ." Callie dropped her head, studying the lines on her palms. "I am the person who fixes things. That's who I am and who I've always been. That's who God created me to be. To do anything else violates everything I am."

Joanne scooted to the edge of her seat, drawing nearer to Callie. "I am about to speak truth, Callie, and this truth may sting. We've had conversations that wade in the edge waters of what I'm about to say, but now it's time to dive all the way in, head underwater. Are you willing to go with me into an uncomfortable space?"

Callie drew in a shaky breath and nodded even though everything within her told her to flee.

"Your need to fix and to rescue is a trauma response from years of neglect and abandonment," Joanne said. "It is a result of having to be the parent and never being allowed to be the child. You've adopted your trauma response as part of your personality. Your very identity. When, in fact, it is a means of survival that you no longer need. You are now safe to let that go."

Her body shook as if it was going into shock. She wrapped her arms around her middle, crumpling. "I can't. I-I can't."

"Tell me why." Joanne's tender voice was like a caress.

Callie swallowed convulsively, fighting for control. "Because I don't know who I am if I'm not her. The one who makes sure everyone else is okay."

Joanne was still and quiet, allowing Callie's words to sink deep. After a few moments she said, "Would you allow me to tell you the person I see sitting in front of me?"

Callie nodded.

"You are a compassionate human being with wants and needs of your own. You said you have everything you need, but I want you to ask yourself if that statement is true. Are all your needs met? Or have you simply learned to make your needs so small that you can pretend they don't exist?"

Callie sat with her heart pierced clean through, unable to reply.

"For just a moment, forget your mother's needs and your difficulty discerning the difference between enabling and helping. Underneath it all, what do you want? What do you need? This is a safe space to be extravagant."

Callie closed her eyes tight, fighting to calm her racing heart. The image of the storefront shattered and fell like shards of glass in her mind's eye. The soaps and candles and images of a house with a nice yard and a dog faded. All that was left was a little girl standing in a darkened corner. Hungry and oh, so tired.

She blew out a slow breath and lifted her chin. The pooled tears that had gathered behind her tight-shut eyes fell in rivers. "I want . . . to not be alone." She swallowed back sobs, causing her throat to ache. "I know I'm strong and capable, but I also want to know that if one day my life fell apart, there would be people in my life able to catch me. Hold my hand. To tell me everything's going to be okay."

She grabbed a tissue and buried her face in it. Joanne asked for extravagant, and she'd given it. And it had almost nothing to do with what she'd been working so hard to achieve.

"Callie, I am incredibly proud of the work you just did. You've just uncovered a great space to begin some deeper work.

"When we're unable to identify our needs, we can't identify when our boundaries are being violated. It makes it nearly impossible to define healthy parameters with the people in our lives."

Callie reflected on the war that had been raging in her heart about the farm, Beck, and her mother's care. "I can't ever figure out if I'm letting people in too much or not enough. It seems safe to keep to myself, but that's not what I really want either. Not even with Mom."

Joanne nodded. "Trauma taught you how to build walls. But if someone starts knocking on those walls, you're not sure if you should tear them down or build them thicker.

"As we do some deeper work on naming your needs, then you get to install doors in those walls. And the beauty of a door is that you can open and close it as needed. The people who respect your doors are the people who are safe to let closer. They are the kind of people you can trust to hold your hand when everything falls apart."

# THIRTY-FIVE

*B*eck wasn't sure how long she sat with the phone still gripped tight before she lowered it to the table. Callie had waited so long to sign, Beck had started to believe she wasn't going to. It would have been the right thing to do.

This was Beck's land. Her inheritance from her father. Anyone could see that it was rightfully hers.

If not for Lindy, Callie probably would walk away. Lindy who had ruined her father's life, wrecked hers, and Callie's too.

She stood from the table and walked to the kitchen window, watching honeybees forage in the bee balm.

All bees were wild things, really. The keeper could make a hive as pleasant a place as possible, but in the end they had no real say if the bees stayed or went.

George Walsh could accept that truth about his bees, but not about his wife. Ever since she'd read her father's letters, Beck had become convinced that he was still trying to save Lindy from herself, even from beyond the grave. Leaving Beck vulnerable with a robber bee bombarding her safe haven, seeking to strip her of everything she'd constructed in order to survive.

Beck walked from the kitchen to the living room and roamed the hall. Everywhere she looked, that hyacinth logo stared back—candles, soaps, lotion bottles.

Had that been his intention? Every time he brought more of Callie's things home from the market, were those hyacinth logos an apology for what he was about to do? That flower sang out its apologetic refrain, echoing in the walls of her home.

She grabbed the trash can from the kitchen and climbed the stairs. In her bedroom, she dropped every hyacinth-labeled vessel into the bag. The crack of glass when the candles collided in the bottom, a satisfying cacophony.

As she worked her way from room to room, purging it of Callie's work, hurt and anger curdled in her stomach. She railed against the man who was not there to hear, struck by the realization that each bottle represented an interaction he'd had with Callie in which he'd come home and presented Beck with a gift in place of words.

He'd taken the time to contact the trust company to add this person to his irrevocable trust, but not once in their hours together had he breathed a word to Beck about Callie and Lindy.

Not once.

She'd thought she'd known the man like she knew the inner workings of a hive. Apparently she'd only known the bees, not their keeper.

In the kitchen, she continued the purge, tossing everything into the trash can. The words burning in her chest broke free. "Why? Why couldn't you have told me? Because you thought I'd shatter? Break?"

She threw a candle into the can. It sang out with a sharp crack on impact. "I'm not glass. You didn't have to cushion me. You didn't." But did she really believe that?

She threw another bottle into the can. "I don't want your apologies." She took a shaky breath. "I . . . I want you." Tears welled, clouding her vision. "I want you here with me. I want you to tell me what to—"

"Cleaning house?"

Beck spun to face the soft voice behind her.

Annette stood in the entrance to the kitchen, a blue pie plate in hand. Bea trotted in and sat at Beck's feet. "I knocked, but no one answered so I let myself in."

Beck swiped at her face.

Annette scanned the disarray Beck had created while clearing the kitchen of Callie's products. "My recipe makes two, and I thought I remembered your dad saying you liked my coconut cream pie."

She reached for it, accepting the extended pie plate. "Thanks." Her voice came out raspy. So often she'd viewed Annette as an intruder who claimed a closeness to her father that she did not deserve, using baked goods as the gateway into their lives.

But maybe Annette understood more than she gave her credit for. There was another person on the planet who understood what it was to love only a part of her father without being privy to the whole of him.

Bea balanced on her hind legs at Beck's feet, begging for attention as she served up two pieces. When both were plated, Beck scooped Bea into her lap and pushed her saucer back so that the pup wouldn't be tempted to sneak a lick.

"I tried talking to him about his marriage to your mother a few times." Annette slipped in a bite of her pie and chewed. Her gaze drifted skyward as if she could pull down answers from heaven. "Morbid curiosity, if I'm being honest." She laughed bitterly. "Not meaning to sound like a jealous schoolgirl or anything, but I never understood his connection to her. It was like an illness."

Apparently it had been a terminal one. Beck drew swirls in her whipped cream with the tines of her fork—cirrus clouds on her jadeite saucer. "Do you think she had something on him? Knew something he didn't want people to know?"

Annette smiled gently. "Your father hardly seemed a likely candidate to have a vault full of secrets."

Beck pictured her quiet father, his work-roughed hands, efficient yet graceful, working in the hives. His weathered face partially hidden under his favorite wide-brimmed hat. The quiet, steady cadence of his voice. Her memories were mere elements of the man—pieces she'd been allowed to see. "Maybe we never really knew him."

Annette reached across the table and squeezed her hand. "Honey, he was your father. You knew him in a way no one else did. That man would do anything for you. You know that."

"Do I?" Beck shook her head. "I literally have given my blood, sweat, and tears to this place. It's my home. And now some person is just going to claim half of it? She signed the paperwork, Annette. It's officially half hers."

"Callie seems a decent sort. There's worse people to be stuck with."

Beck stroked Bea's slick fur. "Worse than a girl who wants me to lose the last of what I have of my father to help the woman who abandoned me?"

"Beck." The gentle warning in Annette's voice nudged her heart back into check. "That proves my point, doesn't it? She's not a charlatan trying to grab quick cash. Think about all the time she's taken to come here, not to mention the long trip to visit your uncle. Doesn't that go to show she's interested in doing right by your father's final wishes? Not a one of us knows what he was thinking, but she's trying to understand. Not just take."

Beck balked at the hint of admonition in her tone. This wasn't about Beck trying to grab all that was due her either. Asking Beck to sell this farm was like expecting a fish to suddenly start breathing air instead of water. "I don't know how I can make it without this place. It's all I've ever known."

"Just because it's all that you've known doesn't mean that it is all that you are." A corner of her mouth lifted. "The farm is kinda like that suit you wear out in the hives. It's just a covering to help you feel safe from the stings. You could work your hives without a suit. It would just be more risky."

Beck shook her head. "You're trying to equate beekeeping without safety gear to living without the farm? No offense, but I don't think that translates." Bea snorted and shifted in her sleep as if in agreement.

"Well. Okay." Annette took another bite of pie, her brow furrowed. "What about this? Even your bees leave the hive. They do what needs to be done to survive. They could get lost. They could get trapped. They could be killed. But still they go. And they find their way back home. You can do that, too, in your new place, if it comes to that."

The sweet, earnest tone of her voice melted Beck's annoyance. She was trying to help. Trying to speak her language. "Do you know much about bees?"

Annette shook her head, sending her dangly earrings swaying. "Just what your father told me about them."

"He sure loved them, didn't he?"

Annette smiled softly. "He loved you. That's what he told me. That he loved the bees because you did." She blinked her watery eyes and reached for her hand again. "I can't promise I'd ever brave the hives for you, but I do want you to know that if you ever need anything, I'm here."

Just like her father had loved bees because of Beck, the emotion filling Annette's eyes seemed to hint that the care this woman felt for Beck sprang from her adoration of the man who loved the bees.

Beck walked Annette out to the porch and passed the pug into her arms. "Thank you. For dessert. For the company." More words followed, a thought only half formed before it slipped through the cracks of her fortress walls. "It helped . . . talking to you."

The woman smiled and dipped her chin. "Of course, dear. It's entirely my pleasure. Take care of yourself." Annette looked out over the farmland, her lips tight. "I don't know what to think about all this trust stuff. But George was a good man. I know he had good intentions. Right or wrong, I have faith that he made his decisions with your good in mind."

As Beck watched Annette's taillights disappear down the drive, she wished she felt the surety that Annette's words bore. But the more she learned, the more her father's actions seemed like a desperate reach for the woman he'd been unable to hold on to.

Beck returned to the living room and sifted through the stack of returned letters. She selected one that had become slightly yellowed with time. She ran her finger beneath the seal that had never been opened, then sucked in a breath as the paper sliced the crease in her knuckle.

Lindy,

It's been five years since the day you left.

Today I find myself replaying that last day with you over and over in my mind. I tried to convince myself it was like all the times before when you'd disappear and come back again.

All I could ever do was look for the signs that you were about to go. That subtle change in mood. The way you moved, almost like you were driven by something outside of yourself. The sweetness in your voice becoming forced.

With a hive on the verge of swarming, you can read the signs, but you never know the exact moment a hive will split. The only hope is to catch them before it's too late and make space for them. Convince them they can stay and thrive right where they are.

I would have made space for you. I wanted to.

I get your postcards. Even if there's no name and no words, I know they're from you. So I hope against hope that one day you'll open my letters instead of sending them back. Why else would you leave this bread crumb trail to lead me back to you?

Sometimes I write just to get the words out of my head, to try and dislodge the barbed stingers you left in my heart, still pumping

242

venom. But then again, there is part of me that wants to keep them there. Because the pain is a reminder of us, and I can never quite shake the notion that I deserve it.

But your girl needs you. She wakes in cold sweats, screaming for a mother who isn't coming. Fighting in her sleep to save you from beasts. To save a mother who won't be saved. Come back to her. Even if you can't stay, say goodbye.

But we'd rather you say hello.

Whatever it is that pulls you away, we can work it out. We can make it right. We can make space.

Come keep bees with me. You always loved the beehive my father kept. Their secret world. The way young bees would fly about the hive to orient themselves so that they always knew the way back home.

Beck loves them too. I hope it will help her. Seeing something leave and still be able to find its way back. But what she really needs is you. Come back home and show her that the world out there won't swallow her whole.

Forever Yours,
George

Beck sat back in her chair slowly folding the note, her index finger still throbbing from the cut. She'd thought the bees were something only she and her father shared. That they had been for the two of them. Maybe her father hadn't loved the bees because of Beck. He'd loved them because of Lindy. Over and over again, he'd tried and failed to lure the absconding queen bee back to her hive.

# THIRTY-SIX

*C*allie gave a tentative knock on the front door of the farmhouse. She hadn't meant to blurt out her decision to sign the paperwork over the phone yesterday afternoon. It was a conversation that was supposed to have happened today, sitting across from Beck so that she could see the care she had taken with this decision.

Not just care for her own interests or for their mother's but for Beck's too.

The raw vulnerability in Beck's voice had collided with her defenses and melted them away. The truth had come out of her mouth. Bald-faced fact, free of her normal compulsion to guard herself.

"Did you come to get another look at your new place?" That same broken voice sounded behind her.

Callie turned around. Beck stood in the doorway of the barn in her white suit, the veiled hat unzipped and hanging down her back. Her arms hung limp at her sides. Fern stepped out from behind Beck, hands propped on her hips, the sassy, pint-size defender at her post.

Callie walked closer. "I needed to talk to you."

"We covered everything yesterday, didn't we?" Beck's voice was hollowed out, as if she had stripped all emotion from the conversation, but Callie saw the fear in her eyes.

"I meant what I said. I don't want us making any firm decisions about how we'll handle the cotenancy. Everything is going to stay just like it is until I get a better understanding of your dad's intentions. Unless you want to make a change?"

Beck's shoulder's rose and fell with a heavy breath. "So, what did you drive all the way here for, then? I've got work to do." Though her words were clipped, she sounded more defeated than angry.

Callie worried her bottom lip between her teeth. "To tell you that to your face. And"—Callie swallowed hard—"because I found out this morning that I might have some of those answers sooner than I expected. Can we talk?"

Beck turned to Fern and said something Callie couldn't decipher. Then she stepped out of her suit and handed it to the girl. Fern nodded and headed for the honey house. Beck crossed the wide graveled parking area between the barn and the house, mopping her brow with a bandanna that had been hanging from her pocket.

"I've got some sun tea in the fridge." Beck walked past her into the house.

Callie followed behind, trying to think of a way to ease the chill between them.

Beck went to the fridge and pulled out a glass pitcher with lemon slices floating in the brew. Callie scanned the room. There was something different that she couldn't quite put her finger on.

Beck filled two mason jars with ice and tea, then passed one to Callie before stepping to the far end of the rectangular table and sitting.

One of Callie's large honey and hyacinth candles had once been at the center. One of her favorites.

She did another quick scan. That was the difference. Her products that had once been sprinkled throughout the room were missing. Not a one remained.

Callie raised her eyebrows. "Decide to clean house after yesterday's conversation?"

Beck ducked her chin. A taut moment passed before she lifted it again and took a long drink of her tea. Her mason jar reflected the redness rising in her cheeks. She sat the glass down with a thunk and let out a slow, heavy breath and then sat taller in her chair. "You said you had answers?"

"Mom's case manager called me this morning. She said that since transferring to the mental health center, Mom has been opening up in both individual and group sessions, making some positive strides. She expressed a desire to meet with me. She even told her therapist there are things she's ready to share about her past." Callie twisted a lock of hair around her finger until it was tight enough to make her fingertip throb. "I didn't really clear it with anyone, and I know what you'll say, but do you want to come with me? You deserve to hear what she has to say about George as much as I do."

"S-see her?" Beck's face pinched and her shoulders inched upward, like a person bracing for a blow. She shook her head slowly. "I-I'd never thought about seeing her again. It's like asking me if I'd like to climb in a car, drive to the North Pole, and meet Santa Claus. Or the tooth fairy. She's a figment from my childhood. A collection of fuzzy memories that I can't quite parse out what was real and what's imaginary."

What a sharp contrast to Callie's experience. She put her hand around the glass, leaving it there until the cold made her fingers ache. Every childhood memory contained the harsh reality of Lindy Peterson.

Beck shook her head and swallowed hard. "I can't. You know I can't. Even if I could, I don't think I want to see her. I have no desire to chase after the mother who left me."

Callie nodded. "I'll call you after we talk."

"Anything else?

Callie studied Beck, considering her indifference to this news that they would have answers soon. And then she understood. Beck didn't care to know the truth about George Walsh, because she already possessed the version of him she wanted—the true and good father. And she was either unwilling or unable to face any other alternative.

Callie, on the other hand, was well-versed in seeing the multiple sides of a person and learning to accept that coexistence between the two—the good and the bad. Though it was tempting to paint the woman who poisoned George's life—who fractured brother from brother, who abandoned both of her daughters in various ways—as the villain, Callie knew there was more to the woman who called herself their mother.

There had been moments. Tender, vulnerable, broken moments that revealed the woman who lived beneath the veil of disease. She could only hope that her mother was ready to talk about things. To heal. To address the roots of the problem, not just the poisoned weeds that sprouted at the surface.

Beck cocked her head, and Callie realized she'd never answered her. "That's all I came to tell you. I wanted to talk face-to-face instead of over the phone."

Beck narrowed her eyes.

Was there any way to get Beck to see her as ally instead of opponent? Not likely. Not when she believed Callie had the power to ruin her life with the stroke of a pen. "I meant what I said. I'm not looking to make any changes at the farm. And I'm going to honor George. And you. I'm not making a move without you on board for it."

Beck's brow furrowed. "And if your mother needs the money for rehab? You need the money? What then?"

Beck's refusal to claim ownership of their mother clanged against Callie's heart. "I . . ." Should she tell her about the other call she'd gotten that morning, the buyer for her storefront? The decision hung in front of her, swinging like the pendulum of a clock. Was this really what she wanted to do? Give up her business plan so that her mother would be cared for and George's estate remained in Beck's hands?

Should she lay all her cards flat before Beck?

Part of her wanted that freedom. And yet there was that old part that hung back. The part that said showing everything to someone made you too vulnerable. That it put them in a position to hurt you. Take from you. Expect more than you had to give. "I . . . uh . . ."

Beck huffed and rose from her chair. "Don't tell me you won't do anything without my blessing and then write in the fine print that you reserve the right to do whatever you think is best." She turned away and walked out of the room.

She'd tell Beck when her building sold, if she could actually make herself pull the trigger on the sale.

*Lord, can You provide a way out? A way where I can keep the building and Beck can keep her farm? And our mother can get the help she needs?*

Beck walked back into the room carrying the stack of letters that were returned to their envelopes and rebound with a rubber band. "Here. Take these to her. They're hers anyway. Maybe for once she'll have the courage to read them. To see the damage she's done and own it. I know at least some of these must have reached her. I found postcards she'd sent to him. No words. Just pretty pictures and her next address."

She wanted to tell Beck that the postcard pictures weren't real—that her mom might have sent George a beautiful print of the Grand Canyon, but the place they'd rested their heads was the back seat of mom's run-down car in some alleyway or on some acquaintance's couch.

Callie took the letters. She wouldn't give them to her mother though. Not yet. There was only so much a body could take at one time, and her mother already had enough explaining to do.

Beck's gaze flicked over her, and her mouth tightened. "The letter on the top is about you. The last one he wrote, I think. You should read it."

Callie's brows shot up. "Me?"

"Yeah. Not that it clears much up." Beck sighed and shrugged. "Listen, I have to go. There's bad weather forecasted over the next couple days, and I need to get some things done. I can't work the hives with even a hint of stormy weather. The bees hate it."

"Of course. I didn't mean to interrupt your work. I'll go." Callie headed to the car, the parcel in her hands too light to contain such heaviness.

As she walked, a little voice whispered, *Ask to stay. Ask to help. To venture into the hives that Beck and George loved so much.*

Honeybees, like Callie, seemed to be particularly skilled at survival. But unlike her, they were not solitary organisms, but parts of a whole.

Callie drove away, her mind thrumming, itching to read the letter. But she couldn't make herself open it until she was tucked safely inside her apartment.

Lindy,

It's been years since my last letter. You've made it abundantly clear that you do not want to hear any of the words I have for you, and I'm not real sure why I am writing now except that I'm desperate for answers.

Two months ago, I was in Chattanooga. Sometimes I get a booth at their Sunday farmers' market. It's a good way to get outside of life at the farm for a little while. As I looked across the crowd, I thought I was seeing a mirage. That my brain had finally become addled by the want of you. But she was no mirage, this new young woman working a booth. She seemed nervous, unsure of how to handle her friendly neighbor. It was like I had jumped in a time machine and gone back to me and you that first day I walked you to school, when I was first trying to find a way into your shuttered world.

Feeling slightly insane, I went over and introduced myself to this young woman who shares your last name. The weeks went by, and I kept on going to her booth with the excuse of buying things for my daughter.

Like when you and I were kids in high school, I watched as a friendship slowly unfolded between Callie and her booth neighbor. The guardedness gave way to laughter and jokes. And then there came the day in May.

Her birthday.

The boy brought her a cake with numbered candles, and I counted back the years and months. This girl, older than our Beck, this girl who had precisely the right number of years and months to match your disappearance that August. I'll never forget your broken whisper in my ear, telling me that you were pregnant. And I told you that it would be okay. That I would take care of you since Chris refused to. But still you ran.

This girl with your hair and eyes and build—where was she when you came back to me? Was she the "friend" you always left Beck and I to help?

I always thought you left because you craved the drink more than you craved Beck and me. I always wondered if I pushed too hard, because I hated what alcohol did to you, diluting all that is wild and wonderful in you into something that was numb and directionless. Was it my fault? Did I hold too hard of a line, forbidding alcohol in our home? In my attempts to help, did I push you away?

But now I'm left with a bigger question. Why would you not let you and me and Beck and your daughter be a family? We could have been. You know that, right? Why did you refuse our love?

When I first met you, I wanted to save you from the misery your father inflicted. But you wouldn't let me. Then I wanted to help save you from the mistake you'd made. And you wouldn't let me support you. And when you came back, I wanted to help you leave your addiction behind, and you wouldn't let me save you from that either. Why?

Please Lindy,
I need to understand.
George

Callie dried her eyes with the back of her hand. Maybe it should concern her, the way George Walsh had so closely watched her, but the sorrowful plea in the letter watered down any discomfort she felt at the scrutiny of this stranger.

She remembered the lifelong struggle Kate had recounted between George and Chris. Of each fighting for ground. How George felt weak and Chris strong. George had seen that same struggle in Lindy, a powerlessness to overcome her circumstances, and he'd tried to deliver her from it. He'd tried to lend his strength to her. But that had been a burden he was never meant to bear.

It was a hard lesson to learn—that you couldn't be the one to fill the holes in another person's life. Working through dysfunctional patterns, finding healthy coping skills, and letting God heal the wounds the past left behind, those were things you couldn't do for another person. No matter how much you wanted to.

Besides, the Lindy Peterson Callie knew had never sought salvation. Only a rescue. There was a stark difference between the two.

She released a soft sigh. There were so many gifts George offered with seemingly unhealthy motives, but his secondhand portrayal of her friendship with Luke was one gift from him that she could freely embrace.

She picked up her phone and dialed Luke's number. When he answered, she said, "Do you want to come over?"

# THIRTY-SEVEN

*W*hat did she want? Why was that woman back?"

Beck and Fern bumped across the terrain, extra honey supers and empty frames clattering in the back of the UTV.

Beck spared a glance in her little guard bee's direction. "Just to talk. She's not a bad person, Fern."

"She wants to sell your farm, doesn't she?"

Beck stopped the vehicle beside the field of hives. "I think she wants to do the right thing. It's just that her idea of the right thing and my idea may not line up, and to be honest, I find that a little scary. You know, not knowing what will happen next. Especially when it's something I really care about."

"I hate that feeling." She peered at Beck and blinked her wide brown eyes, the defensive child shapeshifting into a wise little owl. "My parents are probably getting a divorce. That's why I'm really with Uncle Isaac for the summer. Me being around was just too much."

Beck shook her head. "I don't think so, Fern. I bet they just wanted to keep you out of the thick of it. Parents do that."

Fern straightened. "They don't need to protect me."

Beck nodded, very familiar with that sentiment. "You are about the toughest person I know, but that doesn't mean you should have to deal with their grown-up problems. Kids shouldn't have to carry that."

Fern shrugged. "But sometimes they do."

Yes, sometimes they did. "Can't argue with that."

They hopped from the seat. "What's first, boss?"

"Well, we're supposed to have bad weather the next few days," Beck said. "The girls get a little cranky when you open up the hives when it's windy and damp. And if it ends up raining for several days, we'll get way behind on our inspection schedule, so let's try to get ahead today." Beck smiled. "And I thought we might do a partial honey harvest on some of our fuller hives, swap out some full frames of honey for some empty ones."

With bees, the working never ceased. It was their compulsion, their means of survival. Some creatures had teeth and claws. Others could flee to survive. Bees had their work. Though they could certainly sting, it was really the work that kept them alive.

"So . . ." Fern twirled the end of her braid. "Does that mean I get to take home some honey today?"

"We'll see how much time we have. Our first priority is checking as many hives as possible to make sure we don't see red flags that need to be immediately addressed."

It was strange how things could be appearing to go so right and suddenly take a turn in this secret world of bees.

Beck and Fern worked in companionable silence. Her little apprentice had gotten quite good at knowing Beck's next move. Without her saying a word, Fern would hand over a hive tool to loosen the propolis the bees used to fill any cracks and glue together the stack of boxes that formed their world. She'd pass full frames to Fern, who would then pass her an empty one to replace it. It was like a well-rehearsed dance, one in which her father used to take the lead and Beck would dutifully follow. It was nice having someone to share that rhythm with again.

Beck nudged Fern. "Did you know that bees dance?"

Fern passed her a hive tool to loosen a stuck frame. She eyed Beck doubtfully. "You're making that up."

"It's the honest-to-goodness truth. When a worker bee goes out and finds a prime location for nectar or pollen, she'll come and do what's called a waggle dance. She walks in a little pattern and wriggles her behind in a certain way, telling all her sisters which direction to go and how far to fly to get to the bee grocery store."

Sweat dripped down Fern's nose. "That's wild. I used to watch a single little bee drinking from a flower, and I had no idea what a big life she had. How smart she is. How she's a builder and a gatherer and a caretaker and a maker."

Beck smiled. "She is one of a million and one in a million all at the same time."

Fern let out a little sigh. "I'll miss this when I'm back home."

A knot formed in Beck's chest. "Yeah." This would become a lonely occupation without her bee-impassioned sidekick. An image of Callie flashed in her mind. Where did that desire come from? Did she want a common bond with this strange sister that went beyond a messed-up mother and an undesired cotenancy?

She pushed the thought away and laughed under her breath. Though she had no doubt Callie worked hard at what she did, she couldn't imagine her suited up in the high heat of the day, sweating through her undergarments to tend stinging insects.

A few hours later, they'd collected a super of honey, piecemealed from full frames in several different hives. Fern and Beck headed for the honey house with dusk slowly settling over them. "I bet your uncle is wondering where we've been. We're later than usual."

"Can he help us with the honey?"

"Oh, I don't know that we'll get to that tonight. It's pretty late, and I'm sure we've already kept him waiting." Beck took the wooded path and flicked on the headlights. "Honey will keep, you know. It's one of the few things in life that never spoils."

"Never?"

"As long as it isn't contaminated. They've found honey in Egyptian tombs that was still fit for human consumption. So, I'm pretty sure ours will keep until the next time you come over. Maybe on one of those rainy days we have coming up since we can't do too much out and about."

Fern sighed. "Well, okay."

"I can send you home with a jar."

She frowned and gripped the roll bar when Beck bounced over a rut. "That's okay. I wanted some I harvested."

"Soon enough we'll be bottling so much honey that you'll get sick of the sight of it," Beck told her.

"I will?"

"Probably not. I never get tired of it, anyway. It's like magic, the way the bees take nectar from flowers that fade so quickly and turn it into something that can last forever." It whispered of something beyond this temporal world.

Fern closed her eyes with delight, the breeze blowing tendrils of hair from her face. She looked like the taste of wildflower honey was already on the tip of her tongue.

Beck passed the house where Isaac sat on the porch steps, waiting. He lifted a hand and waved.

Fern called out, "Follow us to the honey house, Uncle Ike."

As soon as Beck parked, Fern leaped from her seat and ran around to the back of the vehicle, then she hoisted the box. Beck's eyes widened. There was more strength in her wiry limbs than she would have anticipated. A full honey super was heavier than it looked.

Isaac strode up.

"Come on, follow us. See what we got from the hives today." Fern tottered to the door, grunting, leaving them no choice but to follow and rescue her from the weight she carried. Beck opened the door, and Isaac lifted the box from her arms. "What do we have here?"

"Honey! And Beck is going to show us how to harvest it."

Isaac smiled as he followed them through the door. "Is she? That sounds fun."

"Oh, well . . . I . . ." Beck shrugged. "I told her another time. I'm sure you need to get going."

Fern skipped happily ahead of them. She pointed to a blank space on the stainless steel countertop. "Put it here."

Isaac set down the honey super. "Nothing urgent on the agenda. We can stay, if you really don't mind. Just say the word, and we'll bounce out of here if it isn't a good time."

A good time? Could there be a better time to have these people invading her life and distracting her from imagining the meeting that would occur between Callie and Lindy Peterson? The things that it could reveal about her father—if they could be believed. Knowing what Callie knew of Lindy, how did Callie see her as a reliable source about her father in the first place?

She picked up the heated knife she used to uncap the honeycomb, that broke the wax barrier and let the sweetness run free.

"Tonight is as good as any, I suppose."

# THIRTY-EIGHT

Callie and Luke walked through her Northshore neighborhood, killing time before her meeting with her mother. She loved how every house on the street was different from the next. Some were well-manicured and recently remodeled while others needed a little TLC. She walked, stepping over the cracks in the sidewalk like she had when she was a girl. She quickstepped, adjusting her stride to miss a weed-riddled crack.

Luke's brow lifted. "What are you doing?"

She shoved her hands into the pockets of her swing skirt. "You know that rhyme, 'Don't step on a crack or you'll break your mother's back'?"

He nodded. "Sure."

"I played my own version of that game growing up. When I'd walk home from school, I'd mince my way around every crack. It must have doubled my time getting home." She pushed a strand of hair from her cheek. "We always lived in places where there were a lot of cracks, and I convinced myself that if I made it the whole walk home without touching a single one, Mom would be okay that day. As I hopped and maneuvered, I imagined her standing at the stove, making dinner. The apartment already cleaned so I didn't have to do it." Callie smiled—a twitch of her cheek that wasn't borne of happiness but rather an attempt to defuse the ache in her chest. "When I inevitably arrived at our empty, dirty place, I'd convince myself that I must've accidentally touched a crack without knowing it. And I'd try again the next day, wanting to believe that something I did could somehow make a difference."

He reached for her hand and gave it a squeeze. When his grip loosened a fraction, she tightened hers, keeping him there.

Luke smiled and their hands swung with their stride.

She sighed. "It's hard to let that go, you know. The belief that I can somehow make it better. Fix it. That I have any measure of control over her addiction." She lifted her shoulders and let them fall. "I'm starting to realize that I'm still skipping over cracks in the sidewalk, but in a different way. I'm trying to take care of her rehab, knowing the whole time that no matter how much I invest, no matter how much I give up, I can't do the work for her. I can't make it stick."

"You're nervous about seeing her?"

"I think when I see her, I'll know. I'll be able to tell if something is different. If she can get better."

"You're different." He squeezed her hand again. "With me, at least."

She glanced his way, hoping he'd explain.

"The story you just told me. About the cracks. Weeks ago, you never would have shared that. You would have talked about your store plans or the last book you read. But just now you volunteered something real."

She nodded. "I've had God as my only safe place for a long time. The only shelter I could cling to. I'm trying to learn that some people are safe too." She narrowed her eyes at him playfully. "Don't prove me wrong."

He was quiet for a moment before he spoke. "I promise to do my very best to be safe for you."

They walked on for a while, her gaze tilted upward, enjoying the way the trees overhead gentled the harsh summer sunlight into golds and greens. Her hand remained tucked in his. She glanced at his profile. "How are you this good at being my friend? I'm a mess and you have this stable life with stable parents. But you always seem to understand."

"My life wasn't like yours, Callie," he said. "But that doesn't mean it was perfect.

"When I was born my mom had postpartum depression. That season was so hard on her and Dad that they actually decided not to have any more children. And then my sister took them by surprise when I was fifteen and Mom had to face it again." Luke focused his gaze ahead, a faraway look in his eyes.

"Watching my mom go through that affected me in a big way. My dad didn't handle it well, and I worried he was going to leave us. We finally had some family therapy sessions to help. If there is anything that I can be thankful for about that time, it's that it taught me how to be there for someone. As a fifteen-year-old, learning how not to take someone else's struggles personally wasn't easy to learn."

She gave him a wry smile. "So you're telling me the answer to how you're such a good friend to a mess like me is that you are, in fact, perfect?"

He shook his head, his expression serious. "I didn't want to tell you this before, but as things have progressed between us, I need to come clean. The last time I brought you coffee, I accidentally gave you my decaf."

She playfully smacked him on the arm. "Ugh. Be serious. Although . . . you drink decaf? That is a serious defect."

They strolled until it was time to meet her mother, walking the odd precipice between friends and more, somehow content to just be.

◇◇◇◇

The hallways of Sunrise Mental Health were warm, bright, and homey, not antiseptic and clinical as she'd pictured them. The grounds were well kept, and the roses were in bloom. The staff was friendly and inviting. It looked like a place that would inspire a person to feel well.

Judy, who had introduced herself as the facilitator for the group sessions, led Callie to the room where her mother was waiting. "Your mother has made some pretty significant strides. Since arriving here from the recovery center, she has been working with our psychiatrist to find the right medication to support her well-being. This, we believe, will help her continue a pattern of growth and health in the long term. Hopefully she'll no longer feel the need to self-medicate with uncontrolled substances."

Callie nodded, noting the art on the walls. Were these therapeutic creations made by the residents?

"And she has been opening up about trauma in her life that seems to have been a catalyst for her addictive behaviors."

Callie snapped her gaze back to Judy.

Some unreadable thing passed across Judy's face that made Callie's pulse quicken.

She fidgeted with the cuff of her thin cardigan. "I know in the past I've requested to speak with her, and I've been turned away either because she was unwilling to speak to me or because it went against her treatment provider recommendations. For today, is there anything I should avoid? Because, I'll be honest, some things have come up lately that I really want some answers for, but I understand if I need to hold off."

Judy's peppy stride slowed to a stop. "Let her lead. Start slow. Ask an open-ended question and let her answer. Don't fear the silence. If you don't jump in to fill it, she'll talk. She has the skills she needs to communicate in a healthy way. She's been working hard on that. But practicing good communication skills with those we have a long-standing history with is often harder. We have a tendency to slip into those old established patterns, which is one reason we don't do visits in the initial weeks."

"Should you sit in with us?"

Judy patted her arm. "It will be fine, dear. We can do some joint therapy sessions at some point, if the two of you would like. But today is just a nice little visit."

Callie nodded and swallowed hard. A nice visit. Maybe today wasn't the day to ask her mother why she had a sister she'd never been told about.

Judy continued walking and led her to a sun-filled room with butter-colored walls. Her mother sat in a rocking chair, gazing out the window, her hair and clothes tidy and clean. Looking somehow diminished and stronger at the same time.

"Lindy, your guest is here."

Her mother rose from the chair with a tremulous smile, her blue eyes brighter and clearer than Callie ever remembered seeing them. "Sweetheart." She held out her arms, and Callie walked into them wanting to take comfort in the difference she saw in her. To embrace it as proof that things really could change.

"I'll leave you two be. Have a nice visit." Judy pointed to the phone on the wall. "Dial seven if either of you need anything."

Her mother released her hold and stepped back. "It's good to see you, Callie."

"You too." Questions clamored inside her brain, begging to be chosen first. "You look well."

Her mother nodded. "It's been no picnic, but I'm getting there." She motioned to the two rocking chairs facing a picture window. "Should we sit?"

Callie chose a seat and looked at the view beyond the glass—rolling hills dotted with trees that looked like they'd lived a hundred years. There was a soft tink-tink sound against the window. A little honeybee was attempting to pass through the pane.

"Bipolar disorder. That's what they are giving me medicine for now." Her mother stared into her cupped hands resting on her lap.

"I never knew . . ." She took a slow breath. "They've been teaching me how one disorder fed the other, two starved creatures feeding off of each other but could never be filled."

Callie listened to her talk awhile, thankful that it seemed her mother was committed to finding a better way forward. But why now? What changed? All the years in which her daughter begged her to get better had had no effect.

"I couldn't have done it without you."

Callie's jaw tightened. The expression of appreciation was nice, but did Mom have any idea how much paying for rehab had impacted her? Did she care? "You could have been honest, Mom. You could have told me that you didn't have health insurance before I dropped you off. Why is it so hard to be transparent with me, of all people? I've been there through all of it." The drunken sobbing. The lost jobs. The moves. The men who used her. The empty refrigerators. The cleanup when her mother was too sick to notice vomit dribbling down her chin.

"The last time we spoke, you were so angry and fed up"—Mom held up a hand like a stop signal, eyes squeezing shut—"and you had every right to be. I wasn't thinking clearly that night, and I was scared. Scared that I had used up all my chances with you, and I didn't want to do or say anything to make it worse."

"So you conveniently left out that you planned to list me as the responsible party? That's the kind of thing you tell a person." Like the fact that you lived a second life and had another child.

"I know." She winced. "I'm not making excuses for my behavior. Part of this whole process is learning how to take responsibility— something I know I haven't done a good job of. But maybe if I told you a little of where I am coming from, it will make more sense?"

Callie rolled her shoulders to work out the rising tension. *Be patient. Be kind. Let her tell her tale.*

"My father was an alcoholic," her mother began. "He wasn't for my whole life, just drank the occasional beer after a long day at work, you know. But when my mother was killed in a car accident, everything changed. Or maybe it didn't really change. Maybe he already had issues and losing her just made his heavy drinking a whole lot harder for him to hide. He lost the job he'd had for years. We had to move my junior year to this small town where he found work. That didn't last long with him coming in late, too hungover to concentrate. I worked to pay our bills while I was finishing up my last year of high school. Looking back, I don't remember him being particularly great as a dad, but before we lost Mom, at least he kept the bills paid."

"So you became an alcoholic because he was one?" Why hadn't she worked harder to avoid giving her daughter the same kind of raising she'd hated?

Her mother released a soft, bitter laugh. "I swore I'd never be him." She swallowed hard and blinked. She tore her gaze from Callie and looked out the window. "Something happened to me the summer after I graduated high school. I went to a party. The guy I was seeing at the time talked me into going. I . . . I was the victim of . . ." Her words trailed away. "I was the victim of an assault. I didn't tell anyone what happened at the party. I didn't even tell my best friend at the time." She shook her head. "Honestly, I put what happened that night away in a box inside my mind. Locked it tight. Went on like nothing happened. It's wild the power that the mind has to do things like that." Her mother wrung her hands, still staring out the window. "Or at least you think that you can lock it away so it won't hurt anymore. For weeks, I kept going with life. Making plans." She shook her head. "The most dangerous lies are the ones you tell yourself."

Callie steeled herself. She wanted to ask who had hurt her but froze. If her mother said George's or Chris's name, would she be able to break that news to Beck?

Her mother shook her head. "I didn't know the guy. He didn't go to our school. Somebody's cousin there for a visit, I think."

Callie's stomach churned. "And that's when you started drinking?"

Her mother turned back to her, the anguish so palpable, Callie's heart clenched. "No. The binge drinking started much later. I found out that I was pregnant because of what had happened to me that night."

For a half second Callie reeled, unable to make sense of her words, imagining that there could be yet another sibling out there Callie hadn't met. Like falling dominos, her thoughts clicked into place. The depth of the pain in her mother's eyes was because she was talking about her pregnancy with Callie.

Callie had spent her life trying to make sure Lindy Peterson could never blame her for her issues. She'd always be the strong, perfect child. But it turned out blame was etched into her DNA.

# THIRTY-NINE

*L*uke, please come get me," Callie whispered the words into her phone. She should have taken him up on the offer of driving her. Just because her mother was getting help didn't mean she'd lost the power to inflict wounds Callie would never see coming.

"I'll be there. Give me ten minutes and I will be there."

She hung up the call and sank to the curb, her phone resting on her floral skirt.

She'd expected information on George Walsh, whom she had no feelings about beyond confusion. Instead, her mother had cracked open her heart and revealed a truth that cut Callie's wide open.

Callie was the embodiment of the very thing her mother drank to escape but could not free herself from, no matter how hard she tried. She had been a constant reminder of the damage another had inflicted upon her. How many times had her mother been tempted to abandon her completely?

As gracefully as she could, Callie had excused herself from that room, telling her mother she would come back and talk again tomorrow after she took a little time. As she'd backed out of the room, her mother apologized over and over again. But for what? For being a victim? For being broken?

Callie grew in her mother's womb, an extension of her mother's pain until she gave birth to it. Was it the very sight of her that caused her mother's alcoholism?

When Luke pulled up in his Jeep, Callie told her legs to stand, but they seemed to have forgotten their function. He hopped out and came to her, extending his hand, pulling her to a stand, and ushering her to the door he opened for her.

Questions swam across his face, but he didn't speak as he drove away other than to say, "Home? Someplace else?"

She shook her head slowly. "I-I don't know."

"Would it be all right if I took you somewhere, then?"

She nodded.

He merged onto the highway and exited at Broad Street. His Jeep took the curves of the road that climbed Lookout Mountain. The war within her quieted. They parked, and he turned to her. "It's not far. But it's a place I like to go if I need to think. Sunset Rock. Have you been?"

She shook her head and climbed out of the car. Feeling like her heart had been shot full of Novocain, she followed him down a gentle trail.

The time was not right for a sunset, and clouds had started to gather on the horizon, thick and dark. The beauty of the serpentine path of the Tennessee River below was obscured by haze.

She followed him farther out on the rocky ledge, then sat beside him. The steady breeze swept over them, soothing the heat rising from her skin.

He looked to her with a furrowed brow. "Did you get some answers about the trust?"

She shook her head. "Didn't get that far. I got a little hung up on the fact that my mother said I was a result of sexual violence she experienced the summer after she graduated high school."

Luke put his hand over the top of hers where it rested on the rock. She blinked back the moisture gathering in her eyes.

"I don't even know how to feel about what she's told me," she went on. "I always knew that I didn't have a father in my life. Anytime I had questions, she deflected them. Based on the various men in her life over the years, I just assumed that she really may not know. I made peace with that as well as I could. But knowing this, it's different somehow. Not only am I a reminder of trauma she's spent her life trying to forget, but it sounds like she even tried living another life. One in which the trauma never happened. A life without me in it."

They watched the darkening clouds be carried across the sky by the wind.

Finally, she stood. "Tomorrow, when I go back, I'll ask her about Beck and George. Tomorrow, I'll make her confess the truth—that she left me with Ms. Ruthie so she could rewrite history. One where I didn't exist. She never brought me to Walsh Farm so that I couldn't poison it with the pain I represent."

Luke pulled her into his arms. The feeling of being drawn in instead of pushed away was exactly what she needed in that moment.

∞∞

The next day, she walked down the halls of Sunrise, heading to the same room she'd met her mother in the day before. A staff member at the front desk had confirmed that she was there waiting, ready for another try at their visit.

Her mother stood when she entered the room. "Callie, I'm sorry about yesterday."

She shook her head. "I'm the one who left. I'm the one who couldn't handle the conversation."

"I hurt you."

"It wasn't the first time, Mom. We'll survive it."

Something glimmered in her mother's eyes, mingling with the sadness. Hope, perhaps? "Should we sit?"

Callie took the chair she'd occupied the day before and drew in a deep breath. Today there was no sunshine lighting the fields. Just a heavy gray that whispered of storms to come. "Just after I took you to rehab, I found out I had been named in a trust. George Walsh's trust."

Callie watched as the words swept over her mother like rolling thunder, her face changing as she processed what Callie had spoken.

"George?" The name came out a whisper. "George is gone?"

Callie nodded. Beck had that same vacant look on her face whenever she talked about the loss of George. "Why did he name me in his trust, Mom?"

"I-I don't know."

"You have to know something. You were married to the man. Had a daughter with him. You, better than anyone else, ought to understand."

"I . . . I . . ." She swallowed hard. "Beckett? You know about Beckett?" Desperation bloomed in her eyes.

Callie tried to ignore the throbbing ache in her heart that asked if her mother had ever looked that way when thinking of her. "She's my younger sister? Right? I was too little to remember you being pregnant or much else about those years you left me with Ms. Ruthie. It wasn't that much different from you leaving me the rest of my life, so I never really thought much about that being out of the ordinary. And let's face it, no matter how long you were gone, my life was far more stable with Ms. Ruthie than after she died and you came back home."

Her mother's breaths quickened, and she stilled like an animal the moment it knows it's become prey.

"What I'm trying to understand is why I was left out of your life with George and Beck," Callie continued. "Did George not want me there because I was a reminder of what had happened to you? Or was it just you who wanted to erase me and start over?"

Her mother's hands trembled in her lap. "It wasn't supposed to be that way. George was my best friend in school. Things were never supposed to get that far."

Callie chewed her lip. "What do you mean?"

"I was just trying to survive high school and figure out if I could make myself start a new life and leave my dad to his own problems. He wasn't a good dad, but we'd gone through a lot together. There was a lot I should have thought about that year but didn't. I didn't mean to come between George and his brother. I didn't mean to lead either of them on. I was just . . . lonely."

Callie didn't want to admit that she could relate. When hunger constantly gnaws at you, you're not always careful with who or what you seek relief in.

Her mother pressed her hands to her brow bones. "And then, the summer after high school happened, and I stopped talking to anyone for weeks. I finally made myself tell George I was pregnant. I'd never seen him so angry. He told me he was going to kill his brother. I believed he was serious. I denied it was Chris's baby, but when he asked me whose it was, my throat closed up, and I couldn't tell him the truth about what happened to me.

"George proposed even though we'd never been more than friends. He told me that he was giving up college to help me. I . . . I left. I thought my absence would fix things, and I guess I could keep pretending nothing had happened to me if I didn't say it out loud. I worked at a diner, lived on the couch of a girl I worked with. She liked to drink pretty heavily on her off weekends." Her mother lifted her gaze, her chin trembling.

"After you were born, I joined her binges. I told myself it was harmless. If I had known about the genetic link to alcoholism and understood the real effect my trauma had on my mental health, I'd like to believe I never would have taken that first sip. But that numb feeling was such a relief. I'd been so raw for so long, every puff of wind made tears pour from my eyes. I just needed it to stop hurting so much."

Her mother went silent and Callie scrambled to process all she'd said.

Her mother continued, "When my father passed away, I went back for the funeral. George was there. We started talking. He asked me to stay. Of course I couldn't. You and I lived in Chattanooga then, just like you do now. I started going to visit him. I always intended to tell him about you. But time went on. You were happy and well cared for while you stayed with Ruthie. He brought up my pregnancy only one time, right when we started seeing each other. He seemed to assume I'd lost that baby, and I couldn't make myself correct him. It never came up again.

"It was like I had fallen into a river, and I was being swept by a current that, instead of drowning me, carried me along. I don't know if I was unable to get myself out of the current or if I just didn't have the willpower to do what was right. I kept your existence secret, tried to hide the binge drinking, and tried to live a double life. Sober when I was with him. Bingeing when I wasn't. He finally found out about the drinking. I was arrested for driving under the influence, and he bailed me out. So, I told him that I left him whenever I couldn't stand to be sober anymore. He didn't say it, but I could see his disappointment. I had become my father, the very person he'd tried to rescue me from when he befriended me."

Callie pinched her lips tight, the pressure grounding her. "Beck and I figured out how you played part-time parent to us both." Even though she thought she knew the answer, she forced out the question. She needed to hear her say it. "What was so hard about telling George about me?"

Her mother shook her head, her voice cracked by a sob trapped in her throat. "I don't know. I don't know. I tried once. Right after Ruthie died, I tried bringing you there, but I couldn't make myself. It was easier to run than tell him how I'd hidden you. Than tell him what had happened to me." A sound rose from her mother. A pitiful sound like a wounded animal who knows death looms. "He never knew. Not until the farmers' market last summer when he saw you."

"You were in contact with him?"

"He found me. Demanded the truth, and I told him. That last Christmas I shared with him and Beck, he'd given me an ultimatum. The drink or them. All that time he thought I left because I chose my addiction. Until he saw you." She sucked in a shuddering breath. "I killed him. My words killed him. Death had been growing inside me, festering in my soul, and I let it out. I told the truth. And it killed him. And it's killing me. And it'll kill you too."

Her mother began to hyperventilate, and Callie hurried for the phone, dialing seven. In moments someone rushed in and ushered her mother back to her room, no doubt administering some sort of sedative to calm her.

Judy came into the room.

"I'm sorry," Callie stammered. "I pushed too hard. After what she confessed yesterday, she seemed fine. I thought . . ."

Judy patted her shoulder. "Sometimes it feels like a person's undoing when they confess the things that hurt the most. It takes a special force of will to compartmentalize and then to yield. To let it free sends the mind into a fight-or-flight response. She's in a safe place to work through this. In the past, this would have been where she spiraled. Here we can help foster growth and healing instead." Judy tilted her head and smiled softly. "Do you have someone who can help you?"

She thought of Luke and Kate and Beck and Joanne, whom she should definitely call. "I'm going to be okay. Can you tell her to call me when she's ready to talk again?"

"Of course."

Callie traversed the long hallway back to where Luke waited in a well-appointed lobby.

He stood when she approached. "Everything okay?"

Callie wrung her hands. "Maybe. Mom had to take a break. It's strange. Today's conversation seemed so much more difficult for her. Yesterday wrecked me. Today hurts, but not like yesterday."

"You were blindsided that first time," he said. "She'd prepared for what she wanted to say to you. But to answer questions about George and Beck? She must not have expected that."

"Yeah. She didn't know George had died."

They walked through the automatic doors and climbed into his Jeep.

"You're sure you're okay?"

She shook her head. "I'm as good as I can be. I really want to get home. Get caught up on some stuff. Make beautiful things that make people smile."

A while later he parked in front of her apartment, then squeezed her hand. "Call me if you need anything."

She nodded and gave an awkward wave in lieu of a goodbye before walking to her porch. Thunder pealed, and she eyed the ugly dishwater color of the sky.

# FORTY

*B*eck watched the storm warnings flashing across her television screen while she folded a load of laundry on the couch. The radar was splotched with a wide swath of yellow and red. The meteorologist talked about winds and other factors that led to the tornado watch for the county, using wording like *shear*, *lift*, and *instability in the atmosphere*.

But she didn't need to worry. Not now. Not yet.

The wind whistled. Limbs clawed at the windowpanes.

She'd expected to hear from Callie after her meeting with her mother, especially after she'd invited her to come. She eyed her phone. She could call.

For a moment in time, she pictured herself standing before a woman she couldn't quite visualize, demanding her to give an account of how she could abandon her daughter. Beck shook her head. What did it matter? She didn't want to hear what Lindy had to say. She'd left—chosen a different life. And whatever the woman might have to say about her father, it didn't matter.

He might not have been a perfect man, but he'd done the best he could. Come what may with this farm, she would make it.

There was a blinding flash, and a sharp crack that jolted her to her core. Her arm hairs stood on end.

And then everything went dark.

The sky opened, and the heavy thunk of hail pounded the roof for several moments before softening to rain. Beck felt her way into the kitchen where she kept her flashlight. Maybe she shouldn't have thrown all Callie's candles away.

With a flashlight illuminating her path, she grabbed the weather radio out of the hall closet and flipped it on. The tinny voice advised anyone in northwest Monroe County to seek immediate shelter. The watch had become a warning.

In direct opposition to the directive, Beck flung on a rain slicker and raced to the barn. Flashlight in one hand, the lead lines for Sparks and Oslo in the other, she led them, willing the nervous animals to stay calm in the slanting rain as wind whipped about them. She freed them in the largest pasture, with farewell pats to their rumps. They were better off being free to get out of the tornado's path should it come to that than to be trapped in a barn unable to escape.

After turning them loose, she jogged back toward the house and opened the goat pen. She dodged limbs and other small debris that scuttled across the ground. The tornado siren sounded. At least she thought that's what that wail was. This was the first time she remembered hearing it. Inside, she opened a few windows. It seemed like she remembered her dad once saying a house could explode in a tornado if it was shut tight. She didn't know if it was true or not, but it was better not to chance it.

She grabbed the radio from inside and sprinted to the root cellar, barring the door from the inside with a broken broom handle she found.

She huddled on the ground, arms wrapped around her knees, praying between panting breaths. Praying for the safety of her neighbors, Fern and Isaac, the animals, her bees. A spider scuttled across the ground, fleeing the beam of her flashlight.

*Keep us safe. Keep us safe. Keep us safe.* It wasn't an eloquent prayer, but it was the most sincere petition she'd uttered for quite some time. She wasn't quite sure when she'd stopped making prayer a part of her life, but this moment seemed as good as any to start up again.

Everything grew quiet and still. The thunder quieted. The rain ceased. And she let out a sigh of relief.

Then another sound rose. A low continuous rumble. At first she thought it a long peal of distant thunder, but it grew louder. More insistent. Her ears popped. The cellar door jumped. Something struck the doors and scraped and scratched like a wraith trying to fight its way in. The screen door of her house slapped in its frame over and over again.

Beck crawled to the corner and crouched in a ball, arms shielding her head. Her heart slammed in her chest. This could be it. This could be the end. Was she ready to meet her Maker? She'd asked Jesus into her heart when she was a tiny thing, but somewhere along the way, when she'd shut herself away from the rest of the world, she stopped pursuing God too. Gotten into this place where she stopped acknowledging His presence. Blips of memories played in her mind like a slideshow, a little girl praying for a mother who never came home.

The roaring grew louder. The air seemed to be sucked from the tight cellar. *Can You love a wandering daughter?*

*Yes.*

There was no way she could have heard a word in the thrashing. The crashing. The roar. But still that word echoed in her being as she waited to walk into the arms of Jesus, hoping to see her father again.

⌀⌀⌀

Callie had risen the next morning, showered, and rehearsed three times what she wanted to tell Beck about her visit with their mother before entering the kitchen and switching on the soft rock station for background noise while she worked on a batch of salt scrubs.

She tapped her foot to the beat.

The song ended and the announcer's voice broke through, the strident tone incongruent with the catchy tune. Mid-sip of her latte, her world stopped turning.

"The National Weather Service estimates the tornado that ripped through the town of Sweetwater yesterday evening, claiming the lives of three people, to be an EF2 tornado. Several area farms have been devastated, and crews are hard at work getting roads cleared and accessible."

Callie set her mug down with a thunk, grabbed her phone, and dialed Beck's number. It rang on and on with no answer. She plucked her keys and purse from the hook by the door and hurried to the car. She connected her phone to the handsfree system and dialed Luke's number as she backed down the driveway. He answered on the third ring.

"Luke, it's Callie. Did you hear about the storm?"

"I just heard. Have you talked to Beck?"

"I can't get through. I'm heading to Sweetwater now."

"Do you want me to come? I can bring tools. I have a friend that I might be able to call who has construction equipment."

"Let me get there and see what's going on first. For all I know, she's perfectly fine, sipping her morning coffee in her kitchen with that crazy chicken perched on her knee, and the calls just aren't getting through." Or she could be one of the few numbered among the deceased. Callie had been so exhausted after her meeting with her mother that she'd worked on a few orders and then went to bed without even a thought about bad weather. Whatever wave of the storm reached Chattanooga, Callie had slept through it.

On the drive, she continued to try Beck's number to no avail. Kate. Surely Beck would have made contact with Kate. She selected her number from her contacts and pressed call.

"Callie? Thank goodness. Have you heard from Beck?"

A weight sank in Callie's middle. "No. I was hoping she'd called you."

Kate conversed quietly with someone in the background. "Martin said we shouldn't worry too much. There is likely a lot of damage in the area. Power is out. Cell service is probably restricted too."

Callie slowed her breathing. "I am on my way there now. I'll try and update you if I can."

"I appreciate it. I am packing a bag and heading that way, but you're a lot closer than I am." There was a pause that seemed to stretch on forever. "Callie?"

"Yeah?"

"I'm sure she's fine."

As she drove, fear gnawed her insides. Mere months ago, she hadn't even known Beckett Walsh existed. This woman who was strong and self-possessed as she worked among millions of stinging insects yet trembled at the thought of venturing beyond her property lines, who possessed an untamed quality that drew Callie to her, a quality that said that rather than being molded by what society expected she'd been shaped by the land that she worked. This sister, maddening in her dichotomized thinking and yet somehow endearing in her simplistic way of seeing the world. Black and white. Good and bad.

Callie hadn't recognized until that moment just how much she desired her sister to count her among the good.

Though she knew that bargaining with God was not a worthwhile endeavor, she said the words anyway. *Lord, if You'll let Beck be okay, I won't let her wonder another minute what will become of the farm. I'll let her have it and walk away. I'll leave it up to her if she wants to be a part of my life. I won't mention Mom's care again. It might not have been fair for me to have carried that burden my whole life, but it's not right to try and force her to carry it too.*

As Callie drew closer, her heart pounded louder in her chest.

Along the highway, trees were snapped in two. Their tops gone. Branches stripped. Leaving the trunks looking like massive sticks some giant's child poked into the ground.

Callie took the exit, unsure if she would be able to pass through this gauntlet of debris to reach her.

# FORTY-ONE

*B*eck? Beck!"

Beck sat up, enveloped in complete darkness. Had that voice been a dream?

She slowed her breathing, repeatedly pressed the flashlight button, but she must have fallen asleep with it on.

The details of the previous evening rushed to the forefront of her mind—the violent tearing sounds that filled her ears. Then the way everything went quiet. And the fact that she was trapped.

She'd remained huddled after the storm passed as if sudden movement could scare away the stillness. She'd eventually crawled for the cellar exit. She removed the broom handle and pushed. It moved but wouldn't yield. She'd shoved her weight against the door over and over again, but whatever was on top of it wouldn't shift enough to free her.

In her rush to get to safety she'd grabbed the radio but not her phone. A mistake that left her trapped with no idea what sort of world waited for her. Would she emerge and find her home gone, save for this small shelter?

The voice of a man calling her name moments ago had been only a dream. A dream in which someone came and rescued her from the tiny corner she'd locked herself into. Beck scrubbed her hands over her face. How long had she slept? It was impossible to know in the dark.

The screech and slap of the screen door sounded. She strained her ears. Footsteps clomped across the wooden porch. She stood, crouching in the low-ceilinged space. "Is someone there? Help!"

"Beck?" The sound of Isaac's voice might just be the most beautiful sound she'd ever heard.

She pounded her fists against the cellar doors and called out. "I'm in the root cellar. I can't get out."

"I'm coming!"

"Isaac?" She just wanted to hear his voice again. To let it register that the sounds coming from beyond the swallowing darkness were in fact real.

"I'm here, Beck. There's a branch. It's pretty big, just give us a second."

A scratching, scrabbling sound permeated the tomblike space. And then the doors opened. She blinked against the sudden light and then grabbed hold of the hand reaching for her.

She stumbled up the two steps, still holding tight to Isaac's hand. He drew her into his arms. "I'm so glad you're okay. I came as soon as I could. The roads have been blocked with downed power lines and trees. We had to cut across the property on foot."

For some reason his words caused her to picture Fern wandering in the storm on some half-baked mission to somehow save the bees.

She pulled back, her stomach clenched. "Where's Fern?"

He smiled. "She's fine. Mrs. Bailey is watching her while I came to check on you. They had a little bit of damage to the roof of their barn, nothing major though."

It was then she noticed Mr. Bailey, standing a couple paces away from them with his hat in his hands.

"You all right, Miss Beck?" he asked.

"None too worse for the wear, I guess." Her eyes having adjusted from the pitch darkness of the cellar could finally tolerate the morning light. She turned a slow circle, taking in the debris. A tree had fallen on the barn, crushing in the roof at one corner. The roof of the house was littered with branches but seemed to be okay. Her picture window was shattered. An enormous pine lay across her drive, blocking anyone from entrance.

Mr. Bailey plopped his hat back on his head. "We're here to help. Whatever you need."

Beck offered her thanks to her neighbor and pulled in a breath of that cool morning air. She was alive. And whatever other damage there might be, her house still stood. *Thank You.* It wasn't much of a prayer, but it was as sincere as the one last night, when she'd thought her life was ending. *Father, I'll get better at this. This will be our new start.*

Isaac cleared his throat. "I was pretty scared coming over here. It looked bad. Trees twisted and snapped off at the tops."

Beck wrapped her arms around herself, still feeling shaky. "I've never experienced anything like it in my life." She scanned the area, the land littered with unfamiliar debris. Even a chunk of a car bumper from a vehicle she didn't own. "I need to look for Sparks and Oslo. See if I can round up all the goats. Make sure the chickens are okay."

Isaac and Mr. Bailey followed as she walked past the damaged barn. From this distance the coop still seemed intact. She rounded the small structure, then shut her eyes against the sight in front of her.

What looked to be the top of a large oak centered the honey house, mangling the tin roof. Seeing this place, where honey flowed, so damaged seemed an omen foretelling a truth she didn't want to face.

She swallowed hard. "I'll have to go see what's become of the bees."

Callie parked in front of Beck's blocked drive. It had taken her an hour and a half to get from the exit to the farm entrance—a drive that normally wasn't more than twenty minutes. So many of the roads were either impassable because of untouched debris or blocked by the road crews at work.

She stared at the farm's sign, half covered by a broken branch.

The foggy memory of another stormy night played in her mind. She was painfully aware of its significance now. How close she'd been to a stable life. Even if her mother had chased her addiction to the ends of the earth, George would have taken Callie in. They would have had each other, the three of them.

If George Walsh could handle loving Lindy all this time, despite her choices, he was a father who could have handled loving a child born out of pain, shame, and brokenness. Her name written in his trust, no matter how impulsive and misguided the action might have been, proved that.

Callie shut off her engine, stepped over branches blocking her way, and traced her fingers over the lettering burned into the wood.

She'd never had the chance to love him back.

*Please, God. Give me the chance to love Beck. To tell her about her father. Maybe it won't give her any comfort. But it might make a difference when I tell her that I don't want the money from the farm. That I want her to have it. That I want to know her more than I want anything from her.*

It was slow going. She picked her way through the downed branches and broken-off trees. She paused when the house came into view. It looked okay for the most part. Maybe some minor repairs. The barn was worse.

Everything was so quiet. She cupped her hands around her mouth and called out. "Beck? Are you there? Can you hear me?"

Nothing.

She called out again. The only sound was a pitiful mewling. A damp cat limped its way out of the barn. Callie knelt and scooped it into her arms. It lay its head over her shoulder, and Callie felt the gentle vibrations of its purr. The infamous Sassy was not feeling up to her name.

Callie walked inside the house. No sign of her sister. When she went to the honey house and witnessed the damage, her heart lurched. "Beck? Are you there? It's Callie. Can you hear me?"

Nothing.

Still carrying the damp cat, she stepped over debris that seemed to have come from some building she didn't recognize and pried open the wedged door to the honey house. "Beck? Are you there?"

No answer came. She stepped deeper inside, hoping the damaged building was as stable as it seemed. Scant light filtered in from the ruined roof. She took another step. Glass crunched under her feet, and something viscous sucked at the sole of her shoe.

Broken jars of honey were scattered everywhere. The heart of the storm had descended here and flung them from their neat rows, dashing them against the walls like a toddler throwing a tantrum.

Of course Beck was not here. If she had any ounce of life in her body, she would be out checking her bees.

# FORTY-TWO

**B**eck walked the trail to the apiary. At least she'd found Sparks and Oslo, neither of them worse for the wear. The chickens were okay, though they'd probably stop laying for a bit due to stress. Half the goats had been found, and she had hope the rest would turn up soon. As much as Isaac was keen on staying by her side, and as tempted as she was to accept that support, she'd sent him and Mr. Bailey to check on Annette.

No matter what had become of the apiary, there was little anyone could do to help anyway. She crested the last small hill that over-looked the field of white boxes and stared. Boxes were scattered like dice thrown from a Yahtzee cup.

Bits of dark cloth littered the ground, having been torn from the brush, some of which draped the crushed and ruined hives. Pain twisted in her chest, and she blinked back the moisture gathering in her eyes. Maybe there were still some that could be saved.

In the field, she stepped around a damaged bee box that was ooz-ing honey. Box after box she checked. Most of them vacant. There were some with a few remaining bees, but they had been overturned and the rain had poured in, chilling the brood. No queens in sight.

Even though she knew the chances of the hives' survival were slim-to-none, she righted every intact brood box, found a lid, and covered it. It seemed sacrilegious, leaving their intimate worlds exposed.

They'd likely all die, queenless and wrecked. Too much of their carefully foraged honey stores were destroyed, but the least she could do was try. She lifted a hive body that was overturned, the wood sides splintered. The frames within mangled. The delicate waxwork smashed. The bees trapped inside had drowned in the collected rainwater.

She retrieved a piece of cloth still clinging to the brush and draped the white box in black—this box her father's hands had built housed one of their oldest hives.

"I'm sorry." The words croaked out of her tightened throat.

She walked through the ruined beeyard, reliving memories. The magic she'd felt every time she opened a hive. Their onyx eyes peering at her from the top edges of the frames, questioning her intrusion, ultimately accepting her clumsy hands bumbling about in their delicate cosmos.

Who else would grieve these tiny beings, their life's work destroyed, their carefully ordered lives thrown into utter chaos? A honeybee could not survive like that.

The wind had stripped away their strength, revealing their true fragility.

Beck stood still in the middle of the field, hoping against all reason for some sign that missing bees would return. More likely the killing wind had carried their corpses away.

A soft buzzing met her ears. Beck stilled. On the ground, next to a broken hive body, she spotted a ball of bees. They'd gathered themselves together into a humming mass.

Could there be a queen hidden in its center, or were they just a collection of workers, damp from the rain, trying to break the chill?

Beck knelt, gently scooping the small living ball into her hands. Their tiny legs and the movement of their wings against her flesh sent a shiver up her spine. She gently separated them with a brush of her thumb. At their center, she discovered the elongated body of a queen bee.

This queen and her attendants, desperate survivors, were still doomed to perish. There weren't enough of them to make it. But it didn't lessen her awe at this nucleus of life. The bees crawled over her hands, regathering around their queen.

"Come back. Your queen is here," she whispered on the gentle wind. "She's waiting for you." How could wind be both a destroyer and a giver of gentle caresses?

The clouds parted and the sun beamed down on her.

More bees landed on her cupped hands, surrounding the queen. Though they'd been scattered far and wide, her daughters knew the scent of her.

The longer she stood there, the more that came. Clinging to her bare arms. Her middle. Her legs. Beck stood stock-still as they moved over her.

The hum of wings filled her ears. They anointed her hands with their tongues, tasting the remnants of honey from the ruined hives.

This queen mother piped, calling for her lost daughters to come home.

Their collective power grew as they increased in number. A single bee was a fragile organism. An entire hive was a life force.

Standing bare, without her protective white garment marking the boundary between her world and theirs, Beck let her head fall back and her breathing slow. Absorbing the sun's warmth and the rising hymn of bee wings, she began humming, matching their tune. Vibrations rose up from the depths of her. A beckoning song of anguish and joy. Power and fragility.

Truth.

And for the first time, Beck fully grasped the language of bees.

The queens of Beck's field were but dainty insects, yet they'd radiated a power that proved stronger than Lindy Peterson. A magnetism that called their children to them. Gave them purpose and direction—to serve its queen and to raise her daughters.

A queen never, ever abandoned her hive, and those matriarchal rulers had not only given the daughters of her hive purpose, but they'd given Beck purpose too.

A wistful smile tugged at the corners of her mouth as a tear trickled down her cheek. She didn't need them in the same way she once had. When and how that had happened, she wasn't entirely sure. Little by little, perhaps, culminating with a dark night in a cellar in which she called out for her Father.

Bees called to bees.

It had been her Father beckoning her.

"Beck!" Callie's panicked voice brought her back to the moment. What a sight she must be, standing in this ruined field, blanketed in bees.

Her sister ran closer and then slowed, eyeing her, unsure of her next move. "Are you okay?"

"I am."

"You're covered in bees."

"It seems so."

Callie circled her at a distance. "Why? What's happening?"

"I never expected for it to end up like this. Can you help me save them?"

"I . . . uh . . . I'd rather save you from the bees than save the bees."

Beck stifled her laughter, not wanting to startle them. "I promise, I'm fine. Bring that hive box over here, the one sitting there that has the lid on top. I need somewhere safe to put the queen. They'll follow wherever she goes."

Callie hoisted the box and drew close by Beck's side, observing warily.

"Okay, now take the cover off."

Callie removed the lid. "Now what? It better not involve me touching bees."

Moving slowly, to avoid unsettling the bees as she bent her body, Beck peered inside. The best she could tell, though the hive had been vacated, it had somehow kept its lid and stayed relatively dry. She bent ever so carefully and placed the ball of bees on top of the frames.

"Now what?"

"Now we wait and see."

Little by little, the bees noticed the absence of their queen, lifted off of Beck, and alighted on the tops and sides of the hive until her skin was bare again.

More and more bees came. No longer scattered daughters but gathered sisters. "This hive could make it. It's possible."

Callie peered at her. "What about the rest?"

Beck shook her head and pushed a breath past the heaviness in her chest. "For the most part, it's a total loss. There may be a few yet that can be salvaged, but my hopes aren't high, even for this one. It's really hard to come back from this kind of damage and exposure to the elements. The balance inside the hive is a delicate one."

"I'll help if I can."

Together they combed the field, trying to find scattered hives that could be put back together again. Even if not a one of them took, Beck felt a release of pressure on her chest for having tried.

# FORTY-THREE

*A*fter scouring the apiary for signs of life, Callie and Beck walked back to the house. Beck solemn beside her, somewhere unreachable in thought.

They'd only found about five hives they thought they could save out of the fifty.

She wanted to ask Beck if the apiary could come back from a loss like this, but given their history, she feared Beck would suspect her to be a circling vulture trying to swoop in instead of the concerned sibling she desired to be.

Today was a day for picking up broken pieces and mending what could be mended. Mourning what could not. Decisions for the future could wait for other days.

Back at the house, Callie helped Beck pile together limbs and brush strewn about the lawn and parking area and on the porch. They fixed a tarp over the broken living room window.

She probably shouldn't have been surprised when Beck came out of the barn with a chainsaw to make quick work of the fallen trees blocking the long drive. This woman who was comfortable with a screaming chainsaw and being covered in a thousand bees made it easy to forget the trembling woman she'd first met in that conference room.

Callie fell in behind her, moving the cut pieces of wood to the side of the driveway. Her stomach rumbled and she knew Beck must be starving too.

When they cleared the final branches from the drive, they walked back to the house, sweaty and exhausted. They rinsed the sawdust from their arms with the cold sluice from the water hose.

Beck dried her hands in the hem of her T-shirt. "Well, at least someone can make it down the drive now. You might want to go get your car. They'll be working up and down the road trying to get power back up, and you don't want your vehicle caught in that fray."

"Should I go pick up some lunch or something? See if anywhere's open? I know you have to be starving."

No sooner were the words out of her mouth than a white hatchback rolled to a stop. Isaac unfolded from the driver's side followed by Annette. Callie noticed the look that passed between Isaac and Beck and smiled at the hint of sweetness in the interaction.

Fern bounded from the back, ran to Beck, and threw her arms around her. "I'm so glad you're okay. I was so scared." She pulled back from the embrace. "Uncle Ike told me that the animals are mostly okay. Have you found the missing goats?"

Beck shook her head. "Not yet. I think they'll turn up though. We're only missing a momma goat and her two kids. If I had to guess, they're just huddled up somewhere in the woods. They'll venture back this way once they're sure things are safe. Sassy and the kittens are fine."

Fern gulped, staring into Beck's eyes. "What about the bees?"

Beck shook her head slowly. "I lost almost all of them."

Fern's eyes welled and spilled over. She wrapped her arms tight around Beck. Beck patted her back.

Fern sniffled. "I wanted to help you save the bees, Beck."

"Oh, Fern." She pulled the child tighter against her. "It was never our job to save the bees. Not really. We can help them, but bees aren't tame things that we can shelter or protect. They fly out from the hive into a world full of dangers outside our control. Predators. Pesticides. Bad weather."

Beck rubbed slow circles on the child's back.

"We do our best to make sure the home we've provided is a good one, that it's healthy and safe. We call ourselves keepers, but we don't keep them, not really. We let them fly free and do what they were made to do, resting in the knowledge that it is in the nature of bees to come back home if they can."

Callie listened to Beck comfort Fern and found a measure of comfort for herself in her sister's words. Was Beck speaking of more than just bees?

Beck's stomach rumbled loud enough for all of them to hear, and Fern pulled her cheek back from Beck's middle. Laughter burst from Fern despite the tears trickling down her face.

"That's my cue." Annette stepped forward with a large basket. "We're eating fancy this afternoon, folks. Good old PB&J is the fare of the day with the power being out." She passed sandwiches wrapped in plastic wrap to each person. "There's cans of cola in the trunk too, but they're a little warm."

They each found a place to settle on the porch. Never in her life had Callie found a peanut butter and jelly sandwich so satisfying.

She turned to Annette. "Did you have any damage at your place?"

Annette shook her head. "Lost a few shingles off the roof but nothing too severe. I'm so thankful it wasn't worse."

Isaac and Fern chimed in, comparing their experiences in the storm with Annette.

Beck sat a few paces away, contemplative. Or perhaps simply exhausted.

Callie rose from her seat and moved closer to Beck. "I spoke with Kate on the way here. She's coming."

Beck gave her a crooked smile. "Thanks for the warning."

"She's not so bad, is she?" Though firm and direct, Kate's love for Beck had always been apparent to Callie.

Beck shook her head. "No. She's not. I've always known she means well, even if she does cramp my style. I have to admit that her administrative skills might come in handy while we sort out what needs to be done."

Beck's use of "we" clanged in Callie's consciousness. How she longed to be included in that we.

Beck lifted her gaze to meet Callie's. "She's had nothing but nice things to say about you since the visit to Uncle Chris. I have a feeling that it's her dearest hope that you can be a good influence on me."

Callie laughed quietly. If that was the case, Kate had underestimated the force of nature that was Beckett Walsh.

Beck glanced away again, looking toward the small pasture where Sparks and Oslo grazed. Her shoulders rose and fell with two heavy breaths. "Did you get to see her like you planned? L-Lindy. M-Mom."

"Yeah. I had been meaning to call you to let you know, but it . . . it was a lot to process."

"Can you tell me?"

Callie nodded, her gaze darting to Fern, Isaac, and Annette. "Could we walk and talk?"

Beck swallowed and stood. "Sure."

She took the lead and Callie followed.

"Was he your father?"

Callie shook her head. "No. But I believe that he might have been one to me if our mother had let him."

The rigid set of Beck's shoulders softened a fraction. "Did you figure out why he named you in the trust?"

"I guess so." Callie recounted the story of the shy, bookish boy who fell in love with the new girl in town, seeing past the ugly rumors, apologizing with purple hyacinths the time he'd hurt her feelings. She talked about the jealousy between twin brothers who couldn't look or behave more differently, and then she told of the night Callie was conceived and the fallout that resulted when Lindy couldn't bring herself to tell the truth.

Beck stared at the ground as she walked.

"I'm not trying to make excuses for her. I'm not," Callie said. "But she's sick, Beck. She is so broken inside. So confused. She sent back his letters without opening them, and at the same time, she couldn't let him go and dropped postcards to tell him every time we moved."

Callie crossed her arms over her chest. "I always thought she was running from something. I think it was the love she was sure she didn't deserve, believing if George knew the truth, he wouldn't be able to love her anymore." Callie uncrossed her arms and massaged her palms. "I want to believe she'll get better. Find peace. She found out that she has bipolar disorder, and she's taking medication to help with that."

Beck slowed her steps. "You think he put your name on the trust instead of hers because he hoped you'd use it to help her?"

Callie shrugged. "Maybe. Or maybe to make up for the mother who kept us apart. When he learned she was pregnant, he wanted to help her, marry her. That's why your uncle thought he'd named me in the trust to spite him. To rub it in his face because Chris hadn't stepped in how George thought he should. He found Mom after seeing me at the market last summer. She said she finally told him the truth. I think he wanted to give me the love and support she'd rejected all those years ago."

"Do you think she ever really loved him?"

Callie shook her head slowly, considering the question. "I'd like to think she loved him in her way, broken as it was. I think he tried to love her enough for both of them. He saw the life she'd had with her father, and he wanted to save her from it."

Beck wrapped her arms around herself. "Yeah. He'd want to see her get all the help she needs, to give her the best chance at getting well." Beck stopped, blocking the path. "We should sell. That way you can keep your shop and help Mom. I'll contribute what I can from my half, but I do need to have enough to get a new place and cover costs while I try to figure out what to do with my life."

"Beck, stop." Callie had a different plan in mind, but Beck was too raw and weary to hear it. "The day you lost your bees is not the day to make that decision. I'll consider what you've said, and we can talk more after you get things settled here."

"Isn't this what you've wanted from the beginning?"

Callie shook her head. "When you met me, I was just scared, afraid I was going to fail all over again in my attempt to help her. For a moment, the trust looked like a lifeline, rescuing me from the repeating pattern in my life. But I never wanted to take away your home. I've never had a decent one of my own, and it wouldn't be right to rob you of yours to save a mother who was incapable of giving either of us a safe place to land."

# FORTY-FOUR

"Beck, have you thought about rearranging the cabinets?" Aunt Kate, having arrived the evening before, just as the electricity returned, now stood at the sink scrubbing the breakfast dishes.

"It makes a lot more sense for the cups to go over there, closer to the fridge, and the plates closer to the stove. Right here above the silverware."

Beck groaned. "If you are looking for something to do, feel free to come help us pick up debris."

Aunt Kate sighed, a hint of mischief lighting her eyes. "All right then. Point taken."

"You have to admit, before the tornado, I was getting on better than you'd expected." Her aunt didn't need to know that Beck had employed a high schooler to be her on-call delivery boy.

Aunt Kate turned to her. "With most of the bees gone, can you start over? Will the insurance cover any of the damages?"

"With any luck. The policy is supposed to cover loss of livestock and crop in the event of a disaster. The guy I spoke to seemed confused on whether the honeybees were considered livestock or crop. I was too tired to keep trying to explain something he should know about the coverage." She rolled her gaze skyward. "I gave up. But I'll call again later today. Get an adjuster out here to assess the damages."

Beck leaned over her aunt and filled cups of water to take out to those who had volunteered to help. "I told Callie I'm okay with selling. Just like this farm was more than a farm to me, her business is more than just a business, and I want to help her."

Aunt Kate placed a dish in the drying rack and turned to her. "What will you do? Do you want to come stay with Martin and me? Would that help?"

Beck held up a hand. "I'll be fine. Somehow. The Baileys have already volunteered to take on Sparks and Oslo if needed. The chickens and goats too. I'll get a small place. Maybe even keep a couple of hives if any of mine survive."

"What did Callie say?"

"Not much. Just that she doesn't want to make decisions now when we're both so raw. But I feel at peace about it. You know, hearing her story. About how our mother kept her life split in two. The two of us split in two . . . I imagine that has to be painful for Callie. Standing on this ground, seeing the life I was allowed to have versus what our mother burdened her with. It seems the right thing. To let this go. She can have the things she's worked her whole life for. I can have a place of my own and start fresh." She shrugged. "I've also thought about seeing a therapist about the panic attacks."

Aunt Kate clasped her hands under her chin. "Really?"

"Callie sees a therapist to help her. She said that growing up with Lindy left marks on her life that she's working on finding healing for," Beck said. "I bear some of those marks even though I didn't grow up with her around. I figure it's worth a try. I can even do therapy over video call if I need to."

Her aunt wrapped her in a hug. "I'm really proud of you."

"My mother never knew she had bipolar disorder. If she had gotten help with that sooner, her life could have been so different." Beck squeezed her aunt tight. "She spent her whole life running from pain. I hid from mine. I could pretend it didn't even exist so long as I never had to face it. I'm starting to believe that there is another way." Beck swallowed hard. "For her too. Part of me hopes that one day I'll be ready to see her. Talk to her. I don't know. One day at a time, I guess."

Beck released her embrace and loaded a tray with glasses of ice water she'd prepared. "I better hydrate the troops."

Fern, Isaac, Mr. Bailey, and even Annette gathered and sorted debris. Stacking brush and wood in one pile to be burned later. Twisted metal, garbage, and broken glass went in another.

Beck perched the tray on the rail. "Come get some water, everyone."

They gathered around her. Though they'd all been working hard to restore the place to order, there was an energy in the air. Joy. Purpose.

When her father died, she'd pictured her life on this farm alone. How different the past several months had been. She backed out of the circle of people so they could all get to the water.

She sighed. Summer was nearly spent. Fern and Isaac would return to Nashville soon. Mr. Bailey would go back to his normal tasks. She'd likely still have Annette—who'd grown on her over time.

She hoped Callie would be there too.

She didn't want her to disappear after the sale of the farm.

⌒⌒⌒⌒

A few days later, Beck sat on her front porch. The sunrise bright and beautiful on the horizon. Satisfied that Beck was well in body and mind, and that she had the help she needed, Aunt Kate had gone home the day before.

Her aunt was a little maddening as always, but full of love.

Callie's car came down the drive and Beck stood, watching her approach. She walked inside and retrieved the package she'd so carefully wrapped the night before.

Callie met her on the porch.

"I have something for you." Beck held out the weighty package and Callie received it, brows raised.

"Special occasion I didn't know about?"

Beck shook her head. "Something I wanted you to have."

Callie peeled back the newsprint and pulled out one of the bars of beeswax that Beck had melted down and refined last night.

"It's from the broken hives. I didn't want it to go to waste."

Callie shot her a wry smile. "Maybe I can use it and make you some new candles to replace the ones you threw out."

Beck ducked her chin. "Sorry about that."

"I'm teasing. I understand. You must have felt so betrayed."

"Yeah."

"And now?"

Beck blew out a breath. "Now I'm just sad he never confided in me. Didn't see me as strong enough to share his burdens. I'm sad he didn't get help with his wounds and heal. I can't go back and change that, but I'm glad it brought us together."

A smile lit Callie's face. "Really?"

Beck chuckled softly. "Yeah. I know in my heart that it was something my dad wanted, and it makes me happy."

They sat side by side on the porch steps, gazing out over the property. The once-lush trees lining the fields were now forlorn and ragged, with their damaged crowns and patchy foliage. How many years of growth would it take to erase the tornado's path?

Callie tucked her knees under her chin. "George wasn't perfect. And maybe he tried too hard to make right what was wrong. With his brother. With Lindy. With you. Even with me. I've tried looking at what he did from every possible angle to understand. In the end I come to one conclusion. Even if he went about it in all the wrong ways, what he really wanted was to restore what was broken."

Beck flashed back to the morning after the storm, walking through her ruined hives, wishing what she was seeing wasn't her reality. Yearning for the ability to rewind time and find some way to save her apiary from destruction. Holding pieces of the broken hive bodies, things her father's hands had touched, now fractured and useless. "That desire for restoration can be like an ache that swallows you whole. When you hold those broken pieces and they are too splintered to fit them back together again. It's a helpless feeling."

Callie nodded, eyes focused on the ground. "He couldn't put Mom back together again. And neither could I." She lifted her chin, determination in her eyes. "But with some divine intervention, even with how messy this all is, I think the three of us could someday have a restored relationship if Mom will stay committed to getting and staying healthy. As we continue to grow and heal, it could be possible." She lifted a bar of beeswax. "It's possible for treasured things to come out of the brokenness. Even if it doesn't happen the way any of us would have wanted. Even if it comes through loss."

∞∞∞

Callie had left later in the afternoon, needing to get back to her workshop. The final farmers' market of the season loomed, and the events of the past week had set her behind. Again, Beck sat on her porch steps, waiting. This time for Isaac and Fern.

This was a hard goodbye. Beck wanted to leave them with promises of coming for visits and declarations of "see you soon." She wanted to believe that the bonds she'd formed over that summer were strong enough to survive distance and time and the hurriedness of life. But she also knew how easy it was to be forgotten. So, she'd resolved to say a simple goodbye and leave them with an open invitation to stay with her if they ever came back.

Her heart ached as the now-familiar hatchback came into view, carrying the little knee sock alien and her uncle.

Fern bolted from the car the second it stopped and wrapped her ropy arms around Beck, squeezing with all her might. "I'll miss you, Beck."

"You too, kiddo."

"I don't want to go back."

Beck glanced up to where Isaac hung back, his hands shoved in his pockets. She returned Fern's tight squeeze. "I don't know how I'll manage without my apprentice."

"How are the bees?"

Beck shrugged, wishing she had happier news to give her in parting. "Not great. There's a few hives hanging on. I'll feed them through the winter and try to keep them going."

"The one where all the bees covered you?" Fern had loved the telling of that tale and had Beck recount it to everyone who would listen.

"So far, so good."

Fern peered into Beck's eyes, her jaw set. "That one will make it. She must have been a strong queen to call all those bees to her."

"I hope so. You'll come back next summer and check on them, won't you? You and your uncle can stay here." If she still owned the place, that is.

Fern let go of her. "Can we, Uncle Ike? Can we?"

He walked to them. "Wild horses couldn't keep us away. Or tornadoes. Or swarms of bees."

Beck smirked. "Swarming bees are some of the gentlest beings on the planet."

He ducked his chin, grinning. "I was just trying to talk your and Fern's language."

Fern propped her hands on her hips. "You'll have to spend more time in the hives next time. Maybe we'll finally teach you a thing or two." She ran to the car and returned, plopping a package in Beck's hands. "It's knee socks! One bee print pair, one daisies. I recommend you mix and match. It's more fun that way."

Beck's heart warmed at the girl's gift. "I love them, Fern."

Isaac patted the girl on the back. "Why don't you go say goodbye to Sparks and the rest of the animals. We'll need to go soon. Your parents will be waiting."

She skipped off toward the pasture where Sparks grazed.

Beck shoved her hands in her overall pockets. "How are things with her parents?"

He lifted a shoulder. "They're trying to work things out. They've started marriage counseling, so that's something. I hope they're able to patch things up."

Beck nodded. "I . . . I'm glad our lives collided this summer." She stifled a laugh. "Meeting Fern was out of this world."

His mouth widened in mock offense. "Fern? What about me?"

"Oh, were you claiming to be a space alien too?"

He snickered. "You hated my guts when we first met."

"No I didn't. I just didn't know why you were so bad at keeping up with your kid."

He gasped. "How dare you?" Then he scrunched his face. "Actually, I was awful. Not that Fern made it easy on me."

Beck peered up at him. "You've made vast improvements."

He laughed and ran a hand through his hair. "I'll take that as a compliment." Catching her completely off guard, he grabbed her hand and threaded her fingers with his. "We will come visit. You're stuck with us now."

Her heart thumped hard in her chest. "I hope so."

"I'd invite you to come visit us in Nashville, but I know that . . ."

"Yeah, well . . ." Beck heaved out a breath, refusing to let her mind travel paths of fear. "Don't count me out entirely. Maybe someday I'll learn how to fly farther afield."

He brushed a strand of hair away from her face that the breeze had pulled loose from her ponytail. "I believe you will."

"Are you two kissing?" Fern's incredulous voice rang out from the hillside.

Beck and Isaac backstepped. Her face likely as red as his.

"Say goodbye to the goats and let us be, you little rascal," Isaac called.

Maybe he would kiss her one day. When they could promise each other more than a "maybe someday we'll see each other again."

He stepped back to her, then gave her hand a squeeze and brushed a kiss to her cheek. "I don't know exactly how this story ends, you and I, but in my humble opinion, it sure has been an interesting start."

Hope tugged at her heart. "We'll see."

# EPILOGUE

*a* soft hum rose from Callie's back seat. A hum that kept her looking over her shoulder to make sure the clustered gold-and-black beings hadn't somehow escaped the mesh-and-wood crate. The last thing she needed was a car full of six-thousand-some-odd honeybees flying free.

She took the Sweetwater exit and drove those long winding lanes.

Over the past few months, Beck had continued to bring up selling Walsh Farm, even after Callie sold her storefront for a tidy sum to an investor wanting to revitalize the entire block.

Callie had gotten far more than she'd paid for her building due to a little financial advising from Isaac. It had been enough to cover the remainder of her mother's care and continue to pay the fees at the therapeutic community her mother moved into after her inpatient care. As it turned out, the building hadn't meant quite as much to Callie as it once had. She'd uncovered something she wanted so much more.

And when her therapist had advised Callie to take risks, buying a building hadn't been what she was referring to. She, too, had meant for Callie to pursue something more.

303

Callie left the main road, zipping past the Walsh Farm sign.

Thankfully George Walsh had arranged for great insurance coverage on the farm, which had provided for the needed repairs and covered the lost income from the disaster. Over the past months, Callie had wanted to tell Beck about the future plans she'd been daydreaming about. It had been hard to wait, but she wanted to make sure that when the time came to make plans, Beck was making choices based on what she really wanted for her life, not because she felt forced into anything. Now that Beck had spent the past several months in therapy, Callie hoped she might be ready.

It was finally spring again. Bee season. Only three hives had survived the winter, one being the hive that had gathered over Beck.

Callie parked and quickly got the package of bees from her back seat. The soft breeze their wings stirred against her hand, mesmerizing.

"Callie?"

Beck stuck her head out of the barn.

Callie held the three-pound box of bees lower, hiding them behind the car. "I called earlier to tell you I was coming, but you didn't answer."

"Sorry, I was out giving Fern a riding lesson."

"I'm so glad she and Isaac could come for her spring break. Are they here now?"

"No. They went into town for ice cream."

"You didn't go with them?" Though her sister had not yet made the drive to Nashville, or even Chattanooga to visit their mother, she now managed to get out and about in her small town on a regular basis.

Beck shook her head. "Not this time." She squinted at her and started walking closer. "Why are you standing behind the car like that? You look suspicious."

Callie lifted the box and forced a smile despite her nerves. "I have a proposal. A bee-posal, if you will."

"Are those bees?" Beck strode toward her.

Callie met her in the middle of the graveled square. "I propose that we don't sell. That we become partners at Walsh Farm. You keep the bees, herbs, flowers. I'll help, of course. And I can continue my company, using only products we grow here on the farm." Her hands trembled. The bees hummed.

Beck had said she was willing to sell. But that didn't mean she wanted to share this place. To live and work together. And if she'd rather do that alone, without her intrusion, so be it. She would refuse to see it as rejection, that she, once again, was unworthy of George Walsh's untainted domain.

Beck stared at the cluster of bees a moment longer and then took the box from Callie's hands. "But you wanted a cute little shop downtown. Not a bedraggled farm in need of updates and repairs and more work than it's fiscally worth. You could still make your dream happen if we sell."

Callie shook her head. "All I ever wanted was permanence. Stability. Something that could weather life's storms. And I found that here with you."

There was a break in the cloudy sky, and the sun spilled rays of light over the distant fields. Luke's crepuscular rays. He was right. They did signify a miracle.

Today those rays marked where two estranged sisters met. Where together they found healing over these many months. Where they'd shared long talks about the meaning of forgiveness and the process of forgiving their mother. And they'd talked about their relationships with Isaac and Luke and how their healing had created fertile soil where new things could bloom.

Callie pointed up. "Do you see those rays? People call them the hand of God. Proof of miracle sightings. Do you know what makes them? Just light on dust, Beck." Thinking of Luke, she said, "If that's not a miracle, that light can make something so common as dust beautiful, then I don't know what is."

"What are you trying to say?"

Callie smiled and shook her head. "I was just remembering something Luke once told me. Though you and I sure have our share of dust, I think God is making something beautiful."

Beck raised an eyebrow as though she were trying to sort through her feelings about Callie's effusive words. "Wedding plans in the works for you and Luke yet?"

Callie's face warmed. "Not just yet. We've talked about our future but nothing official yet. No proposal."

Beck smirked. "Just bee-posals? What does he think about this?"

She shrugged. "He wants what makes me happy."

"And you really think this will make you happy?"

"I do. But only if it's what you want too."

Beck looked out over the hills. "There's plenty of land. We could build a couple of houses. One for you. One for me. The farmhouse could become our store." She shuddered. "Or a bed-and-breakfast, if you're into that sort of thing."

Callie laughed at Beck's feigned horror. "The possibilities are endless. I just want to know if you want me here with you. If you think there could be room for both of our dreams."

Beck chewed her lower lip, looking like a little girl. "We could keep a guest room in the old house. Mom could come for visits when she gets better. If . . . when . . . we're ready."

"Another possibility. But first, there's just one question you need to answer. Beckett Anne Walsh, do you want to revive the apiary and partner in business with me?"

⬡⬡⬡⬡

Beck stared at Callie and then at the clustered, golden bodies in the box she held, Callie's question ringing in her ears. Her heart fluttered in her chest the same way it had the day her father brought home their first package of bees.

He'd inducted her into a realm of magic. A world that became her comfort. A world her broken mother had once loved too.

With all the bees and hyacinths and letters in the world, her father had not been able to fix what was fractured. But he'd tried. And in his fallible way, he'd brought these three women back together. It was up to them what they'd do next.

Beck laughed softly in wonder at this cluster, knowing at the center there was a queen bee who caused them all to gather.

But Beck and Callie were not queen bees. There was room for them both in this kingdom she and her father had loved.

She threw an arm over her sister's shoulder. "I can't believe I'm saying this, but nothing would make me happier than to share this place with you."

# TURN THE PAGE

for a preview of Amanda Cox's

# NEXT MOVING
# NOVEL!

Coming Soon

# PROLOGUE

## NOVEMBER 2, 1941

*C*athleen McCorvey tied off her skiff, the numbness in her fingers slowing her practiced hands. Adrenaline coursed through her body like the spidery tendrils of lightning dashing across the sky. When she straightened, the wind whipped about her head, unfurling her sodden scarf, sending it airborne until it settled somewhere over the seething Atlantic.

Hunched against the slanting rain, she jogged past her faithful light. A light that had guided her to the foolish drunk clinging to a vessel not seaworthy in even the fairest weather. A man who likely didn't merit Cathleen risking her life over. But duty had called. No matter who was at the mercy of the unpredictable currents of the Outer Banks.

She entered the squat stone cottage where she lived, boots squelching on the wood floor. Cathleen sidled up to the fire and added enough wood to coax the embers back to life. She stripped down to her threadbare undergarments, her goose-pimpled skin starved for warmth. She draped her trousers, wool socks, and slicker over the rough-hewn chairs arranged in front of the hearth and wrapped a blanket around her shoulders.

"Cathy?" Her father's voice cut through the silence. Rolling thunder sounded on its heels.

Cathleen cringed. "Yes, Da?"

"Everythin' all right? Why are you up, lass?"

"Just checking the light," she called and then pulled the scratchy wool tighter around her, sending up a silent prayer that he'd accept her answer and go back to sleep. Even though everything was electric now, and the light required far less tending than in days gone by, the old routines were etched in her father's history. And hers too.

She inched closer to the fire, aching for the heat to penetrate her bones. Moments later her father's snores once again echoed through the room, and the tension she carried between her shoulder blades released.

He was having a good night.

Cathleen grabbed a kettle, filled it with water, and hung it over the fire. While the water came to a boil, she rubbed her hands together, trying to turn her blue-tinged nail beds pink. Once she'd downed her tea and her fingers burned white-hot with renewed circulation, Cathleen went to her father's desk and pulled out his sacred book.

"This is our livelihood, Cathy," he'd told her a hundred times. "A lightkeeper is only as good as the records he keeps."

Into the book, she poured her account of the night. She'd woken with an inner urging to check that all was well along the coast, then climbed those endless spiral stairs, chiding herself for dragging herself into this unkind weather without cause. That was when the light beam had glinted off the overturned dinghy being tossed about in the storm.

As she recounted the waves that had crashed over her own vessel as she rowed out to him, recording the wind speed and wave height, her heart expanded in her chest. Not just anyone could have managed swells like that. Especially not someone as young as herself, be they male or female. But sixteen-year-old Cathleen had honed her skills on the water alongside her father since they'd moved to Bleakpoint Island when she was but a toddler. Everything had been preparing her for this night. Her first solo rescue at sea.

Though her skiff had been close on hand, she had to admit that it had been impulsive—taking the skiff instead of her father's larger motorboat—even if she did possess far more confidence maneuvering her own vessel.

She poured words onto the page as the weight of what she'd done crashed over her. Stopping the inebriated man from capsizing her vessel when he'd grasped at the oarlocks to pull himself aboard. The skiff had tipped wildly, but Cathleen had kept a cool head despite her knowledge that a merciless sea cared not whether it was a drunkard or a teenage girl dumped into its depths.

She'd managed to calm the cursing, thrashing man and drag him around to the stern like she'd seen her father do so many times. And she'd saved him. Scarf and storm concealing her identity, she rowed him to where her father kept his large workboat anchored in the sound and then motored him to Ocracoke before disappearing back to her remote island home.

Tonight's events proved she was equal to the task life had handed her. The only thing required was to do whatever it took to continue concealing the fate of the real keeper of Bleakpoint Light.

She stared at the page in which she'd poured out the events of the evening, all written in her scruffy hand. This time she hadn't tried so hard to mimic her father's writing. She added details normally absent from his minimalist record keeping. At the bottom, she impulsively signed a name she wished was her own. A person she craved to know, but who was little more than a legend to Cathleen.

Ever so carefully she tore her account from the precious book, leaving no trace of the torn-out page. As far as anyone knew, this rescue never happened. And that was the way it must remain.

She walked to the fire with the page in her hand. It would make better kindling than anything else. She stretched the paper toward the licking flames. "I am naught but a figment of a drunk man's imagination," she said to the empty room. But instead of releasing it so that the fire could claim it, she clutched the paper to her chest.

# ONE

*J*oey Harris stood from her desk chair and stared out the window of her second-story office. Golden leaves dropped from the trees and pasted themselves to the damp sidewalk bordering the historic town square. Two middle-aged women chatted below, their closed umbrellas propped at their sides. If only they'd move from the sidewalk into her office and write their names down in the blank spaces of her appointment book.

She stepped back from the curtain, letting it fall closed.

A shrill tone permeated the space, and she edged away from its source. What if she just ignored the call and persisted in showing up as scheduled? Refused to accept that her services were no longer required by the inhabitants of Copper Creek, Tennessee.

Joey squared her shoulders and pressed the phone to her ear. "Events by Josephina."

"Hey, honey. Just calling to check in. I've got you on speakerphone." *Mom.* Joey let out the breath she'd been holding. Road noise and the canned voice of a navigational guidance system filled her ears.

Joey sank onto the small sofa that should be occupied by clients at this time of day, then kicked off her heels and tucked her legs beneath her.

"Say hi to your daughter, Ronnie." Her mother hissed as though Joey couldn't hear every word.

"Babe, I'm trying to listen to that GPS woman and change lanes without the U-Haul trailer taking out a minivan. Joey, please tell your mother I'm only capable of doing one thing at a time."

Joey stifled a snicker. "Is your trip going okay so far?"

Early that morning her parents had driven away from the house she'd helped her father build when she was only eight. How she remembered what it was like to be glued to his side, handing him any tool she was big enough to lift.

After saying their goodbyes, it hadn't been easy, denying her ridiculous urge to sneak inside the trailer with their displaced possessions and stowaway on their fresh start.

"We're about four hours outside of St. Petersburg." It was a good sign, this lift of excitement in Mom's voice that had been absent for far too long.

"Sunshine and sea breezes, here we come." Dad's tone was light, but Joey knew better. Her parents had been planning to move to Florida for retirement for years, but not under these circumstances.

Joey ended the call and stared at the empty calendar in front of her. All those erasure marks, traces of plans that were still on, just without her help. Birthday parties. Weddings. Reunions. Graduation celebrations.

Living in a small town where everyone knew your name had its pluses . . . and its minuses. She slapped the calendar shut and stood.

She grabbed her keys and gave a parting look at the pristine space meant to communicate to everyone who walked through the door that she had an eye for beauty and detail. It was a prime location, sandwiched between a day spa and a boutique. She sighed. She wasn't ready to give up on this dream just yet, but she was starting to wonder if it was worth the fight.

Joey locked the door behind her and exited the building, inhaling the scent of damp autumn leaves. Margaret Pierce, the owner of Simple Things Bed-and-Breakfast, walked toward her, her low heels clicking on the pavement. Joey's stomach tightened.

Margaret lifted her head from studying her cell phone screen. She gave Joey a curt nod and chose to cross the street rather than walk past her.

Joey growled under her breath, biting back the words rushing to her lips. She'd tried to explain her family's innocence six months ago, after Margaret convinced her niece to fire Joey as her wedding planner. But if Margaret hadn't listened to reason then, she wouldn't listen now.

A drizzle started, and without missing a step, Margaret snapped open her umbrella and lifted it overhead. Joey peeled her gaze from the woman's retreating form and walked to her car.

She ducked into the driver's side, swiping away the droplets from her bare arms and smoothing the curls that had sprung loose from her bun. Joey pulled out of her reserved space and cruised once around the town square.

As a teenager she'd loved working alongside her father, giving those historic buildings a facelift in preparation for the series of heartwarming movies that were filmed there. Tourists and new residents alike now flocked to Copper Creek, wanting to experience that fairy-tale town they'd watched on the screen.

Too bad the people had forgotten that her father's work had been what charmed those producers in the first place.

As she drove home, she attempted to brainstorm ways to restore honor to the Harris name, but all she could see was that empty appointment book and the determined scowl on Margaret Pierce's face.

Once inside her apartment, she grabbed a cardboard box from the freezer and popped the casserole in the microwave. While it cooked, Joey flopped onto the couch, pulling a tattered patchwork quilt over her lap. She opened her laptop and typed the name of her parents' new neighborhood into the search bar. It was beautiful. Maybe she should have stowed away in that U-Haul, after all. Despite the weight on her chest, she smiled at the mental image of taking up residence in their retirement community at the age of twenty-six and planning posh one-hundredth birthday parties and fiftieth wedding anniversaries for the rest of her life.

Her search then drifted to scrolling through realty listings as she was drawn to beautiful coastal homes well out of her price range. She tried to picture herself standing on the front porch of one of them. In her imagination, a man appeared by her side. The preppy lumberjack wore a buffalo plaid shirt and had her ex-boyfriend Paul's face. She shook her head to clear it. That was weird. Paul never wore flannel, nor had she ever imagined herself marrying him. What was she thinking?

She grabbed her meal from the microwave, which thankfully tasted better than it looked.

Her cell rang. Sophie's name lit up the screen.

Joey set the cardboard tray on the side table, answered the call, and laid back, staring at the popcorn ceiling. "Hey, Soph," she said through a burden-laden exhale.

"Don't sound so excited to talk to me. You'll give me a complex."

Joey laughed under her breath. "Don't take it personally. I said goodbye to my childhood home this morning. Mom and Dad are on their way to a new life in Florida. Plus, my business is in a rapid downhill spiral with no rescue in sight because the Harris name makes me a pariah. Oh, and since we last talked, Paul broke it off with me for someone new."

Sophie sucked in a breath. "Ouch."

"Yeah, I feel like a million bucks." Joey cradled the phone against her ear with her shoulder and unwound her long brown hair from its bun.

"What happened?"

"I thought I had at least two promising events on the books, something to remind Copper Creek that I'm not a scam artist, nor am I a child of one." Joey rolled her eyes skyward. "There's this lady who just moved here to open a gift shop. She asked me to help her plan her grand opening block party." Joey pulled in a breath. "But she stopped me on the street yesterday and said that Ada at the boutique next door said that if she used me, people wouldn't come. I know Margaret is behind this. Because her B&B was almost bankrupted when—"

"Stop the train, Jo-Jo. I meant about Paul, the guy you've been seeing for eight whole months. Why didn't you call me?"

Joey huffed. "It just didn't feel like that big of a deal in light of everything else."

"What happened?"

"Last week he met this girl at the soup kitchen where his men's group volunteers, and he really hit it off with her. He felt like the right thing to do was to break things off with me before even talking to her about his feelings."

"This is the same Paul we went to high school with? Who never even bought a new shirt without taking a month to think about it?"

Joey massaged her scalp, releasing tension brought on by her heavy updo. "He said he's never felt this way about someone before. What can I say to that?"

"What can you say to that? Y'all've been together almost a year, and he ditches you for some girl he just met who might not even like him back? Who does that?" Joey couldn't help but smile. Too bad Sophie didn't live closer. She'd set all of Copper Creek straight for her.

"That's the thing though, Soph. The fact that I didn't cry or feel like throwing something . . . I . . . I just don't know what I'm doing anymore." She grabbed her casserole from the side table and stuffed a generous bite into her mouth.

"Crazy thought. Pack it all up and move to Nashville. The apartment next to me is coming open next month. There would be way more opportunities to event plan here than in touristy Copper Creek. Before you know it, you could be planning parties for the biggest names in country music."

Joey set her casserole aside and sank deeper into her couch. She twirled a brown curl around her finger, examining the way it reflected in the lamplight. "Sophie, I appreciate your vote of confidence, but you and I both know opportunities like that don't just happen. I would be an itty-bitty fish in a far bigger pond. Besides, at the moment, I think I'd prefer anonymity to fame. I just need to stick it out a little longer. I've still got that welcome home bash for Evelyn's son. After I ace that, things are bound to turn around. Aren't they?"

"Why are you so obsessed with making things work in Copper Creek?"

Joey sat up, tucking her knees to her chest. "I . . . it's home." She picked at the French manicure she'd chipped while compulsively tightening down the squeaky floorboards in her office after spending hours with nothing to fill her time.

"After everything that happened?" Sophie scoffed. "Is it really worth it? Working so hard to regain the favor of a group of people who've chosen your family as the scapegoat for all their misery? Any idiot ought to be able to see that the bad things that happened with Harris Construction occurred after your dad sold it. There's more to the world than Copper Creek."

Easy for Sophie to say. She'd left after high school to attend college in Nashville and had never looked back. But Joey had skipped college and had gone straight into doing what she loved in the town she adored. Growing up here had been a lot like living in one of those feel-good movies that had been filmed right outside her office windows. Joey had even played an extra in some of them. But her reality was nothing like the movies that ended with a resurrected family business and a sweet kiss in the town square. "My dad did not deserve what happened to him. Being dragged through the mud like that. I need to—"

"Fix this somehow? Joey, come on . . ." The sound of a baby cry came through the line. "Uh-oh, Liam is awake again. Sorry, friend, I better run. I know Nashville isn't what you're looking for, but think how much fun we'd have as neighbors!"

Joey ended the call and then rested her forehead against her tucked knees.

Starting all over again? Was this really what it had come to? Eight years of building a business down the drain. Did she really have it in her to start from scratch? Did she even want to?

A few hours later, a text came through from Sophie. "You'll probably think I'm nuts, but I think I found the perfect thing for you. Check your email."

Joey opened her laptop. The body of the email read: "You said you wanted to be anonymous." Joey skimmed the attached job listing and eyed the grainy photograph of a lighthouse surrounded by wilderness. Sophie's scheme to get Joey to move to Nashville was absurd enough. But this? She shook her head. She wasn't *that* desperate yet. Was she?

# ACKNOWLEDGMENTS

Thank you to the entire team at Revell for the opportunity to publish another book with you. I am eternally grateful for the time and talent you have invested into helping my work reach its full potential.

To my agent, Tamela Hancock Murray, I am so thankful for your guidance and encouragement on this journey. It is a joy to partner with you.

To Caleb, Ellie, and Levi, your biased and unwavering belief in my abilities is such a precious gift. I hope you always support one another in the same way that you support me. I will forever be your number one cheerleader.

To my husband and hype man, Justin, thanks for always bragging on me to everyone you meet even though I find it insanely embarrassing. I cherish your support. Also, thanks for your patience while I lament my terrible writing and for not laughing too hard when I finally convince myself that I "kinda like" the story after all.

To River, my German shorthair pointer puppy, I want to take a moment to acknowledge the way you completely derailed my morning writing routine during the writing of this book with your insistence that 5:00 a.m. should be playtime instead of the serene writing time it once was. It's a good thing you're cute.

To Tanner, my fifteen-year-old golden retriever, who by the time this book is printed will have crossed that rainbow bridge, you were a good and faithful friend these many years, and the world ought to know.

To Crusoe the cat, how I got to the point that I am acknowledging pets, I'm not entirely sure, but here we are. I didn't want to leave you out. You're a cat, so you already know how awesome you are.

To my honeybees, if not for you, I never would have had the courage to write this book.

Jesus, my writing partner, here is another story "in the books." I did my best to listen as I wrote this tale, to get out of the way and allow the story that You desired to shine through for Your people. Thank You for being my constant, the One in whom I can always trust.

**Amanda Cox** is the author of *The Edge of Belonging* and *The Secret Keepers of Old Depot Grocery*. She holds a bachelor's degree in Bible and theology and a master's degree in professional counseling, but her first love is communicating through story. Her studies and her interactions with hurting families over a decade have allowed her to create multidimensional characters that connect emotionally with readers. She lives in Chattanooga, Tennessee, with her husband and their three children. Learn more at AmandaCoxWrites.com.

# A Beautiful Exploration
## of the Complexity of the
# MOTHER-DAUGHTER
# RELATIONSHIP

"Luminous and lyrical ... storytelling of the finest sort."
**—AMANDA BARRATT,**
author of *The White Rose Resists*

## Don't Miss
### *Amanda Cox's Striking Novel*
# THE EDGE OF BELONGING

**Revell**
*a division of Baker Publishing Group*
www.RevellBooks.com

Available wherever books and ebooks are sold.

# MEET AMANDA

FOLLOW ALONG AT
## AmandaCoxWrites.com
and sign up for Amanda's newsletter—*From the Sparrow's Nest*—to stay up-to-date on exclusive news, upcoming releases, and more!

 AmandaCoxWrites

# If you liked this book, try
## *Almost Home* by Valerie Fraser Luesse

LET'S
TALK
ABOUT
BOOKS

- Share or mention the book on your social media platforms.

- Write a book review on your blog or on a retailer site.

- Pick up a copy for friends, family, or anyone who you think would enjoy and be challenged by its message!

- Recommend this book for your church, workplace, book club, or small group.

- Follow Revell on social media and tell us what you like.

 @RevellFiction

@RevellBooks

@RevellFiction

@RevellBooks